On the Edge

RAFAEL CHIRBES

On the Edge

Translated from the Spanish by
Margaret Jull Costa

Afterword by Valerie Miles

Harvill *Secker*
LONDON

1 3 5 7 9 10 8 6 4 2

Harvill Secker, an imprint of Vintage,
20 Vauxhall Bridge Road,
London SW1V 2SA

Harvill Secker is part of the Penguin Random House group
of companies whose addresses can be found at
global.penguinrandomhouse.com.

Penguin
Random House
UK

First published with the title *En la Orilla* in Spain by Anagrama in 2013

www.vintage-books.co.uk

A CIP catalogue record for this book is available from the British Library

Hardback ISBN 9781846558481
Ebook ISBN 9781448191680

This book has been selected to receive financial assistance from English PEN's 'PEN Translates!'
programme, supported by Arts Council England. English PEN exists to promote literature and our understanding of it, to uphold writers' freedoms around the world, to campaign against the persecution and
imprisonment of writers for stating their views, and to promote the friendly cooperation of writers and the
free exchange of ideas. www.englishpen.org

Supported using public funding by
**ARTS COUNCIL
ENGLAND**

Penguin Random House is committed to a sustainable future for our business,
our readers and our planet. This book is made from
Forest Stewardship Council® certified paper.

MIX
Paper from
responsible sources
FSC® C018179

Typeset in Columbus MT by Palimpsest Book Production Limited,
Falkirk, Stirlingshire
Printed and bound by Clays Ltd, St Ives plc

Fuck away like fucking donkeys, but allow me to say 'fuck';
I'll allow you the action, if you'll allow me the word.

Jacques the Fatalist and his Master by Denis Diderot

I

THE DISCOVERY

The first to spot the carrion is Ahmed Ouallahi.

Every morning, ever since Esteban closed his carpentry business over a month ago, Ahmed walks down Avenida de La Marina. His friend Rachid drives him to the restaurant where he works as a kitchen porter, and Ahmed walks from there to a secluded part of the lagoon where he usually sets up his fishing rod and casts his net in the water. He prefers fishing there in the marshy area, far from the eyes of passers-by and the police. When the restaurant kitchen closes – at 3.30 in the afternoon – Rachid comes to join him and they eat their lunch, sitting on the ground in the shade of the reeds, with a cloth spread out on the grass. They're bound together by friendship, but also by mutual need, sharing the cost of the petrol for Rachid's old Ford Mondeo, a 'bargain' that he bought for less than a thousand euros, but which has turned out to be something of a white elephant because, as he puts it, the car drinks petrol as greedily as a German drinks beer. It's about fifteen kilometres from Misent to the restaurant and, just there and back, the car gollops down three litres of petrol. At nearly one euro thirty a litre, that comes to about four euros a day just for fuel, which means a hundred and twenty euros a month to be deducted from an income of less than a thousand euros; at least those are the figures Rachid gives Ahmed (although he may be exaggerating a little), which is why Ahmed pays his friend ten euros a week for transport. If he could find a job, he'd get a driver's licence and buy his own car. With the crisis, you see, it's easy enough to find second-hand cars and vans at absurdly low prices, although how they perform afterwards is another matter: cars that people have had to get rid of before the bank repossesses them, vans owned by companies that have gone bankrupt, motorhomes, estate cars; it's a golden opportunity for anyone hoping to buy cheap and with a little money to invest. What you don't know is what kind of poison might be concealed beneath the bonnet of these bargains. High petrol consumption, replacement parts, components that break the moment you look at them. You get what you pay for, mutters Rachid, as he puts his foot down. That's another half-litre gone. He accelerates again. And another. They both laugh. The crisis is making itself felt everywhere. Not only among those at the bottom of the heap. Companies are going broke too or are struggling. Rachid's brother used to work in a warehouse that owned seven trucks and employed seven drivers, but that was four years ago. Now, they've fired everyone, and the trucks stand idle in the car park behind the warehouse. When the company has a delivery to make, they hire a freelance driver, who does the job in his own truck, charges them by the hour and the kilometre and then sits, clutching his mobile phone, waiting for the next call. Ahmed and Rachid discuss the possibility of setting up a business buying old cars and reselling them in Morocco.

The restaurant where Rachid works is at the far end of Avenida de La Marina, which, despite the grand-sounding name, is actually a road running parallel to the beach, but behind the back of the first row of apartment buildings, and continuing through the suburbs of Misent for another twenty or so kilometres, as far as the lagoon's first drainage canal. Ahmed has to walk for just over a kilometre to reach the spot where he usually fishes. He carries his rod on his shoulder, his net tied round his waist beneath his tracksuit top, and a basket slung on his back by two chains, like a backpack. Three years ago, countless building sites lined this stretch of La Marina. On either side of the road you'd see piles of rubble and buildings in various stages of construction: sites filling up with machinery; others where a bulldozer was opening up the ground, removing the reddish clay, or where cement mixers were filling in the foundations. Pillars bristling with iron rods, struts, sheets of steel reinforcement mesh, pallets full of bricks, piles of sand, bags of cement. There were teams of bricklayers everywhere. Some houses where the construction work had been completed would be covered in scaffolding heaving with painters, while, nearby, groups of men would be digging and gardening and planting trees and shrubs that are, according to the guidebooks, typical of the ornamental flora of the Mediterranean: oleanders, jasmines, carnations, rose trees and clumps of aromatic herbs – thyme, oregano, rosemary and sage. The roads in the area used to be filled with endless lines of trucks bringing in palm trees, leafy carob trees, and ancient olive trees, all bursting out of the vast pots in which they were transported. The air was filled with the metallic sounds of vehicles carrying building materials or dump trucks, and trailers for transporting bulldozers and cement mixers. The whole place was a hive of activity.

On this sunny morning, everything seems quiet and deserted, not a single crane punctuates the horizon, no metallic noises trouble the air, no buzzing or hammering assails the ears. The first time they made the journey together after Ahmed lost his job, his friend Rachid laughed at him when he said he was going there to look for work on the building sites. Work? Only if you want a job digging graves for suicides, Rachid said mockingly. *Ma keinch al jadima. Oualó.* There's no work, none. There's nothing being built in La Marina. In the good times, a lot of labourers would take their week's wages, then not bother to turn up again because they'd found somewhere else offering more. Now, discouraging signs hang from balconies. Anyone looking for work has become a bit of a pest. NO GARDENING OR MAINTENANCE STAFF REQUIRED. PLEASE DON'T ASK says the sign on the apartments next to the restaurant. Everywhere there are signs in red or black letters – FOR HIRE – FOR SALE – AVAILABLE FOR HIRE WITH AN OPTION TO BUY – FOR SALE GREAT OPPORTUNITY – 40% DISCOUNT – with telephone numbers underneath. All they talk about on the radio every morning is how the building bubble has burst, about the huge national debt, risk premiums, savings banks going bust and the need to cut public spending and reform the country's labour laws. The crisis. Unemployment in Spain stands at more than twenty per cent and this could rise to twenty-three or twenty-four next year. A lot of immigrants live on unemployment benefits, as he will start to do in a few days' time, or so he hopes, because after filling in pages and pages of forms at the social security office and standing in various queues, he was told that it will take some time before he receives his first payment. Five or six years ago, everyone was working. The whole area was one big building site. It seemed that not a centimetre of land would be left unpaved; now it looks rather like an aban-doned battlefield, or a territory under armistice: sites overgrown with weeds, orange groves transformed into building lots; neglected, withered orchards; walls enclosing nothing at all. When he first arrived in Spain, most of the bricklayers in the area were from Morocco like him, and his first jobs were on construction sites; then men from Ecuador, Peru, Bolivia and Colombia began to arrive. Now no one comes from any of those places. The Moroccans are leaving for France or Germany, and the Latin Americans are going back home, even though they had become the most sought-after workers. Employers trusted them – they spoke the same language, they shared a religion and a culture – and, above all, anyone from Morocco, ever since the 2004 Madrid bombings, was considered suspect (most of the bombers were thought to have been Moroccans) as was having anything to do with Islam or Islamism. Ahmed thinks the Moroccans themselves have contributed to increasing this distrust and making things more difficult. His fellow bricklayers, who, before, had always been perfectly happy to drink and smoke and share a joint with the Spaniards on the construction teams, were now declaring themselves to be strict Muslims, haughtily rejecting the bottle of booze being handed round at lunchtime, and never to be seen in a bar after work. They refuse to eat what the company gives them, demanding a halal menu. Some even insist that the work timetable should be changed during Ramadan. *Hamak y Jamak.* Fools and madmen, Ahmed calls them. Muslims and Christians only get together to find out which one can best screw the other. On Sunday afternoons, when the streets of Olba are deserted because everyone's gone to the beach or to have lunch with their families, the Moroccans take solitary walks or sit on the handrails along the Misent road, on the bollards along the pavement. Ahmed quarrels with his fellow Moroccans who, during Ramadan, want the foremen to abandon the lunch break and, instead, shorten the work day. When he was still working at the carpentry workshop and went to deliver a load of doors to one of the sites belonging to Pedrós, one of the managers there said to him: You bloody Moroccans are mad! I never go to Mass, I've got nothing to do with priests, and yet you expect me to fast during Ramadan. What am I supposed to tell the crane operator or the guys driving the bulldozers or working the cement mixers? That they skip lunch and eat later on when they get home? That they don't drink a drop of water while they're slaving away in the sun, when it's

7

humid and thirty or more degrees? To his fellow Moroccans Ahmed says: As if the Christians didn't already have it in for us! It's as if you *wanted* them to get rid of us, he said to Abdeljaq, who had persuaded their other flatmates not to drink beer with Spaniards. But no, Abdeljaq had said: Keep away from the unclean. When he got excited, he would say that it wouldn't be long before they saw the colour of the blood of those Christians. They need us, argued Abdeljaq, and, for as long as they do, they'll have to put up with us, and if they stop needing us, they'll get rid of us soon enough, even if we pray the Our Father stuff they spout or make the sign of the cross.

Abdeljaq had celebrated the bombings at Atocha station. He said he could see the face of Allah more clearly in the sky. He'd performed his ablutions, prayed facing Mecca and cooked a *mechui* of lamb, which he ate wearing a white gandora. It was all done with great formality; he was celebrating martyrdom and vengeance. Look, he said, pointing at the TV screen while puffing on his joint, look, infidel blood. *Bismillah.* On the television, they were showing twisted metal, people covering their faces with bloodied hands. When he was alone with Rachid, Ahmed would criticise Abdeljaq: You see? The Christians don't need us any more, and so we're the first people they get rid of, because we're the ones who make life difficult for them. They'd rather keep the Colombians and the Ecuadorians. Anyway, Abdeljaq is blaspheming when he says he can see the face of Allah. That's the worst blasphemy a Muslim can commit. But Abdeljaq's eyes light up as if he really was seeing that face. A fierce, satisfied face. He talks like some fanatical preacher, a prophet of revenge: The Christians trample on us now, we clean the shit from their toilets, we serve their disgusting wine in bars, we build the houses where they eat *jaluf* and fuck uncleanly, without washing the semen from their foreskins, our women make their beds and smooth their impure sheets, but the day is coming when we will

8

be the ones who lead *them*, on all fours, with a chain about their necks. They will bark outside the doors of our houses, revealed as the things they are: dogs; and they'll polish our leather slippers with their tongues. Our Muslim brethren in America were taken there in ships, in chains, caged up like horses, goats, chickens or pigs. The Black Muslims were just farm animals as far as the Yankee Christians were concerned. The time has come for us to show them that we are men and know how to fight for what is ours. Ahmed argues: But there are rich Muslims too. What about all those sheikhs in the Gulf States. Aren't rich Muslims even worse than rich Christians? Besides, most of the slave traders in Africa were Arabs. Muslims enslaving Muslims. Abdeljaq shakes his head indignantly: Those are infidel lies. But Ahmed has seen documentaries on television and knows that it's true. Those Arabs, those traders in human flesh, were feared from one end of Africa to the other, they were feared in India too, in Indonesia, on the southern coast of China. They didn't care about the religion of the slaves they captured, Christians, Muslims, Animists, Hindus, Buddhists. Any flesh was good enough to fill the cages in the ship's hold. And what about the Turkish Khedives? They were far crueller in their tortures than the Christians. What about our kings? Are we not here because the late Hassan and his son Mohammed and his family threw us out? We are serving the Christian dogs because our own dogs are even fiercer and sink their teeth into us far more deeply. Here they treat us like servants, there they treated us like slaves. All men are bastards, all human beings, regardless of what God they believe in or say they believe in. We're all born from a woman's *tabún*. Do you believe that Allah blesses those filthy rich bastards in Fez or Marrakech who return from Mecca banging tambourines and sounding the horns of their imported Mercedes just so that everyone can see that they have enough money to have made the pilgrimage and be able to call themselves *hajji*? Are they fulfilling the teachings of the Koran any better than the rest of us? Why? Because they've walked seven times round the Kaaba, because they've travelled back and forth seven times between As-Safa and Al-Marwah, and drunk from the Zamzam well? I travel back and forth every day just to scrape a living. And I drink the salt water from the well of my sweat. And yet they, from their luxury hotels in Mecca, humiliate you by telling you that they're better believers because they can go where you can't. Just because they can afford the flight to Mecca – first-class pilgrims in a Boeing – they're convinced that they'll enter Paradise before you do, you poor unfortunate wretch. Do you really think there will be rich and poor in Allah's heaven, people who drive Mercedes and people who clean other people's toilets? What kind of shitty religion is that? Is that Islam? I can assure you, Abdeljaq, that those pilgrims will go to hell before any Christians do. You can be quite sure of that.

Ahmed has walked slightly more than a kilometre from the place where his friend Rachid dropped him off that morning. Two prostitutes, standing at the top of the path to the marsh, eye him suspiciously, or at least so he thinks. He's never sure if people really do look at him suspiciously because he's an Arab or if he's simply getting paranoid and convinced that everyone looks at him like that. He'll have lunch with Rachid in the field next to the lagoon, the field he's walking through now. Before leaving home, he had some tea, bread and oil, a tomato and a tin of sardines, and had prepared himself a lunch of two boiled eggs, a few beans and a couple of lamb chops, but, unfortunately, he'd left the lunch box in the boot of his friend's car. I don't know why you bring anything, you could save what you bring for lunch and have it for supper, I'll get something from the kitchen, it's good food, Rachid tells him every day. The restaurant where he works appears in all the guidebooks, it's one of the best in Misent, but Ahmed is slightly disgusted by the thought of that meat slaughtered any old way, he likes to buy his meat from the halal butcher's and cook it himself at home, he likes what he calls *beldi* food, which is why he takes his own lunch with him every day, even though he usually ends up eating whatever Rachid has brought too. He's been missing his lunch box for some time now. He's hungry. He glances at his watch. Rachid, as he does every day, will bring a couple of Tupperware containers, filled with some sort of stew, which is absolutely fine, but not deemed good enough to serve to the customers, as well as some fruit and vegetables that he's either stolen or which have been given to him because they're not quite perfect. The light is beginning to thin, the fragile winter light gilds everything it touches. It's a mild afternoon: the surface of the water, the reeds, the palm trees far off, the buildings he can see in the distance, are all gradually turning to gold; even the sea, visible if he climbs up one of the dunes, even the sea is no longer its usual intense blue, but has taken on a faintly iridescent sheen. He lights a cigarette to assuage his hunger. He decides to make the most of the time he has until his friend arrives, and when he finishes his cigarette, he goes back to the spot where he left his fishing rod firmly anchored between some large stones, casts the net he's been wearing tied around his waist and studies the mirror-like surface of the lagoon on which insects are tracing geometrical designs with their slender legs. In his basket he has two medium-sized mullets and a rather smaller tench. Not a bad day. Tonight's supper.

When he leans forward to cast his net again, he suddenly hears a lot of barking and growling: a few metres off, two dogs are quarrelling over some scrap of meat and barking at each other. Ahmed picks up a stone and brandishes it threateningly, at the same time showing them the stick he always brings with him to the lagoon. The dogs don't even look at him, too busy growling and baring their teeth. He throws the stone. It bounces off the back of the larger dog, an Alsatian with matted fur, which turns its head, revealing a collar: one of those dogs abandoned by tourists at the end of the season which then wander about, lost, for months, until they're picked up by the local animal protection league. When the stone hits, the dog lets out a yelp and limps off, at which point the other dog grabs whatever it is they were fighting over and disappears into the bushes. The stone hit the Alsatian on the back, but that isn't why the dog is limping. One of its back legs is so mutilated and covered in scabs that the dog can't put any weight on it. Ahmed assumes it must have been run over at some point or that it got caught in a trap or entangled in some barbed wire. It runs awkwardly and fearfully. As it moves off, it glances back a couple of times, as if to make sure the man isn't coming after it to inflict further punishment. A lame, frightened dog and possibly vengeful too, for Ahmed fears that the dog is trying to retain his image, as the dog's aggressor, in the bloodshot mirror of its eyes. But servility cancels out aggression: the dog lowers its head as it trots gracelessly away. Its attitude indicates fear and submission – a creature beaten and made to suffer. Ahmed shudders, with a feeling that combines both sadness and distaste for the murky reality revealed by the dog's wounds. Disgust provoked by the sordid, but also by a dread of cruelty, the cruelty of a vengeful dog and the cruelty of the man or men who beat it. There are open wounds on the dog's skin, bloody welts, the remains of what could be either old and infected wounds or the symptoms of some skin disease. The other dog, smaller and fiercer-looking, has glossy black fur. Surprised by the Alsatian's reaction on being hit by the stone, the smaller dog at first drops the piece of rotten meat as it flees into the bushes, only to immediately snatch it up again. The dog lies down, its body half hidden among the reeds, only occasionally looking up, eyes bright and watchful. The meat hangs from its mouth. Ahmed has been looking with some curiosity at the piece of meat the two dogs were fighting over, and now he begins to look at it with growing horror, because he realises that the blackish lump is taking on a recognisable shape: despite its dark, putrescent appearance, despite the places where it has been gnawed clean, it is clearly a human hand. Curiosity makes him keep looking, overcoming the feelings of repugnance and horror urging him to look away. Ahmed wants to both see and not see; just as he wants to know and not know. He waves his stick at the black dog, forcing it to retreat a few paces. The animal growls, and although it does withdraw a little, it continues to glare at him and refuses to give up its prey, which – and Ahmed has no doubts about this now – is all that remains of a human hand. At the same time, his gaze slides away, again, deliberately and not deliberately, towards certain shapes lying sunk in the mud a few metres further off, to the right of the place where the dogs had been a moment before. He identifies that spot as the source of the pestilential odour he has been aware of for a while and which suddenly grows more intense. Two of the half-buried, mud-coated shapes in the water are clearly human forms. The remains of the third mangled shape could belong to a man who has been mutilated or to a body largely submerged in mud, it could also be the corpse of an animal, a dog, a sheep, a pig. As soon as he realises that these are human remains, Ahmed knows that he must leave at once. Just having seen them makes him an accomplice to something, impregnates him with guilt. His first impulse is to run, but that would make him look still more suspicious: he starts walking quickly, brushing aside the leaves of the reeds that strike his face. He keeps glancing to right and left to see if anyone could have spotted him, but he sees no one. He's unlikely to meet one of those English or German retirees who walk briskly along the side of the road convinced that, as they breathe in the exhaust fumes from cars and trucks, they are, in fact, engaged in healthy exercise; or else one of those excessively thin individuals, more drug addicts than sportsmen, who go jogging along by the irrigation ditches and along the edges of the orange groves: no, none of the fauna prowling the orchards and engaged in various forms of exercise regimes ever comes to that particular piece of marshland.

He moves off as fast as he can, although he can't resist the temptation to turn round a couple of times and look back at that piece of putrid meat, at the tendons and bones with which the black dog is busily playing, beneath the gaze of the Alsatian, which has returned from its brief absence and is again watching from a couple of metres away. Ahmed looks, above all, at the dark shapes half buried in the mud. Despite his haste, he still has time to see, behind one of the dunes and hidden in the undergrowth, the burnt-out carcass of a car, whose presence only increases the sinister air the place has suddenly taken on. He stops breathing. He can't breathe, he can feel a rapid pulse beating in his chest, his temples, his wrists, a buzzing in his head. Esteban told him once that criminals used to throw incriminating weapons into the thick waters of the lagoon. He keeps walking and keeps looking, but can't seem to control the movements of his eyes, which appear to have acquired a life of their own and move at will: they shift from side to side, forcing him to turn his head. He doesn't want to look, but can't help himself, although now he's less concerned about those shapes or about the dogs than about the shadows he thinks he can glimpse behind the reeds or around each bend in the path or in the dips and folds of the dunes. With each step he takes, he grows more confused by the shifting shadows and silhouettes, which take on seemingly human forms. He feels he's being watched. He has a sense that people are observing him from the dunes, from the road, from the reed beds on the far side of the lagoon, even from the slopes of the distant mountains. He suspects that this morning, as he was walking along by the main road, he became an object of interest to passing drivers, to the prostitutes who saw him setting off along the path to the marsh, to the children who were playing by the shacks he passed at the end of Avenida de La Marina, and at that moment, wishing he could erase himself from their memories, he remembers that, in his haste, he has left behind his fishing rod secured between two boulders, his net in the water and his basket on the shore, on the grass. He can't just abandon his belongings there, it would be so easy for a detective to identify both rod and net; especially the fishing rod, which probably still bears the tag from the sports shop in Misent where he bought it seven or eight months ago when he first started coming with Esteban to go fishing, and so he runs back to the place he has just left (now he really is frightened, his whole body trembling), the reeds cut his face, his cheeks, his eyelids. When he pushes them aside, he feels their sharp edges cutting the palm of his hand. As soon as he has retrieved his fishing rod, he must return to the point on the road where he arranged to meet his friend, but it would be stupid to stay there sitting by the kerb, waiting as he usually does where the path meets the road – he'd be leaving all kinds of clues, because that's already the way his mind is working, as if he were one of the guilty parties. No, he can't possibly wait there, but neither can he just leave and have his friend set off down the path looking for him, because when the inevitable investigations begin (no, no, calm down, he tells himself, months and months could pass before anyone else goes to that hidden corner) someone might recognise the car and identify Rachid's clapped-out, rusty fifteen-year-old Ford Mondeo, with its dented doors and its back bumper held on with wire. Besides, there's that burnt-out car in the dunes, and someone is sure to report the disappearances; they'll start dredging the lagoon, although who knows who those bodies might be. Probably immigrants like him, people just passing through, or maybe mafiosi fallen victim to some settling of scores: Moroccans, Colombians, Russians, Ukrainians, Romanians. Perhaps a couple of prostitutes, their throats cut by their pimps, women nobody will take the trouble to look for.

He decides to start walking along the main road, back to La Marina, and trust that Rachid will spot him from his car. Much as he would like to, he can't stay still. He sets off towards Misent, then immediately retraces his steps, watching the passing cars, waiting anxiously for Rachid to appear, as if getting into his friend's car would be like entering a refuge where he could disappear as soon as he sits down, arms hanging loose, breathing under control, head against the headrest, one cheek pressed against the cold glass of the window, relaxing and vanishing completely: the same psychological mechanism that allows children to believe they're invisible when they cover their eyes with their hands: if you can't see, then you can't be seen. Sitting beside the driver of the Mondeo would be proof that he had nothing to do with that putrefying hand, with the stinking shapes buried in the mud, with that burnt-out car; once he has relaxed enough to disappear into the passenger seat of Rachid's Mondeo, when they reach the intersection at the Avenida de La Marina a few kilometres further on, he will roll down the window and lean out to feel the cool evening air on his face, convincing himself that he saw nothing. He will be just another passenger among the thousands of others who travel along Route 332 every day, people filling that overpopulated area for a few seconds and then lost again along the capillaries of the traffic heading for one of the small towns nearby or continuing on to some other part of Europe. At that point, his only thought is that he must tell no one what he's seen (not even Rachid, who will know from his face that something has happened? *Why didn't you wait for me by the roadside? You seem worried, has something happened?*), and yet he needs to tell someone as soon as possible, because he won't be able to rest until he does; only by sharing the fear will he be able to detach it from himself. He approaches the junction and slows his pace to something approaching normal. He stops for a moment to open his basket and throw the fish into the gutter, the fish he caught and that now disgust him. He imagines the crows or the foxes biting greedily into them. He feels like throwing up. The lagoon, which was the colour of cast steel when he arrived, is now smooth and delicate, like old gold, with coppery tints on the waves whipped up by the breeze.

2

EXTERNAL LOCATIONS

14 DECEMBER 2010

I've sat my father down in front of the TV to watch his morning Western, whichever one was on the pay-TV that day. He sits there amazed at the galloping horses, the neighing, the Indians and the noise of gunfire: I know he won't move until I come back. After the Western, they'll put on some film about terrorists, with scowling Arabs speaking a guttural language, translated into subtitles too small to decipher on the TV screen; or one about policemen chasing drug traffickers, Latinos or blacks, with lots of cars screeching round corners, crashing into each other and, finally, hurtling off a high metal bridge. He'll stay there, eyes glued to the screen or, more likely, he'll doze off, eyes closed – it comes to the same thing. In fact, he stares with equal interest at the bathroom wall when I'm washing him or at the ceiling when I put him to bed. The important thing is that he doesn't try to get up and risk hurting himself. To avoid this, I put him in a big armchair that he couldn't get out of even if he wanted to, because it's too deep and too low – not, of course, that he'd have the strength to stand up anyway, but just to make sure he won't fall out, I roll up a sheet, wrap it round his chest and tie it to the chair back, taking care not to tie it too tightly. I check that he can move his body back and forth. Is that all right, not too tight? I ask simply to say something, simply to ask something, because he hasn't spoken for months now, and I can't even tell if he can actually see. That is, he *can* see, because he closes his eyes if I shine a bright light in his face or if I make him turn his head towards a light bulb, and his eyes follow my hand if I move it slowly from side to side in front of him; and he can hear too, although it isn't clear whether he understands me or not; he jumps and looks frightened if I shout at him or if he hears a loud noise immediately behind him. He hasn't spoken since they removed the tumour from his trachea. He doesn't speak, but he could write and ask for things in writing, he could express himself through gestures, but he doesn't – he doesn't show the least interest in communicating. The doctors have run all kinds of tests and scans and tell me that since there's no damage to his brain, they can't understand what's wrong with him. Age. He's over ninety now. He's become a shop-window mannequin. Not that I'm particularly interested in anything he might have to say, although now that Liliana doesn't come any more and I've closed the workshop, I do spend more time observing him. I watch him, study him, learning useless lessons with no practical application. Human life is nature's biggest waste of time and energy: just when it seems that you're beginning to make the most of what you know, you die, and those who come after you have to start all over again from scratch. Helping a child learn how to walk, taking him to school and teaching him to tell a circle from a square, yellow from red, solid from liquid, hard from soft. That's what he taught me. Life – a waste of time. Get used to it. He's always been very bright, the old man, bright and a real bastard too. But that's what he taught me and what I repeated to Liliana, perhaps simply because I wanted to make her feel sorry for me. I'm packing things away: it's time to shut up shop, I told her. And she said: Well, it's never too late to learn something new. One day, I'm going to cook you both a really good *sancocho*, which is like a stew, except that we add vegetables you Spaniards hardly ever use or don't even know about – vegetables like arracacha, corncob, yucca, green plantain, and we season it with coriander, that herb I used to miss so much here until they started selling it in the Colombian shop and in the Muslim shops. A sort of fragrant parsley. We Latin Americans eat it and so do the Arabs. Because it's on my way, I usually buy coriander in that Arab greengrocer's next to the halal butcher. I would never buy meat from that butcher, of course. God knows where they get their lamb and their beef. I saw a TV programme once that said Spain's full of illegal slaughterhouses supplying Muslim shops. Apparently, they have to kill the animal while facing Mecca, well, we all have our little ways, I suppose. In the same programme, they showed you how Chinese restaurants store ducks, dear God, apparently their fridges smell worse than a dead dog, it's enough to make your hair stand on end, and you don't even want to know what else they said they found there. But I was talking about coriander, which you don't use here, or even know about, just as you don't know about real fruit: mangos, papayas, soursops, guayabas, uchuvas, passion fruit, custard apples, pitayas and ahuyama, which you call squash. You're getting more familiar with some of those fruits now, because the supermarkets sell them, but as far as I know, you've only ever eaten tasteless things like bananas, apples, pears, oranges, and that's about it, oh, and those awful pineapples that arrive from Costa Rica and taste of nothing at all and go rotten if you leave them in the fridge for a few days. No, don't laugh, it's true. I bet you've never eaten a decent pineapple in your life. A perfectly ripe pineapple, just picked, with that lovely sweet, honeyed flavour. Her voice, every evening, while I sit him down at the table laid with a plastic tablecloth and on which I will place the larger plate with the vegetables and the smaller plate with the omelette, just as she used to do up until a few days ago. Even in his present helpless state, he's still ruling my life, setting me tasks, imposing a timetable, more or less as he's always done, yes, my diary is still dependent on him. Before, he achieved this by imposing his authority; now he does so through his silence and ineptitude. He is the powerless patient: he's swapped authority for a demand for compassion; and I have become his servant, because I feel sorry for him. On the other hand, we have all been subject to his mood swings for as long as I can remember. His life, on the other hand, has been his property alone. He has behaved much as a king behaves – depending on the constitution – or a certain sort of artist – taking no responsibility for his actions: today I protest and complain, tomorrow I won't utter a word, the day after that I'll be an attention-seeker, the next I won't even be able to bear anyone looking at me. Now that I think about it, he did have an artist's mentality. In his youth, he wanted to be an artist. He loved to read novels, as well as books about history, art and politics. He would borrow them from the local library. On Friday afternoons, he'd get cleaned up, put on a white shirt and a jacket, and go and change his library books. On Sunday afternoons, in other people's houses, when football matches were blaring out from radios, utter silence reigned in ours: my father would be sitting by the window, reading, taking advantage of the afternoon light; then he would lower the blind and turn on the standard lamp next to the only armchair in the house, and remain immersed in his book until supper time, after which he would return to the armchair and resume his reading. The soul of an artist. As a young man, he wanted to be a sculptor, which is what he wanted me to be as well, but the chaos of the civil war put an end to his ambitions. I managed to put an end to my own ambitions all by myself. I was never interested in the skill he'd chosen for me. I lasted only a few months at art college. He and my grandfather made some of the bits of furniture for the house, furniture decorated

24

in a style that was old-fashioned even then, around the time of the Republic and in the years immediately preceding, because, by then, in the late 1920s and early 30s, people were choosing designs that were vaguely art deco, while they, those staunch revolutionaries, adopted a Renaissance style, with carving reminiscent of certain facades that tend to feature in TV documentaries about Salamanca: full of *grottesche*, medallions and acanthus leaves. Obsolete from the day they were born, but no one could deny their excellent quality. They lent a dignity to our house at a time when we had barely enough to eat. More a matter of professional pride than extravagance.

Once I've settled my father in front of the TV, I go down to the shed in the yard to fetch my Sarasqueta shotgun, my cartridge belt and my wellingtons, and I call to the dog in a tone of voice that he understands to mean: Get in the car. I hold open the door of my four-wheel drive and in he jumps and curls up in the back, still watching my every move. He's a very docile creature, a good hunter, but, above all, a good companion. He lies down beside me in the workshop and stays there for hours, and if I sit in the armchair in the living room, he comes over and rests his head on my thigh, as if to say that he's there if I need him, that I can count on him. I've never seen him be aggressive with anyone, far less try to bite them. He does growl if someone – usually the neighbour's cat – goes anywhere near his bowl. Greed is his only defect, but that's more a sign of a healthy dog really. Wherever I sit, he lies down next to me and watches me, but he's always very still, apart from when he wags his tail or comes over to rub against my leg or to stand on his back legs, resting his front paws on my chest (easy does it, you're going to push me over), staring up at me and barking, which is his way of speaking to me, of demanding my attention. He barks, too, when he sees me talking to someone or hears me on my mobile, and then his barking becomes more insistent. He's jealous. If I take him out hunting, he runs a few feet ahead of me, turning round now and then, so as not to lose that contact between man and dog. Sometimes, he runs so fast that his agility (such harmony of movement between legs and back) still fills me with admiration. He returns, panting, sometimes carrying in his mouth the creature I've just brought down.

With the dog sprawled in the back seat, I turn on the engine, which starts on the first try, even though it's been a few days since I've driven it. Tom's a good dog, the Toyota is a good car. We've had some unforgettable times up at the lagoon, plunging into the mud, into the water and the shifting sands of the marshy areas; during the winter, I love driving along the beach, right on the very edge of the sea, where the waves break on the shore. And I've emerged from all those situations unscathed, it's never once let me down. I feel something very special when I take the wheel. The moment I open the door, I enjoy the car and smell the leather of its seats. I enjoy driving; I stroke the wheel and am filled with sadness, already missing that contact, thinking that soon yet another pleasure will be gone. And knowing this causes a wave of melancholy to rise up from my chest into my eyes. Life's a waste of time, my father used to say. Well, yes, you old bastard, yours at the moment is a waste of time several times over, dragging *our* lives down with you. Before setting off, I glanced in the rear-view mirror and caught sight of the dog's alert eyes and thought how sad that the wisdom they express will vanish along with us, will just end up amid the detritus of our own personal rubbish bin. The lives of pets don't seem to be compatible with economic returns either. Despite everything you know, dog, despite everything you've learned, despite the supple movements of your back when you run, despite the skill

26

with which you sniff out your prey and diligently bring it back to me, you, too, are going to have to say goodbye to all this. What's to be done? I think, and only then, with the ignition key between my fingers, my eyes fixed on the dog's eyes, only then do I hesitate and feel like crying. The bloody dog.

First, you mash the maize, then you add the beans and a bay leaf, heat up the stock, peel the plantains, grate the yucca. Liliana's voice. It's really delicious. The dog's eyes. From the workshop, I drive along the road that skirts La Marina beach, past the apartment blocks and the gardens that peer over the walls – palm trees, bougainvilleas, jasmines, thujas, the complete catalogue of plants from the local nurseries – and on as far as the junction with Route 332. The two roads meet in a kind of suburban landscape: abandoned orchards, scrub, rubble that the autumn rains have covered in grass, the characteristic adornment of these areas that were about to be reclassified as urban in the latter years of the economic boom, but which remain in a kind of legal limbo, an apparent no-man's-land on which shacks have sprung up, doubtless built by people from Eastern Europe or by Moroccans who work as agricultural labourers and go marauding for metal, discarded household appliances, old furniture, copper, and whatever else they can find or steal: they'll take anything, they'll rip up pipes, irrigators, cables; they'll make off with tractors, with tons of fruit and even destroy whole orchards; it wouldn't be the first time a farmer has arrived at his orange grove to find that every tree has been chopped down to be sold for firewood. They work as scrap dealers near their local shanty town, piling up scrap metal and strewing around them the mutilated carcasses of cars, fridges, washing machines and old air-conditioning units, and all within sight of the housing developments advertised on the huge roadside billboards as 'luxury estates'. People don't care: as long as the marauders don't throw their rubbish over the wall and the smell of putrefaction doesn't reach their private terrace, the whole world can sink into the shit for all they care.

At the point where the two roads cross, twenty or so prostitutes sit basking in the winter sunshine. They sit on plastic chairs next to the reed beds or walk up and down the hard shoulder; they perch at small rickety plastic tables painting their nails, studying themselves in their powder compacts, playing solitaire or smoking; they wear G-strings that reveal their thighs and buttocks, and tiny unbuttoned jackets that show their tits, even though in the damp air of this muddy area between the lagoon and beach the December sun is too weak to take the edge off the chill, which definitely has its claws out on a day like today, when the wind is from the northwest. Some of the women pace nervously up and down, only a few metres back and forth, as if they were pacing not the hard shoulder of a highway but a narrow prison cell (where several of them doubtless learned this invigorating exercise). They'll gesticulate, perform — opening their legs or crouching down and wiggling their rear ends at any traffic, alerted by the sound of a truck or the beep of a horn. They lift their clothes up above their tits, showing their naked bodies to the truck drivers, to the solitary occupants of vans bearing the logos of locksmiths, couriers, glaziers or food distributors; white thighs or yellowish breasts, pink torsos, flesh the colour of milky coffee or black — or, as people used to say, the colour of ebony, gleaming in the fragile morning light: a sampler of all the races (although only very rarely are there any Asian women — Chinese, Cambodian or Thai — though you can, of course, find them), but the majority are women from Eastern Europe, women with bluish, almost phosphorescent flesh, who seem to emit light rather than receive it. There are loads of

African women and quite a few Latin Americans, although lately I've seen fewer Brazilians, who were the first to appear here. It seems that things are on the up in Brazil, and I imagine the girls setting up business in Rio or São Paulo, hopefully starting their own hair salons or boutiques selling clothes or shoes. Great things seem to be in the offing for Brazil, what with the Olympics being held there and everything. I drive past the women almost without looking. I know one of them, I've seen her here before, and another woman, a Ukrainian I fucked a few months ago, stands looking at the car as I pass, she probably recognised me, but today I drive on – a quick sideways glance and onwards. I'm not on the lookout for sex. I'm on the lookout for locations, for a suitable stage. Or, rather, I'm driving to the spot I've already chosen, to carry out a visual inspection, as they say on the news about the police investigating a crime scene: I'm going back to the very first place I can remember, the place my uncle showed me and that my father always seemed to hanker after, somewhere he would like to have stayed, but couldn't: a second chance. You see, Dad, this time, the postman rang more than twice. You've seen the film, haven't you? Pretty dirty stuff, like everything else in this world. I remember the two main actors, covered in flour, rolling around on the kitchen table. So like life. The theme of the film: the egotism of those who betray and kill for the sake of money and pleasure, the usual tedious story. But then life, basically, is a dirty business; regardless of whether it's pleasure or pain, we all sweat, shit and smell. My old man learned this in the best of all possible schools – war (a war between neighbours too), police stations and prison. The things you can see and smell in places and circumstances like that . . . but let's not go there. Anyway, if I spot some bird I can shoot (and the marsh is a sure-fire place for that), I'll do a little hunting. Small game, of course. That's why I brought my shotgun. It deserves a role in this rehearsal. A key role. It'll play a decisive role in the denouement. When I say hunting, I mean hunting for birds, and not the human kind, today they're off the menu: you want fucky-fucky I'll suck you off without a condom or you can give it to me from behind for thirty euros – from the front, twenty. Nothing much has changed since men were men. Man – a biped buyer of cunts. Not a bad definition. In drachma in sestertius in doubloons in pounds in marks in dollars in roubles. In euros. A buyer of cunts, a hirer of arses, but I don't want to confuse things by mixing up my expeditions; it seems right to impose a certain order on a day like today. The eve of liturgical celebrations calls for a little quiet reflection: confession of one's sins and penance. The purpose of the emendation is irrelevant in this case. There will be no opportunity to reoffend. Before Christmas comes Advent; before Easter comes Lent. Rigorous days of meditation and abstinence that prepare us for the party. Let's do it. Drive out desire, drive out the voices and mouths that ooze desire, the doorways that feed the oven of desire: the velvety voice, the seductive timbre, the soft lips, the poisonous music. Corn pancakes made with eggs, a plantain sandwich, the creamy rice we make in Valle del Cauca. Don Esteban, you have no idea how delicious Colombian food can be. You Spaniards think we Colombians are savages. True enough, Liliana, among the country bumpkins of Olba, you don't exactly get good press, but then they're afraid of anything they haven't seen born and hope to see die. And then there's all the stuff you read in the papers, what you hear on the radio or see on TV – all that doesn't really help: guerrillas, FARC, paramilitaries, drug clans, the cartels in Cali and Medellín, guns, trafficking of this, that and the other, all those shipments that arrive along with consignments of pineapples, canned food, timber, children's clothes or ballet shoes. Yes, you're right, Don Esteban, but we're not all like that, we're not all guerrillas or drug dealers. And anyway, aren't there any Spanish thieves, murderers, traffickers and terrorists? Does no one here ever shoot anyone dead? Are there no cocaine laboratories? And as for terrorism, well, look at all those people who died in the attacks in Madrid, evil is everywhere and probably good is too, although it's harder to find, especially for women, at least you men have your friends, whereas our female friends are more like rivals. Of course there are bad people here too, Liliana. It's her voice, and that little roll of fat between her jeans and her T-shirt, so troubling when you can't sleep: I feel as if she were just a metre ahead of me, reflected in the windscreen, the colour of her skin, the tone, the touch: her skin between my hand and the wheel. Warm, soft, deceptively honey-coloured. But, I tell myself, this is neither the time nor the place for such thoughts, I have to prepare the stage for the performance. On the days when I combined hunting or fishing with paying for the company of a girl, I felt the excitement of that shared intimacy in the silence of the reed beds; and my desire only grew when I'd see her getting more and more frightened as we plunged down barely discernible paths. Where are you taking me? she would ask, a tremor in her voice, while I wondered why fear always adds a little spice to sex: you start out searching for the light and end up in a dark labyrinth, you start out looking for the smooth marble of flesh and end up enmired in the mud of secretions. It's exciting – satisfying – having sex in that dense vegetal boudoir; desire and fear all in one, the ideal combination. And yet, once it was over, I would feel dirtier and guiltier than if I'd done it somewhere else, by which I mean some poky little room with closed windows and a dim light that was sometimes red, sometimes pink and, at others, vaguely blue; or the nocturnal, ghostly back seat of the car, trembling legs next to an open door. Sex that only intensified the post-coital sadness that seems innate in the human animal. Whenever I had sex here, by the lagoon, I was looking for a sense of freedom, and yet it seemed to me I wasn't the only one left feeling soiled, which is how I usually feel after my venal contacts in those ill-lit rooms (I relieve it with a vigorous shower when I get home, sponging myself down with plenty of soap and finishing off with a generous sprinkling of eau de cologne); except for one woman, it always felt as if I was soiling the place itself, which is rather paradoxical, given that the lagoon has long been a kind of neglected backyard for the neighbouring towns, one where everything was permitted and where decades of rubbish and filth have been allowed to accumulate. It's only with the latest fad for conservation and ecology that the area has acquired some symbolic value, and the newspapers and the local TV station describe it as the area's great green lung (the sea is the other great, powerful lung, the one that growls and hisses and grows angry and washes us all), and they refer to it as a refuge for indigenous species and a special place for migrating birds to nest. Until about ten years ago, Bernal, the manufacturer of asphalt roofing felt, used the lagoon as a dumping ground for any defective material. Everyone knew about it and yet it never occurred to anyone to report it. Bernal went entirely unpunished. Just like his father, although he was apparently more civilised than his father. I'm not joking. In the 1940s, his father, who owned a few fishing boats, used to get rid of the occasional awkward corpse by putting it in a boat, tying a stone around its neck and then dropping it over the side into the vast, merciful Canal de Ibiza, where the waters separating Spain from the island are at their deepest: you find the best prawns and the best red tuna there, the kind that they say is going extinct. A corpse is organic matter, nutrients. The sea washes everything clean or else drives it out or gobbles it up, purifies with iodine and saltpetre, uses and recycles: one assumes the water there is healthy, not like the lagoon, which is always viewed by the people living nearby as an unhealthy, fetid place, stagnant water that can't be trusted, liquid that grows

warm and putrid in the spring sun and is only washed clean
again when the first cold drops of rain fall in the autumn. The
sea cleanses and oxygenates, the lagoon rots – like wars, police
stations and prisons. They rot you, don't they, Dad? They stink.
Lagoons don't get a very good press: fever, malaria, filth. The
Romans drained lakes like this for reasons of health and economy,
I've seen it on TV documentaries: Rome was surrounded by
infectious swamps, like our own dear marsh, beads in the malarial
necklace of the Mediterranean, a marshy chain scattered along
the coast; until very recently, farmers, with their hunger for
arable land, have always systematically drained all the lakes in
the area. The novelist Blasco Ibáñez described the process, which
nowadays is considered highly prejudicial to the environment,
but thanks to which a lot of people managed to make a living
here. Anyone who hasn't read the novel is sure to have seen the
TV series. I've read the book: the edition my grandfather bought
before the war must still be knocking around in the house
somewhere (we saved half a dozen or so of the books from one
of the boxes my grandmother buried, I don't think there can
be many more than that in the whole house), and I watched
the series they showed a few years back. The seashore has never
been a hospitable place and, apart from a few promontories, it
remained deserted until a few decades ago, when they started
building wherever they wanted. In Misent, for example, there
are housing developments right on the beach with names like
La Laguna, Las Balsas, Saladar or El Marjal, whose inhabitants
all complain that their houses get flooded with the onset of the
autumn rains. But what sensible person would think of buying
a place in a development with a name like that? The names of
the places retain the memory of what they were. Lagoons.
Quagmires. Ponds. Bogs. Salt pans. My father felt a particular
scorn for people who bought houses and apartments in areas
reclaimed from the lagoon. In fact, he scorned all those who

arrived in the area drawn by the call of the sea. Layabouts. Adventurers. Speculators. The coast is an evil place, he used to say. The sea either washes up or attracts rubbish, and only the scum remains. It's always been like that: con men, card sharps, thugs. Although now that the human animal has become the least protected species, the ecologists probably consider what Bernal Jr did as less forgivable than what his father did, because the worst sin has always been to destroy the eternal (no sin committed against the Holy Spirit can ever be forgiven) and for our materialistic society the eternal is no longer God, which means that the human body doesn't merit the respect it once enjoyed when it was deemed to be the temple of the Holy Spirit, no, now the great shrine of the divinity is nature: impregnating water and mud with asphalt roofing felt – bituminous matter, glass fibre, carcinogenic asbestos – which is what Bernal Jr did – seems far worse than the murders his father committed. If you throw a corpse into the sea, you're doing the environment a favour, supplying food for the fish to nibble on with their small cold mouths. The sins of the gunmen – who turned ditches into graves and peppered the walls of cemeteries with bullets, who fed the fishes out at sea – those were all absolved by the Transition, because apparently they were only venial sins, whereas the sins committed against the environment have no expiry date and no judge can absolve them. Let's not deceive ourselves, man is nothing very special. In fact, there are so many of us that our governments don't know what to do with us all. Six billion humans on the planet and only six or seven thousand Bengal tigers: tell me – who needs protecting most? Yes, you decide who needs most care. A dying African, Chinaman or Scotsman or a beautiful tiger killed by a hunter. A tiger with its pelt of matchless colours and its flashing eyes is far more beautiful than a varicose-veined old git like me. What a difference in the way it carries itself. How elegant the one and how clumsy the other.

Look how they move. Put them next to each other in a cage in the zoo. The children gather round the old man's cage and laugh as they watch him delousing himself or crouching down to defecate; outside the tiger's cage, though, they open their eyes wide with admiration. The sleight of hand that made man the centre of the universe no longer convinces. It's true that we can recognise human animals by their gestures, faces and voices, and this arouses our sympathy, but we can also recognise the features of the domestic cat or dog we live with, we can attribute feelings to them too. Voices are another matter: Could you help me fold the sheets. No, not like that, the other way. God, those great clumsy hands of yours make me laugh, oh, sorry, I only meant that you look as if you could tear the cloth just by touching it. And when I said 'clumsy', I didn't mean that your hands were ugly – they're very strong, no, not ugly at all, you have lovely hands, virile hands, a man's hands.

We turn the sheet this way and that before we can agree on which way we're going to fold it. Our hands touch when I hand her the folded sheet and again when she gives me the pillow to hold while she smooths the pillowcase. Do you know how many varieties of potato there are in Colombia? The pores of our skin give off the warm sweat in which we gently cook during the night.

There are two girls (I don't think they can even be eighteen yet) standing at the end of the road where I turn off to reach the lagoon, at a point where the reed beds come right up to the hard shoulder. They're chatting to each other, blocking the way, standing right in front of my car, doubtless assuming I'm a potential customer. I stop for a moment so as not to run them over. Each one runs her tongue over her lips, smiles, strokes her

35

crotch, and one girl reveals a brush of fair, well-trimmed pubic hair, as she elbows her friend and guffaws, pointing at me, perhaps meaning, look at that old man. That dirty old man. A disgusting old man – a lech. At least, that's the unpleasant thought that passes through my head. I pap my hooter and put my foot down on the accelerator. The car lurches forward with an aggressive roar that makes them step hurriedly aside. They wave their arms about and shout things in Russian or Romanian, and it doesn't take much intelligence to understand that they're telling me that for all they care I can fuck off. Despite that earlier depressing thought (of the dirty old man, so proud of his sixty-thousand-euro four-wheel drive that I saw reflected back at me in the mirror of their eyes), they've nevertheless managed to arouse me and I drive the rest of the way with my left hand pressed down on my flies. My cock deflates beneath the weight of my hand, at the same time as the two whores disappear from my rear-view mirror – at the bend in the road, their gesticulating figures have vanished behind the vegetation. The road surface (if you can call it that) is pure mud and full of deep potholes filled with rainwater. I advance very slowly. At the first intersection, I turn left along a dirt road just before you get to the river, or whatever you want to call that stretch of water which, like another half-dozen or so similar stretches of water further north, forms the system of canals through which the lagoon flows into the sea. I park the car by the water's edge, on the grassy bank. The pleasure I get from driving down these diabolical roads comes in large measure from knowing that I won't meet any police – no civil guards or nature protection police or environmental police – or even other fishermen or hunters: no one ventures down these dirt roads buried in scrub (the lagoon has been declared a nature reserve, but no one keeps watch over it or guards it: there's no budget for that), and no one else knows the complicated grid you have to reconstruct each time you visit, given that it's used less and less, and the people who once knew every inch of the area and kept the pathways reasonably clear have also disappeared. I've known this place for over sixty years. I've come here either alone or with Francisco, Álvaro, Julio and, lately, Ahmed. I've been coming here ever since my Uncle Ramón started bringing me when I was a child, once or twice a week, to hunt for coots, crakes, mallards or one of those ducks that we call mute ducks and the French call Barbary ducks, creatures that added a touch of highly valued protein to our stews, along with a bit of rice – the inevitable local vegetable – some spinach, a few potatoes, a handful of beans, some chard or a few cardoon stalks, protein that was considered a luxury at the market, although most country people, instead of eating what they caught, sold it to restaurants back then or to distributors who sent it off to the butchers' shops in Valencia. The protein gleaned from the lagoon paid for the inferior protein and fat we bought in the market: bacon, offal, chorizo and black pudding.

Go on, then, tell me how many varieties of potato you have in your country?

Well, they say we have over a thousand, *tuquerreña, pastusa, roja nariño, mambera, criolla paisa*. You hardly know anything about my country really. On television, the only time Colombia gets a mention is when there's an item about drug trafficking or there's been another massacre by some guerrilla group.

I've known these paths for as long as I can remember. My uncle showed me how to use a shotgun when I was only eleven or twelve: children matured much earlier then; by the age of nine or ten, we were helping in the fields, on building sites, in work-shops. The first shot I fired nearly knocked me off my feet and left me with a huge bruise on my shoulder. As you can imagine, I completely missed the target and turned to my uncle, red-faced with embarrassment. I thought he would make fun of me, but he didn't laugh as I'd feared he would, instead, he tousled my hair and said: You have just acquired the power to take away life, which is a pretty pathetic power really, because if you had real power – the power nobody has – not even God, I mean who ever believed that business with Lazarus? – you'd be able to restore life to the dead. *Taking* life is easy, anyone can do that. They do it every day all over the world. Just read the newspaper and you'll see. Even you could do it, take someone's life I mean, although obviously you'd have to improve your aim a little (and then he did smile teasingly, the corners of his lively grey eyes etched with a web of delicate lines). Mankind may have constructed vast buildings, destroyed whole mountains, built canals and bridges, but we've never yet succeeded in opening the eyes of a child who has just died. Sometimes it's the biggest, heaviest things that are easiest to move. Huge stones in the back of a truck, vans laden with heavy metals. And yet everything that's inside you – what you think, what you want – all of which apparently weighs nothing – no strong man can lift that onto his shoulder and move it somewhere else. No truck can transport it. Loving someone you despise or don't really care for is a lot harder than flooring him with a punch. Men hit each other out of a sense of powerlessness. They think that by using force they can get what they can't get by using tenderness or intelligence.

He must have absorbed these ideas from my grandfather, who read them in the Russian novels he borrowed from the community library in Misent (there was no library in Olba at the time); he would cycle there wearing his best clothes, with his carefully pressed trousers folded into his bicycle clips, just as my father used to do on Friday afternoons, years later, although, by then, the community library had gone and there probably weren't a lot of Russian novels in the municipal library. The men in my family liked those books. We kept them in the house until the war ended (and with it, my grandfather's life), gospels of a code that was about to impose itself, the violence of the masses, the chronicle of the workers' epic struggle. Russia came to mean the Soviet Union, the mother of all the world's workers. Francisco and I have often remarked on how the bright light of all things Russian inspired a couple of generations of Spaniards (although Francisco's uncles, grandparents and parents experienced it more as a blinding threat). Now, when you say 'Russian', you think the worst: extortion, mafias, the trafficking of women and of human flesh in general, flesh, which, as with herds of animals, seems so dull and undifferentiated when seen from a distance, and yet so magnificent in the one individual you have before you, in those bodies in roadside brothels that can be yours for forty or fifty euros. Soviet Russia. The class struggle. My father always refused to expand the workshop. We take on just enough work to keep us busy. And that's that. We don't live off other people's work, but our own. We don't exploit anyone. Apart from Álvaro, that is. But Álvaro, he would say, is family, his father helped me when I was in prison with him and stuck by me when I came out. For my father, Álvaro was a son, a relationship I'm not sure I could presume to claim for myself. I was *take this, pick that up, carry this, assemble that.* He never once called me by my name, never used any term of endearment – my dear, sweetheart, sweetie – as I so often have with Liliana: Why buy light bulbs in the hardware store for two euros, when you can buy them in the Chinese shop for just thirty céntimos? Why buy rubbish bags in the supermarket, when you can get twice as many at the Chinese shop for less? I'll buy the bags next time, because all you're doing is paying more for the same thing. You're right, Liliana, you're a much better shopper – you're more careful with money. You notice prices, add up the céntimos, work out distances – how much you'd save or what you'd waste on petrol, how much you get in a packet, twelve or fifteen, you sniff out bargains, clip coupons, accumulate points on your loyalty card.

We sometimes caught a wild boar, which we finished off with the shotgun my uncle kept hidden beneath a trapdoor in the workshop. My uncle could never get a gun licence: he was too young to have been in the war, but was paying the price for his family's political allegiances. When he got married and left home, he gave the gun to me (I've caught my deer now, I just hope she doesn't stick a pair of antlers on me, he said, beaming and kissing his new wife) as well as his fishing tackle so that I could catch fish in the marsh, possibly easier to catch than the fish in the sea, and they were the best we could get at the time, given that we couldn't go out to sea and cast our nets like some of our neighbours in Olba, who owned small boats that they kept moored in the nearby harbour of Misent. The marsh was like a fish farm: shrimps, mullet, frogs, tench, barbel; eels and elvers: we didn't catch the elvers to eat, no, we didn't eat them; the sight of that seething mass in the bucket disgusted my grandmother, who called them maggots; my uncle would hold them close to her face, laughing, and my father would watch, sitting on a bench in one corner of the kitchen, leave your mother in peace, can't you see she doesn't like it, his mask about to crack into the merest hint of a smile. We sold them to a dealer who had a contact in Bilbao, and we made good money like that. The price shot up just before Christmas: later, I found out just how much people were prepared to pay at that time of year for what my grandmother thought were repulsive maggots. In stormy weather or at high tide, the sea bass would swim in from the sea. Nowadays, you only find those borderline fish in the canals of the lagoon. My uncle could pinpoint them with uncanny accuracy. I used to say he had a good nose, but what he had was common sense. He kept a list in his head, a system – every freshwater species, every saltwater species, every creature: The environment is irrelevant, and that applies to birds as well, and if you push me, to human beings too – they all have a right time and a right place, and need to be caught in a particular way and using a particular bait, he would tell me, while he was baiting the hook. I didn't initially understand what he meant: the fisherman who fails to choose the right bait does so because he doesn't know how fish think, and a fisherman or a hunter has to become the thing he's hunting, to think the same way. That's why the real hunter, the real fisherman, falls in love with his victim: he's hunting himself. And he feels sorry both for his prey and for himself. Hold the hook like this, no, we're not going to use the dough we normally use for bait, today we'll use this stuff. Smell it. Disgusting, isn't it? What a stink! Well, fish love that smell. And so do crabs. Everything rots. We'll end up rotting as well and we'll smell quite a lot worse. Many years from now, you'll rot too – and it's that rotten smell that the fish like. When you get older, you'll realise that they're like humans in that respect. Don't go thinking you're not going to end up smelling like a dead fish, Esteban. Ultimately, we all end up smelling like that, and just as a doctor prescribes particular medicines for each patient, Uncle Ramón offered each creature its particular bait and taught me how to think like a fish, like an eel, like a mallard, and to think about life's baits too. You will rot too, my boy. You will stink. Like everyone. See how beautiful the colour and design of the duck's neck feathers. But now it's dead.

And sixty years have passed, long enough for the web of veins to climb up the legs of that once young boy and form a network of blotches which, in the arch of the foot, has become a dark mass. The scaly skin on arms and chest is now the jaundiced colour of old ivory, I have age spots on my face and on the back of my hands, and then there's that old man's smell, like sour milk, Liliana, that aura of rust and urine. The body is no longer certainty, but doubt, suspicion. You think you'll make it through to tomorrow, but you know things won't be getting any better. Are the blue patches on my left foot turning black? Sometimes, with old men, our feet turn gangrenous and have to be amputated.

According to my uncle's strict code, every creature caught dies its own death, a ritual so precise it verges on the religious: after all, neither he, my father, nor my grandfather, and none of the men in this household, ever had any other religion than that of submitting to the codes imposed on them by nature, or dictated by their profession (perhaps more than most professions, carpentry is an extension of nature: a man goes into a forest armed with an axe, and with the help of his hands and his tools, he transforms nature into some useful civilised object). They put away the other codes – lacking in civilian life (the ones promised in those old Russian books) – to which they'd aspired, and in whose stormy sea they drowned. As for nature's codes, they managed to learn the rudiments. The civil war cut short any aspirations for justice and a harmonious life lived in common. With my grandfather, all it took was a few gunshots beside a wall outside Olba (it was only one shot, Esteban, why would they waste ammunition, he was found the following morning, along with five other men, next to the cemetery wall, right where the cemetery meets the rocks at the foot of the mountain, a buzzing of wasps announced the presence of the bodies on that spring morning, and there was a burn mark from the bullet in the back of his neck). With my father, any aspirations were frozen during his year and a bit of war and three years in prison, and by the prejudice that has pursued him ever since. Long enough to corrupt and rot any aspirations or hopes, which also die and stink once they're dead, poisoning everything around them, like fish, like bodies. My uncle was barely an adolescent, two eyes staring in horror at this sombre collection of images. My father never complained about being sidelined: he was too proud. Nor did he consider that he'd given up his aspirations (we don't live by exploiting other people, but from our own work: these words saved him), but he blamed us for the limitations placed on him. Decomposing, fermenting aspirations, just a hint of putrefaction: justice more like a punishment than a balm. He pretended to be above it all, crouched and waiting for these difficult times to pass, as if his own life were on hold, and the effort required to believe this was the fluid sustaining him, keeping him strong enough so that the outside world would not break him. Or so he believed. But he was already broken, he already had a deformity, a kind of monstrous hernia. And we should not dismiss the energy it takes to tell yourself a lie and maintain it. He could do that. He had that constancy of mind, the necessary willpower. After leaving prison, he grew a shell around himself on which the outside world could batter in vain. The shell protected him, sheltered his aspirations (Álvaro's father was the only one who helped me when I left prison, and Álvaro is like a son to me, the son of my best friend, the friend who never called me 'comrade', because he thought the word, in my ears, might be demeaning), and he has probably kept those aspirations to the end, like wine turning sour in the barrel. I said he shut himself away, but that's not true, he always had his antenna alert to a rather remote outer world: he didn't live outside the world, but in opposition to it, and that included his wife and children, who, I suppose, he made unhappy, if it's possible to make other people happy or unhappy.

★

Yesterday, as I do every evening, I went to the bar. First, a game of dominoes, then the chance to get your revenge with a few hands of cards. My partner's Justino – he's an occasional associate of Pedrós, whereas I'm an associate around whose neck Pedrós has tied a very large stone, just as Bernal's father – Bernal is partnering Francisco today – did with the corpses he threw into the Canal de Ibiza. After the game of dominoes – the losing pair pay for the coffee – we bet a couple of drinks on a few hands of tute, and that's when Justino announces that Pedrós' businesses – the hardware store, the domestic appliances shop, the offices – have been 'intervened'.

'"Intervened"? Like what happens to banks or to EU member states? What does that mean? That they've sent in the men in black?' asks Francisco.

And Justino says:

'They've impounded the delivery vans, the trucks; they've confiscated all the stuff in the warehouse, they've sealed off the shops, they've even confiscated the blowtorches, and not only have they halted all work on all the sites, they've taken away the accounts books. Apparently, Pedrós has disappeared from Olba, vanished, and no one knows where he is. His creditors are looking for him. Some of them have sworn they'll have him killed when they find him and I believe a few of them have clubbed together to pay some Moldavian or Ukrainian mafiosi, ready to scour the entire planet to find him.'

'Cut the bureaucratic language, Justino. "Intervene" is what the EU is doing with the PIGS. What's happening to Pedrós, here and elsewhere, is what we call "seizure of goods". You mean he's bankrupt, that they've seized his property,' says Francisco. 'Anyway, I knew about it already, we all did, didn't we?'

I had been convinced for some days that the subject would come up eventually – and probably because of me. But until today, not a word. And no one asks me now if Pedrós going bankrupt will affect me at all, knowing as they do, because I've been boasting about it for ages, that I'm responsible – or was responsible – for all the carpentry work in his developments. Fortunately, I've never told anyone that I'm also his partner in the construction company, that I put all my savings into his company and mortgaged my properties. It seemed so profitable and, yes, even the safest thing to do. I didn't tell them about that, but it will leak out eventually, these things always do, Pedrós himself might have announced it at suppers, at bars, at social gatherings. They'd probably been talking about it, about me, before I arrived. Carlos, the manager of the savings bank in Olba, may have mentioned it when he came in for his post-lunch coffee and sat – as he always does – in the bar opposite the bank. Or here, over a game of cards. I don't think he cares much about confidentiality. He'd be spilling the beans – quite openly now that the creditors have come knocking at the door: now that my account with the savings bank is no longer an account but a black hole. The only reason the people here haven't asked me is because they already know; besides, Álvaro must have told them that the workshop isn't just closed until further notice for renovation, as it says on the sign I pinned on the door. You don't start renovating when you're seventy; and the only things that are likely to give you notice at that age are your heart, your colon or your prostate. You just have to see the way the police have sealed off the building sites. It's obvious that I'm not trotting down to the market each morning with my shopping bag because I'm retired now, having simply chosen not to take myself off to a spa or to the Mexican Riviera Maya. Of course they know, and they probably know more than I do, there's bound to have been gossip about what Pedrós has done with my money and just where my participation in his business has landed me, namely in the rubbish dump. They've probably known about his bankruptcy for some time and, indirectly, about mine, and in fact, they probably knew before I did. The cuckold is always the last to find out and, of course, the one who knows least about the kinky things his wife gets up to with her lover. But these bastards are perfectly capable of keeping quiet and waiting for me to be the one to give in and confess, for me to break down in tears in the arms of my childhood friend and reveal all, to open up my heart: dear Francisco, Pedrós has bankrupted me. Help me. Save me. At least console me. That's what they want me to say. Or else I should get drunk with Justino and – stumbling and stuttering – tell him what everyone already knows: that I'm bankrupt and about to land in jail, and ask him tearfully not to forget me, not to abandon me; not to leave me alone behind bars, but to come and visit on the odd weekend and bring me a couple of slices of tortilla and a few packs of cigarettes. Of course I will, don't you worry, Esteban, I'll come with my plastic bucket and the tortilla wrapped in aluminium foil, I'll stand in line with the gypsy women, the criminals from Eastern Europe, the mothers of junkies from nice families who keep their faces half covered with scarves and tell you: my husband and I are only here because of our son, poor thing. He got into bad company, and, well, you know what boys are like when they get into drugs. We're not like these other people queuing up, and I could see at once that you're from a different class as well. And I can see it's your first time (and I have to laugh at the thought of Justino as the innocent virgin, *ha*), I'll tell you what you have to do, no, no need to thank me. And in a low voice: just take a look at them – it's frightening. Gypsies, Romanians, Colombians, Italian Mafia, Russians. Riff-raff the lot of them. I could see at once that you weren't like them. Anyway, let me explain: you have to put any clothes in one of those big black rubbish bags; and any food or soap or shampoo has to go in a plastic bucket. The gypsies on the corner sell them . . . Yes, that's what the bastards in this bar are waiting for. There's a simple reason why they're in no hurry to get the prisoner to tell all – they've already passed sentence on him. But I'm a wise old dog, and over the years, I've learned how to deal with interrogations because, as the saying goes, it's as easy to say a No that could save you as a Yes that could condemn you: I glance at the other card players and all three are impassively studying their hands. You're late today, Esteban, says Francisco. We played a game of tute to pass the time until you came. And Justino: Come on, let's finish this hand and have a game of dominoes. They all know. Word of Pedrós' bankruptcy came out more than two weeks ago, although news of his disappearance only reached this table today, and it's nearly two months since I put that sign up on the workshop door. The police sealed it all off ten days ago. But it's the details they like here, they want to squeeze every bit of juice out of the orange. I can feel them squeezing me gently with their fingers to see if they can get the first drops. They know they have time to squeeze hard, to milk me properly or stick me in the juicer. No hurry, they're not being pushy. Like Francisco said, it's what we call 'seizure of goods' (and that's just the prologue, the easiest part to admit). Every little dart they stick into Pedrós this afternoon will hurt me too. I'm the real target. I need to give myself an epidural: I close my eyes. That's it. The needle hurts when it goes in, but afterwards you feel nice and calm. Let them say what they like. Let the birth begin. If the baby's got a beard, we'll call him St Anthony and, if not, then La Purisima Concepción. Francisco smiles when he says the word 'seizure'. He's above all this: anything that doesn't affect him directly he just brushes off, and the truth is, he doesn't give a shit about what might affect us. As Justino says – mind you, Justino is jealous because he's no longer the centre of attention as he was for so many years – Francisco only comes to the bar in order to take notes, to pick up a bit of local colour to give his books

47

some street cred – jargon, stock phrases, gestures, atmosphere. He studies our meals and our drinks, which once were also his; our customs, our traditions: like an anthropologist, he asks us when exactly our mothers used to add the paprika to a dish of *all-i-pebre*, should you or should you not sauté the paella rice first? Was there a special name for those esparto shopping baskets or for the wicker baskets they used to collect the grapes in – even I don't remember that. My friend Francisco should know, after all his family owned a vineyard and even had shares in the winery where they made moscatel. He could have asked his father about the baskets, and also about how his family came by those vineyards and those shares in the first place, and what became of the people who owned them before the war. To reconstruct that episode of village life, he could have arranged for his father and the father of Bernal – the same Bernal who's sitting here right now – to sit down together and get them talking. That would be a real surf-and-turf menu, as the chefs of the restaurants he frequents might call it, restaurants he may still frequent when *he* disappears from Olba. His father would provide the turf, Bernal's father the surf. It's a shame he never did that, never got them together for a good long chat, that he didn't order them a coffee and a glass of wine and leave them to natter away, swapping anecdotes about the old days. That would have been real ethnology. But they both disappeared a long time ago. As far as Francisco is concerned, our evening get-togethers at Bar Castañer are pure anecdote, whereas for us, the bar is an indispensable part of our lives, or has been; for him, it's an exotic landscape, and we are his own personal *tristes tropiques*, colourful local figures. He observes us the way anthropologists observe a Bedouin village, the desert, the pyramids, the Arab with his turban and his camel; or the pot-bellied, loin-clothed inhabitants of the Amazonian jungle, the cannibal with a bone through his nose or worn as an ornamental comb,

48

a bone saved from the missionary he ate earlier. For a time, Bar Castañer stopped being my sole refuge: I had wanted to leave that village forever and perhaps only return as he has returned, like a professor with a camera, butterfly net and tape recorder; that had been my intention. When I returned, I'd been convinced I'd only stay a short time. I thought I was coming back in order to gather strength for the great leap, but, instead, I settled back onto a soft flesh mattress, and what was temporary ended up becoming permanent. I lost the mattress years ago and have been sleeping on the floor ever since. That's what usually happens, it happens to a lot of people: they think the situation they're in is merely temporary and that all they're doing is living their life, the life they've been given or the life they wanted – Olba, until my last breath.

I've left and returned a few times over the years – I don't mean the village, but the bar; there have been periods when I've abandoned it entirely, but I've always come back in the end, to that stimulating daily journey, the one that prises me out of my solitude at the workshop in the evenings: down Calle de San Ramón where I live, along Calle del Carmen, Calle de la Paz, Paseo de la Constitución (formerly known as General Mola), and here I am – as on so many evenings for so many years – in Bar Castañer, my refuge: the protective gauze of cigarette smoke, which, today, like the snows of yesteryear, has vanished. You can't smoke inside any more. Although, even after all these months of the smoking ban, the smell of nicotine that used to impregnate walls and tables may have gone, but other components of that comforting olfactory gauze linger on: the smell of old cooking oil, damp wool, sweaty vests and overalls, the smell of cheap beer and sour wine. All of these still allow me to recognise the place, to snuggle down in my nest and shuffle the cards. Lately, I've been coming almost every evening. Saying goodbye to all this was the dream of an empty-headed youth who ended up staying and who has, in the meantime, become a decrepit old man without ever passing through maturity. I think I was trying to avoid maturity, and there was the added attraction of getting away, of not thinking too much and leaving it to Time to resolve everything. The result: I have adorned my old age with bankruptcy, a little twist of angostura bitters to spice up my last drink. I'll say goodbye before they put a name to the disease (because they've already detected it, this transmittable disease, to be kept at arm's length), before they hang the leper's bell around my neck. I'll snatch victory from under their noses when they've already prepared the pyre, guns at the ready; leaving them without any prey in their sights. Screw them all. I finally feel able to say goodbye: burnt cooking oil coffee beer anis wine and damp wool. Goodbye to the overflowing ashtray outside the street door which we visit from time to time, stretching our legs and receiving, cigarette clamped firmly between our lips, a breath of clean winter air.

But Justino is speaking:

'At least he doesn't have to spend money any more on radio ads or appear in the directors' box at the football stadium or preside at their suppers along with the players and the powers that be paying homage to him, the generous builder of their new changing room with its hot and cold showers, to the man who gave them the south stand. Right now, his creditors are providing him with an ad campaign gratis, for nothing. If he wanted to be talked about, he's certainly succeeded, because he's left an awful lot of people in the lurch: suppliers, clients who've paid for materials he's never delivered, would-be owners of apartments who've put down a deposit they're never going to recoup, not to mention paid for all the stuff that's already installed in those unfinished buildings. No, he's on the run, who knows where, to China or Brazil perhaps, to some more or less civilised place where there's no extradition treaty.'

Francisco says:

'Given how few such places are left, things don't look so good for our friend. I can't see Pedrós plunging into darkest Africa armed with pistol, pith helmet and insect repellent. He's not exactly into *extreme travel*, as they say, he's more your civilised, cosmopolitan, urban tourist, looking for a nice central hotel and some Cartier perfumes.'

Bernal adds:

'What with the Schengen Agreement and the mess the Swiss bankers have got into, it's not so easy now to bury money, it's really difficult to find a nice quiet resting place, a mausoleum where your money can safely repose; and it's even harder for the owner of the money to disappear. There must be places, of course, certainly for the money, gigantic black holes where by day you can stash the cash that races back and forth in the night: between drug traffickers, Arab sheikhs, financiers in London and New York, the owners of oil wells, the people who attend art auctions, because they're the truly rich. If you yourself want to disappear, there's always the Pitanguy option, one of those plastic surgery magicians who can change your face and even swap your fingerprints for those of some anonymous Third World corpse who was never fingerprinted while alive, there must be hundreds of thousands of them.'

Justino clearly knows a lot about the subject: 'Why, just down the road, a drug dealer got caught because he'd replaced the skin on his fingertips with the skin on the ends of his toes, just so that he could change the prints on his passport. I'm not making it up. It was in the newspapers.'

'Well, I can't see Pedrós and his lady wife doing anything like that, they're your typical lazy, comfortably off bourgeoisie, although who knows . . . when needs must . . .' says Francisco.

And Bernal says:

'What's the point in getting rich if you end up enjoying your fortune in a prison cell surrounded by psychopaths, wife-murderers, Russian hitmen and faggots with huge cocks.'

'Well, where could he go?' ponders Francisco, taking this opportunity to give us a lesson in human geography. 'I seem to remember that one of the countries that has no extradition treaty with Spain is Indonesia, and they certainly know how to enjoy money there: women, jewels, good food. Bali belongs to Indonesia – celebrities go there to get married. Beautiful girls carrying trays of fruit and flowers on their heads (and if you don't like small, dark girls, there's a whole collection of big, buxom Australians holidaying there), beaches lined with coconut palms, good discotheques. But that's too handy for the creditor's hitmen, those Bulgarians who are such experts in tracking people down and in the ancient art of inflicting pain.'

'They're not usually Bulgarians, they're Moldavians,' Justino states, with his encyclopaedic knowledge of dark subjects. 'People say the Moldavians are worse, even more ruthless.'

For a second, I wonder if I, too, in order to recover what I'm owed, should get in touch with that band of pursuers. But I immediately think, no, it's too late, the horse has well and truly bolted. Sometimes I forget and continue to think as if I have years ahead of me, not just hours. While he talks, Justino skilfully cuts the cards, shuffles them like a magician or like the card sharp he is, although at this hour of the evening, he behaves more like a modest pensioner, as most of us do, as Francisco does, and as I have also started to do: pure theatre. The money which, to frighten his rivals, he places on the table in the clandestine card games he plays at night – when he takes off his mask and shows his teeth – had its origins in Switzerland and Germany in the 1960s (those German marks and Swiss francs begat pesetas that then begat euros, three monetary generations). Thanks to contacts he had with who knows what mafias, he earned his money by charging commissions on the work contracts and permits he acquired for men from the area seeking employment abroad. He took men from the villages to work as road sweepers, waiters, bricklayers or navvies, and he alone knows all the shady dealings involved. He'd housed the men in large, freezing-cold huts, where they would have died of hypothermia if they hadn't paid separately for coal, or oil for the heater, and then, on top of what they'd shelled out for the journey and the work permit, he had deducted some twenty or thirty per cent from their wages in payment for continued protection and accommodation. What puzzles me is that the survivors of those expeditions still speak to him, even buy him a drink and think he did well by them. Forty years later, they still say: the guy's so smart, a genius really. I mean we're talking about Germany and Switzerland here – they're so finicky about who they let in. But he could smuggle you across three frontiers under a blanket, feeding you sips of brandy to keep you warm during the time you spent in the boot of a car or sharing a refrigerated trunk with a cargo of Galician fish; and when you got there, everything was already sorted and the next day you were working. The victims speak of him with almost religious awe, and you might think that they still haven't realised that they were slaves in the hands of a trafficker of human flesh. However, when the same grateful guy has had a few drinks things change radically. Then the whole story changes, and at that point, you do get a glimpse of the cannibal, of our very own Hannibal Lecter. The predator. In Olba, he has continued to do more or less same thing, just variants of slave-trading: taking vanloads of workmen to jobs he finds for them in exchange for keeping twenty or twenty-five per cent of what they earn. That's just an example. He's a protean being who has a finger in every pie: agriculture, construction, import-export, banking. And he dabbles in all the professions too: teams of orange-pickers, groups of bricklayers, electricians, plumbers, whole brigades of drivers. Not to mention the white-collar sector: customs men and port agents, superintendents, lawyers, notaries, town councillors, mayors. He makes them all employees in his service company which, of course, has no legal existence. He could be seen as a champion in the struggle against unemployment: he has all kinds of ways to keep other people working. Wherever he goes, work flows forth. He always collects the money himself and then distributes it as he sees fit. If you meet him, if you stop to talk to him, it won't be long before he's offering you some little job too: Listen, I've been meaning to talk to you. Would you do me a favour? He'd make an ideal candidate for the post of Minister for Social Affairs. Some years ago, he got into trouble because, it seems, he sent phantom teams of orange-pickers into orchards that weren't his and where he hadn't been invited. In a matter of hours, entirely without the permission of the owner, the workers had picked clean two whole orchards and, immediately afterwards, our very own Hannibal Lecter was either selling the stolen fruit to warehouses that don't ask too many questions, or else warehousing it himself and distributing it throughout half of Europe, including the former Iron Curtain countries, crating up the fruit with stickers that someone had managed to forge or steal for him, or which were given to him by the warehouses themselves for a trifling amount, on condition that no one ever found out about their involvement. I can't quite remember what exactly happened or how things panned out, but, depending on who you talk to, he either narrowly escaped prison or ended up doing time. Anyway, he disappeared for a while, and various reasons were given for his absence. There are lots of businessmen who spend prolonged periods in limbo or at imaginary spas, when they're actually in the clink or in a clinic somewhere detoxing from alcohol and cocaine. Such retreats are all part of the businessman's busy life. Ahmed knows him because he worked for a while as a fruit-picker, before finding work as a bricklayer and then with me in the workshop, and I've noticed that he always greets Justino with a nod whenever we pass him; these Arabs know all about murky dealings – in fruit, clothes, scrap metal or the routes taken by the boats carrying marijuana from the Alboran Sea to Spain or about the ads on the Internet for gigolos and rent boys; on that vague frontier with the lumpen-proletariat, the Arabs offer their own complicated services, although they doubtless make more modest profits; they compete, not always on friendly terms, with the gypsies, although at present the kings of all this trafficking are the Romanians, Bulgarians, Poles, Ukrainians, Georgians and Lithuanians – in short, that unstable multitude we describe as Eastern European, specialists in copper, top-of-the-range cars, burglaries, break-ins, and in the use of backhoes to wrench cash machines or safes from walls; they're experts, above all, in the exercise of disproportionate violence: capable of smashing in the skulls of two pensioners just to make them reveal where they were hiding the fifty euros they needed to see them through to the end of the month.

The slave trader continues:

'No one wants to lead a life like everyone else's, no one wants his obituary to read: He was born, he lived, he worked, he reproduced and he died – and so people try to attract attention. They do absurd, tedious, painful things they'd refuse to do if they were required to by their work contract – it's been the same since the world began. Tomás Pedrós thought he could grow as big as El Corte Inglés, Inditex or Mercadona, or like that Bañuelos guy – making his fortune here and now building like mad in Brazil apparently.'

And then there's Pedrós, growing like a malignant tumour, yes, and Justino has been a malignant tumour himself: and like all tumours, he grows in darkness and in silence. We laugh, yes, so do I, although I'm afraid they might notice that my laughter is somewhat forced, because I feel utterly wretched.

'Well, yes, he always had to cause a stir, and have a finger in every pie,' Bernal comments mildly, and it seems to me that he looks at me out of the corner of his eye when he says this, or is that just my paranoia?

Justino returns to the charge:

'Exactly, the self-made man. All those films from the 1950s and 1960s – or even today – all contain that same poisonous hidden message. The Kennedy saga, the Obama story. Pedrós was always so keen on all that freedom of the individual crap, about will power and hard work, the winner burning his excess energy at the gym or on the tennis court, and he encountering other alpha males, who help him make his way thanks to a spider's web of influences they call synergies. Sure, he was very ambitious, but there was that touch of the mythomaniac, the fantasist: he was just too much in love with himself, the butterfly, the show-off.'

'And the times were ripe for men like him,' says Bernal sagely.

'Yes,' says Justino, 'but not everyone fell into the trap.'

Of course they didn't, and our Hannibal Lecter is no show-off. Justino's no butterfly – more of a moth. He moves among the shadows of the night, where evil lurks and where his succubi have their beds, the labourers who stoke our nightmares with filthy coal. Justino covers up, dissembles, hides. His life is a mystery, you have to decipher the meaning slithering about beneath his words, he's the oracle of all things murky, the sibyl of the unsavoury: he conceals the truth with lies and conceals lies with half-truths. You always have the feeling that he's deceiving you; if he says it's a nice day and points up at the sun, you can be sure this is merely a diversionary tactic so that you won't notice what's going on down below. And he takes every precaution and successfully fends off the tax people – he's a past master at hiding any so-called 'signs of ostentatious living' – but we all know that he leads a secret life and that, in the shadows, he lives far beyond his theoretical means. I'm not talking about the watches and chains he wears, or the fact that his wife looks like a walking jewellery shop: those are mere trinkets, the equivalent of the finger pointing at the sun; I'm talking about land transactions, property transfers, estates registered in the name of nephews, brothers- and sisters-in-law, his retired mother- and father-in-law who both have Alzheimer's or senile dementia, poor defenceless stooges whose signatures he has forged and who, even in their wildest meanderings, would never dream they were the owners of apartments, business premises, import-export companies, orange groves and building sites like the ones they possess thanks to Justino: underhand deals that you hear others mention only obliquely and sotto voce. And then there are the occasional disappearances, the mysterious periods spent in limbo, trips you know nothing about but which – as I said – you imagine to be to some spa to cure his arthritis or to an exclusive clinic to control his hyperglycaemia or his high triglyceride levels, trips that his enemies say are time spent in prison or on journeys to some dangerously borderline country (Thailand, Colombia, Mexico) to coordinate the transport of illegal substances and about which his vanity will eventually lead him to spill the beans one night when he's had a couple of drinks and you're alone with him and he's telling you about a wife-swapping club in Paris (*you didn't take your wife, did you?* I asked, and he replied: *Don't be an idiot, where she's concerned I have exclusive rights*), or a place in Miami (ah, wonderful, chaotic Miami, so popular with wheeler-dealers up to no good) where at the reception desk, you have to leave not just the money for the ticket, but all your clothes (yes, even your underpants, he laughs, adding with a touch of vulgar humour, and your jock-strap: your wallet and your watch are put in a safe with a secret code), and only then can you go over to the bar and order a whisky or a glass of champagne and, finally, enter the spa, the main room with its sofas, swimming pools, jacuzzis and saunas, and the tortuous labyrinth of small rooms with beds of various sizes. He can't resist telling these secrets – out of sheer boastfulness and egotism, he can't help it: they make him seem different, more interesting, more mysterious, in the eyes of the person he's talking to, in my eyes too, me, the bored carpenter who, for the last four decades, has barely gone any further than back and forth to the marsh or to some small room at the Lovely Ladies Club, but who, in his now distant youth, did his fair share of globetrotting too and can, therefore, be of use as a confidant (you know what I'm talking about, Esteban, you've been around a bit, you travelled when you were a young man, although you rarely leave the house now, I mean, would you ever even go to the local pickup joint if I didn't drag you there? – and you're single, for heaven's sake, you don't have to account to anyone), and these confidences make him grow in his own eyes too, because among us prestige is consolidated by such anecdotes, which seem to slip out as unexpectedly as farts, but which he has learned to ration out, knowing that such stories are as easily transmitted as flu, and are vague enough not to get him into any trouble with the authorities. In order to make sure that everyone finds out, he only has to use the words: This is just between you and me, in confidence.

'I told you *that*? I certainly didn't mean to. Had we had too much to drink that night? I've really got to drink less and be more careful and watch what I say when I leave the house. Please, not a word to anyone else.'

Even though he was supposedly as drunk as a lord, he still couldn't resist whispering to me – his mouth pressed to my ear – about the oysters in champagne that he ate in Monte Carlo (*I won't tell you why I went there*, he says, adding further to the mystery, while I yelp: *ugh, you're sticking your tongue in my ear*, and wipe away the saliva). He boasts about the luck he had at roulette that night, the Russian bitch I was with seemed to have seriously lucky nipples – she kept sticking her roulette chips down her front and rubbing them on her tits before putting them down, and the ball stopped on her number every time; then he tells me about the journey from Monte Carlo to Paris in her convertible BMW (*la douce brise de la Provence sur mes joues, la huître au vent*: needless to say, she wasn't wearing any knickers, and while she drove, my hands went walkabout) and about the quarter of a kilo of caviar that they bought in Kaspia – on the Place de la Madeleine, next door to Fauchon – and ate in their room in the Hotel Lutetia on the Boulevard Raspail. Actually, the hotel's a real disappointment. The furniture, the bathroom fittings, the room with its dusty corners, all very shabby and dated, hotels in Spain are much better maintained and a much better deal too – it really needs a complete overhaul, he says. He probably suggested to the manager that he could carry out the renovation himself (his architects, his teams of bricklayers, his decorators, leaving the Lutetia like new), he probably left his card on the desk and, in exchange, got a free bottle of champagne, although it's hard to get anything out of the French – stingy bastards. But – oh, and the champagne I drank out of that Russian oyster was Krug Millésimé, so rich, so nutty, so strong, have you never tried it? Ask your friend Francisco about it. He'll tell you. Ask his opinion as an expert, as a connoisseur. It's certainly my favourite, and I know more about champagne than you might think, in fact, I know a lot. Krug champagne is, now how would your friend Francisco describe it? – serious, elegant, noble. Justino continues to allow himself to be carried away by details: do you know that French painting called *The Origin of the World*? Do you know the one I mean? With that great furry hole in the foreground. Well, that was the scene I had before me, the original black hole — albeit pink and fair in this case — from which everything emerges and through which everything enters, I caressed it with my teeth, with the tip of my tongue, I stuck my whole tongue into that dense jungle and touched the genesis, no, it wasn't shaven, but a good dense mat of hair, neat and trimmed, but furry, I like pubic hair, the fair, silky kind, which makes the thing itself look like a shy, delicate little animal, it makes you want to caress it, bite it, eat it, we Spaniards call it *el conejo*, the rabbit, while the French call it *la chatte*: well, I gobbled up the first day of creation along with a sip of champagne. And I ate the end of the world, I ate the world from beginning to end, I stuck my tongue into that other retractile, slightly brownish hole where everything ends, but through which one can begin the excavation in reverse, travelling from darkness to light. I dug my tongue into that sweet, dark well, and then I plunged my steam hammer into that place where, it must be said, *hélas*, others had fervently dug before. She was, after all, a high-class whore. But that night, I voyaged from alpha to omega. I penetrated the very beginning and the very end.

He prattles on, he laughs, he grabs you by the lapels with his great mitts and pulls you towards him, splattering your shirt front and your face with spit, which you wipe away, not that he notices, of course. You feel like asking: When was that? Why didn't you tell me at the time? But you don't, because his hairy hand is now on your shoulder and his face is now resting between his hand and the bit of your throat that his hand isn't touching, the place where a vampire would bite, and you feel on your neck the warmth of his breath, the tickling of his mobile tongue, your neck sticky with saliva, and the girls at the bar have started looking at us, thinking that, tonight, one of them will be making up a threesome.

★

The watching birds who fly up at the first morning light, the waiting wild boar who come down at dawn from the nearby mountains to drink in the ponds, the murmur of the reeds that bend or break as they advance. For nearly half a century, the shed in the backyard has been filled with all the necessary tackle and tools for fishing and hunting: rifles, ramrods, straps and cartridge belts, rubber waders, wellington boots, rods, nets and baskets of various shapes and with various uses, and which, locally, are given different names according to their shape and purpose. To every animal its own death, to every tool its own name: *ralls, mornells, gamberes* and *tresmalls*. It's like a small collection ready to be exhibited on one of those TV programmes about hunting, with titles like *Rod and Gun, Forest and Stream*, or the other kind – which are the opposite really – that you get on those cute little local television stations or the no less cute national ones, with titles like *Environment, Blue Planet, Territories* or *Our Traditions*, which show, with reverential sanctimoniousness, the landscapes that mankind has supposedly not yet destroyed; they talk about old rural customs, visit some ethnological museum where they keep tools once used for cultivating, threshing, pruning, as well as millstones, oil presses and wagons, programmes that try to make a near-paradise or a precious natural park out of the place I knew as a child. On the road leading out of Olba, the sewers flowing into the dried-up riverbed transmitted infections to the neighbouring houses, which were built in areas regularly flooded by the torrential autumn rains. As children we used to play among piles of rubbish, would plunge up to our knees in quagmires plagued with mosquitoes and rats, among the remains of dead animals, old clothing, dry excrement, filthy mattresses and bloodstained bandages and gauze nibbled by vermin. We were looking for comics, cigarette cards showing footballers or film stars, pages torn from illustrated magazines, movie posters, scraps of old film strips, discarded tools that we could use as toys, a spinning top, a broken doll, a mutilated cardboard horse, a punctured ball that could be mended with a rubber patch of the sort used by the man in the bicycle repair shop or that we would simply kick around half inflated. We particularly liked the little penicillin bottles, widely used as the recently discovered remedy for tuberculosis and venereal diseases, and which we would adopt as containers for our tiny treasures. My mother would fly into a rage whenever she discovered, hidden in my pencil case or my satchel, one of those glass bottles with the rubber stopper still bearing the scar left by the syringe, and now with an insect for my collection. She thought those bottles would bring into the house the very diseases they were supposed to cure. Who knows who might have touched it, people with TB or some other infectious disease, throw it away right now. She would make me get rid of them however much I protested and explained how useful they were and how I had washed them thoroughly (which wasn't always true), and I would cry whenever she, with an abrupt movement of her arm, tossed one of them over the wall. The river and the pools around the marsh were full of all kinds of detritus – old furniture, the sweepings from backyards, dead animals – the assumption being that the mud would swallow it all up, that the next flood would carry it off or that vermin would eat whatever was edible. This hobby of mine, which would now be described as ethnological, has led to me preserving and adding to my uncle's collection of tackle and tools. Francisco often accompanied us on our trips to the marsh and, despite never wanting to fire a shot, he actively helped in casting the nets and would hold the rod and get excited when he felt a fish tugging near the shore. However, he would contemplate all this equipment as if it were part of some museum of torture. He would say to me:

'I don't know how you can bring yourself to shoot an inoffensive animal.'

'Fishing is just as cruel. A fish seems to me more helpless than a wild boar, and more worthy of compassion.'

'But fishing seems less aggressive somehow.'

'How can you say that? They're caught on a hook that pierces their jaw. They die slowly from asphyxia in the net, those innocent little creatures,' I would say mockingly.

'But fish are cold-blooded things that you can't really feel much empathy for, but if you see a mammal dying, soaked in blood, you have a sense that a creature like you is dying, and when you skin one, the body is disconcertingly like a human body, like our body.'

'Try observing the death of an insect through a magnifying glass. You'll see the same frightening convulsions, the same contortions, the desperate opening and closing of the mouth, the frantically waving legs. It's really awful.'

At the time, neither of us had seen anyone die, although I had caught glimpses of my grandmother on her deathbed.

Francisco used the word 'human' – a human being – whenever he wanted to describe something worthy of pity, perhaps the soul he imagines we carry inside us; 'human' is a word with a powerful emotive impact. He knew how to use it. Now, when we've witnessed several deaths, the resemblance strikes us as even more troubling. And I say 'us', even though I haven't stopped hunting and even though he no longer finds it repugnant. With age, we become more knowledgeable about the unpleasant side of life and, doubtless as a way of making it slightly more bearable, we become less sensitive too. Wars and massacres are usually topics of conversation for hardened old men, the young are mere pawns moved by arthritic fingers. What they see in war sweeps away their innocence, prepares them to follow in the footsteps of their fathers and grandfathers. Turning,

63

turning, turning, that's what this world has been doing for millennia. It makes the young suddenly old, and they become those fingers capable of moving the pawns. *Gira, il mondo, gira, nello spazio senza fine*, Jimmy Fontana used to sing. I watched my grandmother dying (in secret, through a crack in the door, a disfigured creature, railing and moaning, I was six or seven), I've seen my mother die, my mother's brothers, Uncle Ramón, my brother Germán, defenceless hares trembling in their beds, I've seen them gasping and flailing just like the various dogs who have died on me, the same struggle, the same harsh, intermittent breathing. Francisco watched Leonor dying for months, an animal gradually being consumed despite all the stratagems of doctors and family members, her dying must have cost them a fortune, what with trips to Houston, treatments in private hospitals here and there. Right now, I'm watching the endless dying of my father who, at this point, could easily be hunted and dispatched without too many ethical qualms.

But we were only twenty-something then, and I would say:

'My father has always hated hunting, which is understandable after what he saw during the war, but Uncle Ramón and my grandfather had to hunt in order to eat.'

They finally managed to hunt down my grandfather (with a bullet in the back of the neck), a fruitless, cruel bit of hunting, we never used to talk about those things, we didn't even know about them, I thought my grandfather had died in an accident. 'It's just the food chain, so why go digging around for any deeper meaning, it's cruelty without the guilt. It was simply a matter of staying alive. Now that need has disappeared, we've become corrupted, sophisticated, and nothing has that same necessary, urgent character that carries within it its own absolution. We argue about whether hunting, since it's no longer a matter of survival, is a pleasure or a hobby, a pastime or a vice, or if we simply carry in our genes a death impulse, some mechanism in our system that drives us to want to continue freeing ourselves from those who are not like us . . .'

'Unfortunately, there are far too many instances of people viciously freeing themselves from those who are all too like them.'

'Of course, and you free yourself from yourself precisely because you are too like yourself. No, don't laugh, Francisco. You commit suicide because you are who you are and not the person you'd like to be, you put a bullet through your head because you can't bear yourself. Out of pure hatred. To resist that, to remain alive, you need a good dose of idealism. The ability to lie to yourself. The only people who survive are those who manage to believe that they are what they are not.'

'Are you trying to convince me that you hunters are looking for some unnecessary guilt to load onto yourselves, like a belated payment for the innocence of your ancestors?'

'To call a man innocent is an oxymoron. Is that what they call putting two contradictory words together to create a strange effect? You taught me that. Oxymoron. A thunderous silence, an innocent man. The first is good for poetry, the second for sociology, religion or politics. Our ancestors ate the putrid remains of whatever the wild beasts had hunted and left half eaten. They had no skills, they couldn't run or jump like their prey, they weren't able to hurl themselves on a deer and sink their teeth into its jugular. On the other hand, they carried the seed of evil within them: they invented traps and tools. The things I still use for hunting and fishing. Up until then, they fought with dogs and vultures over scraps of food. I don't see innocence anywhere. Cunning and duplicity, yes. What can I say, Francisco? We don't always do what we should. There is such a thing as negative egotism, the desire for what will destroy us. Perhaps that's the best thing about us, that uncertainty, that fragility. Humans are strange creatures, we think with a logic

65

that is quite different from what we feel, and all too often what we feel goes against what we need – love, passion and, yes, hatred, those are the feelings that can bring about our downfall, and we go towards that downfall knowingly, we seem to need to keep doing that, and no one can explain why.'

I could have talked to him about that, about the magnetic attraction that drew me to Leonor – to each his own trap – but that was a secret I promised her I would keep. We met in secret. I'd left art school in Madrid and decided to work where I'd never wanted to work, in my father's carpentry workshop, and I didn't even want to admit to myself that she was the thing holding me there, sucking dry my ambitions. In fact, the work was purely incidental, unimportant. I hated carpentry, but that wasn't the problem, that was by the by. I felt superior. It seemed to me stupid to spend time learning the aesthetic codes our teachers at art school were trying to drill into us – what was the point? It all seemed to me as futile as what Francisco was studying at the faculty of philosophy and letters; his political, artistic or theological debates, the search for the message contained in books and films, were mere adolescent trifles I thought, because I was involved in something real, something adult for which it was worthwhile putting up with any job, even putting up with my father: an undertaking worthy of a man seeking ways to keep a woman at his disposal, a woman who says: again, fuck me again. That was what it was about: doing a job you don't like, just as grown-ups do; having a woman who wants you, not your sympathy, not your intelligence, but your flesh, that's how desire works between grown-ups. At least, that's what I thought. That was my idea of maturity. While Francisco talked about Plato, Marx or Antonioni, infantile babblings, I had a woman who obeyed me, who begged me, yes, like that, I want to feel you inside me. It wasn't just hot air about the meaning or the truth about life. It *was* the truth.

Possessing that flesh, defending it from other men's desires, knowing it was there at my disposal and off limits to other men. Being a man. The call of the primordial pack.

'But God –'

'God arrived quite a lot later, when your ancestors had already been killing and eating each other for millennia, and sucking the marrow from the bones of their neighbour, poking fingers and tongue into their hollow bones. I think the real reason people suck each other's cocks is because they can't suck their bones. It's a leftover from cannibalism. After all, we bite each other when we fuck, don't we? And when we're screwing, we say "eat me, eat me".' I said this as a joke, secretly mocking him, enjoying the fact that he would think I was just joking, because I knew those were the words that poured from my lips into her ear. And there he was talking to me about God and about some amazing book he'd just read.

'I say that God gives no one the right to make even the most insignificant of His creatures suffer,' Francisco insisted, more mystic than anthropologist. He believed not in the primordial pack, but in the placid primordial family circle. Papa and Mama, the puppies gambolling about in the shade of the leafy trees, the grandparents observing the scene, and a pot of stew bubbling gently away (don't ask about the ingredients). He had become an active member of two of the Catholic youth movements in vogue at the time, the Juventud Española Católica and the Hermandad Obrera de Acción Católica. In his house, what with the draper's shop, the grocery store (which, later, with the arrival of tourism, became a chain of supermarkets), the orange groves and the vineyards and, above all, his father's membership of the Falangist Party, which opened so many doors to the family – hence the blue shirt of the Falangists that he strutted about in once the war was over – they could allow themselves the luxury of buying the necessary protein for their meals without having

67

to hunt for it. If money serves any purpose at all, it at least buys innocence for your descendants. Which is no small thing. It removes you from the animal kingdom and places you in the moral kingdom. It humanises you. Thanks to money, it had completely slipped the Marsal family's feeble memory that they had participated in the hunt for resistance fighters in the mountains and around the lagoon: the months during which his father placed his gleaming Hispania motor car at the service of the Falangists (they really were a pack of hounds, survivors of the primordial pack). The assistant at the grocery store, in his grey overalls, would polish the car before the owner, Don Gregorio Marsal, set off to act as chauffeur to the Falangist patrols swarming everywhere. They would appear suddenly, block the roads, pursue any cyclists carrying a couple of sacks of black-market rice or sugar or oil. They would confiscate any goods, demand to see documentation, and hand out beatings to any black marketeers or drunks or other unfortunates unable to justify their presence on the road at that hour, or those suspected of having fought for one of the Popular Front parties who were unlucky enough to be passing by. My uncle and, quite a long time later, my father told me these stories, although I always found them rather boring. I didn't understand the epic of resistance that they, especially my father, wanted to pass on to me. The sinister black car would circulate the streets at night, its headlights off, and park outside the door of some house, laughter wafting from the car windows left open to the hot night. The summer of 1939. Shots fired into the air was their letter of introduction, along with the crunch of plaster flaking off a wall where, the following morning, the neighbours would see the holes left by the bullets. A butcher's car, a whiff of carrion. But those were the dark days, which, one way or another, are inevitable in what Marxists term 'primitive accumulation'. For the plant to grow, you must first add manure. Those raids weren't as youthful and carefree as the accompanying jokes, laughter and drinks might appear to indicate, they were calculated steps necessary for continued growth, rites of passage, stages in the formation of the new entrepreneurial generations: during those skirmishes, the grocer's features began to grow rounder, his eyes took on a jovial glint, his voice a frank, manly tone, his gestures became more authoritative (*don't you try it on with me*), a satisfied smile parted his plump, pink lips. It's an ill wind that blows nobody any good. Money, among its many other virtues, has a detergent quality. And many nutritious qualities too. It puts a sparkle in your eyes, fills out your cheeks, allows you to sit in an armchair, stretch out your legs, and read the newspaper. It gives you those immaculate hands that emerge from starched white shirt cuffs. It's no longer you prowling the night. You employ assistants and servants to trap, kill and skin the creatures from which one obtains the vital ingredients for the Sunday stew or paella. The wealthy have always enjoyed that privilege. The master of the house doesn't deliver the mortal blow to the rabbit, the mistress of the house doesn't slit the throat of the chicken and pluck it, holding between her legs the bowl full of breadcrumbs to soak up the blood to make the dumplings for the stew. The animals have always arrived ready-cooked, in a dish, served on a tray covered by a gleaming silver dome and so transformed as to be unrecognisable and, for that very reason, delicious in their false innocence. That's how it has always been and remains so today; it has taken only a few years for us to acquire that privileged status, the illusion that we are all lords and ladies of the manor, while in remote factories, workers kill and skin and carve and package the animals we eat once they've become acceptably aseptic: pink fillets that look more like salmon than veal thanks to the substances they add so that the meat doesn't darken and is therefore attractive to look at (yes, *attractive*, the cut-up, dismembered corpse like the corpse of the victim of some deflagration): shanks, chops, steaks, entrecôtes, shoulders; chicken thighs and breasts placed in little white polyurethane containers covered in transparent cling film, as pure as it can be, given that it's the small coffin of something that died a violent death. In the meat section of the supermarket they can't quite get rid of all trace of blood, we sense its presence, but avoid it. We force ourselves not to decipher the signs, so that the dismembered corpse doesn't shock us, just as we're not shocked by what we see on television, figures lying sprawled on some dusty avenue with palm trees in the background. In the lower social orders (from which we think we have escaped in recent years), there's no room for metaphysical discussions about what limitations can be placed on us when we exercise our right over other animals. Things are as they are. There's no moral kingdom anywhere to be seen. You're in the lower orders because you haven't sufficiently de-animalised yourself. The lower orders worry more about work strategies, questions of method, ways of increasing efficiency with the least waste of energy. They exist on the technical plane, searching for more results with less effort; empiricism: how to tie together the wings of a duck so that it doesn't struggle when you sacrifice it, how to deliver the punch to the back of the rabbit's neck so that it dies the first time, how to stick the knife into the pig's gullet so that the blood flows into the pot prepared by the sausage-maker, a pot containing finely chopped onion and paprika, ready to make the blood puddings. No halfway intelligent rich man commits murder. They're not psychopaths. They have no reason to be. That's what employees are for: to be murderers and psychopaths.

I rejected Francisco's opinions (God gives no one the right to make even the most insignificant of His creatures suffer). As if reason could do anything against faith. No one had yet told me about his father's nocturnal expeditions or his strange idea of what constituted big game; I didn't even know at the time how my grandfather had died, nor that my father had been in prison for three years and that I'd been born during his absence. Uncle Ramón filled me in on just how much the war had influenced my life.

'Your father has always insisted that you should know nothing until you were older. "They," your father would say, meaning you and your siblings, "have nothing to do with it. They'll find out soon enough. I'll tell them how it was."'

Later, my father did try to talk to me, but, by then, I wasn't very interested in his stories, the delicate thread connecting us had broken. Besides, none of that information entered my discussions with Francisco. We debated more on the level of metaphysics than of history – the history that so tormented my father – and which, to us, seemed too recent, too lacking in poetry: smelly, badly ventilated rooms; the chamberpot in which my grandfather had done his business after being given an enema; sprigs of lavender and sugar warming on the stove to disguise the stench in the patient's room; the smell of rotting entrails in the rubbish bin, that was what recent history meant to us. It was what we had seen and smelled at home, what we used to be and from which we wanted to escape. Far better to be in places where words do what you want them to and where blood doesn't smell because it's set down in ink on the page; history traps you, forces you to follow a prearranged script, one that didn't interest me in the least:

'But how can you talk like that after reading the Bible? God doesn't just grant the right to kill, He spends His time sowing discord among humans so that they end up killing each other. Right at the very beginning of beginnings, Genesis, there's Cain. There are other examples too: Moses, the first supporter of liberation through violence, doesn't hesitate to kill the man oppressing his people; the adulterer David, cruel Salomé, or that decapitator so beloved of feminists, Judith, who beheads the gallant Holofernes: his only crime was admiring her beauty, presenting her with his finest treasures, serving her the most succulent of dishes and, we assume, after all those hours spent alone in that luxurious tent, giving her a good seeing-to as well – and is that how you repay me after I placed in you the seed of the most glorious of Assyrian generals, something most women would consider the very best of gifts, namely, the possibility of engendering an heir to all my glory, and you repay me by cutting off my head? That woman wasn't a hero, she was an ungrateful wretch and very rude to boot: that's hardly the way to behave at supper, or to treat a host who receives you with open arms (appropriately enough). When someone invites you to supper, it's not even acceptable to say you didn't enjoy the food. Killing the owner of the household certainly doesn't appear in any of the etiquette books. The Bible is the mother of bad manners.'

'But that's the Old Testament God . . . no, I know you, you're just winding me up, taking the piss. Go to hell!' says Francisco, half smiling and dismissing me with a wave of the hand.

'The heroic story of Judith, the criminal story of Judith, the sad story of Judith, as you prefer. The adjective you choose depends on your ideology.'

The story of Judith and Holofernes is, let's say, a story shorn of adjectives. What do you think, Liliana? You Spaniards don't even know what a really good potato or *papa* or *patata* is. I mean, if you go to the market here, in Olba, or in Misent, which is quite a lot bigger, or go to Eroski or to Mercadona, how many types of potato do you have to choose from? Red and white, new and old, and that's it, but in Colombia you'll find a whole selection of different varieties on any small street stall, and each one is perfect for a particular recipe, and there are even some recipes that call for three or four different varieties, because some are floury and good for thickening stews, while others stay firm and only give when you bite into them or prick them with a fork. I'm not saying your country isn't a more peaceable place, because it is, although it's rapidly getting less so, but it's boring too, things don't have much colour, much variety, and the people, well, they're all right, I suppose, but not all of them, they call us Colombians blacks even though we're not, I mean there *are* a few blacks in Colombia, just as there are here in Spain, the guys who sell stuff on the streets, for example, but they're from outside Colombia, and there are others who were taken there as slaves. And they did come from Africa, like the blacks here. But we Colombians are Latin Americans and yet here they call us blacks or *conguitos*, apparently because of some ad for sweets that was on the TV years ago, which showed little fat black coffee beans with legs, dancing about, they may even have shown them wearing Colombian hats. No, they didn't, Liliana, they called them *conguitos* because they came from Africa, from the Congo, you see, chocolate sweets or coffee beans from Africa not Colombia. That's as maybe, but now they call us Colombians *conguitos*, I know this because my husband told me so, he says that when he worked on a building site, that's what they used to call the Colombian workers, *conguitos*, *panchitos*, blacks, darkies. That's just because people are ignorant, Liliana, they have no idea. Sometimes my husband would just laugh and, at others, he'd get really angry and say that the next person who called him that would get his head smashed in with a bottle. Of course, he only gets angry when he's had a few drinks, when he's drunk too much; otherwise, he's really quiet, but when he drinks, he shouts and shouts until he's so tired he goes to bed without any supper and is soon fast asleep and snoring like a pig – if you'll pardon the expression. I wish he was more like you, quiet and polite, I'm sure you'd never shout like that or threaten anyone. The trouble is that when you get married, you're young and full of hope, you're not thinking clearly, because when you're going out with someone, they only show you their best side, they might even be pretending to be good. You only really get to know the other person once you're married. Our mothers know that and tell us it's always been the same, exactly the same, but we young people take no notice, love blinds us and we don't want to listen to the voice of experience because we're stupid enough to believe we're the very first people in the world ever to fall in love, as if we'd invented it. You're different, though, I think that if you had got married, your wife certainly wouldn't have been disappointed, it's a real shame you didn't marry, because marriage would simply have confirmed to her that she was living with a good man, why, you're almost like a father to me, more than a father really, because my father didn't care about us, about me and my brothers and sisters; on the contrary, he sent us out to work and got all the money he could out of us so that he could go off with his friends and spend it all on drinks in the local bar. Sometimes he wouldn't come home for three or four days, and you can imagine the state he was in when he did come home, he'd be completely out of it, his clothes in shreds, stinking of other women, high on cocaine, and with all the money gone. You're exactly the kind of father anyone could possibly want, and the other gentleman, your father, even though he doesn't talk now, he's so tall and slim, he must have been very handsome as a young man, and I'm not saying that because you're shorter and stockier, I mean everyone's different, but he's so distin-guished-looking – there he is not saying a word, we don't even know what he might be thinking, my sense, though, is that he must have been very kind and polite too, you can tell from his appearance, his presence, and even though the poor thing can't speak, you can see his good thoughts in his eyes, in the way he looks at us. You can see his kindness. You must have been a lovely family. It's just such a shame your mama isn't still with us, but, of course, if she were alive, she'd be as old as your father, so better to let her rest in peace, don't you think? I'm sure she deserves it. She's waiting up there in heaven for you all to join her.

What do these people want, what do they expect a man to do when the fridge is empty? In day-to-day living, you're constrained by your kids, by your wife; if it wasn't for them, you'd do all kinds of crazy things, but when you're in really deep trouble, when you reach that final tipping point, the very opposite happens: it's precisely your wife and kids who make you do the crazy thing that, before, they seemed to be stopping you from doing. The same people who saved you become your downfall. You ruin your life because of them. You're capable of taking a rifle and stealing the takings from the local butcher just to be able to put some chicken breasts in the fridge, have a few chicken bones to make stock and a bit of blood pudding for the stew; sausages, hamburgers, cheese triangles, yogurt. To get a packet of Ariel for the washing machine, nappies for the baby. I don't know exactly what I would be capable of doing to you people – to you, the ones who've got everything – but I do have a rifle at home. I have the right licences, so the crime of illegal possession of weapons wouldn't appear on the sentence; homicide, murder, premeditation, execution, they might appear, but not illegal possession, because I do have a gun licence. Legal possession. It was my cousin who persuaded me to take out a licence, he wanted me to go hunting with him at some game reserve he's a member of in La Mancha, near Badajoz, near Luciana and Arroba de los Montes (no, you won't know where they are, they're tiny villages, barely visible on the map), and at the time I could afford it, I could afford to go on little trips like that, just head off with my rifle to shoot a few partridges, the odd hare, a wild boar even. Sometimes we went hunting for boar and deer on an estate you could have spent three or four days roaming and still not have seen it all. I used to like

75

coming back in his van, smelling of mud, grass and damp hair, of animal blood and our own sweat, smelling of wild boar during the whole journey on cold, clear winter days or on misty, drizzly days, the smell of bitter coffee, brandy, or coffee with a dash of rum (we always used to make three or four stops en route); sometimes, too, we'd come back stinking of whores, because we'd call in at a pickup joint along the way, near Albacete, then, when you got home, you'd take off your shoes, take what you'd caught out of your game bag, and have a good long shower so that your wife wouldn't smell the whore's lipstick and make-up on your neck or between your legs, or that really penetrating cologne they always wear, never taking account of the fact that most of us have wives, and that a wife can smell a whore at fifty paces. What more could you ask for? Well, Esteban has taken me with him to the marsh now and then: come on, Julio, we'll spend the morning there, have lunch, and with a bit of luck, we'll bring back an eel or a duck, but it's not the same, the marsh is so confined, and muddy and smelly, whereas out in the open, with fields disappearing off into the distance, one hill after another, you can breathe freely. We could manage then. I could cope. We never imagined the shit we'd be in now, when you don't know who to borrow money from next, and it's so embarrassing walking around and seeing the look of alarm on the face of any acquaintance when he sees you coming and crosses the road pretending he hasn't seen you, because he's sure you're going to touch him for a loan the way you did a couple of weeks before. It really gets to you, spending all day plotting, going over and over things in your head, wondering how you're going to get by on your four hundred euros of family allowance and the six hundred euros your wife earns, and doing endless calculations that never work out, always more debits than credits, however you juggle the figures, how are you going to pay for the books and the other things for the kids' school, which went up to seven hundred euros this year, then there's the new uniform, because last year's is too small and, besides, it's worn out, shoes, car insurance, mortgage, council tax, it all feeds into the same nightmare, a nightmare you never suspected when things were going well, but which, as soon as everything goes pear-shaped, becomes your sole preoccupation: how to fill the fridge. It's only when you've lost everything that you realise you have to eat every day, isn't that ridiculous? Of course you have to eat. Everyone knows that. When conditions are normal, you don't even notice, but when you haven't so much as a euro in your pocket, it becomes your one great obsession: you have to eat every single day. You have to put food on the table, and the children have to take their little carton of juice to school as well as a sandwich filled with mortadella or with tuna, out of that small round metal tin containing just a few scraps, barely enough; and this isn't just today, it's every day, because every day they have to have their afternoon snack and every day they have to eat supper. And the little one has to have her nappy changed every morning. I go to bed and dream that I'm drowning, then sit bolt upright, scrabbling for air and screaming. My wife gets frightened. Whatever's wrong? I thought I heard a burglar, I say, but that's not it, I take the anxiety to bed with me, because what used not to be a problem at all has turned into four daily problems that I have to find some way of solving one after the other: breakfast, lunch, tea and supper. Could you spare a bit of money (addressed to one of the acquaintances who didn't have time to cross the road when he saw me)? I can't afford to buy a loaf of bread or the children's juice. They can't go to school with nothing. It breaks my heart when I hear them say to my wife: Mama, there's no more yogurt, no more biscuits, no more cakes. I tiptoe out of the house, close the door behind me as quietly as I can, get into the car (don't waste petrol now, the tank's almost empty, and how am I going to fill it up?), drive to the first bit of wasteland I come to and weep. I sit there on my own, weeping. About the children asking for juice and my wife shouting at me and telling me to do something, because she can't stand it any more; I can't perform miracles, the mean cow says to me – encouragingly – as if this was all my fault. Get your arse off the sofa. The other little girl: Mama, look, my brother's eaten all the bread and you can't make me my snack. And they take to school a little bottle of tap water with strict instructions not to remove the label, so that it looks as if they're drinking mineral water, because it's healthier, *when the other kids have all got their pineapple juice or orange juice or multi-fruit juice with added vitamins and calcium and who knows what else, every enriched juice costs one euro at the supermarket. How do I pay for that, if there isn't even enough money to buy potatoes? It's three months since Esteban stopped paying us, and when I pick up my unemployment benefit, I can accept that my family will only be able to buy the cheaper juice, but there are many days when there isn't even enough money for that: tap water with a posh label on the bottle or a few drops of squeezed orange juice if it's in a bottle bearing the label Zumosol.*

And you pounce unscrupulously on the person who didn't have time to cross the road when he saw you: just give me whatever you can, you know I wouldn't ask if things weren't really tight, and I've always paid back any money you've lent me before, it's just that now . . . The victim feels nervously in his pocket as if he had a knife in his back. He does. I'm holding the knife. Sorry, I can't, I haven't got anything on me, it's just that . . . And I know what he means: this is a kind of mugging, but I pretend not to understand. The man produces a crumpled five-euro note and holds it out to me. That's all I have, he says and quickly moves off, as if any further contact might infect him with the leprosy of poverty. He leaves without waiting for my proffered thank you, thanks a lot. He doesn't stop to listen when I say that I fully intend to pay back those five euros. Thank you, I say more loudly, I'll pay you back as soon as I can, and he, from a safe distance away, explains: Look, I'm broke too. I really haven't any more to give you, we're all getting by as best we can. Then he averts his face, turns beetroot red: he feels more ashamed than I do, and I, on the other hand, feel not the slightest gratitude – bastard, I think, even though the man was under no obligation to give me that crumpled note. Bastard, I say again under my breath, and I say it because he's alive, because he can afford to give me that surplus note, because he doubtless has more notes, whether many or few, in the wallet he hurriedly put back in his pocket (he covered it with his hand, so that I couldn't see how much was in it), not to mention the money he'll have at home, and what he certainly has in the bank. The rotten bastard, I think to myself. But, Julio, where is the feeling that priests, teachers and all good parents call gratitude and which they taught you when you were a child? No, I feel no gratitude at all. I don't feel it in myself, and I don't think it's out there in the world either. I never thought I would ever experience something like this – no one told us, no one prepared us for this. Now I miss what I probably didn't appreciate enough at the time: the chilly mornings with the gradually lifting mist: it would float like a piece of cloth among the trees, above the streams, above the river, the sickly smell of rock roses, the aftertaste of aniseed on your tongue as you advance through the scrub, the dry cold that cleanses your mouth, lungs, nose. I've taken part in retraining courses for the long-term unemployed, for people who have exhausted the family allowance, courses that, instead of actually teaching you something, are intended to be incentives to take your mind off this particular stretch of the journey as you blunder on into the black space of that non-future, and they're an expression of profound pessimism: they teach you how to write a CV and how to sell yourself to people taking on staff; or how to optimise the use of your mobile phone when it comes to asking for work (that's what they say, optimise*); how to save on transport when you go out and about delivering your CV to different companies, and how to make the best use of your time by drawing up your route beforehand; they even explain – plumbing the very depths of despondency – how to have a balanced diet based on the food they give you at food banks, the little packet of pasta or rice or chickpeas, the tin of passata, the sugar, and how to use those few ingredients to prepare a varied and imaginative menu. A healthy Mediterranean diet. I looked for work in other local carpentry businesses, saying that I've already worked in a carpentry workshop, but are you a trained carpenter, they ask me, and I explain that I've spent the last few months working with Esteban, but illegally, because I'm not getting unemployment benefits any more, only family allowance, but how can anyone live on 425 euros? How exactly did you help Esteban, in what way, they ask, did you measure up, did you use a saw, a plane, a lathe, a milling cutter, a drill, a sander, do you know how to put together a mitre joint, or a* *tongue-and-groove joint or how to use dowels? Did Esteban actually let you use any of the tools? Or work the machines? No, he didn't, did he? You were just the driver, you used to help that Moroccan guy load and unload, you delivered the tools Esteban asked you to bring him and sometimes you didn't even know what they were called and you'd bring him the wrong ones, and then he'd shout at you and call you an idiot. Everyone knows everything in a village. So why are you trying to pull the wool over my eyes — you're not a carpenter. Anyone could do what you did. You were just Esteban's errand boy. Yes, everyone knows everything here. It's a village. But at least ask him if he had any complaints about me, if I was a good worker. Oh, I'm sure you were, but if I needed to take on anyone new, it would be a qualified carpenter. I've got plenty of people to load and unload. And he's right, there was no need to tell him all that stuff about unemployment benefit and family allowance — everyone in Olba knows that I asked Esteban to take me on illegally because I was still getting unemployment benefit and didn't want to lose it, because on the wages he was offering, I couldn't afford to pay the mortgage or the car loan, and then I stopped getting unemployment benefit and now all I have is the family allowance, and how, with only those 425 euros and the six hundred euros my wife earns, how am I supposed to pay the mortgage, pay for the children's books and clothes, the electricity and water and gas bills and the petrol, at least I managed to pay off the car, because, otherwise, they would have impounded it, and if I go elsewhere and say I've been employed in a carpentry workshop for the last few months, I haven't even got a reference to prove it, and it wouldn't be any good anyway, because they know, everyone I speak to knows, because here in Olba, we all know each other, like I say, it's a village, but they think I deserve what's happened to me, because I chose to work illegally, and they don't realise that the reason I had done that was because what Esteban was paying me wasn't enough to survive on, but people are naturally envious, and they'd say to me: you're getting paid twice, as if I was earning millions, they get a kick out of seeing you down and out and they don't like it if you try to lift your head and, instead, they push you under again, give you a shove so that you fall back into the pond you were only just crawling out of.*

As I leave the workshop where I'd gone looking for a job, I wonder how people can be so cruel, so rude. You have to be pretty hard-nosed to say such things to a married man with three children, without even knowing him. They throw all your limitations in your face. How do they expect a man, a worker, to recover his pride? What right do they have, these people you don't even know, to call you useless, to play with you, the way a cat plays with a frightened mouse. They stand in the doorway to watch you leave, a cigarette between their lips, hands in their pockets, lips twisted into a half-smile. They don't have to look for work, they don't have to humble themselves or borrow money. They have plenty of bread on the table, and the haves have always acted cruelly towards the have-nots. Their power comes from knowing that they can decide whether other people's mouths are empty or full, that's the origin of that half-smile, that cigarette clamped between the lips. During military service, the mess sergeants wore the same disgustingly smug smile, the smile of someone who has what others need and want. My father often used to say the same.

The biggest treat my grandfather gave my uncle was to sit him on his knee and allow him to lick the stamp for the letter he'd written to a supplier ordering something for the workshop. He would let him stick on the stamp, then walk with him, hand in hand, to the post office, where he would lift him up so that he could reach the open mouth of the bronze lion that served as the letter box and slip the envelope into his mouth. This became a kind of hereditary game, because my uncle went on to have the same ritual with me. When I came home from nursery school, he would sit me on his knee and place before me a few envelopes and a diminishing sheet of stamps. I would then tear along the perforated edge, taking great care not to damage the stamps, and once I'd removed a single stamp, I would lick it very carefully, stick it on the top right-hand corner of the envelope, and thump it hard several times with my fist. On this bright morning, I can still remember that sickly glue taste on the tip of my tongue and the sadness I felt at letting go of those little bits of coloured paper when I posted them in the postbox. Why don't you make a stamp collection from the letters you receive at home my grandfather suggested, but we didn't receive enough letters at the carpentry workshop to make a collection, and the few that did arrive, from suppliers or from the savings bank, had stamps all stained by the postmark.

'But,' he insisted, 'those are the stamps some collectors value most, the postmarked ones, showing the date the letter was sent and where it came from.'

It was my Uncle Ramón who let me stick the stamps on, who gave me a little wooden cart and a real bird tied by a thread to a perch, the person who took me to the fair and won me a tin truck at the shooting gallery. If I look up now, I can see – through the sharp leaves of the reeds – the bare, blue, rocky mountains on which a small clump of pine trees somehow manages to grow, and the lower slopes, their terraces dotted with olive trees and the occasional dense green stain of a carob tree. It's the same landscape I used to look at with him. On this cold morning, I can still feel the sickly taste of glue on my tongue.

When he came back from the war, my father considered hiding in the reed beds near the lagoon until the worst was over, but my mother persuaded him to go to the town hall and turn himself in.

My grandmother's suspicions about my mother date from that time, with my mother asking him to give himself up and my grandmother telling him to leave, to hide somewhere no one could find him. She had a vague sense that my mother selfishly wanted to have him near even if that meant putting his life in danger. During his time in prison, though, the idea lodged in my grandmother's head that her daughter-in-law, all revolutionary fervour gone, now regretted her earlier 'indiscretion' as well as her Republican wedding in the presence of other comrades, her first child – Germán, my older brother – who was already running around the house, and her second child, namely me, who was chewing on her dry, malnourished breasts, a child whom her husband didn't even know because, for months, she refused to take me with her to visit him in prison, saying that I was too small and frail for such a difficult, dangerous journey. I don't want to put the child at risk, she said, who knows what might happen in the train or outside the prison. She and my grandmother used to take my brother, but not every time. Often her parents would look after him. My grandmother believed that my mother wanted another husband, perhaps one in a better position to face the new era that was just beginning. After all, those civil marriages were invalid now, null and void. There remains something confusing about this story, however, something no one has ever explained to me. My grandmother didn't trust or even like my mother, a clumsy, empty-headed girl, who poured all her energies into cleaning the house, doing the laundry and the cooking, but always sulky and tearful, because my father was away and she was left at the mercy of her authoritarian mother-in-law. My grandmother expected a different kind of energy from her. They had been driven apart by the arguments that raged between them about having my father hand himself over to the authorities. And that rift remained for as long as my grandmother lived. Your father gave himself up so as to get away from those women and their bickering, Uncle Ramón would joke when he told me about it years later.

Anyway, my father duly handed himself in and spent nearly three years in prison waiting for a death sentence that was, in the end, commuted. He survived, but he felt like a deserter from an army that existed only in his head, the ghostly army of those who did what he wished he had done – fighters who did not surrender, who managed to cross the frontier or join the resistance or stay hidden near the lagoon, surviving for several years on whatever they could hunt or catch. Some village men did this, innocuous Robinson Crusoes, whose enforced lakeside life did not, for the most part, go well: they caught malaria, any wounds they had became infected, and in that dank atmosphere, the slightest scratch from a reed gave them tetanus, condemning them to a horrible death, added to which they were constantly being hunted by the civil guard, who pursued them like animals, even burning down vegetation. The crackle of the reed beds burning and the sticky smell of the smoke suffocating the other marsh creatures would reach as far as Olba. To make the fire spread more rapidly, they would pour petrol on the reed beds and the scrub, which were often small islands of floating vegetation. It wasn't all about repression though. There was a business aspect too. On the excuse that they had to hunt down those poor wretches, the authorities encouraged the draining of the lagoons, promoted the idea of filling them in, giving swathes of swampy land to a few friends and ex-combatants, granting them authority to drain and cultivate it. Greed was enough of an incentive to mobilise the volunteers for the hunts. Properties like Dalmau and La Citrícola were born out of those redistributions. The export company Dalmau was created on the newly cultivated areas given to General Santomé, who was, in fact, little more than a jumped-up officer risen from the ranks and mentioned in dispatches (as I found out later, he was also the instigator in the rearguard of indiscriminate shootings, bullets in the back of the neck like the one that killed my grandfather, the burning down of houses with their inhabitants still inside: farm workers accused of providing food, clothes, blankets or of simply talking to fugitives and sharing a cigarette with them), and La Citrícola was born out of the part of the lake handed over to Pallarés to be drained, another blue shirt who strutted about with a pistol in his shoulder holster, generally tyrannising the area until the late 1960s, when his legal heirs took over the estate, and while they – a sign of the times – have behaved rather more discreetly, they have been just as greedy, and all their dealings wiped clean of the old ideological cobwebs: clean money without the packaging of patriotic speeches, proclamations or sabre-rattling. These calculated acts of aggression were a mixture of military strategy, political vengeance and economic pillaging. The perfect storm, as glib commentators like to say nowadays to describe the moment when the conditions for some disaster to occur are just right. Whenever the civil guard captured one of the escapees, they would display his corpse on a cart or on the back of a truck and parade it through the streets of the village. The locals proudly allowed themselves to be photographed standing next to these putrefying bodies. Someone must still have those photos, identical to the ones that hunters take after a wild-boar hunt. Those human trophies have dark stains on their cheekbones, foreheads, shirts, on the crotches of their trousers. They were the succubi who pursued my father. For years afterwards, he kept watch on those huntsmen, thanks to information given him by his wife and children and possibly by some other secret informant. Our words fed him. I know now that words can do that, can nourish you. Yes, I've learned that too: I can make you a proper Colombian chicken soup now because here, in the local shop, they sell all the ingredients, as well as yucca and yam and all the things I could never find in the usual stores, but now, ever since they opened up on the corner, I can get everything I need, it's just like being in Manizales or Medellín or Popayán: I can cook plantain fritters, a few arracachas, potato, peanut and pork tamales, I can cook all those things for you here whenever you like. And don't tell me you don't like food you've never even eaten. You have to try it first. Your father would probably have liked it too, he must have been a very gentle soul, he reminds me of my grandfather.

He got annoyed when he heard that my uncle was doing well in Misent. There's no shortage of work, tourists are buying apartments and houses, and they need doors, window frames and shutters, my uncle would say, adding a dash of cognac to his coffee, and my father would reply that here nothing much had changed: we're freshwater people in Olba. And fresh water only attracts mosquitoes. He would make fun of my uncle: I suppose now you go fishing in the sea – I know you left your freshwater fishing tackle to him (he didn't say 'my son' or 'Esteban', or even 'the boy': he said 'him'). Next time you visit, bring us a grouper or a bit of salted tuna or some red mullet. When he spoke of saltwater people, he wasn't referring to the fishermen in the port of Misent, who'd always formed a marginal colony of poor folk (have you forgotten that, Leonor? the houses that got flooded in the storms, with no toilets, no mod cons), but to those people who were drawn by the strong magnet, the magical spell of the sea, who have generated so much coming and going over the last few decades, so much speculation, an invasion of which my uncle was beginning to be a part. Misent. At the beginning of the twentieth century, the sea attracted the first tourists to Misent, a few bourgeois families with aristocratic pretensions, just as in the preceding centuries it had attracted merchants, adventurers, smugglers (the sea as a source of violence), invaders who forced the freshwater men to protect themselves, filling the coastline with watchtowers and fortresses built in the middle of the marshes, the uncertain sea as a metaphor for moral ambiguity: the casinos of Misent, the brothels, the cheap boarding houses and bars that attracted the sailors who moored in the port and the farmers from the villages inland. They would buy supplies from the warehouses, go for a check-up at the doctor's, visit the notary's office to sign any legal documents, go to the bars, casinos and gambling dens, until, that is, the bombardments during the war left the port unused for decades, and Misent became almost a ghost town: no ships arrived to unload timber or cement and then load up again with raisins and figs, oranges, grapefruit, pomegranates, brightly painted wooden crates carefully packed with fruit wrapped up in delicate tissue paper. It's true that bourgeois families continued to spend their summers there, and they had their own cafes in Avenida Orts, but they were not invaders, no, those who came in the summer were like guests: they lived in elegant houses with stucco facades built behind high walls overgrown with jasmine and wisteria, houses built on the low hills with views over the vineyards; for those people, the sea was like a blue fringe on the horizon; they were not the invasion that came later: thousands and thousands of complete nutters (that's what he called them, nutters, idiots), who bought apartments right on the seashore – who in their right mind would choose to live right by the sea, he would say, that's where the poorest houses have always been built, for fishermen and unskilled labourers, as well, of course, as the merchants' warehouses, which had to be where the business was, and the boarding houses and lodgings for sailors and prostitutes. I myself see things in rather the same way, and in the midst of all this confusion, the lagoon seems to me the sole surviving nucleus of a timeless world that remains both fragile and forceful, in the centre of that diminishing tapestry – sharkskin green – formed by the orange and grapefruit plantations, the orchards, the fields that drink from the lagoon thanks to a complicated system of irrigation channels. We use the word 'nature' to describe any forms of artifice that preceded ours, we don't stop to consider that landscapes are not eternal, they exist and are – like us – condemned to die, and not always more slowly either. I can testify to that. You just have to look at what's happened in the last twenty years. But what's wrong? Nothing's wrong, it's all right, don't worry, it's nothing, I'm not crying, yes, I am, Don Esteban, but I'm crying over nothing really, just my own problems, which I don't want to dump onto you, they're my problems after all. But, sweetheart, calm down, tell me what's wrong. No, stop. Tell me why you're crying, just calm down a little, that's it, here's my handkerchief, dry your eyes, come on, raise your head a little and I'll dry your eyes. That's better, there you are, you're so pretty when you smile, and you look ugly when you cry, no, that's not true, you never look ugly, you're always pretty, but I do hate to see you sad, let me wipe away your tears again, I'm really sorry to get so upset, don't worry, you can rest your head on my shoulder if that helps to calm you, that's it, relax, what tiny hands you have, next to mine they look like toys, like a doll's hands, look, I can wrap my hand around one of yours and it's gone, vanished, that's better, it's good to see you laughing again, with those lovely eyes of yours, you really do have tiny hands, put them on top of mine, and, look, if I close my hands, they vanish, they're lost, such small hands and such big eyes. That's right, relax. Everything passes, but there's always light at the end of the tunnel, whenever anything bad happens, just remember that nothing lasts forever, that's what life is like, we're born and we die, everything passes, nothing remains the same, everything dies, us too, my mother died more than twenty years ago, and how long ago is it since Uncle Ramón died, the one who wasn't born in time to take part in the war, the one my grandmother kept slapping even while she was clutching him to her when the fascists burst in, can't you see he's just a child, she said, clutching the one who married late, was soon widowed and never had children, although I often think that he did have a son in me, just as he was the closest thing I ever had to a father. In his later years, he came back to Olba, he'd closed his workshop in Misent when his wife died: everything reminds me of her, I can't bear to be in the workshop or the house or down by the port, or in the cafes or shops or the banks in Avenida Orts. He even took to blaming a God he didn't believe in. Men, he used to say, can fuck you up your whole life, but, as the mystics said, at least we're allowed all eternity to rest or to continue cursing your enemies. Each man contains his own particular evil and you can prepare yourself to confront him (he talked about men as he did about fish and wild boar, each with his particular bait, each with his particular appetites, each with his particular trap). I'm not afraid of men, but I'm afraid to think that God might exist. He's the one who created the evil in each of us, the one we keep inside us, the one that emerges into the open only to screw everything up. I hate to think what's in that divine head of His, or what He shits out of His sacred arse, Mars and the Sun and Jupiter and the Moon are all His turds, and we and the rats and the cockroaches are just stinking little bits of His crap.

One evening, he asked me to drive him to the local brothel. He went upstairs with one of the women, but didn't even take his clothes off: how can I take my clothes off with all this flab hanging off me (he had continued to put on weight, widowhood had made him greedier, his eyes grew smaller, pillowed in fat) and all these bulging veins? He rolled up one trouser leg and showed me his varicose veins, which covered the complete colour spectrum, from sky blue to navy blue, from lilac to black. He paid, sat down on the bed, looked at the naked girl for half an hour, reached out to touch her, a single caress, and came unsteadily back down the stairs, one hand pressed against the wall to support himself. On the way home, I looked at him out of the corner of one eye, where he was sitting in the passenger seat, and I saw his flushed face and the tears rolling down his cheeks. How could those two men possibly be brothers, the sensual man who, in his old age, could still take pleasure in merely looking at a woman's flesh, and who had only fallen out with life because he loved it so, and then my father, that lugubrious bat who often didn't leave the house for weeks on end and kept the windows closed to avoid the sun's dazzling gaze. And yet, with the universe's usual senseless logic, the one who was full of life was the first to die, while the other has lingered on, growing ever sourer: the one who for more than seventy years has shown no interest in life is still slowly rotting and infecting everything around him with his bitterness.

My older brother Germán and I weren't alike either; a variant on the same biblical theme, Cain and Abel, dark and light, although, in this case, I was the bat who survived, while he died of incurable lung cancer (and he didn't even smoke). Right from the start, he said he didn't want to be a carpenter. He liked mechanical things, taking cars and motorbikes apart and putting them back together again. Initially, my father was adamantly opposed, but finally gave in and helped Germán open a garage which ended up in the hands of Germán's wife and her brothers, an unseemly, rather tawdry ending. It's hard to understand how that young woman, Laura (apparently her father named her after the film, which came out the year she was born, she was seven or eight years younger than my brother),

90

who was apparently so in love, always taking my brother's arm and giving him sloppy kisses, how that cheerful, helpful girl, so ready to help with the lunch and serve at table, always so house-proud and considerate, especially when it came to our family, giving my mother presents and calling her Mama, kissing my father and calling him Papa, the only one who could ever kiss him without him groaning and who could get his eyes to fill with tears when he received her gift of socks or a sweater, how that same selfless, hard-working woman became the one to cut all ties with our family as soon as Germán died. She'd been almost as ruthless with her husband when she found out that his cancer was terminal. She became cool and indifferent towards us, her in-laws, and even towards him. My mother took better care of Germán than she did, for she was too busy during his final days, rushing about between the land registry and the bank, from the notary to the lawyer's office, determined not to leave any loose ends, and getting my brother to sign papers when he was almost too weak to hold a pen. She even phoned up my father to get him to sign a few documents too. It's for the children's sake, she said, by way of justification. In the end, she managed to keep the garage and the house my brother had set up with our father's money. For several years, my father had to continue paying the mortgage. So, what was it all about, then, the soft voice (she wasn't remotely like the highly stylised Gene Tierney who'd played Laura in the film, she was short and chubby, but with a very animated face), the domestic hyperactivity whenever they came to lunch at our house, the eagerness to lay the table, to smooth and iron the tablecloth, and help in the kitchen, the charming, industrious little ant who called my parents Mama and Papa, and kissed my brother and straightened his collar and patted his bottom, put her arms around his waist, intertwined her fingers with his while she gazed adoringly into his eyes? Was it all an act? Are we all just actors, who might at any moment grow tired of the role we're playing and remove our disguise? Or are there also real people? But what does that mean? What does 'real people' mean? And if it means nothing, *is* nothing, what sense is there in life? What happens to us if real people don't exist? We tend to think that people's true nature comes out at decisive moments, when the going gets tough, when they're pushed to the limit. The moment for heroes and saints. And yet, strange though it may seem, at such moments, human behaviour is usually neither exemplary nor encouraging. The group who elbow their way to the head of the queue where the concert tickets are being handed out; the spectators who flee the burning theatre, trampling over the weaker members of the audience, not even noticing them, the child, the withered flesh of the old man, crushed beneath the soles of the anxious fugitives, pierced by the heels of young women elegantly dressed for an evening out; the honest citizens, including the women – from middle- and working-class families, it makes no odds – who use their oars to furiously beat back the other shipwreck victims trying to clamber into the overcrowded lifeboat. It's every man for himself. As we know, Dad, it's not hard to arrive at the point where you are now; day after day, life insists on proving you right. The great human family. Of the two grandchildren your older son gave you, we haven't heard a word – they've vanished. My mother would occasionally weep for them: I do have grandchildren, but it's as if they had never existed. That shameless hussy (she was a hussy now, no longer *my dear, I've put some croquettes by for you so that you can fry them up later this evening when you get home, because the children love them freshly cooked, nice and hot*), that shameless hussy, my mother would say, she took them from me. She stole them. Just as she stole everything that belongs to our son. Just as she stole what was ours.

My sister's children helped somewhat to assuage the resurgence of maternal feelings that grandchildren tend to provoke in women. At least she had them, even though they were far away, in Barcelona. At least they came to see her sometimes. She never spoke ill of her daughter, but I know that it pained her never to have been invited to their house in Barcelona. Not once. Either because they found her presence bothersome and didn't know what to do with her in the big city, or – as Carmen herself said – because their house really was too small. My mother interpreted this as indifference, but that, in turn, became a stimulus. Suffering diverted her, gave meaning to time, gave focus; and it allowed her to complain, to give vent to her bitterness: her grandchildren were there and she, their grandmother, was here, 450 endless kilometres away. She would knit sweaters for them, buy them jackets, and I imagine that my sister gave these away to some needy child or neighbour, provincial sweaters and cardigans and old-fashioned jackets that no one with any ambition would dream of wearing in the big city. She never saw Germán's children again, they didn't even come to her funeral, I can't remember now if they were still living in Misent when she died, because that was where my brother moved to when he got married and where he'd set up his business. I know they don't live there any more. My sister-in-law sold the house and the garage years ago when she remarried – the garage went to one of Leonor's brothers – and then the whole family moved away, possibly to Madrid. Needless to say, I never saw them again either. I imagine they'll remember us, though, when they find out that my father is dead and that I have no heirs. Then they'll be happy enough to sit down with the rest of the family to divide up the spoils. The grandchildren and great-grandchildren, if there are any, there must be some, and Carmen's children and grandchildren (I know she has grandchildren, not that she's ever brought them here to visit, I've only seen photos – she blames her daughters-in-law, *well, you know what they're like*). The dish we make by frying up the leftovers from the previous day's meal is called *ropavieja*, old clothes. That's what Germán's family will be eating when they come; they'll meet their aunt and uncle: Uncle Juan (who was born after me), the ne'er-do-well, who will arrive from some far-flung part of the world to join them in the notary's office; they'll meet their Aunt Carmen and the cousins and nephews from Barcelona, they'll greet each other gladly, exchange phone numbers, addresses, all of them in excellent spirits, looking forward to the prospect of the money that will come to them from the division of spoils, the sale of the house and the carpentry workshop, a magnificent plot right in the middle of the village, although don't even think of selling it now, there's no point, prices are at rock-bottom; but they'll be pleased at the valuation placed on the land in Montdor, even though the price of land up there is in free fall: it's worth only a third of what you would have paid for it six or seven years ago, but it's still a decent sum of money; they'll be pleased, too, about the orange grove that my father tended until not that long ago, land now reclassified as suitable for development, but which, like everything else, would be almost impossible to sell at the moment. The old man was unlucky even in death, they'll remark jovially as they sit in the visiting room at the funeral home, the coffin containing my father's body safe behind a discreetly drawn curtain, because, although the funeral home has done an excellent job, he really isn't a pretty sight. Our father was always a complainer, a sourpuss, his once favourite daughter will say. And Uncle Juan, the ne'er-do-well, will call him a miser, an egotist, remembering all the times that his father ignored his cries for help. For a few hours, the surviving brother and sister, the nephews, the children and grandchildren of Carmen and Germán, will all be drawn closer by greed, until they discover that the coffers are empty and there's nothing left in the bank, and that the land and the house and the workshop no longer belong to the family, then that sense of fraternal togetherness will rapidly evaporate and family ties will be replaced by documents from the private limited company set up for legal reasons, by requests for a special levy to pay for a lawyer (*a good lawyer*, one of them, possibly Germán's widow, will say – *we need the very best, remember we're up against the banks here, and things are looking really black*), by arguments because the restless, ne'er-do-well brother will, of course, think that what his sister in Barcelona and her offspring are proposing is far too expensive (that's probably why her husband comes along too, *you don't think I'd let you go there alone, do you?* in order to keep a close eye on the business, two pairs of eyes are better than one), and by the children and possible grandchildren and the wife of the husband who has been lying in a grave in Misent for years now. And after a while, after the initial skirmishes, and after looking at the problem from every possible angle, the great battle will commence, the family Waterloo, a return to the natural human state, everyone pitted against everyone else, ruthlessly and unreservedly, using every weapon available, siblings against siblings, siblings-in-law against siblings-in-law, aunts and uncles against nieces and nephews, grandchildren against grandparents, cousins locked in combat, with no holds barred, because the prospect of their getting anything at all is now highly unlikely (don't forget, *we're up against the banks, it's a very tricky business*), and they've had no luck with the legal steps they've taken so far, despite the exorbitant lawyer's fees (they dropped the one I suggested as the best option, Germán's widow will say, because they didn't like the way things were going to be shared out, honestly, they're mean sods even when it comes to acquiring money, and *they* chose this lawyer, not me, and he's turned out to be not only more expensive, but an out-and-out crook), and the inevitable suspicions that there's some kind of agreement between one section of the family and the lawyer, an agreement intended to plunder the others; and on and on it goes, the great family war by other means and in other places, the cold, damp Ardennes, dusty El Alamein. And once they're convinced that the only thing they're going to inherit are debts, and that what they're defending is a ruin (the scene now is more like Monte Casino in May 1945, a scorched landscape in which all that remains are blackened walls, stinking corpses and half a dozen dying men), the private limited company will be dissolved and they'll part with no hard feelings. Then, the ne'er-do-well brother will distribute kisses all round, just in case he can still touch one of them for a loan, an advance, a supper or a place at the dinner table and a warm bed, now that he has their addresses and, above all, their phone numbers and email addresses, the catflaps through which modern-day intruders creep; anyway, kisses all round and let's say goodbye like brothers and sisters, with no hard feelings. All that's left is despair and disillusionment with the family in which they had invested so much hope, and which, for a moment, they even thought would require the occasional get-together, just to enjoy the warmth of belonging to a clan: we don't want to meet in Madrid, where you live, or in Barcelona, where we live, so why don't we meet up once a year somewhere halfway between the two, like Zaragoza or Teruel, for example, the Monasterio de Piedra is gorgeous, isn't it, Pedro? (Carmen addresses this rhetorical question to her husband.) We were there a couple of years ago and we saw the waterfall and, as I was saying, it was just lovely; we could meet once a year to have a slap-up meal together (presumably spending any remnants of the booty they manage to scrape together). It seems incredible, such selfishness between brothers and sisters, between cousins, blood of our blood, my sister Carmen will complain to her closest friends once back in Barcelona. I can't believe they could be so stingy, she will say charitably, angelically. It wasn't a very enlightening experience for the children. Or was it? Perhaps it's best that they learn what life is really like.

Oh well, too bad. Brothers and sisters. So far, there's been one definite disappearance (death is always definite), that of Germán, and two less strident disappearances, two subtle, gradual, stealthy escapes: that of Carmen and of Juan, familiar shadows moving in the distance, too far off for their presence to warm us: Juan sends out few signals from his nomadic and, as I imagine, turbulent existence, although perhaps, with time, he's calmed down a little: time tames us all, calms us, sedates us, lulls us gently to sleep. When Juan last phoned, a few years ago now, it was to announce that he'd become involved in property management or something of the sort in Málaga. That's what he told me. Everything's fine, really good, he said in the voice of a snake-oil salesman. I'll tell you all about it later. Put Dad on the line, will you? But Dad didn't want to be put on the line, he made a gesture with one hand as if batting away a wasp. Dad's not here right now, I said, he's gone out and won't be back until late. What's wrong, Juan said, doesn't he want to speak to me? I said nothing. Silence. He cleared his throat and: Well, you can both go . . . he began to say as he was about to hang up, one-tenth of a second after I had hung up on him, without waiting to hear what it was that we could both go and do. Ever since, silence. I'm sure he was lying then too, there was no Málaga, no property to manage, no everything's fine. He hasn't told the truth once in his more than sixty years of existence. He could be anywhere, in La Coruña, in Bilbao, in Bangkok, dealing cards in a gambling den in the private room of a roadside casino, a cigarette in his mouth and a line of cocaine waiting for him in the toilet for when he's finished his round; clipping his toenails in a prison cell or pressing his elbows hard into a mattress as he struggles to elicit a moan of pleasure from some international bit of totty. Or else he's just been released from jail and is phoning someone because he senses that tomorrow he might land up in another jail, and he has to make the most of this moment when he has access to a phone booth and enough money to make a call and try and persuade someone to stand bail for him and get him out of tomorrow's prison. The last time he came here, he turned up with a Ukrainian woman, to whom, according to him, he was married (she must have been about thirty years his junior); this, it turned out, was a lie, there had been no wedding, no happy couple, not even a relatively stable relationship: she was just a prostitute who had joined him on the journey, because he'd happened to meet her on the road a few days before, she was a whore and he was a crook, she was merely an accomplice he had brought along to assist him in whatever thieving opportunities came his way, including thieving from us. This fake couple moved in and stayed for a month or two: flies buzzing around us, repeating over and over the word 'money', because that's what they wanted, the money that my brother said he needed in order to set up some deal that would bring him stability and us wealth. Although in order to launch this fabulous business opportunity he needed cash, dosh, dough. They want money up front, he told me and my father, to set up this big deal, and because, as everyone knows, banks don't give credit without guarantees, he wanted us to sign over all our money to the bank as a guarantee for the mountain of crisp banknotes he would receive in exchange. You just lend it to me (he had forgotten all about *give me my part of the inheritance now, and I'll sign whatever I need to sign*, that trick hadn't worked). Or, easier still, I don't even touch your money, you sign a document saying that the bank can keep it for a fixed term while I pay back what they lend me. A kind of guarantee that wouldn't be a guarantee, that would continue to give you interest, more or less the same as happens now, I imagine, because I'm sure you have a fixed-term deposit account somewhere, don't you? Everyone does. What I'm proposing is really simple, and you don't have to release your money or put it at risk. It's a kind of guarantee that doesn't endanger your money. The smell of money – for someone who knows that it's near, but not exactly where or how to get at it – must jangle all the other senses, because I don't know how he could possibly imagine he was going to get a single céntimo out of our father, because there was no way he was going to fool him into doing that. No con trick, no hustle, no scam would work, no one has ever got anything out of him with kind words or begging or threats. Not even the approach of death made my father generous. What does the old git want the dosh for anyway? my younger brother would ask, hoping to make me his accomplice, as if we were both driven by the same interests rather than by entirely opposing interests, what you gain I lose and vice versa: that tired old Cain and Abel story yet again – when is he ever going to spend it, and on what, because there's no money in the next world. Besides, he would conclude, he's a communist and doesn't believe in the afterlife. I just played dumb: you can see how he treats me, I would say, he virtually keeps me on bread and water. Although I was also careful to look after number one: I don't honestly think he's got that much money. My brother: but the workshop's doing well, isn't it? Hm, I said, meaning only so-so. Needless to say, he wasn't going to get money out of us by feigning affection. He wasn't going to get anything out of our father or me, because during the months he was with us, I didn't even give him money to buy cigarettes, as he sometimes asked me to. He would say, lend me five hundred pesetas to buy some cigarettes, a coffee, a beer, we're completely broke. Me too, I would say. I never gave him anything, but I would see them smoking (the Ukrainian woman smoked even more heavily than he did), or drinking beer in La Amistad, the bar opposite our house, and sometimes they would roll up in a taxi from Misent.

99

I preferred not to know what they got up to, where they got their money. At any rate, as far as food goes, they didn't go without. When it suited them, they ate with us. We did allow them that. The old man may have been strict, but in that respect he was a good father. Meals were for the whole family, everyone got the same portion of rice, greens, fish, the same slice of potato omelette that was there for anyone to take. Nothing luxurious, but nutritious. Justicialism: from each according to his abilities, to each according to his needs. Pure Marx. But apart from that, apart from providing food, at least as long as my father kept his marbles, no one ever got a céntimo out of him. His method is very simple: he doesn't show you the money, he doesn't talk about it, he doesn't think about it, it's as if it didn't exist, and as long as his mind was intact, it didn't exist (we are neither exploiters nor speculators). And that's what drove Juan crazy, knowing that it must exist, that it was there somewhere but not knowing where. He assumed there must be some money, either a lot or a little, and it drove him to distraction, smelling it: like a dog getting all worked up because it can smell the hare's urine, skin and even the blood beating in the hare's little heart, but can't find the entrance to the hole where the animal is hiding. The dog pants, growls, scratches at the ground. I did know where the entrance was, I could see its mouth, but I couldn't take one step inside. In fact, the hare wasn't very large, it was a tiny creature hidden away in three separate holes, the Caja de Ahorros del Mediterraneo, the Banco de Santander and the Banco de Valencia. As far as I knew, there was no money in the house, no locked cash boxes, no wall safe concealed behind a painting. It was a bit like the Holy Trinity: the money was one in three, glowing dimly in three different bank accounts, that's where the suppliers' invoices got paid, where we deposited customers' cheques, where the electricity and water bills and the council tax had their home. And our father had exclusive use of the key to those three doors. He did as he pleased. He was the sole signatory. When, two years ago, I took out the money I needed to become a partner in Pedrós' business and, shortly afterwards, withdrew the rest in order to buy a still larger share, I was terrified by the thought that my father might suddenly regain his reason and speak and call me a thief. Although calling what I did theft is not quite accurate. It would be fairer to call it restitution, an advance on or a settlement of what he owes me, an historic debt as the politicians in the autonomous regions call it when they demand more capital transfers from the state. That I made a mistake, took too great a risk, is quite another matter, but what could I do, who could possibly have foreseen what happened, that what seemed like an unstoppable rise, a hot-air balloon, would deflate and fall to earth and burst into flames? I needed to see the tiny bit of capital I'd been saving for so many years grow larger, to see our own hot-air balloon take off and fly along with the others I could see drifting proudly across the sky, money that was as much mine as his, the fruit of our work in the carpentry workshop; I needed it to grow more quickly to ensure myself a dignified ending. I needed to pay for our euthanasia, his and mine, our place of rest, home care (or independent living to use the term invented by the social democrats my father has always so wholeheartedly loathed) or palliative care, and the deal with Pedrós would have the same effect as anabolic steroids, it would help build up our flaccid accounts: that was all, but it was my money *and* his, our money. I was the hare, I was my own urine and skin, I could smell my own trail, I was hunting myself. When I finally caught myself, I also lost the prey. Oh well.

My brother: If you don't like any of the solutions I'm proposing, all you need do is sign a guarantee written in such a way that the bank can never trace it back to you. I know how to do it – he insisted tirelessly – a guarantee that passes the ball to someone else, a sort of chain guarantee – he went on. I have a friend in Barcelona who has drawn up a few trick contracts of the kind that has the bank tearing its hair out for ever having signed them: that's how he tried to get round us, to deceive us, but when has anyone passed off a false guarantee to a bank? The bankers can cheat you, but you cheat them? Ha. Still he goes on: I've never asked for anything. Another of his lies: he's done nothing but ask ever since he was a child. He was always asking, in all kinds of ways, on any excuse, adopting every possible tone of voice: seductive, threatening, pleading, imploring. He was asking from the moment he learned how to speak, and before he could speak, he used gestures. He used to wheedle things out of my mother when she was still alive; and when I was an adolescent, he still managed to get the odd bit of money out of me too (not much, I never had much: for sweets or for the cinema when he was small; for cigarettes and the occasional beer once he started shaving), he may even have got something out of my sister (and though she may be an utter cow, you can milk her as hard as you like and you won't get much out of her dried-up teats), he tried to cajole money out of neighbours and friends, and we never did find out how everything slipped through his fingers so very fast. So young and such as spend-thrift, such as scrounger, such a layabout. When he was twelve, he discovered where my mother hid her money and he stole it to buy a racing bike. He had to take the bike straight back to the shop, but they couldn't accept it, because he'd already managed to scratch the saddle.

On that visit, his last, he would either be talking about this latest new business opportunity or, a couple of days later, bemoaning the fact that he was getting older and really *needed* to buy an apartment, to have somewhere of his own to live so that he wouldn't find himself a penniless old man, living on the streets, it really frightens me the thought of ending up homeless, eating in soup kitchens and sleeping in hostels, or, worse still, sitting in a doorway, covered by cardboard boxes, with only a piece of stale bread to eat and a carton of red wine to stave off the cold. There was such anguish in his eyes, it broke your heart. He just needed a really small apartment, the bare essentials. He would look for a job and retire to live somewhere near us. I said: We have empty rooms here and you could work in the workshop. But no, that wasn't what he wanted: a little apartment just for me, he said pouring all his tenderness into that word 'little'. My father continued eating, staring down at his plate; he paused for a moment, a spoonful of succulent rice suspended between plate and mouth, his gaze fixed on the minute hand of the clock on the wall: Juan's torpedo had missed its target again. He changed tactics. A day or so later, what he wanted was to *rent* an apartment, yes, he would settle for that: he'd seen a tiny third-floor one-bedroom apartment, nice and bright, with a kitchen-cum-living room and a bathroom with a full-length bath, and it was a snip, the owners were asking almost nothing for the sale price and an equally ridiculous sum for the rent, but there was one small problem: they were demanding a guarantee for the very large deposit they wanted, and not only that, they also required payment of the first four or five months' rent in advance and, until he managed to get himself organised and find a job locally, that was what he was asking us to provide in order for him to fulfil his dream: having a little place of his own to live. Another torpedo is launched, the spoon pauses, suspended in the air, my father's eyes are fixed on the clock, and again, nothing. The ship remains afloat, impassive, sailing straight ahead. My father raises to his lips the spoon containing the saffron-flavoured stock and the grains of rice and makes more noise than usual as he slurps it up. Hot stuff, he says. And one assumes that when he says this, he's referring to the rice. Days later, Juan had come down to earth and what he wanted now was to buy a ground-floor business premises, a warehouse – or rather than buy it, he wanted to rent. We're no longer on the third floor (in the cosy, comfortable one-bedroom apartment with the full-length bath), but on the ground floor; his business ambitions drop several storeys and hit the ground when he sees that, once again, my father fails to avert his gaze from either his spoon or the clock, while I raise my eyebrows to form something like an ironic question mark. He was finally about to achieve his life's ambition. In the last few weeks he had pulled out all the stops, done everything he could, and, eureka, the miracle had happened (he addressed that word 'miracle' to my father, who, for a millisecond, interrupted the journey of spoon to mouth, he's never believed in miracles, you idiot, but in Marx, the republic and the class struggle), and the chance for him to open a car dealership was within reach. He had all the municipal paperwork in order, the approval of the manufacturer, the paperwork for the franchise was ready to be signed, but to do that – who would have thought it – he needed, surprise, surprise, a certain amount of money. Not much, just the deposit and the first three months' rent in advance for the premises plus the deposit and the guarantees that would allow Hyundai to release the cars to him. He realised that this was much more than he had asked for the deposit on the apartment, about a thousand or two thousand times more, but, of course, this was something really important, not a loan, not a guarantee, but a family business with guaranteed short-term profits, profits that he would, of course, share with us. It would be shared out equally, I would just be the employee, the manager, and you would be the capitalists. We would immediately be able to begin paying back the large loan we had asked for and begin putting coins in our piggy banks. *Dinero, argent,* money, *flus, Geld.* That's what he needed, that's what we would have to pay back and that's what we would share out and, in our free moments, we

104

would be happy. All paths led to the same place. To the hare's hiding place, where the fuck *was* it? I can smell it. He wasn't asking very much. A few days later, another change of direction, while the Ukrainian was sticking her knife into a meatball, tasting a mouthful and saying: it's good, really good, and in Spanish you call this a *pelota*? – they had something similar in Ukraine and called it by a name that was either much longer or a little shorter. Meanwhile, he was still intent on finding that hare. Trying every trick in the book. The hare with its agile legs, its twitching mouth behind which you could see its sharp teeth: the stiff little moustache, the nice ears, and the back feet with which it scratches its nose. He told us that he had been given the Hyundai concession for the whole region – he apparently had exceptionally good contacts in the land of the rising sun – this was, quite simply, an unmissable opportunity. He said this with an absolutely straight face, as if I hadn't driven past the Hyundai concession a hundred times when leaving Misent. Whenever I have a delivery to make there, I see those second-hand Japanese cars glinting in the sunlight, warming their undersides on the heat coming off the tarmac, and I see the signs with the price written in bright red and the slogans, UNIQUE OPPORTUNITY emblazoned in garish colours on the bonnets of the second-hand cars: BARGAIN OF THE YEAR. They keep the new cars inside, behind the big smoked-glass windows, and there they sit, cool and protected by the air conditioning, neatly lined up, gleaming, and saying: Buy me if you can. Take me, I'm yours for €25,000.

Never has there been so much talk of business in this house as there was during those weeks over lunch. The little dining room with the sideboard and the chairs made by my grandfather or my father or by both; the walnut frames surrounding sepia photos of couples arm in arm, with her clutching her bouquet in both hands and him clutching her arm; the modernist lamp with its green glass shade; the china cabinet with the little porcelain cups that had been my mother's pride and joy and which, if they had actually been worth anything, Juan would have tried to sell. That dining room saw more economic debate than the Cristal de Maldón, Leonor Gelabert's restaurant, at whose tables, according to Francisco, sat secretaries of state for the economy, for the treasury and for public works and even the occasional minister (Leonor, you left without saying goodbye, on both occasions). Renting, buying, selling, mortgaging, conveying, building, decorating, distributing, warehousing, guaranteeing, endorsing, signing. For a couple of months, those were the sole topics of conversation at mealtimes, until my father could stand it no longer and had had enough of them ruining risottos and paellas, soups, fish, croquettes, omelettes and hamburgers – it all came heavily garnished with bundles of virtual money, piles of bank drafts ready to be signed and hundreds of square metres for sale or to rent, with or without a lease – and one afternoon, after drinking his coffee and lighting the cigar he always smoked after lunch, he put their luggage, Juan's and the Ukrainian's, out in the street. They found the suitcases there, by the front door, when they came back in the early hours. The suitcases out on the pavement, and the door locked and, just in case, bolted twice with the key left inside in the lock. I imagine that my father knew that, even though the luggage would be left out on the pavement for hours, where anyone could take the suitcases, they would contain nothing of any great value. No cash, no chequebooks or credit cards, no bank drafts, no deeds, no priceless painting cut from its frame and rolled up, no jewel case containing a diamond bracelet and a white-gold Piaget ring encrusted with emeralds. *Oualó*, as Ahmed would say. *Rien de rien*. Nothing. Tired old clothes given a quick spin in the washing machine to save on soap. Juan and the Ukrainian had, as usual, spent the hours after lunch shut in their room, screaming at each other, my father sitting in front of the television, as he is now, but holding a glass of brandy, with his cup of coffee and the ashtray on the small table next to the sofa, while he took sips of his brandy and puffed on his cigar. He'd raise the glass to his lips, then set it down next to the ashtray exactly where I now place his glass of milk before I put him to bed. He'd fill the glass a couple of times and drink its contents very slowly, as if gathering strength. It was the same every afternoon before we opened the workshop at four o'clock. They would hurl insults at each other, and he would seem not to hear, but on that day, his face was becoming ever greyer, the skin on his cheeks tighter, his cheekbones more pronounced. I was very familiar with the way he displayed his anger. When, after a while, the Barrow gang – our very own Bonnie and Clyde – left the house, he got up, went into the room they'd been staying in (the one with the double bed where he and my mother used to sleep until she died, and which was a sanctuary forbidden to us kids when he was listening to the BBC or to the banned communist radio station La Pirenaica, I still can't understand why he let them stay there), and he himself gathered their clothes and began stuffing them willy-nilly into suitcases and bags, while he growled and grunted (the double bed profaned, the smell of her cologne replacing the delicate Maderas de Oriente perfume my mother used to wear and that still impregnated the room – in fact, I think the idea of profanation only really struck him then). This is nothing to do with you, go downstairs and open the shutters in the workshop, he said when he saw me leaning in the doorway, watching him. Nothing is ever to do with me in this house. In the workshop, I lit a cigarette and sat down, not in the little office, but on the floor, my back against the power saw. My father never allowed anyone to smoke there, not with all the sawdust, wood shavings, glue, varnish, enamel – we work with flammable materials: you can smoke in the house and in the street, you can smoke in the office, but not in the workshop, he used to say, and yet he himself often walked around with a cigar clamped between his lips, although it was rarely lit. This thing wouldn't light if you doused it in petrol, he would grumble, tapping the cigar with his forefinger as if to justify his lack of consistency. Meanwhile, he threw the couple's luggage out into the street. He locked the door from inside, left the key in the lock, and bolted it twice. That afternoon, he didn't come down to work and didn't want to have supper with me. That night, from my room, I heard someone scrabbling at the lock. Then I began to hear my brother's voice in different tones and registers: at first, it was a whisper, then he began to call to us, softly at first, as if with deep affection, then angrily and, finally, shouting; Fucking hell, he kept growling, spitting out oaths in a crescendo that ended with a long, noisy drum solo – him repeatedly kicking the door. Then, the silence of the night, the shrill *cricri* of crickets, a car engine, the distant barking of a dog. The peaceful Olba night.

That was the last time I heard Juan's voice in the flesh so to speak. Since then, we've had no further news of him. Not a letter, not a postcard, only that mysterious phone call from Málaga a few years ago (seven or eight years after my father chucked him out), telling me – for reasons known only to him, but probably simply to find out if our father was still alive, or if he could drop by to pick up his inheritance – how well his new business was going, something to do with property management (or was it construction work? I can't quite remember now). My father had refused to take the phone when I held it out to him as soon as I heard Juan's voice. His final words – 'you can both just go' – included me in his curse. But as soon as the old man dies, I'm sure he'll turn up in order to demand his part of the inheritance, the part he wanted us to give him in advance; he'll come back, convinced that the inheritance has continued to grow fatter and fatter (he has always believed whatever he wanted to believe, taking no account of reality) because in his febrile imagination, the carpentry workshop is a fabulously successful business – well, it must have been in the years of the building boom – and that, hidden away somewhere in the cellar – the place he could smell but not locate – there's a pile of gold ingots, bundles of purple notes arranged by serial number, as well as sheaves of share certificates. It won't take him long to realise his mistake. By the way, before that pair of frustrated thieves made their hasty departure, I saw the Ukrainian woman naked. It was one morning when he'd left the house alone. Olena – that's what they said she was called – appeared at the door of my bedroom, dressed (if you can call it that) in a transparent bathrobe. She wasn't wearing any underwear, just that brief robe, left open to reveal one pink nipple and the reddish shadow of her pubic hair between her very white thighs, which the gauze, or whatever that subtle fabric was, signally failed to cover. She asked to borrow some nail clippers. Who knows why. The nails on fingers and toes were long and carefully painted. Perhaps she needed to remove a hangnail, that's possible, although I'm convinced that my brother sent her, a variant on his many ways of begging, and her appearance at my door that morning was a commercial proposition. The minuscule robe, the nipple and the reddish shadow sheltering between those white marble thighs were, I thought, an invitation for me to become part of the gang and collaborate in the task of finding the treasure chest, a way of allowing me in as a new associate. If not, why the hell had he got up so early and left the house without her, leaving at my disposal that hint of reddish pubic hair, when the two of them always went everywhere together, because he wanted to keep a watchful eye on the owner of the pubic hair. It was clearly a proposal to make this a family enterprise. I rejected the offer to be a part of that company – whether limited liability or just limited I don't know – of which the gauze allowed me a glimpse. In return, I lost the nail clippers that I lent to Olena and which she never gave back.

I couldn't believe it when I saw him lying there gasping for air, his little paws quivering, and the blood spreading out around him as he grew still, I called to him, as if calling could bring him back, but no, after a few more spasms, he lay there, mouth open, and you could see his teeth, which looked suddenly rather threatening. A creature with no feelings, unfamiliar and cruel. As if death had revealed his true nature. Suddenly, I didn't know him, didn't love him. I didn't want to stroke him or even look at him. Those glassy eyes, sharp canine teeth, the stiffness that overtook him almost instantaneously. A carnivorous animal causing me only pain and filling me with fear and disgust. He just wasn't him any more. I looked away. I don't know why people insist on gazing at the corpses of their loved ones, because they're not them any more, they don't even look like them. Then you're stuck with that final image forever, it comes back to you when you least expect it and sullies the memory of what went before, of the time when you loved that creature; when you thought it beautiful to see him running about and you felt like stroking him and even weeping with emotion when he looked tenderly up at you. The driver of the car hadn't even stopped. People said he probably didn't realise he'd run him over, he was so small. Perhaps that's true, although personally I think the driver was some heartless man, who simply drove off. I couldn't believe it, my neighbours had to take me to the hospital because I became hysterical. There they gave me an injection. I couldn't stop crying, my little dog so full of life was now as stiff and lifeless as a toy.

I'm so alone now, my children live far away, and the truth is they don't seem to care about me that much, they don't come and see me very often, and as for my marriage, well, I hardly speak to my husband, not even now that he spends most of his time at home after losing his job at the workshop. He sits down in front of the computer, gets onto the Internet, and snaps at me whenever I speak to him — I'll ask him to go with me to Lidl or Mercadona: *Why don't you come too, Álvaro, it'll help clear your head? No, you go, I'm not in the mood.* And what mood does he think I've been in since I had to give up my job and was put on permanent disability leave? What kind of life is this? The visits to the hospital, which at least provide some distraction. The waiting room where you sit until the door to the doctor's consulting room opens, or the door to the little room where they do the tests or that other room where there's a small bed against the wall that no one uses and where I wait to have my warfarin levels checked, having first asked who's last in the queue. Yes, it is a distraction, although it seems wrong to say that: I don't go there for fun, I go there for them to test my blood *(if you're the last in the queue, then I'll go behind you)*, but I like seeing the same faces every month, people who are going there for the same reason as me, and where there's always a new face to be seen. Some faces disappear too, and I prefer not to ask about them, people do disappear in hospitals, that's why it's so lovely to see someone again when you haven't seen them for a few months, people you see periodically, not the people you've seen every day for the last forty years, but people you're pleased to see because they're new in your life, do you know what I mean? Even though you've probably been going to the same hospital for a couple of years, it's not the kind of daily event that becomes boring after a while, it's just a matter of a smile and a few words of greeting; after you've met a few times, some will ask how you are or make some other casual remark, that it's hotter than usual for the time of year, and we all know how badly the heat affects those of us with heart problems . . . that's why, because these meetings only last as long as the waiting time at the hospital, that's why you begin to think that the person might be holding something back and that one day they'll surprise you with a story or might themselves feel pleasantly surprised by a story of yours, they might see in you something that none of the people who've lived with you all these years have ever seen before. You have no idea how crowded hospitals are until you start going there, the noise and bustle in the outpatients' clinics, the hours spent waiting on benches in corridors, the clip-clop of the nurses' clogs as they walk past, chatting and laughing and leaving behind them a trail of perfume, not the smell of alcohol, not a medicinal smell, but a healthy smell; and how grateful you feel when, among all those people, you find some old acquaintance you haven't seen for ages. At first, Álvaro used to come with me, taking time off from the workshop, time that he would make up afterwards by working late. Now I go on my own. I'm so glad I got my driver's licence, I only learned to drive so as to be able to go shopping and to the doctor's, because I never needed it for getting to work. Álvaro's so unsociable – I was fed up with having to depend on him – he would get annoyed if I started chatting to someone, he thinks small talk is a waste of time. He used to get bored waiting, he'd get up from his chair, scratch the back of his neck, and whenever a nurse passed by, he'd say in a loud voice, Hmmm – it looks like we're here for the day, as if their appointment system was her fault. I was always worried, ever since I had the blood clot, about what would happen to the dog when I wasn't there, because my husband wouldn't bother to buy his food or keep his litter tray clean, so who would look after him, poor little thing. He's – no, he was – as old and infirm as his mistress, and it made me sad to think of leaving him all alone without me there, and then he went and died before I did, taking with him all his joy and a large part of mine too. I'm the one who's been left alone.

I wrapped him up in newspaper, trying not to look at the threatening teeth death had given him, and then I put him in a plastic bag until I got back to the house, where I placed him inside a wooden toolbox Álvaro had made ages ago, but never used. I thought he'd tell me off when he saw this, that he'd be offended because I'd given a box he didn't even care about to the dead dog, that he would immediately see that box as a work of art, something he'd taken great pains over and which I clearly despised. I could already hear him saying: You treat everything I do as if it was rubbish. But that isn't what happened. He didn't say anything about the box, although he did make fun of me for putting the dog's toys in with the body, his ball, his plastic bone, and the blanket he used to sleep on, as well as the little coat he wore when I took him out for walks in winter. I thought they would keep him company. I put the box with the dog and his things in the living room and then, much later that night, we buried him under the magnolia tree in the small square near the house. I made Álvaro go with me in the early hours, despite his protests (it gives me the creeps, with the dog inside the box), and we dug a grave, taking great care that the civil guards wouldn't find us and that none of the neighbours would see. You're mad, he said, and the trouble is that if they catch me here, they'll say I'm mad too, he grumbled, but in a low voice, without shouting or getting angry, because he knew I wouldn't stand for it. Not that night. I was too upset and sad and irritable. I didn't care what he said – the important thing is to have my dog close to me.

I talk to him. Alone, at night, in the bedroom, because I keep his photo on the bedside table next to the photos of my children, but I often talk to him as well when I sit on the bench near the magnolia tree. And in spring, when I see those big flowers open, like raw silk, I'll think of him lying there underneath, taking joy in his presence even after his death. I think: the memory of you makes me happy, it's as if you're immortal, because you'll be there to keep me company for as long as I live – I'm still alive, and you'll only die when I do, not a moment before: then we'll both die at the same time. My husband says I'm completely mad, but I don't know why we're so sure that only humans have a soul, I mean, why make that stark division? His eyes, the way he used to look at me, a creature like that must have some kind of soul, I'm sure of it, a small, fragile soul. He was always so overjoyed when I came home laden down with the shopping, and he'd return my kisses too, putting out his little pink tongue and licking my face, he was a far more joyful and affectionate child than most of those I see in Olba with their jeans half falling down, showing their underpants, with their iPods stuck in their ears, or racing through the park on those noisy skateboards, not caring that there are older people sitting on the benches. A creature like that must have some kind of soul, the joy in his eyes, the sadness, the fear, aren't *those all qualities of the soul? And even if he didn't have a soul, if he's now nowhere to be found, he still consoles me, for me he's still here, at least I have someone I can speak to. I'm ashamed to say so, but that's how it is, especially now that Álvaro no longer goes to work and spends all day lying on the sofa, drinking beer, because he's taken to drinking beer now, when he only used to drink a glass of wine before lunch and another before supper, but now he drinks can after can of beer, filling the whole house with its sour smell, tapping away on the computer or watching TV. I can understand him feeling disorientated, depressed. It must be hard to get used to his new situation because carpentry has been his whole life, but wasn't he saying that he wanted to give it up anyway, didn't he say that, when he retired, we'd go off travelling in a motorhome, moving from place to place, a life on the road? With what we have left, we could still do it, sell the apartment, buy a motorhome, put any remaining money in a fixed-term deposit account and head off, me with my EU health card in my handbag. Now, though, I pray to my dog to free us from the misfortune that might befall us if Álvaro carries on like this.*

It's been a very long time since my sister Carmen came to stay with us as she used to, a couple of times a year, bringing the children and, sometimes, her husband. She did make a lightning visit at the time of my father's operation, but back when the kids were small, the family would spend the whole summer here; of course, they only set foot in the house to sleep, because they'd spend all day at the beach and every evening on the terrace of one of the ice-cream parlours on Avenida Orts in Misent. Her husband would join them when he was on holiday from the textile factory, usually the last two weeks of August. The house would fill with voices and the colourful detritus that always surrounds children: plastic planes and cars, little bags of sweets and dried fruit, bits of chewing gum stuck to the bathroom shelf, and with rubber rings, flippers, snorkel and mask abandoned on the chairs in the hallway, much to my father's annoyance. Don't you know that salt eats into the varnish and ruins the wood? You should leave those things outside. The kids were a nuisance, it's true, but they brought life into the house, so silent and even gloomy the rest of the year, especially after my mother died – she always used to sing to herself, almost right up until the end, while she scrubbed the floor, dusted the furniture and hung out the clothes in the backyard. *La bien pagá, Picadita de viruelas, Angelitos negros, Ay mi Rocío.* If, one year, they came later than usual or didn't come at all, like the summer they went to Galicia instead, Carmen would at least send photos so that we could see how the children were growing up (with the passing years, these became the photos of those grandchildren she never once brought to see us, and my mother laid the blame for this, as I said before, on her daughters-in-law), I think Carmen wanted us – my parents and me, the bachelor uncle from whom they assume the children are going to inherit – to fall in love with them. But such long-distance courtships no longer happen, that was in the old days, when kings would receive a portrait of their future wife and gradually fall in love with her over the years, until she eventually arrived at the palace gates. Indian men would get married to some poor girl with whom they'd exchanged photos and letters, the girl would travel across the ocean, docile and frightened, to find a husband who was really a complete stranger, but who did at least provide a means of escaping the poverty she had known at home. In Olba, in the mid-1950s, there was still the occasional case of a girl hoping to do the same by falling into the arms of some supposedly rich emigrant she didn't even know, and who, not infrequently, turned out to be a cruel, penniless bastard. Now we take it for granted that, in order to fall in love with someone, you have to get to know them, to live with them, to let them become a daily presence, someone you miss if he or she goes away, and, as I say, we only saw my sister, my brother-in-law and their children at breakfast on Saturdays and Sundays, the days when my father and I used to get up a little later. During the week, I would really only see my nephews at night, in the room I had to share with them, both of them asleep in the bed next to mine. I found them annoying while they were in the house, but missed them when they'd left. With the advent of the Internet, the old custom of long-distance courtships has, in part, been revived; adolescents – and older people too – show each other arousing photographs, this is my cunt, this is my dick, NINETEEN CENTIMETRES, they talk dirty in emails and get excited, watching each other on the computer screen jerking off (have you got a webcam?) or on their mobile phone, more or less as happened before (the usual thing: text and images, the ways in which we humans have chosen to present ourselves to others have remained unchanged for millennia. Before, heirs to the throne would send an oil painting, a locket containing a portrait and would accompany these with a letter, as I said: text and images), but now everything happens with more immediacy. In the past, you'd have had to be the Marquis de Sade or, at the very least, Casanova to write such filth. In the photo you can't even see her little turned-up nose or his Brylcreemed toupee. I occasionally join these chat rooms and pass myself off as someone else, attractive thirty-six-year-old lawyer, 1.82, 78 kg; single forty-year-old architect seeks sex; sometimes I even pretend to be a woman and flirt with various dickheads who say I really excite them and even claim to be falling in love with me. When you check that particular email address months later, you'll still find messages from them. They miss you. I know you don't want anything more to do with me, they sob. I imagine them suffering, and they deserve to. If you don't even really know the people you've lived with for decades, how can you possibly trust someone hiding behind a screen? The script is always pretty much the same: given what you've told me about your tits and arse, you really sound like my type of woman; besides, whenever I receive a message from you, I always feel that we're two beings who understand each other, twin souls. I'm sending you a couple of photos of my cock, in one it's relaxed. Not bad, eh? How would you like to lick it? The head sticks out a bit from the foreskin, because when I was little, I had an operation for phimosis, and they removed a bit of the skin. In the other photo it's erect, quite a decent-sized prick, don't you think? Do you like it? Well, this fat shiny prick is knocking at your door. Will you open up? Or will I have to batter my way in? It's all yours. It will enter you up to the very hilt. I want you to feel it deep inside you. I can't send you a photo of my arse, because I can't work out how to take one on my mobile phone. I'd have to ask someone else to take the photo for me and who could I ask? But it's nice and firm and perky. And as you can see, my stomach is pure muscle, a real six-pack. When you send me a photo of your face, I'll send you one of mine, and may I know where you live? You say you live in this same province, but you haven't said whether you live in the capital or in a village. Why don't you want to tell me the name of your village? Why so mysterious? Don't you trust me? You probably live next door. That is the mechanics of communication. With a few variants: if instead of presenting yourself as a muscular male chest in the prime of life, you pass yourself off as a young girl with small, firm boobs, then the mature married men will immediately start buzzing around, predatory paedophiles, just how young are you, are you sure you're telling me the truth about your age, I bet you're older, more like nineteen, no fourteen-year-old girl would talk like you, unless, of course, you're very advanced for your age. Has someone already given you a good shafting or is your little pussy not yet open for business? I bet you've been fucked every which way, you little bitch. Fucking hell, a hot fourteen-year-old. I can't believe it. Shall I send you a photo of my prick, you little slut? I bet you've never seen anything like it (the photo of the huge prick will have been downloaded from some Internet archive). On the other hand, if you adopt the personality of a mature woman, your inbox instantly fills up with propositions from excited little boys who want to have access to what they think of as the wisdom of some remote future. The fetish of experience. All of this has very little to do with love and, if you press me, not much to do with sex either. It's all a lot of hot air. If you want to fuck someone, just find a prostitute, male or female depending on your tastes, but don't spend all day sending little messages in order to get aroused. And besides, love, or whatever you want to call it, is something else entirely: if even the normal way of doing things doesn't work – meeting and getting to know someone gradually over the years – how is looking at a photo of a cunt going to do the trick, while you drink your morning coffee? I mean, putting sex aside for the moment, I've known my father for sixty-seven or sixty-eight years (ever since he came out of prison), and I still haven't learned to love him. Most of the time I haven't wanted to have anything to do with him, only on very rare occasions have I felt I understood him, and I could count the times we've achieved anything like closeness: I wasn't the son he wanted, from him I almost never experienced the kind of warmth and energy I felt from being with my uncle when he used to take me hunting by the lagoon, when he would sit me on his knees to stick the stamp on a letter, when he made me a little wooden cart to play with – a catalogue of the toys of the poor: a stick between your legs is a horse you're riding; a bird tethered by a piece of string is the pet I adopted as a friend, that I talked to and fed with little bits of bread soaked in milk, and whose sudden disappearance one morning I experienced as an act both of betrayal and abandonment, and over which I wept bitter tears. I presume the bird simply died, and that my mother removed it from view before I could see it, not realising how much more upsetting it is for someone to leave without explanation, more troubling than death itself, which doesn't depend on an act of will, which isn't a decision made by the individual, at least not usually, but something that happens; and when it *is* the result of an individual decision, it causes infinite pain and remorse to the people left behind, because that's a way of escaping, abandoning, punishing. What did we do to make him leave us like that? He had everything he could possibly have wanted, he could never have accused me of not loving him enough, didn't I always treat him like a prince, cries the widow, I gave him the best food, the best armchair, the TV remote control. Why did he have to go and kill himself? That won't be my problem. Leonor and Liliana, two birds of passage. The new pain covers up the pain left by the old wounds.

What my father taught me. At home: hold your knife and fork properly, you've got two hands, haven't you, can't you close a door without slamming it, what are those stupid posters you're putting up, you're ruining the walls with those drawing pins, the walls have got more holes in them than a colander. At work: that isn't how you use a saw, you'll slice your hand off one of these days, and then I'll end up with a crippled son, yet another burden, it's high time you learned how to use the glue without making such a mess. He always spoke harshly (spare the rod and spoil the child: always the threat of cruelty), drawing attention to my lack of skill and, above all, crushing any ambitions I might have, just as life had crushed his. What the victors from the civil war did to him, he did to me, the only son he had handy. I can't say I've ever loved him. And I've paid for my refusal to fulfil the ambitions he placed in me. Just as the suicide kills himself because he can't accept himself, he probably hated me because, while appearing to be his opposite (I never wanted to be an artist and never took any interest in his political aspirations), I've turned out to be just like him. My physique, though, is completely different; he was tall, slim, with an angular face and large eyes, and the intense gaze and the deep lines that have marked his face for decades now both contributed to giving him a vaguely dramatic air. I imagine women must have found him attractive. Women are attracted to men like that, men who seem full of inner life. Liliana says he's still handsome even now, when he's in his nineties; and when she looks at the wedding photo on the sideboard, she says again: He really was a very handsome man. But basically, he and I are identical. The same pessimism, the same idea that all men are nothing but a bag of shit tied up in the middle. I think it's that idea that makes my post-coital depressions even worse: the sense that I'm drawn to that filth, that I've clasped one of those putrid bags of shit to me and released part of my own filth into it. I wonder why I even accepted this servile role, if, given that we're just the same, we should have been associates or at least rivals on equal terms. It's not easy to find the reasons, it's not like opening up a corpse and finding heart, liver and spleen. Fears and desires are beyond the reach of scalpels. Although, to be honest, it doesn't seem such a very grave fault not to love someone, after all, what does the word 'love' mean? Most of us live together without feeling any need for an emotion we know nothing about until we read about it in novels or see it in the cinema. I think the fact that we don't instinctively know what it is tells us that perhaps it's something that doesn't naturally exist in us, but is inculcated into us, imported. I think it was an old French philosopher who said that when a man declares his love for the lady marchioness

– saying how much he admires her intelligence, her physical grace, her remarkable ideas, her sensitivity – what he's really saying is that he can't wait to screw her like a hot bitch. There is some truth in that. We confuse sympathy or pity with desire, we believe we want to cradle and protect when what we really want is to enter and violate. But that's not true. I've often called Liliana 'my child', I've wanted to protect her, and that was quite different, a different kind of language. Despite what that French philosopher thought, language does put things in their place, either raising them up or dragging them down. Speaking well of someone confers elevation and nobility. I call Liliana what my father used to call his beloved Carmen. I say 'my child'. My little child, my dear little child, my father used to say, kissing her. You're going so far away, my child. To Barcelona. How lonely we're going to be without you. That day was the only time I actually saw him break down in tears. The only time. Those words can't possibly have been contaminated. Did you know that the flower of the coffee tree smells as sweet as orange blossom? It looks the same too, flowers like little white stars: all those plants, orange blossom, jasmine, *galán de noche*, or that colourful little flower called *dompedro*, all have a scent, but I think the flower of the coffee tree is the most delicate. In Colombia, we call a black coffee *tinto*, but here that means red wine. Your father reminds me of my grandpa, you know, I couldn't say why exactly, he has the same serious face, the same rather sad eyes. He must have been a very good man, your father. It's awful to see him like this. He has such kind eyes. What would you know, Liliana? You know about your own life, your own domestic sorrows of which I, too, know a little, because you've told me about them. Your sorrow touches me as if it were my own, makes me feel like embracing you, like drinking those warm tears that roll down your cheeks. *Piel canela.* Cinnamon skin. No, you don't know that song, do you, *ojos negros, piel canela*, dark eyes, cinnamon skin, no, you're too young, all I care about is you and you and you and only you, says the song. You're my only child. I have no other. At least as far as I know, none that I recognise. I did have a child, but it never got past being a little cluster of cells. What does that mean, Señor Esteban? Ah, you're laughing. I like to see you laughing, Liliana, not like the other day. Oh, the reason I was in such a state then was because I didn't even have enough money to make the children their lunch, the shelves in the fridge were bare and the vegetable drawer was empty. My husband's company hadn't paid him his month's wages, so it's just as well you were able to lend me some money, because, otherwise, I don't know what we would have done. Yes, I know about your problems, Liliana, for me you're my child, and I'm a father to you, one you can talk to about anything. Your problems, your dreams, your desires. Just pay me back when you can. Money doesn't matter. Or, rather, it's money that corrupts everything, spoils everything, a bad father, a cruel father, but which – oddly enough – seems to bring together so many apparently incompatible lives. That's one of its virtues. It has others. You could say that it's a bad father who grants his children's every wish, who spoils them. Without the cement of money, though, think of all the broken families, all the lives set adrift. They have loans and bills to pay, obligations to fulfil, and they remain bound together until death does them part, just as they promised; although there are a lot of people who can think of nothing better to do than spend every day bickering and generally making each other's lives miserable, and they're afraid to change a situation they consider safe because at least it's stable. Resentment guarantees you company, and hurling insults at each other every night does confer a certain stability. People think: What's the alternative? Being alone? To hear them talk you'd think that being left alone was the worst of all fates. Solitude, abandonment. Sad, threatening words.

Terrible: just wait and see what old age has in store for you if you make the mistake of staying single. They try to frighten you. They say: If you carry on like this, you'll be left all alone. How terrible to die alone, like a dog, they say. And that seems to be the very worst of misfortunes; you have to die, we all have to die, but we want to do so in company, not like a dog. Dying alone is so bleak, so shameful somehow, it reveals a lack in the human being (to use Francisco's favourite and much more touching term), a lack that should remain hidden, swept away into the shadows, behind the screen they put around the bed in the hospital ward when they're going to do something nasty to the patient. You could also say that dying alone reveals a certain arrogance, what you might describe as excess pride. You have to share, people say, in other words, go begging for affection, for sympathy, calling in old debts: I brought you up, fed you, clothed you, lent you money, did this for you, gave you that. Now it's your turn. Take up the sponge, the antiseptic wipes, and start washing this grubby flesh of mine, give me back some of what I gave you. Pay me what you owe me. Success in life, what people call 'a good end', consists in managing to get everyone around your bed. Putting them to work, having a whole multitude ready to wipe your arse. The more the merrier. As if the intensive care unit were a Christmas party attended by all the family, that thrilling moment when parents, children, grandchildren, cousins, nieces and nephews burst into a rendition of 'Silent Night', with the cattle lowing and the shepherds watching their flocks, as if you weren't lying there with your tubes, your probes, your oxygen mask and with more hypodermic needles in you than a modern-day St Sebastian, or that poor bull in Tordesillas who is chased every year by village brutes armed with lances. What do you care about anyone else at such moments? Are they being pierced or lanced? Or is it a question – again we're back in the realm of economics – of not wanting

123

to perform something as moving as death to an empty theatre. Exploiting it to the full. Generously allocating seats so that the audience can watch the death, a high-voltage show and a useful experience on life's Grand Tour. Capitalising on the energy of those final moments. Being alone or accompanied seems essential to give meaning to their lives. Bringing family members and neighbours in to see the burst blood vessels, the bruises, the ecchymoses, the endless lesions caused by all those pointed instruments, by the intravenous drip that perforates and blackens the back of your hand and through which they pump serums and poisons; the probes, the cannulae, the tubes that drain viscous fluids from some other part of your body; the suction pads stuck to your chest where the nurse has used an electric shaver to remove any body hair, leaving patches of whitish skin, the tangle of cables and tubes emerging from somewhere or other, including from your index finger, the ventilator they've stuck up your nose or through a hole in your throat, the metal of the stretchers and the IV drips, the plastic bags with their troubling liquids, serums and solutions that flow directly into the blood, the huge amount of money invested in the health industry. The visitors contemplate the dying man, unrecognisable now (he's so thin, and his skin is almost grey, he won't get out of this alive) and, as if in passing, they also admire the progress, the advances made in our hospital system in the ward for the terminally ill, they gaze, reverently, fearfully, at all that complex apparatus. And this vast input of skill is wasted if you experience and suffer it in solitude. My mother used to say to me: before I die, I want to see you married to a nice girl who loves you and who'll take care of you if anything happens. You have to remember, my son (I was my mother's son, just as Carmen was my father's daughter), that right now you're all set to go out and conquer the world because you're a young man, because you're healthy, the young only think about the present, they don't notice the leaves from the calendar falling one by one. You may laugh, but when the time comes, you'll see how important it is to have someone by your side, how important affection is as the years pass. Someone to be with you and to clasp your hand in the final moments (although what other part of a dying man's body would you be likely to clasp?). And while you're listening to people talking like that, listening to your mother, you feel anxious, and you can actually imagine yourself being unable to get out of bed, lurching from chair back to chair back in order to move around inside the house, feeling your way along the walls to reach the toilet, your body drenched in sour, senile sweat; or choking on something, a piece of half-chewed meat, a sip of water, a bread-crumb, one of those pills you take for your blood pressure or for cholesterol or hyperglycaemia; you're choking on your own spit: you cough, gasp for air, with no one beside you to slap you on the back or put their fingers down your throat to help you cough up the thing choking you, someone to call the ambulance or bundle you into a car and drive at top speed to the hospital or the nearest clinic. People think loneliness is the worst of all evils. What can I say? It may well be, because, in the end, loneliness – like nakedness, malnutrition, excessive heat or cold – is only a manifestation of the one real evil, a truly terrible evil, one that anyone with any intelligence should avoid at all costs, and that is poverty, yes, Liliana, poverty has been the only real evil since the world began, not that I'm telling you anything you don't know already. What else were you running away from, what were you escaping from when you came to live here in Spain? The philosopher said: I am I and my circum-stances. Exactly. Well, you'd better get used to the idea that 'I' is the money that allows you to fund your circumstances; if there's no money, you're stuck with your empty 'I', a mere shell without any circumstances worthy of the name: and that oppor-tune hand ready to slap you on the back to help you cough up the piece of half-chewed chicken currently blocking your epiglottis, that hand won't be there (I don't mean you, Liliana, how could you even think such a thing, I'm talking in general, I know *you* would never abandon me); on the other hand, if you have money, you can pay for company, for a nurse, male or female. Right up until the very last moment, you can pay for a chiropodist to buff away the hard skin on your feet and cut your toenails – a task that has become more exhausting each time you attempt it – and to trim your nails so that they don't become ingrown, a delicate, expert fellow who removes your corns and treats the dangerous sores on the bottom of your foot which, because of your hyperglycaemia, threaten to become chronic, and which, if they fail to heal and begin to spread, can become gangrenous and might then lead to you having your foot or leg amputated; money allows you to pay for a masseur and a barber who cuts your hair and shaves you in bed, a pharmacist who gives you the most effective sedatives to help you up to heaven quickly, to hear the celestial bells and see the soft wings of the angels (did you know that in the church of a nearby village, they worship a feather from the archangel Michael's wing?), and you can even afford to pay some gorgeous piece of arse (and forgive the crude language, Liliana) to give you a handjob. And all this in a comfortable house or clinic in Lucerne, a lovely bright room with views of a lake, green meadows, the cows from the Milka chocolate bars and the snows of Kilimanjaro, while you recline on a memory foam (is that what it's called?) mattress, on which you are dying like someone taking their four o'clock tea if you're English or a pre-lunch beer and a dish of calamares *a la romana* if, like me, you're Spanish, and the whole thing takes place at an ideal, pre-programmed temperature. With your final pill they give you a glass of champagne. But you're looking very serious, Liliana, no, don't take it like that, when I talk about paying someone, about buying that kind of care, don't be offended, I'm not talking about you, you mean something quite different to me, you're my child, what my sister Carmen was to my father, you're very special to my father and to me: you're family, a kind of belated daughter, there are three of us in the family now, two sad old men and one young woman who brings life into the house, I like to hear you singing when you're doing the dishes, for instance, when you're hanging out the clothes, you remind me of my mother, or hearing the radio when you have it on in the kitchen to keep you company while you're doing the ironing, and I think my mother would have liked that too, although we can't possibly know, because we can't ask her, she's not here, no, don't cry, I feel like putting my arms around you, lifting your chin and making you look into my eyes. That's it. But, Don Esteban, you know that even if you couldn't pay me at all, I'd still come and see you both. You've already seen that nothing fazes me: I can wash and feed your father and do whatever else he needs me to, and it would be the same with you. For as long as I'm alive, this nurse, or if you'll allow me, this friend, will always be with you. You know I like it when you call me 'my child', don't you? Yes, I know, Liliana, now give me a little kiss and stop looking so sad. You're not crying again, are you? It's just that I love you as much as I do my own parents, or, rather, my mother, because my father took away any love I felt for him with the blows and the beatings. We're not talking about love, are we, Liliana? Don't trust that word. No, don't take offence, I'm not saying that because of you, but it's far better to say that we treat each other with mutual respect because we like each other, rather than love each other. And don't even think about what might happen between us in the future. That's what distinguishes liking from loving. We are the people we are today, and we're living and sharing this moment and this same desire to weep today, because we understand each other, but tomorrow, who knows? No, Don Esteban, tomorrow and the day after and the day after that, you can count on me until you die. You and your father are my family. I'd still come even if you couldn't pay me. After all, what does money matter? I know, my child, but, Liliana, just look at my sister Carmen, my father's beloved daughter, his favourite, she doesn't even phone any more. She used to be so loving and affectionate, and now? Nothing. Who would have thought it, my father's beloved favourite has turned out to be *nothing*. A stranger. Worse than a stranger, because with a stranger you can begin to have some fellow feeling for him or her, but here it's the other way round, a fire has burned out, and a fire that burns out leaves the ground it burned on black with soot and there's no getting rid of that stain. When they operated on my father's trachea, she was here for only as long as was absolutely necessary: the day of the operation, she spent the night at the hospital, but the following morning, she said she had to leave: he's out of danger now, it's just a matter of recovering, they won't keep him in for very long, they'll probably discharge him tomorrow or, at most, the day after, they try nowadays to get patients out of hospital as soon as they can; besides, with the new, less invasive techniques they use, the incision leaves scarcely any mark, any scar, and the patient is better within a few days. And that was the sum total of her loving contribution. And off she went: Bye bye. Everything else, coping with the anxiety and the sleepless nights because he kept choking, using the blender to make the purées he could barely swallow, doing the laundry, getting him showered, dressed and undressed, changing his incontinence pads, all that was left to someone who didn't love him and whom he didn't love, someone who didn't and still doesn't like him. It was a mere prolongation of what we did in the carpentry workshop, of the way society functions. Do you see how commercial obligations bind people more closely than love? One of the many changing manifestations

128

of that bad father, money. She cried repeatedly on the phone when I told her how our father was becoming a virtual vegetable. He couldn't speak and appeared not to understand, he had to have everything done for him: he had to be washed, fed, helped into and out of bed. How sad. And she would cry. They loved each other. It really was very sad. It broke your heart. Those sobs down the telephone line. It even made me cry, and I don't cry easily. But she still didn't come and see him: all she sent were those tears. And just in case I didn't pick these up over the phone line, just in case she failed to transmit them down the almost five hundred kilometres of copper and fibre wires separating us, she would break off halfway through a word, sigh, pause for a few seconds, clear her throat, begin to talk again, her voice hoarse now (one had to presume she was crying, had a lump in her throat, was uttering sorrowful sighs): You'll have to find someone to help, you can't look after him all on your own as well as work, cook, do the dishes, wash the clothes and hang them out. Of course I won't be able to do that, of course I'll have to find someone. But not a word was said about who was going to pay the eight euros an hour to that someone (who turned out to be you) or how much it might cost if I had to make special arrangments for that person to be here all day. Nothing but deep, sorrowful sighs. She behaved as if it were in bad taste to debase her grief with talk of money, as if it were unseemly to mix paternal love with filthy lucre, to apply an economic yardstick to love. No, love can't be judged according to market values. It's too personal, too private. It's free of all ties. This isn't a matter of money. Months later, when his bronchial tubes became blocked up and he had to be rushed to the emergency room and given oxygen, and was kept in the hospital for another week, I phoned to tell her, more in order to annoy her than because I thought she was actually going to give me any support, and, just as I imagined, all I got were excuses: her

129

husband, her children, her work, the economy, everything was against her. She didn't even bother to cry this time, but gave me a long litany of problems: I can't take much more to be honest, later, when things calm down, I'll tell you about the chaos my life is at the moment, we've got the workmen in, changing the old drains, and as you know, Pedro is too immersed in his work to help me, and so I have to deal with the plumbers, the bricklayers, and all the various traps they set for me and the dirt they leave everywhere, and how much they want to charge us, I've no idea where we're going to get the money. Anyway, the fact is she never came. Poor thing, she had enough on her plate. She phoned about a week later, and before I could say anything, jumped in with: He's better, isn't he? (On that occasion, her voice was clear and hopeful, the voice of a bright, sunny morning – a winter morning like today, with that intensely blue sky above the lagoon – a cool breeze blowing away all trace of tragedy.) And again: You have found someone to take care of him and look after him, haven't you? You can't possibly keep him clean, wash his clothes and cook his meals, not on your own. She was worried about our father and she was worried about me. And I was grateful for that. It was true, I couldn't keep him clean, or sew the buttons back on his shirts or on his flies, which he would tear off if he got upset because I didn't respond to his first imperative gesture, his first grunt; I probably wasn't even capable of keeping myself clean, and the thought of that kept her awake at night. She came up with a solution: hire someone to look after you both. So considerate. Let's hire someone to look after us, to keep us clean and well fed. You see how easy it is? It's assumed that I've been the major beneficiary in all family affairs, I have a house at my disposal, I've inherited a job and, above all, it's assumed that I am the signatory for all the bank accounts. She was concerned about that too, the soul of generosity; she said: Given the state Papa is in, we'll have to organise things so that we don't have problems later on with the bank, so that they don't freeze the savings accounts, and to make sure we all have equal access. I laughed: You're not going to make Juan a signatory, are you? No, perish the thought, she said at once, he'd clean out the accounts in a week. And, of course, the point was that while she wanted my father and me to be kept nice and clean, she didn't want the accounts to be equally clean, she wanted them to stay full of lovely green, yellow and purple banknotes, and when the time came for us to get hold of the money – what Carmen called cleaning out the accounts – that was to be done by the two of us, jointly. And then there are Germán's children and his possible grandchildren, and his widow. They would also have to have access to the bank accounts. We can't be the only ones to do that. That would be wrong, even illegal.

The assumption is that Dad is spending the money he has coming in and occasionally dipping into his savings, and that the two of us are getting the benefit of that. And I understand Carmen's annoyance, her indifference, her caution. This isn't a particularly appetising dessert; the end of life's banquet is not exactly sweet, but let's not talk here about love. Do you under-stand, Liliana? No one likes the idea of living with a zombie who wanders down the corridor and sits staring at the TV screen, or who lies there, open-mouthed, when you lay him down on the bed, his vacant eyes fixed on the ceiling, a zombie from a real-life horror film who clicks his false teeth at you the way the skeletons do on the ghost train, and pushes them out with his tongue until you can see the teeth in their pink plastic, a zombie who still wolfs down his food and, above all (and this is the most unpleasant bit: a zombie-tamagotchi), continues to defecate twice a day (always assuming he doesn't have diarrhoea). She, like Juan, like Germán's widow and children, will turn up when the corpse has finally stopped twitching and it's time to share out the treasure hidden beneath the skull. Then they'll come to inspect the accounts, they'll want to see the deeds of the workshop and the house, and of the former orange grove (now a potental building plot) and the piece of land in Montdor, where I would like to build a little house to retire to alone with my dog Tom, the two of us going for walks in the countryside, him trotting ahead and constantly stopping to wait for me, as he does when we go to the marsh, the two of us getting old together. He's four years old and could have kept me company until the end. He's got at least another ten or twelve years of life ahead of him, or did have; now he has only what the others have. And to grow some fruit and vegetables and fill a wicker basket with loquats, peaches, cherries, apples, quinces, and adorn the centre of the table with those multicoloured fruits, those fruits that Liliana says we don't have here, to put them in a bowl, a fruit bowl on the tablecloth, so that when you open the door, you're greeted by the scent of ripe fruit. They'll come and sit in the notary's office and confidently discuss what they believe to be their legal share of the estate, having already booked a return flight home, convinced they can afford this extravagance because of what they're going to get from the scrum (the complete cleaning out of the accounts that the industrious Carmen suspects will happen, the sale of property). The living feed and grow fat at the expense of the dead. That's nature for you. You only have to watch those wildlife programmes on the TV, huge birds pecking at their victim's innards and squabbling among themselves; the lioness picking at the bloody flesh of the zebra. But there's no need to look to nature for examples; the gondolas in the supermarkets – that's what they call them, gondolas, although they are, in fact, shelves – are grim cemeteries: shoulders of dead lamb, bones and steaks from a deceased ox, the viscera of a sacrificed cow, loin of electrocuted pork, all packaged in containers made from the remains of slaughtered trees. We live off what we kill. We live from killing, from what is served up to us dead: the inheritors consume the spoils of their predecessors, which nourish and strengthen them when it's time to take flight. The more carrion they eat, the higher and more majestic the flight. And, of course, more elegant. And none of this is in any way at odds with the natural condition of the world.

When I get home, I'll find him still sitting in front of the television, although what mood he'll be in is hard to predict – people with dementia are prone to mood swings – so, on some afternoons, he'll be quietly dozing, snoring away, his head bent over his chest, while on others, he'll look at me, eyes glinting, needle-sharp, as if he were high on drugs or something: he kicks out when he sees me, moves his head back and forth, moans or grunts, and punches me in the chest and tries to punch my face too. Regardless of his mood, I have to untie the sheet, get him out of the armchair, warm up the food, put it on the table and serve it up, you'll be having a late lunch today, Dad, so enjoy your few remaining hours; you may or may not know it, but it's a lovely day; nature has put on all her finery to bid us farewell; winter has disguised itself as spring for us, and the weatherman is forecasting an equally bright day tomorrow. Enjoy your vegetables: one small potato, some chard and an artichoke, because vegetables are really beneficial to your health, artichoke is a diuretic and chard is good for the heart; fortunately, the market in Olba, though small, is very well stocked, and you can supplement products from the nearby farms with imported goods, plus the packaged stuff you can buy in the big local supermarkets: the day before yesterday, I looked at the bag containing the mixture of dried fruit and nuts – Exotic Cocktail, the label said — that I was munching my way through while I watched TV with you, and it turns out that the peanuts were from China, the corn from Peru, the raisins from Argentina and only the almonds, it seems, were Spanish: a true citizen of the world, a real cosmopolitan, that packager of titbits, who, according to the tiny lettering which, even with my glasses on, I had difficulty deciphering, is a company from near here, from Alcásser or from Picassent, a village in the province of Valencia, I can't remember where. Once fertile villages or villages in what was the once fertile province of Valencia, which, instead of green beans, tomatoes and broad beans, now produce plastic packaging for fruit cultivated and picked ten or twelve thousand kilometres away. They've become the dormitory suburbs of the industrial estates surrounding them. Places full of nobodies: abandoned factories, closed warehouses, concrete esplanades where skateboarders career noisily past empty cans and broken bottles. Doubtless located in one of those depressing industrial estates, the warehouse that packaged the dried fruits and nuts concentrates the energies of all five continents in the form of beans, peanuts, macadamia nuts, roasted chickpeas or corn. Where had those fruits and nuts been before they reached the plastic bag, in what warehouses and in what ports were they stored and how long had they taken to get here? Which company brought them here, piled up alongside what other merchandise? Pineapples packed with cocaine, valuable tropical timber that has lent them the smell of its resins, which is why the macadamia nuts have a very faint taste of cedar or pine, a taste that a wine connoisseur like Francisco would be quick to detect. And once here, in Spain, what other cargo were they stored next to? What other aromas have they retained from their long journey? Diesel? Acrylic paint? Rubber? Rat piss? Rubber, paint, rat piss and diesel: the smells of our contemporary *tristes tropiques*. The employee of the packaging company which opens and closes its doors in a non-place that was once fertile agricultural land, is surrounded by sacks that have come from other non-places situated in the four corners of the earth, and into the bag he puts a little of each, a pinch of sunflower seeds, another of roasted chickpeas, walnuts, pistachios, macadamia nuts, a few raisins, and, having finished his selection, he shrink-wraps the plastic bag, sealing together all those fruits and nuts into happy cohabitation as one heterogeneous, globalised, multicultural family. On the outside of the bag, each product is listed under the heading INGREDIENTS, written in a font the size of fly droppings, which again obliges me to put on my glasses in order to decipher it. The size of the lettering doesn't dissuade me, because I like to find out where things have come from, to know what I'm taking off the shelf (or gondola as they insist on calling it) and putting into my shopping trolley and then transferring from the shopping trolley to my car, from my car to the fridge and, finally, to my mouth. I like to know what I'm eating, what it is that's going to share my inner life and make its home inside me. Whether you like it or not, the distance those products have travelled, the sense of alienation, inevitably arouses a feeling of distrust, which is perfectly normal (am I going to put *that* in my body?), who knows what food safety rules or non-rules exist in those countries of origin, but it also excites me to know that I'm biting into the fruit of a plant that someone grew and fertilised and picked in places I will never set foot in. While I savour the taste, I imagine the faces of the pickers: almond eyes, olive skins burned by the sun, the intent gaze of the women shelling the nuts, which, at this precise moment, belong exclusively to me: I've bought their intent gaze, their quick movements, the bead of sweat rolling down between their breasts while they work in a zinc-roofed warehouse. With each nut, each seed, each fruit, I'm eating the houses in which they live: small huts with corrugated-iron roofs, bamboo shacks; the smell of chilli in their stews (the

stews that Liliana prepares in her fifty-five-square-metre apartment, that she cooks and eats with her children and her husband),
the smell of coconut and ginger, of the forests or jungles that
surround those places where the pickers of my pre-supper nibbles
live. That – eyes, skins, landscapes, lush vegetation – is what
I'm eating, what delights and nourishes me. Another day, I
noticed that, on the shelves in the fruit section of Mas y Mas,
even though we were in September – harvest time for the sweet,
perfumed local muscatel grapes – the white grapes they were
selling came from Argentina (but if it's September here, isn't it
springtime in Argentina – are there grapes in springtime?). I've
no idea what variety they could have been: large, golden grapes,
glossy and insipid; and the little bundle of green asparagus
almost always bears a strip of paper declaring its Peruvian origins.
Peru isn't a country you ever think about, it rarely comes up in
conversations in the bar, it's a country no one ever mentions,
and yet you just happen to read what's printed on that strip of
paper and there it is: Country of origin: Peru. You think: did
we Europeans take asparagus to America or did they already
grow it there and did the Incas eat it at the banquets they held
among those enormous carved stones that appear in TV
programmes about Cuzco and Machu Picchu? Which came first,
chicken or egg? And there on the counter is a piece of really
fresh fish: before you buy it, you have to choose, scrutinise the
tiny letters on the tiny label intended to make it as hard as
possible for you to find out where it comes from, but on which
the price is perfectly legible: €6.50, €8.50, €9.25, €14.35, followed
by North Atlantic South Atlantic Pacific Arctic Chile Indonesia
Peru Ecuador India; port of unloading Marin Vigo Burela
Mazarrón: good God, what a journey they've taken those hake,
those anglerfish, those Hindustani prawns. For us, Dad, I always
try and buy the fish you imagine would be the freshest, caught
off our own coast and unloaded in one of our ports, although

our fishermen – doubtless mindful of the Andalusians and the trouble they've had about who could or couldn't fish for hake and plaice in the Bay of Cádiz – have, for a while now, been claiming that their catch comes from the Bays of Misent, Calpe, Peñiscola or Alicante, and those – which one assumes were caught here – are given special labels – RED MULLET FROM THE BAY OF MISENT, PRAWNS FROM THE BAY OF DENIA, OR GROUPER FROM THE BAY OF ALICANTE – and you end up paying far more for them, and suddenly it turns out that every bay is one in which wild fish graze, which means that you and I have to pay more for them. Buy fish caught locally. That's what the government-sponsored TV ads say, as if the fish had their own health insurance card just as we bipeds do, and paid their local taxes. Stonefish, *mavra*, parrot fish, bar jack, *roig*, *furó*. The delicious oil to fry it in, brought from the Sierra de Mariola, or, even better, from the Sierra de Espadán, the one bottle I have left in the house. Come on, eat up. That's your job, to eat and take your pills – I had my own chemical menu at breakfast; for you, it's six pills in the morning, preceded by the miracle-working omeprazole (so cheap and effective anyone would think it had been made by those Soviets you dreamed of in your youth), four at midday and four (or is it five?) at night, now sit on the toilet and try hard, that's something I can't do for you, go on, squeeze, but keep calm, we have all the time in the world, don't get agitated, just stay calm, but don't stop squeezing, OK? Keep relaxed but squeeze, don't make me have to give you an enema on this our last night. And once you've done your work, completed your task, just watch the TV and don't hassle me. Not tonight. Although I don't really need to encourage you to eat, you've never lost your appetite. Not in all these months. That's another of your contradictions: so little interest in life, but such an appetite for food. Can you explain that? You'll die ruminating, chewing, grinding your false teeth. A little oil drizzled over the potatoes and the green beans, I know you like that, you always have. The Mediterranean sun is concentrated in those golden drops, bringing health and life. For some years now, everyone has agreed that each drop of oil is packed with energy, with hope, the balm with which Greek athletes and Roman patricians anointed themselves, with which the church anoints the dying, the fruit of that sacred tree – like olive shoots around your table, Lord, they sing in the Catholic Mass. That's what they tell us on the radio, on the TV, in the newspapers. It's the other fats that are dangerous: things like margarine, animal fat, butter, full-fat milk; and other oils too: sunflower oil, peanut oil, palm oil, corn or soya oil, the kind of oils eaten by those poor black people with vast bottoms, tremulous as a jelly on a plate, who drag themselves around the streets of New York and who we see on TV; huge black women, hippopotami on two feet, whose thighs rub together when they walk and cause sores to form; not to mention the elephantine white failures, stinking alcoholics with a purple nose and cheeks covered with a network of purplish veins, people about to lose their jobs or their homes or who have already lost them and now form part of the hopeless hordes, bodies that can't even sit down on the bus because their buttocks overflow the seat and their belly is too large to fit in the space between them and the seat in front, however wide they open their legs in a vain attempt to make optimum use of space, individuals who turn up wearing shapeless tracksuits, talking to a TV presenter and explaining that the bank has repossessed their house because they can't pay back the loans they signed up for when they weighed a few kilos less and could still go to work. Go on, Dad, eat up, have a slice of that omelette perfuming the air with the smell of good honest olive oil. Good cholesterol – that's what the scientists say – to help the blood flow unobstructed through the arteries. The holy supper, the last supper. Most of the houses in Olba had that picture hanging on their dining-room wall, in frames made of metal or porcelain, engravings of the original painting by Juan de Juanes. Jesus with his twelve apostles, the traitor sitting diagonally across from him, holding his money bag behind his back. We never had that kind of rubbish in our house, and so yes, there are things I should be grateful to you for.

Then I'll put you back in your armchair (I won't need to tie you in with the sheet this time, I'm here standing guard), and we can watch some more TV: he'll fall asleep, after lunch he usually goes to sleep until it's time for tea. He'll be having a late lunch today, poor thing, lunch and tea all in one, but I had to come here, you see, to this marsh, these reed beds, this stagnant water. I wanted to check out the scene, to drink in the dubious or perhaps contradictory perfume of the place where we're going to stage our play. Just as the growers of those exotic fruits have their backdrop of coconut palms, coffee trees and bamboo, so we have our backdrop, this putrid, life-giving marsh, and I want to make sure that everything is in order on the eve of our premiere, which will also be our *dernière*, isn't that what they say in French? *La première* and *la dernière*. I do remember some things from my Paris days and from the years I spent at school, the alpha and omega of the Greeks, I learned that on the trips you helped me pay for when we still had some hopes of each other, a journey essential to the education of any artist, isn't that what they all used to do? The obligatory trip to Italy. Donatello, Della Robbia and Michelangelo were intended to inspire the artistic vocation of a son who had to be what you were not allowed to be or could not be. A world premiere with only one performance: dunes, reeds, rushes, the watercress whose presence signals the spot where the water in the lagoon is cleanest, and the maidenhair fern that grows in the shade, the blue irises and the yellow irises: all that's missing is poor Uncle Ramón, but, don't worry, we'll see him too, one of these days we'll meet him when we're strolling about in that place where the days and nights no longer pass, where nothing worthy of mention happens (no historians have left any record of it in their annals): he's waiting for us there, impatiently, you'll see, you're finally going back to the place where you almost turned your back on us in order to preserve your dignity. That was what it came down to, that stark choice: us or your dignity, and you, generously, chose us – those of us who were already here and those of us yet to come – you sacrificed the treasure of your dignity, but, convinced that this show of generosity was, in a way, a betrayal of your comrades, you hated it and, consequently, could never love those of us who had benefited from it. I owe you the pain of that moment when I had not even yet been born. I have to repay you. And I will give you what we took from you, don't worry, I will restore the dignity you gave to me then, always assuming that the priceless gift of your dignity really does exist and that one can ever recover what is lost: a foot, a leg, an arm, a face, these can all now be restored to those who've lost them, as long as you act quickly, and if not, they can reconstruct them: that's what the surgeon Dr Pedro Cavadas of Valencia does, but you can't recover what you lost, and, besides, how can you possibly reconstruct it after all these years, when it's already rotted away? But I will free you of the obliga-tions you took on, the obligations that prevented you from being a proper man: feeding us, clothing us, educating us, the sticky web in which your biography became trapped, but don't think about that now, what's the point, it's too late: I'm afraid we don't have time to recover anything, however hard we try. Here you are, drink up, I say, handing him the glass of warm milk (mind you don't burn yourself); he grabs it with his two hands, holds it tight and raises it to his lips, he picks up the packet of biscuits which he eats greedily until I take them away. They'll make you ill, I say, not knowing if he can hear me: he clings on to the packet when I try to take them away, he grunts: a kind of dull groan, his bony fingers gripping the package.

We all know that the world is divided between what I am and what others are. The great existential chasm. The whole history of philosophy turns on that divide, and it's something we take for granted as soon as we begin to form our own first perceptions. It's part of the essential baggage of life, but, for you, that is all the world has ever been, the struggle between the I, your I, and the others, us, who formed a society of accomplices, a guilty family from which you felt excluded. You weren't entirely wrong: almost all of them were, yes, accomplices. There they were, kneeling at Mass, grovelling fearfully before the authorities, responding to the police superintendent's questions in a quavering, little old lady's voice and, above all, hurling themselves like a pack of wolves on the remains of the fallen, shamelessly gobbling them up. They denounced each other in order to wipe from their own police record the memory of the half-dozen or so years when they had puffed out their chests and openly said what they thought; they elbowed each other out of the way, bidding at the auction of confiscated goods. You remembered seeing your neighbours wrapped in the tricolour during the years of the Republic and in the days shortly after the military uprising, when they were convinced they were going to win the war, and you saw them when they came back, when everything was over: they queued up at the town hall to denounce their comrades, they couldn't wait to squeal to the local thugs, telling them in whispers where they could find the person they were looking for, in which hiding place, in which country house, in which attic, in which barn, in which cave, in which corner of the marsh. Anything to save themselves. Suddenly, pride did not consist in raising a clenched fist, singing the Internationale and waving the tricolour. It meant wearing a reasonably new jacket (they didn't yet dare to wear the Falangist blue shirt, that would mean risking a beating, *you*, how do *you* of all people dare to wear the sacred blue shirt that José Antonio embroidered with his own red blood?). Or speaking with a nicely judged degree of confidence to the local leader of the Movimiento Nacional or the commander of the civil guard; it meant having your wife, wearing her black lace mantilla, genuflecting at the head of the queue for midday Mass, High Mass (waddling slowly along, head up, she would walk from the house to the church, so that people could see her, mantilla covering her hair, hands clasping prayer book and rosary). I'm not afraid of anyone, they would say whenever they had the opportunity, but would fearfully greet the Falangist scum – the fifth columnist – who had spent the war in hiding and had joined the entourage of the victors to tell them about everything that had happened in Olba during the war years. They would doff their cap and bow their head when they passed a town councillor or the civil guard, they would kiss the priest's hand. Big strong men would bend low and press their lips to the soft little hand of Father Vicente, smiling at him like devout fools. The same men who, during the Transition, ransacked their attics, rummaged around in chests, in hiding places beneath the floorboards or in holes in the backyard to dig out the photos that capture the glory of those proud times, but who have carefully buried, erased, expunged any photos that record the post-war complicities and miseries that followed. The same men who fought off others in order to be allowed to help carry the saint in the procession; who, having only escaped execution by the skin of their teeth, now present the priest with a crate of oranges (the sweetest in the whole region, Father Vicente, they say unctuously), meanwhile offering to decorate the parish house for free; who stand next to a pillar in church, listening to Mass with head bowed and clutching their rolled-up beret; who sit on the front pew during religious ceremonies and earnestly read their prayer book, having previously thrown their incriminating copy of Manuel Azaña's *The Garden of the Friars* onto the kitchen fire.

Even though you didn't go into hiding in the marsh as you wanted to, you weren't one of those men. You stayed in your hole. Others did too. They lived as if they hadn't really lived. They didn't count somehow, they weren't part of their own times. They gradually died off, without ever having existed. They would walk quickly, cautiously along the pavement, keeping close to the wall, looking at the world out of the corner of one eye. Shut up in their houses, they would silently brood over their sadness. You are part of that legion of shadows, as dignified as you are insignificant. Fresh out of prison, you make a note of all the cowards, all the traitors. You're preparing for the next act. You're reviewing your troops. Counting your money. You ask my mother and my uncle to tell you about this man or that man: if they bow their head or stop to greet members of the Falangist Party when they meet them in the street; you send me, when I'm only seven or eight years old, to see if so-and-so is taking part in the religious processions this year, if he's helping to carry the saint, if he's barefoot and wearing chains round his ankles or if he's donned the purple shirt of the penitent. Idiot, you say, when I confirm that the man was, indeed, barefoot. Idiots, what can one think of men who accept without complaint what they're told from the pulpit by someone who says the first thing that comes into his head, because he knows no one can contradict him. What kind of common sense is that, grown men dumbly nodding at what the priest is saying: virgins who give birth, fishermen who can speak every language in the world, dead men come back to life, devils using their three-pronged forks to prod a few wretches being boiled in pots or stretched out on a grill. And those same grown men said nothing. Have we all gone mad? You should have seen the meetings and assemblies held in the Cine Tivoli or in the town hall square during the Republic: they would all shout at once, talking over each other, arguing, threatening each other, grabbing each other by the lapels. You suddenly fall silent. You remember that it's me you're talking to. You probably notice my bored expression. You're not talking to a comrade or even to your eldest son, who does at least appear to be listening, even though, later on, he'll betray you, but to this other son who is bored by your stories, and you think that it's because of him — because of this son and your other children and your wife, at this point you make no distinctions — that you're here in the workshop and at home, mere prolongations of prison, as, indeed, they were. For years, he received regular visits from the Falangist brigade, he was forbidden to go into the village, he had to present himself each week at the headquarters of the civil guard in order to sign on and, as a way of getting by, of surviving, he tried to decipher what seemed to him to be the signs of something yet to come. They had won the battle, but the war remained unresolved. When he left prison, he preferred to go for solitary walks on Montdor. So as not to see 'them', he would say. Then he shut himself up in the house, probably because there was no way of avoiding seeing 'them'. He only left the house for work reasons. He didn't go to the bar because he didn't want to bump into the blue shirts who, each time they threw down a card on the green baize tabletop, would smugly pat the shoulder holster in which they kept a pistol with its mother-of-pearl butt, or the other men who laughed at their jokes, people who, now that everything has changed, have brought out their photos of the time when they were young Republicans, before they ran like little dogs tied to the victors' cart. God knows where they kept those photos hidden, the cap with the tassel at the front, the flag whose colours are not visible in the black-and-white photo, but which we know were red, yellow and purple, the raised fist. The 1980s: when you see the faces of the children of post-war opportunists on electoral campaign posters, you groan: who does he think he is? So his father and grandfather made a fortune out of ham and chorizo, big deal, but they're still butchers. And what does the son and grandson of a butcher have to teach us? he asks me.

Even though I've never taken any interest in your political obsessions, I must acknowledge that I've inherited a few drops of that poison: expecting only the worst of human beings, seeing man as a factory for shit in various stages of preparation, a bag of rubbish tied up with string you used to say when you were in a bad mood (although your actual words were 'a bag of shit'). But I've never given this pessimism of mine a social dimension. I've kept it to myself. I've felt my frustration without ever thinking it was part of this fallen world, rather, I've lived with the conviction that everything to do with me will die when I disappear because it's merely a manifestation of the little nucleus that is my life. An easily replaceable being among thousands and millions of other easily replaceable beings. That is where we disagree. You have had the capacity, the gift of being able to read your biography as part of the great tableau of the world, convinced that the ups and downs of your own life contain part of the tragedy of history, present-day history, the gossip and meanness of Olba, as well as the old history of the disloyalties and betrayals of the war, and the history going on thousands of kilometres from here and several centuries away: you are touched by the wars going on in the mountains of Afghanistan, in Baghdad or in some tiny village in Colombia: your suffering is a suffering to be found everywhere, in the very heart of every misfortune, just as, for Christians, the body of Christ is present in each and every communion wafer: Christ's whole sleek, vigorous body is there in those fragile wafers given out time and again to the faithful in any of the churches of the world, the same whole identical body in wafers that have been given out century after century. Your attitude, like that of those church-goers, confirms me in my belief that what most successfully survives the passing of time is a lie. You can embrace a lie and hold on to it without it ever deteriorating. Truth, on the other hand, is unstable, it rots, dilutes, slips away, escapes. The lie is like water, colourless, odourless, tasteless, and yet even though we can't taste it on our palate, it nonetheless refreshes us.

A sect with no members, no accomplices: just you and your comrades, as ubiquitous and as invisible as the body of Christ hidden in those communion wafers, golems made to the measure of your own desires. You celebrate your rituals at home: the little office at the workshop with its small glazed windows, the shed in the yard, the solitude of your bedroom, where, on top of a small dressing table, you keep your radio. In the fifties and sixties, you press your ear to the speaker, which you keep at a barely audible volume. You listen to the news about Spain broadcast by the BBC in London, by Radio Paris, Radio Pirenaica. In order to muffle the sound further, you cover the radio and your head with a towel; none of us is allowed to enter the room while you're listening to the news; and underneath the workbench, in an invisible place (I happen upon it one day when I'm playing, crawling about on the floor) you stick photos of Marx's bearded face and of La Pasionaria, cut out from some old book or maga-zine. A long time passed before I found out who those people

146

were, those faces you kept hidden away, just as the painters of the Altamira caves hid their images of fetish animals. And after your release from prison you used the back of the calendars hanging in the office to mark in pencil any dates you believed were decisive steps towards the circumstances that would allow you to restore the manhood you felt had been diminished the moment you decided to hand yourself over to the authorities. You kept those annotated calendar leaves, just as I imagine you believed you were keeping back any feelings of husbandly love or fatherly affection until that hoped-for future normality arrived, when the dark times and the years that had transformed us into nonentities would end; not that you ever put into practice those feelings of compassion and solidarity, or if you did, I certainly never noticed (yours was a future solidarity whose time never came, a bird with no branch on which to perch and make its nest). I came upon some of those calendar leaves a while ago now. You kept them at the bottom of one of the boxes piled up in the office. Messages from the past, a feeding ground for future affections, the days preceding the coming celebration of solidarity. On the page corresponding to August 1944, only a few months after you were granted provisional release from prison, you had written: *Warsaw uprising; 25th: Leclerc division commanded by our compatriot Amado Granell, a r. from Burriana* (r. doubtless meant Republican), *takes Paris, and the Spanish t.* (i.e. the tricolour) *flies over the Arc de Triomphe.* And written in red pen, in large almost angry capital letters: OUTSIDE THEY'RE WINNING WHAT IS BEING LOST INSIDE. I was born four years earlier (I must been conceived during the very last days of the war when you were wondering whether or not you should hand yourself in), when you were still in prison, which meant, of course, that you couldn't make a note of my birth on one of your calendars, but Juan and Carmen were born in 1944 and 1947, and yet they didn't merit any mention either, you presumably saw their births as being of no future significance, you saw no hope in them and therefore no hope *for* them, just as I believe you saw no hope in me. On the back of one of the leaves the following year, you had written: *13 February, the Russians take Budapest;* on another: *13 April, Soviet troops occupy Vienna;* on the following: *2 May,* THE NAZIS SURRENDER BERLIN TO THE SOVIETS. In 1949: *1 October, Mao Tse Tung* (that's how it was written then) *establishes people's republic in China.* 1959: *8 January, Fidel Castro enters Havana. Is he with us or with them? Don't ask because time will tell.* And he had added: *time, goddamn time, how quickly it passes too, it's been twenty years since all that, but it seems like yesterday; and how slowly it passes, each day seems like a century to me. For the moment, Batista is out* (no insulting adjective, you don't say 'that bastard Batista', or even 'the dictator Batista', you just give his name: you have to be careful what you write, those bits of paper could be dangerous, they could fall into the wrong hands, and reveal that the virus isn't dead, only sleeping, I'm surprised you even dare to write 'us' and 'them' because, at the time, they had a single, dangerous meaning). 1968: *Russian tanks take Prague. What the hell is going on? I don't understand. I could weep.* Your writing is there on the back of coloured pictures of landscapes, paintings by Velázquez and Murillo, photos of cathedrals in Spain, of singers, footballers and bullfighters. Clandestine, sterile notes, condemned to grow mouldy, their faces to the wall, although I imagine, too, that you took a certain perverse delight in that secrecy, because what was on show in your little office – those vulgar, innocuous images – was concealing your pride: the virus wasn't even sleeping, it was still working away, stealthily but indefatigably. The solid nucleus that nothing had managed to destroy – not the years in prison or in the vacuum to which your neighbours subsequently relegated you – was still there, intact. The old mole was still tunnelling in the night, or so you believed, because the truth is that those written notes neither changed nor nourished anything, you were the only one who read them. We didn't know of their existence. In the solitude of Olba, which condemns you to melancholy walks in the countryside (going with someone else would only cast suspicion on them, you used to say, but I think it was more that you couldn't stand to be with anyone, perhaps not even your comrade, Álvaro's father), it was you yourself who you were nourishing with those notes: they're the nutrients that allow you to survive until your moment comes again. *How quickly time passes, and how slowly it passes too,* you wrote, *each day seems like a century to me*: time, while it was busily devouring terrible memories, continued to generate new variants on the ominous. As I said, there's no mention of us, of your wife, your children; not even your mother or your siblings appear in the notes. According to those notes, we are not born, we have no birthdays, we don't fall ill, we don't start school; your mother dies during those years, in 1950 or 1951, and yet her death doesn't appear either. We don't merit so much as a mention, we don't form part of the progress of the world, no god watches over us, we're outside the universal system of pain and injustice and rebellion, we're not part of that legion of transubstantiated bodies, pale comrades you can just make out on the horizon; we have no access to the great concepts that nourish them. We represent the personal, which is to be deplored, which binds you and keeps you earthbound, on the level of animal nature: being born, eating and defecating, working, reproducing: and what a wretched way we have of reproducing, how low down the scale of species that mode of reproduction places us. Dying: another moment not worthy of being recorded, again that closeness to our animal nature, a regression that only confirms you in your ideas. Everything you learn and know dissolves into nothing. Beings with no public importance, individual selves that fall like leaves in autumn. Others will begin to sprout in a few months' time and replace them and you won't even be able to tell the difference.

★

When Francisco bought the house from the Civera family and set about renovating it, he didn't ask me to do the carpentry work; he wanted an expert. The builders had uncovered the original limestone facade and doorway. The man he had put in charge of restoring the woodwork left the main door and the beams – all made of pinewood – like new. They had also restored all the dining-room furniture (you know about wood, Esteban, and, as you can see, these are an antiquarian's dream, they could fill a room in a museum), along with all the wardrobes, free-standing and fitted, all the dressers, coffee tables, beds, cupboards, shelves and mantelpieces around the house. The furniture was made of walnut, cherry, lime, kingwood, jacaranda, a veritable catalogue of styles and materials, the furnishings in the kitchen, living room and dressing rooms were all included in the price of the house, everything: tables, beds, bedside tables, dressers, wardrobes, they didn't take a thing, look, I'll show you, they even left this bargueño desk, can you imagine, and this little marquetry table, inlaid with ivory. The house looks like new now or even better, because we've improved the varnishes, stripped off any botched retouching done twenty or thirty years ago using really bad-quality varnish that was damaging the wood and corroding it, plus, we've treated the woodwork for termites and got rid of a patch of woodworm too. The Civera siblings couldn't stand each other and so they sold the house as a job lot – no argument about what's yours and what's mine, just cash in hand; imagine how much all this would have fetched if sold at auction or in antique shops, but no, they preferred just to take the money and run. They got far less than they could have, but at least that way they didn't have to suffer the humiliation of arguing about it face-to-face or giving in to each other: they paid for their pride – an extremely expensive and old-fashioned piece of merchandise. And then, along the way, they'd lost more of their inheritance to the Lord so to speak, because, as was the case with so many houses in those days, the wills weren't drawn up by notaries, but by priests, and part of the inheritance went to a very devout aunt, who gave it to the church, and so the sharing-out of spoils proved fairly ruinous for the family, victims of both religious and human prejudices – well, money and religion do tend to make for a fairly poisonous combination. The foolish squabbles of one of those old families that had been going downhill for decades. Francisco wanted to show me the exquisite woodwork, as well as the restoration work that was being carried out. I knew the house already, having been there a couple of times to carry out a few minor jobs with my father, who, many years before, had repaired a kitchen cabinet for them and a few cupboards in the ironing room. He eyed the furniture in those rooms with dread. He trembled, he had no confidence in himself, frightened in case he bungled a job that was not only the most important he'd ever been given, but had been given to him by what was certainly his most important customer to date, the head of the Civera household. Even though the work we were called on to do was only in the servants' quarters, everything around us oozed class. The cabinets in the kitchen and the pantry were made of limewood, and the kitchen cabinets had a carved geometric design on them. All he had to do was repair some doors under the sink and on a couple of cabinets and, in the ironing room, to refurbish some cupboards decorated with a floral motif. These were by no means routine jobs, however, and, in the case of those cupboards, required a certain degree of skill. The skill of a cabinetmaker. But he was frightened. He tried to hide this from me, but I could tell he was nervous. When we arrived, the maid led us to the back of the house, and, on the way, with a lift of his chin, my father indicated to me the many fine pieces of furniture, and whispered in my ear, showing off his expert knowledge: the display cabinets, the ornamentation on the banisters, the delicate work on the oak handrails, the carved newel caps, but also the filigree ironwork on the balconies, and the leaded stained-glass window on the mirador. His eyes shone with tears. That same afternoon, he asked me not to go with him: you'll just get in the way, he said, but I knew it was because he didn't want me to see his lack of skill or, rather, his fear of that lack of skill, because that isn't the story he had told me, and those weren't the hands capable of carving the table in his office, with its medallions, human figures and *grottesche*, the skills of someone who'd once wanted to be a sculptor.

Half a century later, I visited the house again: the living room, the kitchen, the bedrooms; I saw what I remembered and what I didn't remember, what I recognised and what I'd forgotten, what I hadn't seen on that first visit when we saw only the part of the house where we were going to work – the rooms and corridors that led there. You don't show your house to a couple of carpenters or to a carpenter and his assistant, you don't show them around the way you would your guests. You say *this is here and it's like this and I'd like it to be like that*. On this visit, Francisco asked my opinion about the restoration that was taking place and explained that they were superb examples of workmanship that no one could possibly afford nowadays, museum pieces. He invited me to run my hand along the edges of tables and sideboards, to open doors and drawers, to admire the perfect finish, the precision with which they had been repaired, saying again that this furniture was a hundred years old: doors that still fitted and drawers that slid smoothly in and out after a century of use. He had found the only furniture and woodwork restorer in the whole region:

'He uses natural, non-aggressive oils – he's truly a miracle worker – reconstructing what's damaged, rotten, splintered, worm-eaten or broken, I've seen some amazing work he's done before, on a fifteenth-century coffered ceiling in a palace in Valencia, on a couple of Renaissance bargueño desks. He's worked marvels here too, as you can see, although, everything in the house was in a remarkably good state of preservation, generally speaking, it was just a matter of cleaning it up and using the best treatments to protect the wood, you must know him, though he's not a local, there's no one around here now who does this kind of work; he gets calls not just from people in Valencia and Barcelona, but from people in Paris and even Italy, even though he says he's not that keen on travelling. I travel, he says, because I enjoy the challenges they're offering me. He's quite a lot older than us. He must be about eighty, but he looks like a young man. And he has no intention of retiring. He shows me his hands sometimes, and not a tremor. He's very thin, pure muscle and bone, and yet he can carry a plank of wood on his shoulders that I'm not even sure I could pick up. He says to me: I work with wood that's three times my age and it hasn't given up the ghost yet, it's still looking after clothes and china or holding up roofs, it's three hundred years old and still doing its duty, so why should I retire at eighty if my materials are good for three centuries? I'm not going to have that wood look down at me, thinking it's better than I am. He laughs and takes a sip of wine, a little glass at breakfast, another with his lunch and another at supper time. A bit of wine never hurt anyone. And then, after supper, a drop of brandy.'

I don't blame him for taking on that man. It's only logical that he should choose the best, someone equal to the task; it's what the house deserves; we've been friends for a long time, but he was talking to me about a world of which I know nothing, a world my father once aspired to, or so he said, but it's never really interested me, I despised it, and have been a mere jobbing carpenter, doing mundane work, a minor industrialist with no ambition, that's all I've wanted to be ever since it became clear to me that I was going to abandon any aspirations I had in order to accept a future that would be circumscribed by the workshop and by the shadow cast by my father's tutelary presence. Basic carpentry: I've produced work more quickly and with better tools than your average DIY enthusiast, but with only slightly better results, or possibly not even as good, I've just never been able to get up the enthusiasm to take on anything more complicated. I've stuck to turning out well-finished, but undemanding stuff: doors, windows, wardrobes, shelving, all very elementary and functional, plank to plank or plank fitted into plank, nothing too difficult, and of course carpentry for the building trade. Bog-standard, nothing fancy. That's how it was to the end. I don't know if I regret it or not. Having no ambition, I mean. Perhaps, if I'd had ambition, I would have been even more bitter, would have become impregnated with the bile that has always filled my father, contaminating everything around him. I can't say that I lost my business because I aspired to something better, that I bet to win and lost: no, I don't have that excuse, nor am I looking for an excuse. I made that bet in order to survive, simply to get by. Or to help myself to die better. My objective had nothing to do with my profession, it was the house, or rather the small refuge I was going to build for myself in the mountains; going for walks with the dog, hunting near the lagoon. I didn't even lose because I did something wrong, but because Tomás Pedrós failed to meet my expectations, because he drew me in or I wanted to be drawn in or allowed myself to be. *He* was certainly gambling, that's what he's done all his life, he's younger than me, he'll survive all this and continue to gamble. He had another business before, towards the end of the 1980s, and he made a lot of money too, but according to Bernal, that business went down the tubes. He left his partner in the lurch, without a penny. According to Bernal's version of events, Pedrós kept his own money on ice for a while, then used it to set up the hardware store and then began to expand from there: the shop, his partnership in the waste management company, his first forays into property development. People said he'd won the lottery or that he'd been involved in some kind of dodgy deal, smuggled something in from one of his trips abroad; that he'd worked as a courier for that Mexican drugs lord Guillén, that we all know where he got the money. On the other hand, for me, the business with Pedrós was simply the straw that broke the camel's back. I see that now. He went into partnership with me because he knew he was taking a risk with this latest wager of his. He didn't know whether or not the property development deal would work, and it wasn't so much a question of splitting the profits if the roulette ball happened to land on the lucky number, but of minimising his losses if, as was only logical, it didn't. His wager was my disaster, added to the long chain of unpaid bills over the last two years: whenever he commissioned any carpentry work, he always wanted it done very quickly, with poor-quality materials, chipboard doors and panels; his idea of good-quality wood was newly cut, unseasoned pine put together quickly, hastily: but why am I even bothering to explain, that's the way everyone was doing business, commissions taken on just to pay the next bill and to dupe clients who think they're middle-class simply because they don't work with a shovel and pickaxe but who are merely the saddest of our lower classes nowadays. The deal with Pedrós would have allowed me to sell off the paternal home and workshop, sharing the spoils among the heirs in the same impatient, rapacious spirit as the Civera siblings, to put an end once and for all to what had already gone on for far too long, and with what I obtained from this operation (yes, operation) and the savings I'd been squirrelling away behind my father's back, to build a house in the mountains where I would retire with my dog, even taking a few tools with me so that I could begin to work on some new carpentry caprice, perhaps an old-fashioned Renaissance-style table, complete with *grottesche* and medallions like the one made by my grandfather or father, or that they made together.

Slamming down an ace of clubs on the table, Francisco, who has never liked Pedrós – perhaps because he feels that, in the bar and in local society, Pedrós is stealing some of the limelight he doesn't want to share with anyone – completes our piratical Lecter's thought (strange times make for strange bedfellows):

'Yes, the local radio and TV ads – the football club director, the local events committee chairman. Sheer greed. The man's a glutton; he's tried to stick all the spoons in his mouth at once. At Chinese feasts, they put all the different dishes on the table, serve them up at the same time, but you take a little from each dish on the turntable in the middle, a bit like a roulette wheel, except that you decide where the wheel should stop. You don't put everything in your mouth at one time. The hardware store, the electrical goods store, the property development business, the shares in the waste management company and the water treatment plant: that man has, or had, more departments than one of the giant superstores.'

'Yes – using what he calls synergies (in the language of the big multinationals) to make his way on every front – with his taste for bossing people around, showing off, and cutting a prominent figure in society – add that up and you get a very explosive mix, ready to go off at any moment: envy is a very dangerous thing. If someone sticks his head above the parapet, everyone wants to chop it off; if someone's winning the marathon, there's always some spectator ready to stick out a leg and trip him up. What can you do, if that's how the good Lord or nature made us? People can't bear to see anyone rising to the top. The more relationships you maintain and the more friends you seek, the more enemies you acquire and the more threads you weave in to your own failure. I don't know if he was hoping to become mayor or deputy. There isn't a councillor he hasn't had in his pocket, who he hasn't done favours for: invited to suppers, presented with crates of champagne, anointed with money from some business deal or other, or taken to a brothel or sent on a cruise. That's all very well day-to-day, but in the end, it just evaporates. The councillor doesn't get re-elected or another associate with more possibilities turns up and then that's all wasted time and money and you ask yourself: what was it all for? Feast or famine,' concludes Bernal, who's always been jealous of Pedrós.

Justino disagrees, even though Francisco and Bernal have basically been saying more or less what he said. He tries to differentiate his position by focusing on some nuance. Proud of his own pride, he doesn't like to always agree with Francisco, he needs to show that he has his own criteria and isn't going to have someone from Madrid come along and explain to us how things work here:

'If he'd wanted to be a politician, he would have stood for election. You have more power and more control if you stay in the wings, you're free then, not controlled by any one party, out of sight of the journalists and politicians, free from their in-fighting, better to be lurking in the shadows, pulling the puppets' strings.' The slave-driver, the gangmaster, the exploiter of the workforce – as, when he was young, Francisco would have described him – but now his partner at the card table tonight in the village bar where the most anyone ever bets is a round of coffees or drinks, at least during the day.

At night, after closing time, things get more serious – players will sometimes bet hundreds or even thousands of euros or offer a kind of IOU in the form of the price of a night out at the local so-called gentleman's club. But, by then, Francisco is no longer in the bar. Cinderella has gone home before his carriage turns into a pumpkin, leaving no delicate glass slipper to mark his trail; he hides away in his lair to read and write, or so he tells me:

'At night, there's no noise, no phone calls, no one ringing the doorbell. That's my favourite time,' he says, as if his night were not as crowded with ghosts as any other seventy-year-old's. The body sleeps, but ambition continues to labour away. Seated at his fine desk made of lignum vitae wood, Francisco scribbles on paper or types at his computer, working on the novel or memoir he hopes will bring him the prestige that the last few agitated years have denied him. Wine tastings, reviews of books and restaurants, the wittily written fortnightly editorial, the half-dozen pages of an article on some particular wine region, minor works that will never bring with them the posterity that ambitious writers always demand, that promise of life after death, even if it means ruining their nerves and health spending long, difficult nights writing, not to mention the terrible frustration when their present-day voice fails to produce the expected strokes of genius. At seventy years of age, late at night, you're besieged not by brilliant ideas but by the half-buried dead – although which of our dead could be said to be entirely buried? Not a single one, they all have at least one limb or another sticking out. For some reason, you end up having an outstanding debt with each of them, a debt that requires repayment. You've either done something you shouldn't have done to all of them, or else failed to do something you should have done. As I well know. But Francisco, that night owl, probably has enough sangfroid to meet them face-to-face; he has what I lack and he always has. He'll form alliances with a few ghosts and pit them against the others and he'll choose his allies wisely. He'll flip the coin and make an educated guess, heads or tails. At night, he shuts himself up at home. That, he says, is when he sits down to work, but I think his need to keep to himself springs not only from the tiredness that comes with age – and, really, who wants to go flitting about at night at seventy? – but even so, with Francisco, it has more to do with image. He takes great care not to fall into the dark holes that open up late at night in the outside world, even in a village like Olba: the card games after the bar has closed its doors that go on until sunrise, the constantly replenished glasses (*another drink? I've already had nine or it is ten?*), the fluorescent lighting at the Lovely Ladies Club, the electric-blue flesh, which one imagines must be white or pink or golden when out of those lights, the deceptive glare, flesh you can buy by the hour. This is what Francisco is protecting himself from – with his supposed contentment with his own personal abysses – his ascetic solitude – saying that he prefers it or finds it more bearable; he is also – I would say – keeping scrupulous guard over his reputation as a connoisseur of other, more prestigious vices. He has a lot to gain by not letting himself be contaminated by the vulgarity of those open-all-hours places, the laughter, the slaps on the back, the off-colour jokes, the obscenities, the kidding around. Even as a young man, he kept well away from that world frequented then by his father's friends, and he'll give it an even wider berth now. If he didn't, he would immediately be labelled a dirty old man. Being slapped on the back or on the arse amid loud guffaws, being seen groping the Ukrainian girl or French-kissing the Romanian, and having the bulge in your trousers reveal the hard-on you've got from getting up close and personal with that soft, bright, eminently touchable flesh, which only costs forty euros for half an hour and has been handled by plumbers, bricklayers and Latin American or African immigrants – no, that would be to fall very low. That would involve a head-on collision with his image as a rigorous connoisseur of *le grand monde*. It just isn't Francisco's style. When he was young, he would try and impress me by bringing back from Madrid a ball of cocaine wrapped in cling film. He would place it on a small mirror he kept in the glove compartment, balancing the mirror on his right leg, which he rested against the gearstick. An alluringly sleazy atmosphere filled the car, parked, at night, in the middle of nowhere. Inside, the only light comes from the moon glinting on the phosphorescent white lines on the mirror, the ambiguous intimacy of sharing something forbidden, combined with Francisco's cosmopolitanism and my own cosmopolitan melancholy (cocaine, heroin, David Bowie, Lou Reed and the Velvet Underground, whose posters and records I collected at the time), the ritual of breaking up the lumps and using a credit card to chop the loose powder into neat lines, ready to be snorted through a rolled-up five-thousand-peseta note, the two of us alone in the night, something almost as alluring as sex, like screwing a complete stranger in the toilet of a disco, keeping the unlocked door jammed shut with one part of your body so that no one can open it, or doing the deed out in the open somewhere, leaning against the trunk of a carob tree, protected from the moon's impertinent spotlight by the broad, densely leaved branches. He bends towards me, holding out the mirror so that I can lick the surface before he returns it to the glove compartment; I notice, briefly, the pressure of his elbow in my stomach, then the weight of his forearm on my thigh, we're close friends, two friends set talking and talking and talking by the cocaine until a smudge of pink appears on the horizon, something superhuman growing on the black surface of the sea, which, in turn, becomes milk-white and silver then gold and blue, all of this seen through the blood-splattered veil formed by the thousands of insects sticking to the windscreen. Sometimes he would offer me a small silver spoon, like the protagonist of a novel we had read at the time. A distant, dazzling dandy. His path was already on an upward trajectory that would take him out of that world in whose bargain basements he and I had rummaged around a few years before, when we went off travelling together, on those journeys that, for me, were supposed to be the prologue to something, but ended up being the epilogue to everything, with me trapped in the web of a weaver of dreams (or, rather, desires), a weaver called Leonor. Not for him though. For him they were the goose on which he flew above the world, like Nils Holgersson in the story we read as children. But I digress: he was adding chapters to the formative story of his life. He would return to Olba and, each time, I had the impression he was growing before my eyes, as if in one of those low-angle shots we were told were characteristic of Orson Welles when he made *Citizen Kane*, a way of making the main character seem larger than life, a giant: from his lofty position, he was seducing me, crushing me; our conversations, rather than being shot and counter-shot, were low-angle (him) and high-angle (me). You choose, Francisco – you're the one who's just come back from abroad, I've been here all year, we can do whatever you fancy doing or discovering, I know this place like the back of my hand, it's not very exciting for me, not even the starry sky and the smell of orange blossom, which you say you really miss when you're away, to me it's all very dull and everyday. I would follow him and, at the same time, loathe him, because I loathed the image of myself that he reflected back at me. I followed him the way a lamb follows the shepherd, the way ducklings will follow any moving object that becomes a protective, maternal presence. I would meekly snort cocaine with him or stand at the bar drinking and listening to him, or trudge up to the rooms in the roadside brothel with my usual apathy, him first and me second, preceded by the two whores. He hadn't got lost, as I was getting lost, along a path which – like the paths through the marsh – ends up buried beneath scrub. He kept going. I would have needed to prove that I had my own personality, my own criteria, even if that meant simply picking up on some detail as Justino does whenever we get into a discussion. I'm talking now about the early 1980s. I'd been buried in sawdust for eight or even ten years by then, years when I'd lost all hope. Leonor was no longer mine, and never had been. The woman-goose, who flew wherever she wanted, had abandoned me – a mere pastime – in favour of egotistical calculation – she'd shaken off the person riding on her back. Nowadays, cocaine has lost all its glamour, it's handed round by young men who left school to go into the building trade and are now unemployed: come into the toilets, the coke's all ready and waiting. Needless to say, they don't offer it to me, because of my age and my image as a serious, sensible fellow, even though being single and alone does lend one a faintly bohemian aura: those boys know nothing about my past, and they aren't interested either – people in villages only manage to rub along thanks to the periodical layers of forgetting that are thrown over past events; otherwise, life would be unbearable; like any other old man my age, for them I'm a photo, fixed in its frame, beyond evolution, solidified sediment. Old people reach a state of atemporality, we become immutable, changeless, it's assumed that there are no intermediate stages between growing old and dying, however many decades that may take. You grow old and then you die; if they happen to see a picture of you when you were their age – I have four on the office wall, and I have shoulder-length hair in one – they're amazed that you look so much like them. Fuck, check out that hair, and the T-shirt's really cool. In the photo, I'm wearing a T-shirt and my hair is long and fair and straight; and in another one next to it, I'm wearing a baggy linen shirt, open at the neck to reveal a shark-tooth necklace and a medallion with a large A in the middle: You look like a hippy in that one, but you look youngest in this one with the Beatle haircut and one of those buttoned-up jackets. How old would you have been then? Eighteen? Twenty? That was fashionable for a while. At the time, they called it a Mao jacket, after the uniform Mao used to wear. What do you mean, you've never heard of Mao? Haven't you ever seen any documentaries about the Chinese revolution? Oh, fuck, that's not really you, is it? You look just like Leonardo DiCaprio. God, you've put on a bit of weight . . . and your face has changed. And look at that great mane of hair. You're as bald as a coot now. Of course, you don't think I've always had this moon face and a drum for a belly, do you? The worst of it is that most of the men who sported necklaces with shark's teeth and shells or wore Mao collars are all dead – they were killed or they're past retirement age, they have grandchildren and great-grandchildren, hyperglycaemia, triglycerides, high cholesterol, triple bypasses, pacemakers, varicose veins, prostate problems and osteoarthritis. Or else they're lying awake in the early hours wondering if they'll survive the chemotherapy for their colon cancer. They're old men like me – moon-faced, over-stuffed sausages – or doubles for a B-movie Dracula, thin and grey, sallow-complexioned, with deep lines criss-crossing their face; a profusion of bald heads, toothless mouths, huge dentures and white hair. Ruined prostates, with the proof of their radio-therapy sessions there in their dull gaze and in their sharp, frightened little eyes glancing cautiously about in case they should stumble into death – the faces of Jews who have been through the Auschwitz of modern medicine.

The older Francisco despises Olba's *petits vices*, he wouldn't sink that low, just the occasional gin and tonic made with Bombay Sapphire or Citadelle gin, which the owner of the Bar Castañer reserves for him. He keeps two bottles on the shelf just for Francisco, who is the only one who'd ever think of asking for either. Other customers order a Larios or a Gordon's, or, for more fanciful ones, a Tanqueray. Francisco asks for a Citadelle gin and tonic, easy on the gin, purely for medicinal purposes, you understand, to relieve the treacherous drop in blood pressure that occurs each evening, his hypoglycaemia, but he never goes in for any heavy drinking. Poker, prostitutes, gambling and drugs are out: he wrinkles his small, decrepit rabbit nose when he hears comments from the other old men (whores, gambling) or from the young men (lines of coke, a joint: marijuana grows well in these sunny climes, young people grow their own, half a dozen plants in the backyard or up on the roof), because, one assumes, he has better things to do, or the same things on a different, but higher level – yes, only the best, far removed from what's on offer in some poky room complete with a Romanian whore who has removed any body hair with a razor or with wax because she hasn't yet heard about laser technology or perhaps can't afford it; rooms equipped with a toy jacuzzi. I always wonder how those jacuzzis can possibly hold the great carcasses propping up the bar at the Lovely Ladies Club, men weighing in at ninety, a hundred, a hundred and ten kilos or more, strapping farmers, burly bricklayers, obese truck drivers and mechanics, sedentary estate agents or bank clerks, arses of all dimensions, fat, soft and low-slung, men with wide hips, who rock from side to side when they walk, like the clapper in a bell. The Mediterranean amphora-shape which one always thought of as female has become unisex. I know many a whore-monger with wide hips, but have no idea why that should be. I can't imagine those carcasses fitting in one of those mini-jacuzzis. *I* only just fit. Instead of splashing about in the pool with all those high-pressure jets, they presumably crouch over the bidet as I do when I visit, mounted on the pony (isn't that what the French word means, a small horse? I'll have to look it up in the French dictionary I've kept from my schooldays) while she scrubs your bottom and your arsehole with antiparasitic soap to flush out any lice hiding inside; the pool-cum-jacuzzi is pure decoration to bump up the price of the session, an illusion of luxury that even the starving can afford. You pay for it, it's there, but it's so difficult to use that you give it up as a bad job. Another time, you say, next time, or in the next few months, when I've lost a bit of weight on the diet the doctor has put me on to lower my cholesterol levels and triglycerides. He said I have to lose nearly fifteen kilos and eat a lot of grilled chicken breasts and salads, otherwise, he said, my arteries and my heart will explode like a well-stuffed piñata. Anyway, I came here to fuck not to have a bath. I can do that at home. No, Francisco doesn't go to places like that. In Olba one bad move is all it takes to tarnish your image, if you lose your name and reputation, you can never get it back, your picture remains sullied forever; my childhood friend, our local celebrity: while we were drinking wine from the local Misent cooperative and ordering paellas at some open-air cafe, he was working as a journalist in Madrid, for a national magazine, *Vinofórum*, as well as being a co-owner of a swish restaurant. His wife was nominally the owner (on marriage they had opted for separation of property just in case) and, thanks to a few Castilian businessmen in Salamanca and Valladolid, he was a partner in a couple of boutique wine hotels, selling *vinos de pago* – that's what they call them, not that they're so expensive, but because it's the rather twee translation of what the French call *cru*, domain or estate: *pago* is a would-be medieval word and, believe me, he would say, there are still plenty of medieval *Franquistas* in this wretched country of ours – and he would talk to me, too, about the slopes of Burgundy and Corton-Charlemagne, which produce white wines because the emperor was fair-haired and red wine stained his beard; and about Romanée-Conti, Médoc and Château Latour. He would explain the virtues of *botrytis cinerea*, the grey mould used to sweeten the wines of Sauternes; and he would lecture me about the decantation time required by each wine, on which he was an expert, as well as being a writer of cookery books and articles and travelogues. He was no longer interested in St Paul's epistles to the Romans and the Thessalonians, nor in the ideas of the lay theologian Enrique Miret Magdalena; and he couldn't care less about the Second Vatican Council and didn't even remember it had existed (when *was* that? in the far-off sixties) or about Karl Liebknecht and Rosa Luxemburg, whose books he used to read a few years ago, indeed, we spent many nights discussing their ideas. Long before that, he used to tell me about St Paul, although, to be honest, I was never a believer, I slightly preferred – although not by much – those German revolutionaries: they had more interesting adventures, although I was always bored by the political vein running through their various trials and tribulations; that was more my father's territory. Francisco would have enjoyed debating with him, had my father ever agreed to such a debate, but he could never forgive Francisco for being his father's son, and I've always been allergic to heroes and saints, feeling incapable of following their example, but Francisco and I used to talk about all those things, not just here, but in Paris and London and Ibiza during the months of my great escape, my Indian summer that ended with me caught in Leonor's web. Then came those forty long years of winter. Those people from the German Weimar Republic were like family to Francisco (he had aligned himself with some really fine specimens that would have delighted his hunter father Gregorio Marsal), and the landscapes were familiar, the frozen canal into which Rosa Luxemburg was thrown by her social democrat comrades. Indeed, we knew more about their trials and tribulations than we did about those suffered by our grandparents. I had been given certain hints about how my grandfather met his end, although only in the vaguest of terms, I still knew nothing about the bullet in the back of the neck administered just a few hundred metres from our house, but I knew about the bodies of revolutionaries floating in the icy waters of the River Spree (whenever anyone mentions crime and Germany, there's always night and fog and the waters have to be icy: even Marx in the *Communist Manifesto* speaks of the icy waters, although in his case they're the icy waters of egotistical calculation, that I do remember). Nor do I think he knew of his father's hunting tastes in the 1940s. We were in the early 1980s then and concerned with other things. It wasn't a time of prisons or of corpses floating in cold, murky rivers, except as chapters in an adventure story, something like the exploits of Jules Verne's hero, Michel Strogoff, in the waters of the Yenisey River, adventures in which Francisco had wished that he, too, could be a protagonist, while I opted instead for the role of curious onlooker reading about them in some book. Is it a sin to have no interest in revolution or in digging up the past? Then again, after putting out many feelers, he also turned his back on history and the struggle of the proletariat. He chose rather cosier places for his adventures, while I opted not to find out about such things even in books (or, rather, in the book of life itself). After all, the positive option, not to destroy, but to choose the best of what's on offer – a dilemma that preoccupied him – and which he resolved at the time – seemed more in keeping with social propriety or his family's status or, more precisely, with his family's aspirations and pretensions, because his family enjoyed high status in the village, but in a rather confused fashion; it was best not to talk about the origin of that status (Falangist father: pistols, land seizures, black-market dealings, the pursuit through the mountains of famished, fugitive scarecrows in rags) to the half-dozen families who had inherited their wealth (the so-called 'good families' who had always lived in Olba and who had been able to hang on to their wealth and status without too much fuss or too much vulgar probing), the nouveau riche, however, swallowed whole the farce put on by the Marsal family, along with their pretensions, Don Gregorio this and Don Gregorio that, the uniformed maid serving at table when they had guests; as did other post-civil war upstarts and those who made their money in the 1960s, people who, in a way, considered themselves Don Gregorio's heirs – following the path opened up by him in the immediate post-war years – and saw themselves reflected in his mirror: second-generation predators, some of them the children of those who used to run with the pack – of which Don Gregorio was a member in his gleaming Hispania motor car – gangmasters, riff-raff, a rabble with their newly acquired wealth and a gun licence just in case some bastard breaks into your house and wants to steal your undeclared earnings. Their even more credulous children have the Spanish flag emblazoned on their key rings and on their watch straps, and a racist joke always on the tip of their tongues, convinced that barrack-room humour is really classy, failing to realise, the poor ignorant fools, that it is, in fact, merely the province of the buffoon. The Marsal family are held in high esteem by the local developers, the dealers in construction materials, paints and ironmongery, the bar owners, as well as the multitude of new arrivals who, over the last thirty years, have vied to be even more fascist than their immediate predecessors: the children of the winning side. Put Adolfo Suárez up against the wall. Santiago Carrillo wasn't just a commie, he was a war criminal. Hitler didn't go far enough in killing the Jews. This is how they show their colours, by socialising with Don So-and-So and Don Somebody-or-Other, supporters of the regime, brothers of the air commandant or the colonel of the civil guard and, inevitably, by sporting the Spanish flag on their key ring, which they proudly brandish whenever they start the car, or having their mobile belt out the Spanish national anthem in the middle of lunch in a restaurant, and letting the Falangist anthem, 'Cara al sol', blare forth on their CD player as soon as you climb into their 4x4, not to mention the camouflage gear they wear in this most urban of settings, and their taste for weapons lightly disguised as a passion for hunting. This was very far from being Francisco's world when he left, nor would it have become his world had he stayed. On the contrary, these people were his nightmare, his shifting sands, the ones who might reveal his shame, the half-buried corpse that lies behind any recently acquired fortune. He left precisely in order to escape from this world, he wasn't prepared to be a buffoon, a flunky, which – when all's said and done – was what his father and his cronies had been, entertaining governors, deputies and high-ranking officers visiting the area. Preparing paellas and eels *all-i-pebre*, taking them out on boat trips to see the cliffs of Misent while they bit off the head of a prawn (*the head is the tastiest bit, General*) and to the club where the best-looking whores could be found. When he began to learn more about his family history, he spat on the photos his father had pinned up on his office wall, photos of his father as a young man, blue shirt and military belt, the yoke and arrows embroidered on his shirt front – although he was careful to wipe away any traces of spit before his father came in – and he was not amused by the bronze bust of José Antonio used as a paper weight. He kept that sanctuary, with its proof of original sin, hidden away from his friends. I think I was the only one ever allowed to see the room, which he considered ignoble because it revealed the murky origins of Gregorio Marsal, his father. He rejects that room, because he has escaped into another world in which, like an astronaut, he enjoys zero gravity, with nothing binding him to the solid ground of recent history, which is pure vulgarity: Don Gregorio's card games, which he presided over wearing his shoulder holster, cheap music, Mum's croquettes, the chamberpot under the bed, his grandfather's enema, he erases all of that; he enjoys not having to set foot in the dust from which he sprang, he lives in a state of weightlessness in which one can build a new, improved self. His new world: crepinette and crème parmentier, foie gras from Perigord and *poulardes de Bresse*, the golden forests of France in autumn, the vineyards somewhere in Burgundy, the red vine tendrils glinting in the fragile October sun. I – like everyone – we're now in the 1980s, in what seems to be the new Spain – would listen open-mouthed. His little hare's nose discovering a whole fruit stall in a glass of wine: cherry, apricot, plum; a whole timberyard: cedar, oak; a complete grocer's store: honey, sugar, coffee; a submerged garden: there's a background of aquatic flowers – he would say – irises, water lilies, clear still water. As if he didn't know that irises and water lilies, like all marsh plants, stink of rotten fish. Gastronomic and oenological knowledge, a mastery of haute cuisine. At night, I would search the sparse bookshelves in my bedroom, looking for something by Luxemburg, Gramsci or Marx, and I discovered that my copies had disappeared too, although how I didn't know. Not one remained. I couldn't even remember what I could have done with them. I had probably only read them because Francisco lent them to me. Or perhaps I hadn't even bothered to read them. I talked about them without having glanced at a single page. They were there in the air. A dense, Middle-European fog, *Nacht und Nebel*, icy water, filled my brain and swamped all memories of the life I had abandoned when I decided to come back to Olba, an epic narrative I never really felt was mine. When I returned to the workshop, the past had ceased to exist. I couldn't bear my father's – always mysterious – allusions to things that had happened. At first, I didn't understand the allusions; later, I found them boring and, ultimately, disgusting. He thought I had accepted carpentry as a kind of vocation, and then he felt an urgent need to talk to me about the past, to tell me that he had been part of that epic narrative, but I didn't want to listen. I said to him: All that bitterness just keeps you from living. It's over, don't you see? Like Francisco, I, too, had landed on a weightless planet. Leonor had set me floating, then dropped me. I learned something from all of that, from that time of adaptation, the spell of decompression divers need before returning to the surface, although what I did mostly was suffer horribly, she was there in everything I saw and touched: it wasn't love, love doesn't last that long, because, by then, a few years had passed; it was probably bitterness, which has no expiry date, she flies off and escapes, and I remain alone, anchored to the earth, flailing around in the mud, and I rage at her, it's not fair – I can't bear it, you bitch – me coming home late at night, sometimes furious, sometimes barely able to keep from crying, and always very drunk. I'd brood on what I had lost by not being brave enough to leave. I could have freed myself from those German martyrs and icy canals without necessarily coming back home to my father and the workshop. Francisco managed to step free and yet he had believed in them in a way I never did. My father was a domestic Liebknecht, and I had shut myself up with him, drowning in the same icy canal. We were both floating, but my planet bore no relation to his. Saw, hammer, chisel, lathe, brace and bit, my father's voice, the voices of the cardplayers in the bar, the compulsive drinking, totting up my earnings at the end of the week to see if I could afford half an hour in a room at the Lovely Ladies Club, forty years in a world as coarse as sandpaper, vulgar, sordid, and with my one love – who didn't want to be the mother of my child – married to my best friend, living in a paradise filled with *dinde farci aux truffes, poulardes, canard à la Rouennaise*, polyglot people and hotel rooms with a view over Lake Geneva. I felt like a useless astronaut, left behind on an inhospitable meteorite, watching the rest of the crew travel on to an unknown blue planet, covered in lush vegetation, with a scattering of lakes and a population of temptress nymphs and eager fauns. Lack of ambition, environmental factors – I used to think: I am the owner of my own deficiencies. The only thing I own is what I lack, what I cannot reach, what I've lost, that's what I have, what is actually mine, the empty vacuum that is me. I have what I don't have. And I felt infinitely sorry for myself, filled with a bitterness that sometimes verged on hatred of her, a false hatred (no, I don't think I ever hated her, I still felt aroused whenever I saw her, I desired her, yes, I desired her right up until the end, she was the only woman for me), and a false hatred of Francisco which extended to my father (and did I really hate him, do I still hate him?), or vice versa: love *in absentia.* They were two sides of the same coin – on one side, what seemed to me unattainable and, on the other, what was denied to me: Francisco showing me what could have been, and my father showing me the depths of the nothingness that had become my sole property. He rubbed my nose in what was not to be: the workshop, the furnished apartment where I had no space to call my own, the caged goldfinches that I took care of after Mum died, Saturday afternoons spent in my tiny room whose walls were covered in posters of Deep Purple, Jimi Hendrix and Lou Reed until they grew too old and faded and I tore them down; the velvety bluish or reddish flesh standing at the bar of a club that changed locations and names over the years, but always remained the same, the half-vanished paths traversing the marsh, the smell of damp, rotting vegetation, the feathers of a coot, wet with mud and sticky with blood, the steam given off by the skin of a panting dog. The only things that were mine – before the word 'mine' became only the empty space left by what I had lost – were the few escapes into adventure that I squandered and that Francisco was able to turn to his advantage. We undertook those adventures together, or, rather, Francisco dragged me along in his wake: a few months in Paris, probably for the sole reason that, in order to live life in style or at least try to, it was assumed you had to go to Paris; a spell in London because, at the time, that was where the avant-garde was happening – op art and pop art, everything that was 'in' was there; a few months in Ibiza, before the hippies arrived, but where there were already a few people who grew marijuana and somehow or other got hold of Mexican or Guatemalan peyote, which they chewed slowly with religious unction, following the teachings of their shaman, Castaneda. Laila used to make some delicious hemp-seed cakes and, after eating them, we would laugh or cry at the memory of something or other, and end up snuggled against somebody's chest. I *think* her name was Laila, although I'm not sure now. And I can't remember either if I had anything much else on my mind then. I occasionally returned from those adventures feeling slightly disgusted (although now I couldn't say quite why) and flat broke (and I do know the reason for that). In bullfighting terms, I would say that I felt the bull's tendency to return to the same spot in the ring, I was building my own corral, voluntarily fencing myself in, drawn by the call of house and cradle; if you press me, I would say I was answering the call of the womb, and Leonor gave me that: after all, what is sex but the desire to be enclosed again in that soft, pink arena: to climb back inside someone through any one of her orifices, a desire to return to that warm, dark inner space, to be rocked in amniotic fluid, cradled by mucous secretions. Equally uterine were the washed shirts, ironed and neatly put away in the chest of drawers, the dazzling white underwear (my mother's block of Lagarto soap, her laundry bluing bleach, the clothes swaying in the sun on the washing lines on the terrace roof beneath the blue dome of the sky, I can see it, smell it), the hot succulent risotto in a bowl on the tablecloth and made variously with beans, turnips, greens, pig's trotters or ears, and blood sausage. And yet even now I blame my father for my frequent scamperings back home. That's the version I've given to other people, although not to anyone in the village, I haven't told them anything, what would be the point, I'd just be providing them with fodder for jokes or sideswipes, it's not a good idea to tell people in Olba any truths, but I did talk about it to the friends I met abroad, with some of whom I remained in touch either by letter or phone (what will have become of them? nearly fifty years have passed since then and yet I still remember them, how many of them will now be nothing but skin and bone?), who were friends for a while, and with whom I used to drink a cafe Calva near the Bastille in Paris, opposite the stop for some bus heading out into the suburbs (Vitry, Ivry, Maisons-Alfort, Vincennes), or a pint of beer in Camden; the friends I made during the few months I spent at art school and never saw again, it's the story I've always told myself, whining on about what I could have become but didn't. I tell myself that it was my father who tied me to the workshop, who clipped my wings the way farmers clip the wings of the geese in the pen so that they won't fly away when they hear the call of the migrating birds heading north from the lagoon (ornithologists ring them every year and have proved that they migrate to England, Russia and Sweden, all the great-great-grandchildren of the goose who carried Nils Holgersson in the books I read as a child), the *padre padrone* who demanded that I stay by his side, because all the other children had flown the coop. One of them had travelled beyond the nebulous destination of those migrating geese: Germán had, for some months already, been living in the land of no return. Carmen had just escaped to Barcelona, *almost a child*, said my father with tears in his eyes – the only time I've ever seen him cry – and the third, the quick-change artiste, Juan, was flitting about who knows where. I returned home to the rule of staying put. My father's insistence on this had become more urgent since my eldest brother died. His need to possess. He wanted me here, to be with him, he wanted an assistant and an heir who would give meaning to his work (*at least try to be a carpenter*, he said), he wanted me to give meaning to his life. A workshop in which he was the only carpenter lay bare his empty futurist rhetoric, his egotism, as if everything he had was for him alone. If he wasn't working for someone else's sake, to safeguard someone else's future, his life had no meaning, his betrayal (which is how he saw it) would only have benefited him. He would have been a coward not a martyr, not a cornered bull, like me. My mother was too small a territory over which to exercise his authority. He felt he was too important to govern only a timid little woman whose love he had never been sure of and whose family of well-to-do farmers had never forgiven her precipitate civil marriage to an adolescent carpenter, the son of a poor, left-wing carpenter, who had given her a child. He needed to expand his territory. My brother German's death kept me tied to the workshop, even though he had never wanted to stay there, or precisely because he hadn't wanted to stay and ended up paying for this with disease and death. That's the official version. It sounds pretty convincing, *Death Kept Me Tied to the Workshop* could be the title of some Soviet tragedy or a socialist variant on one of Sergio Leone's spaghetti westerns. But that feeling of guilt has stayed with me right up until now, although I've always had a sense that, biologically, I'm a slave in search of a master, and whether that docility is in my genes or I imbibed it with my mother's milk, I can't tell. A son worthy of my mother, that queen of sighs and of tears, falling as if to be seen by no one, but that were, in fact, intended to be seen by everyone, the apparently furtive dabbing at her eyes with a handkerchief always managed to make her tears the undisputed protagonists of the moment, be it a farewell, an argument, a disagreement, an order flouted or a sudden sharp word. Instant tears and sighs. With my father's growing rage as counterpoint. I've often wondered if perhaps my grandmother wasn't right to doubt that my mother was still in love with him after insisting he give himself up, yes, I've thought that many times, because those falsely modest tears and recriminations were a way of bringing out the worst in him, of stripping away the little pride he had left. His uncontrollable rage at seeing her cry, the slammed doors and the ensuing hours of tense silence as he took refuge in his workshop or in the small room he called his office, with her crying and him furious and then doubtless hating his own brutality and sinking into self-pity for days at a time, despising himself and realising that his whole life had been a mistake. And it's been in that climate, or in the silence that filled it after her death, that I've spent my almost fifty years in the workshop, trying to erase the pages of the past, to leave them blank, adapting my habits and aspirations to those of everyone else – pure nothingness, a glass of brandy at lunchtime, a game of cards in the evening, a visit to the Lovely Ladies Club a couple of times a month (before that, it was called the Cosy Corner and, before that, Caresses, and, as I said, while it may have changed name and location, it's remained essentially the same). Since the 1980s and 1990s, the end of the twentieth century and the beginning of the twenty-first, I've always been alone, avoiding all witnesses, and some people take me for a queer now, no girlfriends now, no lovers, no more prostitutes, I know what some people say behind my back; and others I've run into sometimes, propping up the same bar, consider me an oddball; the workshop, meals with my parents, then just with my father, the two of us alone, not talking to each other, moving about among the machinery and the wood panels, passing each other tools: a gesture, an order, pick that up, grab that plank, we've got to finish this today before we close so that we can deliver it to the customer tomorrow; the house with its three closed bedrooms and my room with its two beds, one of them empty (Uncle Ramón used to sleep there when my brothers were still living at home), except when my sister and her children used to visit, and then the two kids would sleep in the bed next to mine; the rest of the time, I was like the residue of what had once been a family: initially, I used to read and listen to music; then, after my mother died, my father took to sleeping in the room next to mine (why that room and not the one he'd shared with his wife at the far end of the corridor? or the one that used to be my sister's room, also down the corridor? why was he spying on me through the wall, listening to my sighs, to the creakings of my bed, turning them all into guilty secrets?) and banging on the wall whenever I turned up the volume on the record player. I haven't read a book or listened to music for years now, but I do listen to those radio stations that the lonely can call up in the early hours: desertions, unsatisfactory sex, broken hearts, terrible incurable diseases, that's what you hear; at night, the world reveals its unsavoury underbelly. The radio captures it, showing it to us as if wanting to make it more palatable or make us believe that it's more palatable than it really is, and while I listen to this caramel-coated catalogue of woes, I think every night about all the people I knew but haven't seen again; with some I only remember their names, and I wouldn't know how to get in touch with any of them, since we're not connected by a single mutual acquaintance, nothing – people who've fallen through the cracks – and I think of those who've gone – which ones? how many? – and that I'm about to go too, and that when I do, no one will remember them and no one will remember me. No one is thinking about me in the early hours of the morning. I myself am appropriate fodder for such a phone-in: feeling that you're a shadow you could walk through, that you lack all substance, that you're someone who isn't like the others but who tries very hard to conform, except that you're trying to be what the others no longer want to be. I'm a stranger in a house that has never been mine, either by law or habit: the doors never opened or closed when I wanted; my father's anger when, as a young man, I came home late: this isn't a hotel, you know, the next time you can sleep out in the street; I wasn't allowed to put up the paintings or posters I would have liked, my own bedroom has been a burrow guarded by a ferocious ferret: we're not thieves in this house, you know, there's no need to shut your door. Take that rubbish off the walls, by which he meant a few political posters – he was calling 'rubbish' things that were a continuation of his own aspirations, but which, in me, in my ignorance, seemed to him, quite rightly, mere frivolousness – and a few pictures of pop groups that Francisco brought for me: Crosby, Stills, Nash & Young, the Rolling Stones, David Bowie, Lou Reed, Janis Joplin. Whenever anyone comes to Bernal with a problem, he always laughs: *The Lord is good enough to keep us alive, so what are you complaining about?* What *do* I have to complain about? I'm in relatively good health for someone of seventy. Many people would envy me. My cholesterol and my triglyceride levels are on the high side, so are my blood pressure and pulse rate, but then the same could be said of anyone my age lucky enough not to be suffering from something far worse. What is happening to me, what has happened to me, is all of my own making. I snipe at Francisco, and it's true that I'm not as fond of him as when I was a boy or a young man, I don't know when that resentment first began to brew inside me, it was before the business with Leonor, I'm sure, but I don't envy him now as I did for all those years: I recognise that he did, at least, dare to take a chance. He had, of course, put down more solid foundations than I had. In between escapades, he'd found time to study philosophy, take some courses in law and, after that, journalism. He learned to think, to write and to do business as dictated by the rules you need to abide by if you want to succeed. I trotted along beside him like a puppy, but my adventures were pure dissipation, pure prodigality, I thought I was squandering my time, but really I was squandering myself. If you have no idea where you're going, any path will do. I failed to realise this and, as it turns out, I was using up the few provisions Providence had placed in my knapsack. On the other hand, let's not forget that his engine was running on the top-quality fuel his parents were pumping into him, the money he pretended to despise (or that we both pretended to despise), that and a few discreet but useful contacts. These are not venial sins. You shouldn't exclude any details if you want your story to be credible. But apart from that, and perhaps because of that, he had a plan. Travelling, screwing around, taking drugs, going to the cinema, listening to music, discussing this and that with whoever happened to be around, was all part of what Marx calls the primitive accumulation of capital. For his father this had taken the form of those night-time raids, trips with the powers that be to view the cliffs of Misent or visit the local nightclubs. The methods had changed, but the mechanisms still worked. Even spitting on his Falangist father's photo was part of his education. It was a matter of laying the foundations on which to build the business-of-all-businesses that has been Francisco Marsal. This is doubtless easier when your accumulation of capital is not exactly primitive, but a second-generation increment, because your father, in his accu-mulative labours and during his own educative process, did things that were far less instructive than the things you do, which meant that you didn't have to actually dig in the manure one usually needs in order to create a plantation: having a little bit of capital behind you already gives you a sense of continuity, of multiplying synergies, the kind of capital you can't acquire when you jump from one job to another, from one temporary post to another, which is what I did in London and Paris, doing the odd cleaning job here and there, mixing with all kinds of different people, as the Charles Aznavour song says, *rien de vrai-ment précis*: you end up in a tunnel with no light at its end, a suffocatingly hot tunnel that wears you down. It's very unlikely that a dynamic like that will produce a miracle. He was

179

fabricating, or should I say constructing, his CV – I don't know which is the better way of putting it – beginning with a rapid exit from a badly paid job as a schoolteacher, a job he had accepted not because he needed the money, but as one of the rites of passage demanded by his own particular *Bildungsroman*: first it was the Catholic youth movements he belonged to, then the visits to working-class areas, his political engagement, which he again abandoned to devote himself entirely to politics proper, which he also soon tired of, as soon, in fact, as he had woven the web that would allow him to entrap his prey.

'All this stuff about wines and restaurants keeps me on the margins – everyone else wants to get into politics, be a councillor, an adviser, a deputy or a parliamentary hack,' he told me.

That's what he said in the mid-1980s, once he'd got over his political fever. From the great illusion to the great opportunity. The times were in his favour. I doubt very much if we will see such a period of instability and social upheaval in many decades. And so Francisco Marsal did not go on to offer to an expectant humanity treatises on Marxist ethics, if such a discipline exists; or essays on the relationship between the political struggle and the class struggle, or the concept of citizenship in St Paul and St Augustine; nor the great novel he sometimes said he wanted to write (who doesn't want to write a novel? I don't, for one – I didn't want to write novels, I didn't want to be a sculptor, nor had I any desire to be a carpenter, still less work for my father – I wanted to live and yet I didn't know what that meant: for me, living was screwing Leonor until I had screwed myself dry, having her there, at my disposal), no, he wrote articles on such insubstantial subjects as wine, food and travel. I'm not saying those subjects are in themselves insubstantial, Francisco wrote articles about wine and gastronomy, and it's true that wine and food are important, of course they are: we are what we eat and drink. What's so fragile about it is trying to capture in words something that vanishes and ceases to exist the moment it's consumed, you can't write or theorise about or try to hold on to such a non-communicable experience. The mystics wrote a lot about this. How, for example, do you describe ecstasy? Each bottle of wine is different. Each dish tastes different, even if you cook it using the same recipe. On one of his visits to Olba, he was soon proudly handing me a card: Vinofórum *Francisco Marsal. Editor.* He was no longer the young hack writing pieces about wine under the pseudonym *Pinot Grigio* (an ironic name, since he did not consider himself to be grey at all: his articles fizzed with wit). The word 'Editor' beneath the name of a prestigious magazine instilled respect – that was all in the late 1980s, when a food magazine was no longer a newsletter for restaurant owners, nor a recipe book for housewives, something suitable for a largely female public, but a product to be read by successful men looking for information about the expensive eateries that appeared in its pages, about which wines they should buy and where. They wanted to know how much they should pay and what social kudos they could gain from eating in a certain place or ordering a particular bottle of wine or a particular dish, because they now had access to anything they wanted, but (like bewildered children in a toy shop or sweetshop) they had still not yet learned how to behave in that world; they had to learn very quickly to differentiate themselves from the other waves of arrivistes coming up fast behind, who were equally eager to succeed and hungry for contact with what they believed would soon be their world, so that, when they did finally arrive, they would no longer have to behave like bewildered children. They wanted to know those things before they actually got them, they wanted to know their names, qualities and defects, know their price and their value, not so much their use value, but their exchange value, their image value, because the actual moment of tasting was of little importance, what mattered was the previous stage, adorning the table with those bottles, adorning themselves with those bottles and those table-cloths in those restaurants. We are not just what we eat, as the old philosophers said and as I myself had assumed; we are, above all, where we eat and with whom and how correctly we name the things that we eat, and correctly order the correct things from the menu and do so before witnesses, and we are, most especially, the person who then tells others what we ate and with whom. If you know all that about someone, you know precisely what kind of animal you're dealing with. And how high he can fly. Whether he's worth wasting fifteen minutes of your time on or standing him a drink and even arranging to meet for supper another night and establishing a relationship. Or whether, on the other hand, he's the one eager to get into conversation with you and you're the one making excuses, saying you're late for a meeting and glancing at your watch before hurriedly making your escape, even though he wants to invite you to supper. And then there are those who gab on to you for half an hour about the virtues of a wine they've never tasted in their life or about a restaurant they'll never visit. Francisco explained it to me: That's what upstarts do; the first phase of ambition; the Genesis: In the beginning was the word. The word precedes being (or at least provides a temporary substitute, an *Ersatz*) – finding out from books and magazines what other people experience on a daily basis. Theory preceding empirical knowledge, the performative value of words as the first step up the ladder. All you had to say was 'I want' – you say those words and everything's set in motion. I didn't dare. It seemed to me that Francisco had actually arrived somewhere, it didn't matter where, and so I failed to realise that the job of editing the magazine didn't use up enough of his energy or, more import-antly, his ambition: he was on the road to somewhere else. He had moved on from standing in the pulpit as the apostle of wine and food to being the sleeping partner of the restaurant that Leonor ran right up until the end, and which was soon declared one of the country's gastronomic temples: calling it a sanctuary rather than a temple would have been to devalue the perfection of Leonor's croquettes, which were, in the words of restaurant critics, sublime: critics like to use such extravagant language; the four last things – death, judgement, hell or glory – to describe a Béarnaise sauce. That's gourmands for you. A dish of *bacalao al pilpil* can send them straight up to heaven, the lucky souls. I read Francisco's articles in the Sunday papers, again following in his footsteps, pursuing him, watching him. Leonor's bacalao, woodcock cooked à la Leonor, ah, yes, *la bécasse*, Leonor's *bécasse*. I know that, over time, her enemies began to call her La Bécasse, as her thin face and pointed nose grew sharper, her anorexia became more marked, first signs of the illness eating away at her flesh. I read about that in a newspaper article. Francisco told me that customers from as far away as the Basque country would come to eat there: every lunchtime, a dozen or so politicians and financiers would gather round the tables of the Cristal de Maldón restaurant: smelling and tasting and chewing over fashion, prestige, the avant-garde, feeling between their teeth the crunch of power along with the toast on which they spread the purée made from the woodcock's guts. A few years later, the restaurant was awarded two Michelin stars, although I didn't need Francisco to tell me that – besides, he and Leonor almost never came back to Olba, well, she never returned and he did only very rarely, for his father's funeral, for family matters, to divide up the inheritance with his siblings. No, the two Michelin stars were reported on the evening news, and I read about them later over a coffee in the bar. It was in the morning newspapers too. I leaf through them every day when I'm standing at the bar. I encountered Leonor again on the TV while I was peeling an orange after lunch in my dining room, they repeated it on

Channel 1 news and showed a brief interview with her, the first woman in Spain to be awarded two Michelin stars, an extraordinary achievement in the macho world of haute cuisine, in a publication as thoroughly machista as *Michelin*. (How many female chefs have been awarded two stars in France? Or indeed in the rest of the world? I can't remember if they said there was one in France or not.) I saw her often after that, as chefs occupied more and more TV space, and as Leonor embarked on a series of programmes about taste: the cuisine of aromas, the cuisine of the senses, molecular gastronomy. I would watch her, in her chef's hat and white coat, posing behind a tray of fish, holding a bunch of asparagus, a bouquet of greens, or a porcelain dish on which lay a grouper, Leonor smiling, her teeth glinting under the spotlights as if she were in a toothpaste ad (do they use that tooth-whitening stuff on your teeth before they film you, you bitch?), and I would have to turn off the television before she finished preparing whatever it was she was demonstrating and before she answered the questions put to her by the presenter, because the image on the screen immediately fused with the pictures I still had stored away in my head and which suddenly leapt out, interposing themselves over and over, preventing me from seeing her actual image and instead dragging me back into a world of confused memories, both real and invented, and all unbearable. By then, Francisco, on his rare visits to Olba, no longer talked to me as a journalist or a writer; he talked to me about his powerful position on the magazine, his powerful position in certain wineries, his vital advice when it came to blending wines – what he called *le coupage* – choosing the casks, approving the labels and – most important of all – determining what he called 'the philosophy of the wine', which dictated its price. The more philosophy, the higher the price. And then there were his other businesses, Leonor's restaurant, his various hotel projects, which involved hobnobbing with businessmen and politicians. The long nose of La Bécasse would appear on the screen, and what I would see was Leonor lying naked in Francisco's arms. I can see her now. Leonor with her legs locked around him; Leonor's face peering over that male shoulder, her eyes fixed on mine, her mouth half open, and his buttocks pumping up and down, her feet drumming on them. Leonor on the front cover of a fashion magazine, holding a platter on which lies an intensely red, cardinal-red lobster, which, when I look more closely, is actually a bloody doll curled up in a foetal position. I sit bolt upright in bed. I scream. I demand to be left in peace. Memories. The Francisco you see now, so good-natured and simple, playing a game of cards in the evening with his fellow villagers, out walking in the country, strolling along the beach at Misent, hiking up Montdor, using a stick to help himself along, because Montdor is all rocks and thorny shrubs, the perfect backdrop for one of those re-enactments of the Passion that many villages put on at Easter, it's the most inhospitable place you can imagine, a vertiginous forty-five- or fifty-degree slope, sharp, skittering pebbles among which grow thorn bushes of every variety nature can dream up: thistles, gorse, scrub oak, and God knows what else: I can see him on some mornings from the balcony of my house, heading for the mountain, panting hard, I imagine, climbing that steep slope, a born-again countryside lover and guardian of its traditions and symbols: the harsh sacred mountain, the earth fertilised by the bones of his ancestors, or, rather, the bones of the fugitives hunted down by his ancestors, by his own father, some of whom must still be there, their bones crumbling into the soil, a surf-and-turf landscape, irrigated and unirrigated land, against a backdrop of sea and marsh; our ancestors used to make that rich, succulent risotto with turnips, pig's trotters and black pudding, more or less as we make it today, I suppose, and he records this in the book he's writing, manifestations of the spirit

185

of the race, the *Volkgeist*, the homeland to which the pilgrim has returned to take refuge: with what joy, my home, I now behold thee (that was the version we sang in the school choir, the song of the pilgrims at the end of *Tannhäuser* as they gaze down upon Rome: we also sang the Falangist anthem, 'Cara al sol' and another Falangist hymn: 'Montañas nevadas'; it was obligatory, and it drove my father mad, but there was no other school I could go to), the land appropriated by man, the culture that has grown up there: the rocky slopes and the risotto, the anisettes and herb liqueurs, and the groves of oranges and grapefruits and gardens full of climbing beans twining about canes, and the fields of broad beans bent low by the rain that the east wind draws up from the sea, and the green leaves of pepper and tomato plants; and the marsh, which was once the basis of our cuisine and is now an abandoned swamp that no one visits. He records all these things. There you have it: the endless lunches with local bigwigs, slippery Justino and the now vanished Pedrós; Carlos, the manager of the local bank, who says he chose to be transferred here rather than to Misent, so he can stay in touch with nature, but above all, although he doesn't say this, because in Misent a house like the one he owns at the foot of Montdor would cost him a fortune; Mateu, the dealer in fruit and vegetables, who exports to half of Europe; Bernal, who contaminated the lagoon with his roofing felt (how many centuries does it take for poisonous asbestos to disappear?); the card games in the evening in the Bar Castañer, where the cream of Olba gathers, by which I mean the property owners, the car dealers, the owners of supermarkets and whole hectares of fruit trees; bank clerks, council workers; active participants in deals both clean and murky, a fauna as prickly as the shrubs on Montdor: all gathered around the marble tables that echo to the sound of dominoes being slammed down; the one who wanted to imitate the Kennedys and who has disappeared, carrying off with him all my savings; the trafficker of human flesh; the one leaving half the population of Olba homeless (ah, those mortgages so blithely taken out in a happier decade); the teacher who conducts the local band, and, sometimes, even the pleasant, absent-minded philosophy teacher from the secondary school in Misent, who lives in Olba because – and here the Epicurean philosopher and the ruthless bank manager agree – it's a more peaceful, authentic place: once again, the homeland, *with what joy, my home, I now behold thee*, covering up the economic fact that a house in Olba costs exactly half what a house in Misent would cost; like Francisco, some are peacefully retired, others – like the man from the bank – are in the first phase of their socio-economic rise. A card game that enjoys great local prestige has been joined by the local carpenter, who, since Francisco's return, has changed tables and now plays with the crème de la crème, legitimised by his vaguely well-travelled, vaguely adventurous, vaguely hippy past and by his vaguely cultivated present (you can have a conversation with the carpenter, he knows what he's talking about), and by his mysterious, solitary, sedentary life, shut away from the world, which has gone on for decades now; legitimised by the fact that I often used to join Pedrós at the bar and, above all, because Francisco slaps me on the back and refers to me openly as his childhood friend, his travelling companion, his colleague who has rejected the vanities of this world to embrace the profession of those who prefer a simple life on the margins, saints like St Joseph, a good artisan. More like the perfect profession for a cuckold, I think. Francisco casually stirs his post-prandial coffee, as if that ritual and that way of life were the only acceptable ones, the same nonchalance with which, at one time, he aligned himself – as if inadvertently – with what my old friend Morán, whom I met in Ibiza and whose articles I also used to read in the national press (I don't know what's become of him either), defined as 'an elite poised to plunder'. Now, *beatus ille*, he has, in the serenity of his mature years, embraced scorn for the court and praise of the village. Here the days and months pass, and there's not so much as a hint of Francisco's former alliance with that ruthless, voracious elite, no sense of what was once the very hub of his existence. It's as if nothing had happened between us or within us since those shared years of childhood and adolescence; I even find myself believing it, I can even understand why he bought that house, after all, who doesn't want the perfect place in which to spend his declining years, a luxurious monastery, until, that is, you go to Misent with him one day, and, as if by chance and after much random wandering about, we find that our walk – apparently unplanned – has led us to the marina. And he distractedly raises one arm and points, saying, look, Esteban, just perfect for a little trip around the bay one morning, his finger still pointing, inviting me to look, and what he's inviting me to look at, what, according to him, is *just perfect for a little trip around the bay one morning*, is a sailing boat moored in the port, an elegant sailing boat that turns out to be his, the little boat he'd mentioned once, as if in passing, while you were discussing something else, and whose existence you'd completely forgotten about, because you didn't believe there was much truth in it: a little boat, you assumed, the kind that any poor sod could afford during the boom years, what people call a motorboat and which is little more than a dingy. But no, you suddenly realise that the reason he's taken you on this excursion is so you won't die without seeing it, yes, he has to make sure that the carpenter sees it, he has to deliver the *coup de grâce* before the carpenter bites the dust of a natural death, pretty much as a matador does with a bull, finishing the animal off quickly before the spectators start booing because the bull is taking too long to die, and as we all know, no one is so young that he might not die tomorrow, so it's just as well that the carpenter should see the sailing boat and feel envy and pain and sadness, I may have lost Leonor – except that you lost her first, I think to myself. I wonder, did he ever find out about us? Did Leonor ever tell him? I don't believe so, a relationship with no added value is just a piece of junk you get rid of – but I have a beautiful house and a sailing boat (it's like that nursery rhyme: I have, I have, but you have nothing, I have three sheep, one to milk and another to keep), and so he invites you to jump on board, you walk across the teak deck, he takes you down to the saloon with its kitchen and its dining table, which is laid as if for some imminent banquet, and the little bar with its shelves of bottles, and he opens the door of the bathroom, and then shows you the two bedrooms, bloody hell, this is just amazing, says the artisan, the cuckolded St Joseph, so skilled at planing a piece of wood, who climbs up a few steps to see the screens of blinking lights on the instrument panel. It's very comfortable, says Francisco, adding for further emphasis, yes, it really is very comfortable. As if I were trembling with admiration and emotion and pride just to know that what I see and touch and caress belongs to my old friend, my travelling companion, and as if he wanted to bring me back down to a modest reality. There's the plain language he uses as proof: yes, she's a cosy old thing. You can sail her or use the motor, she's got a 200-horsepower engine. But this cosy old thing isn't moored in the harbour built by the town council for the small boats of those who define themselves as the new middle class and who are, in fact, a conglomerate of variants of the conscienceless working class created by Thatcherism and which the current crisis is sweeping away, taking them down a peg or two, and, as a consequence, many of the small boats moored in that popular, municipal harbour now have cardboard signs saying FOR SALE BARGAIN PRICE. No, Francisco doesn't have his yacht moored there, but in the Marina Esmeralda, where the yachts of German or Gibraltarian or Russian millionaires rub shoulders, thirty-metre-long boats that belong to traffickers of something or other – sausages, mass-produced bread and cakes, works of art, money or weapons – yachts owned by builders who've put more tons of cocaine into the market than they have cement; launderers of dollars, euros, pounds. Is there anyone in that marina who has earned an honest living, apart from the waiters, who, tray in hand, ply the quayside bars, alongside the shops offering yachts for sale at more than half a million euros? And even those waiters can be rather alarming if they happen to meet your eye while pouring out the whisky-on-the-rocks you ordered. They're not waiters, they're thugs, bodyguards, dealers in stolen goods and illegal substances, pimps, hit men, mules, drug smugglers, the rent boys of yacht owners, the servants of smarmy mafiosi who, when interviewed on the local TV news, describe themselves as owners of nocturnal marketing businesses. Yes, Francisco, that's what *le grand monde* is. I know the good life is essentially contrary to the law and to justice, and is rigorously incompatible with charity, but life is short, and no one is so young that he cannot die tomorrow and no one so old as to think he cannot live another year. Do you remember that quote? You studied philosophy at university and you read it out to me once, to this idiot whose father was forcing him to be an artist and who didn't know what he wanted to be, but knew absolutely what he didn't want to be. In showing me his yacht – as when he showed me his house – Francisco is confirming that for him the rustic life – playing cards at the Bar Castañer included – is merely a game in a toy shop, and that these are the rules imposed by the game he has chosen to play, like in the game of the goose, where, if you land on a square with a goose on it, that allows you to jump over your competitors; or when you play Battleship, you call out the number and letter of the target square and the other player says hit or miss, and you can then either cross it out or not: every game has its rules, rules that are only valid for as long as the game lasts, and that's certainly so in his case, the rules governing his game as humble villager last only as long as the evening round of cards, and those rules no longer obtain (one day, we really must share a fantastic peaty whisky I've put aside especially for us, he says, closing a small wooden door) when he allows you a second viewing of his house, the now restored Civera house; and the carpenter who never even made it to cabinetmaker grade sees the furniture: kingwood, rosewood, mahogany, the glass cabinets in which Francisco keeps ancient volumes bound in silk or shagreen, then there are the paintings by Gordillo, engravings by Tàpies, watercolours by Barceló and Broto. But all this must be worth a fortune, I say, and he laughs, yes, I haven't done too badly, I'll tell you about it some time, and so with him I always have the impression that when he talks about the people he hates (he specialises in public rants against unscrupulous businessmen and unethical bankers, fulminating against the mad speculative property bubble of the last few years, although not, of course, when he's with Pedrós, Justino or Bernal), he is, in fact, inveighing against himself, shitting on his own biography – the cosmopolitan Mr Hyde versus the card-playing country bumpkin Dr Jekyll. But all this paints a very hasty, even clumsy portrait. We need to delve back into his past as a young Catholic with a social vocation, a member of JEC, JOC and HOAC and so on. He even considered becoming a seminarian; he yearned for justice, aspired to a universal, egalitarian happiness, well, who didn't at the time, with all that talk of liberation theology: becoming a worker-priest in Franco's Spain or a guerrilla priest – as Camilo Torres went on to be – somewhere in Latin America, but his cock was made of a material all too susceptible to the magnet of sex, a psycho-physiological remora that many priests manage to transform into a precious pastoral tool thanks to the invaluable collaboration of that authentic network of erotic contacts – the confessional;

although what closed that particular path to him was, I believe, his realisation that power within the Church was being offered to him as a very demanding fruit, born of a combination of overly complex codes and rhetorics, strict regulations, and, at the same time, certain very subtle movements, insinuations, hints, a slightly raised eyebrow, an imperceptible pursing of the lips. He preferred to take more direct action than was usual among the clergy, whose complicated labyrinth, designed on baroque lines, was the legacy of the Council of Trent, which required that any advances should be made very slowly indeed; going through the motions of submitting to the hierarchy, engaging in secret intrigues, irrational surrenders or acts of obedience, too much whispering and not enough shouting, and shouting was precisely what politics offered him when he took it by the horns in the late 1970s: politics, it must be said, was a far franker world, its tactics and strategies more overt (the very opposite of his father's modus operandi), and one's own image had a public dimension, true, Francisco's first steps were taken in the age of clandestinity – even though the transition had already begun – but all the people involved knew each other, and there were no secret negotiations in the corridors of parishes, sacristies and archbishops' palaces: you ran the cells, you held semi-clandestine meetings and you gained a certain prestige, still under your *nom de guerre*, while the dictatorless dictatorship continued to crumble, but once democracy was in place, that was it – stripped of your *nom de guerre*, you appeared under your real name, and with this one slogan, politics as the supreme and almost unique value, far superior to any other form of social activism: you would climb onto the platform and shout, your shouts amplified thanks to a superb sound system (paid for by your Swedish, German and French comrades, social democrats showing their solidarity with the anti-Franco struggle) and accompanied by drums and flutes played at full blast, *a desalambrar, a desalambrar, dale tu mano al indio, dale que te hará bien* – and this was a real going out into the world, not spending your life shuffling around gloomy sacristies, dark corridors and damp offices full of crucifixes and paintings of martyred or wounded saints, pale as boiled chard, darkened by hundreds of years of exposure to the smoke of candles that appeared to be made of the same yellowish substance as the faces inhabiting those rooms, places on the very borders of the dread continent of eschatology: a narrow frontier where the living merge with the dead, down a path between today's shadows and the deep abyss of the shadows waiting for us just around the corner. Although, in reality, as long as he remained involved in politics – or, later on, in his professional life as a writer or businessman or whatever he was – he still appeared to behave like a priest, and showed a definite penchant for secret meetings and behind-the-scenes scheming: he carefully hid the tips of his fingers when he was pulling the strings, a born operator, that was what his fellow party members called him: he showed his eyes, full of convincing, encouraging fire; his lips, from which proclamations issued forth; his chest which filled with air when he was about to bellow out the relevant slogan, but he always hid his nimble hands, capable of pulling dozens of different strings at once. He would tell me all this with great amusement, proud of his own deviousness. It was quite safe to tell me; after all, I knew no one to whom I could pass on the information. His taste for intrigue has never left him: when he abandoned politics, he went on to manipulate a number of winery owners from behind the tasting tables, because the price of their wines depended in large measure on the points awarded them by *Vinofórum*, the magazine he ended up editing, having stabbed a few rivals in the back, rivals who, it seems – at least according to him – resisted with unusual ferocity, resorting to an email war, sending the then editor reports linking Francisco to all those wineries who were paying him for his services, and

193

with whom he, with jesuitical sangfroid, denied ever having had any contact (it's a speciality of his co-religionists, whether religious or political, to do the opposite of what they say, and not to let the left hand they're showing know what their thieving right hand is up to); from the dark den of the magazine's office in which he had taken refuge as a fugitive from political intrigues, he rose as inexorably as a bubble in a glass of champagne, until he reached a prominent position on the board of the editorial group (the surface of the champagne, from which one can see − as if from a high-angle camera − the other bubbles rising up from below: the office was on the thirty-somethingth floor of a skyscraper in Madrid's elegant Paseo de la Castellana), producing magazines, wine guides, publications about hotels and restaurants, a couple of monthly travel magazines (one for upmarket clients and another for downmarket clients: on the cover of the former the ten best hotels in the world; on the latter the ten best-value campsites on the Costa Dorada), as well as a stake in various hotel chains and wine and spirits distributors. He told me about this on his visits to Olba, much as Stanley would tell his friends about his journey into darkest Africa. An exciting adventure. From there − and more to amuse himself than anything − he was at liberty to raise up to the skies or trample into the mud the faithful legions of chefs, who would distribute his photo among waiters and waitresses, who had been given express orders to raise the alarm the moment Francisco crossed the threshold: take a good look at this bastard and remember his face. As soon as he appears, tell me, we don't want to let him escape (chefs weren't exactly stars then, this was an earlier phase, when, as restaurateur Arzak said, chefs were just beginning to merit the same respect as engineers, architects and doctors). The chefs − like men on a Gothic altarpiece condemned to the fires of hell, surrounded by flames and prodded by a legion of kitchen boys in the guise of dark devils − scurried about among saucepans and ovens whenever the head waiter appeared in the kitchen to announce that the critic, Francisco Marsal, formerly known as *Pinot Grigio*, had just walked into the restaurant. He extorted money from oenologists who would work themselves to death experimenting with Merlots, Syrahs and Viogniers, foreign stock in which he believed and which he had recommended, assuring the oenologists that he would back them all the way in their experiments. You'll get a ninety-three at the tasting table. Guaranteed. With a bit of luck, three or four points more. That would put you up there among the very best. It's your choice whether you want to accept the offer. Afterwards, they might or might not get a ninety-three: they would have to hold further discussions about the fine print, talk actual numbers, and then there were the ads in the magazines belonging to the group, the confidential contract to design their publicity campaign, including fold-out brochures and labels, establishing the all-important philosophy of the wine, and all this began with a suggestion that they change the original oenologist for another man who the publishing company was interested in turning into a media figure, following his appointment to a big consortium for a wine and spirits distributor with which the magazine had a close relationship, and which was, in fact, one of its main sources of finance. Francisco's articles in the group's magazines, his carefully honed 'letters from the editor', his judgements at tastings, all had quite a lot to do with consolidating the prestige of what are now some of the most expensive wineries. And he succeeded in transforming his wife from a cook who'd opened a small restaurant simply to stave off boredom into a gastronomic star: four tables and an oven, they said modestly when they came to Olba shortly before the restaurant opened in Madrid (I think that was the last time she came with him), something very simple, rather like those small bourgeois restaurants of yesteryear. I wish you'd come and see it, promise me you will, Francisco said, knowing that I would never dream of doing so. To start with, I had no suit, no tie. I had nothing that would satisfy the dress codes of the new age. Leonor sat silently beside him, as if we only knew each other by sight. Soon afterwards, she was saying that standing in front of an oven in the restaurant was just an extension of her role as housewife, that's what she said in the interviews her husband arranged for her in the colour pages of the Sunday papers, while he travelled the world training his nose and taste buds on Burgundies, Rhine wines and Moselles. (I don't know how you can taste anything. Your sense of smell must be completely fucked by all that cocaine. Don't exaggerate, I only snort it once in a blue moon, when I come here, just so that I can switch off from everything and talk to you, ah, yes, the good old days.) And the crepinettes flavoured with Piedmontese truffles, the Kobe beef carpaccio, and filling the cunts of five continents with whipped cream – speciality of the house. The housewife in her modest restaurant with just half a dozen tables became the first Spanish woman to be awarded two Michelin stars, as well as garnering the highest number of points in all the food guides, including the one published by *Vinofórum*. But she's no longer here, and the stars she was so proud of have burned out, and her widower husband gently places his three of clubs on the table and says:

'The easiest way to attract attention is to do extravagant, stupid things. Standing out from the crowd because of your work is a lot harder. Appearing in the newspaper signing a contract to refurbish the dressing room of the football pitch or the south stand, or handing over a cheque to the local events committee that will pay for all the bulls for this year's bullfights. That's easy. Who else is going to waste money on such stupidities? They applaud you on the opening day or when, in front of the press and the mayor, you hand over your cheque to the councillor in charge of sports, but there's an end to it, and even then, at that very moment, someone will doubt-less be slagging you off, the locals – including the ones who will benefit most from your generosity – will be calling you a spendthrift, a braggart, and wondering aloud if you're into some form of trafficking, drugs or guns or money laundering, in order to earn the cash you're spending like there's no tomorrow. And instead of climbing up the ladder, you're on your way down. A few months later, everyone has forgotten your generous gift, but not your dubious reputation.'

'Yes, if you're hoping to be remembered for doing something no one else is fool enough to do, namely, throwing away your money, well, even though people are more than happy to pick it up, you're on your own there,' says Bernal.

Nevertheless, on this luminous winter morning, I – one of the innocuous ones – am the person looking for a stage on which to recreate the natural order, at least in part, with an intimate little drama, a chamber work, offering to restore what history destroyed. I'm preparing the moment, Dad, I've taken it upon myself to return you to the place where you would have gone if it hadn't been for us, I'm restoring the mutilated body of your dignity to make you once more fully a man, a man I never knew, because my other brother, my sister and I only arrived after the mutilation, the children of a reluctantly accepted servitude, beings with no real shape, domestic creatures with no aspirations. The whole country had been deprived of aspirations, and nothing could grow in the midst of all that greyness. It's up to me now to fulfil your long-postponed wish and return you to your comrades. In fact, I'm putting into practice the lesson my uncle taught me: grant an appropriate death to each creature you hunt, as a restorative act of gratitude to nature, which – like the great tragedy of history or the miracle of transubstantiation – fills with its essence even the tinest particle, for it is born, lives and dies in each and every one of its manifestations. Use the appropriate bait for each fish. I'm returning to him what I owe him as a son, my life in exchange for several lives, I'm fulfilling my anonymous role in the chain of history, I'm going with him so that in the final act he will lack for nothing, it's a decisive role, and one that he himself cannot undertake. Civilised peoples honour their dead with a feast held at the graveside. As a proxy at your funeral ceremony, I am a fly growing gradually desiccated, trapped in the sticky web, an insect condemned to be encrypted and caught in the spider's web of other people's voices, an echo without a voice: yes, Don Esteban, of course the smell of the orange groves here is good, I'm not saying it isn't, but the smell of the coffee plant seems to me finer, more delicate, more elegant, you only say you prefer the smell of orange blossom because you've never smelled the flowers of a coffee plant, isn't that right? The perfume is sweeter and the flowers are prettier, like little white, perfumed roses which, in that warm, welcoming climate, fill the air with a scent so dense you can almost touch it. Everything smells of coffee and cinnamon and cocoa. Tropical smells. You've never seen a coffee flower, have you, or the fruit of the cacao tree? You never see them here, not even cacao pods. All you can buy is that powdered stuff they sell in the supermarket, and it's anyone's guess what that's really made of. The Indians valued the pods and seeds of the cacao tree so highly that they used them as currency. Hot chocolate, they believed, was the drink of the gods. The other great advantage of those plantations is the unobstructed view: it's proper countryside, plantation upon plantation growing on the sides of the hills, with the occasional small ranch or a bigger farm in the background, or else on a slope with the snowy peaks of the volcanoes behind, not like here, where all you see are buildings under construction and rubbish dumps, the landscape here isn't calm and quiet, I mean, even on the really narrow streets you have to take care because of all the traffic, the cars and the trucks, it's like that even now, and yet Wilson tells me that all the building work has stopped. It's completely different over there: everything is so beautiful, really it is. It's not the land or the climate that makes us leave, it's the situation. Men have destroyed paradise, and I don't think God, who they say can do all things, will ever be able to forgive them for that. He may not want to. The web of voices entrapping you, like an insect caught in a web that suddenly breaks.

Shall I change channels, Dad? Do you want to watch another Western or would you prefer the one about the suicide bombers who are about to explode at any moment? The afternoon is gone in a flash, it gets dark depressingly early in winter, so as soon as we've finished eating, I'll draw the curtains so that we can't see the night outside and can continue prowling around for a while with these rustlers, beneath the implacable desert sun in Texas or Kansas. So much desert, so much dryness. I need to go and get myself a beer because the dust kicked up by those cowboys is starting to irritate my throat, even though the radiator is barely enough to warm the room or absorb the damp in the air. Here, in Olba, it's the damp rather than the cold that makes winter evenings so unpleasant. I leave you watching a film while I take a stroll around Olba, I leave you securely tethered to your chair with the sheet and join Justino and Francisco in the bar for a couple of games of cards or dominoes, and here I am, back in time to watch the news, in time, too, to eat our last supper: the Eucharist of a slice of ham and a glass of milk, our sacred nightly ritual, communion in the form of a solid Christ and a liquid one, just like the early Christians, a custom restored by the Second Vatican Council. It doesn't matter if I get back a little later tonight, because you'll be having your midday meal late anyway, which means you won't have your lunch and supper too close together. After supper, I'll leave you in your armchair for a while before changing your incontinence pads and washing you. At night, I only wash between your legs. A light immersion, like the priest, who, after Mass, dips just the tips of his fingers in a little holy water. It's the same in our ceremony, a dribble of warm water applied between pad and skin. Latex gloves, warm water and one of those soapy wipes that nurses use to wash patients in hospitals, and then more warm water, until I've left his bottom looking like a newborn baby's: like a wrinkled, purplish prune. I've taken to applying some methylated spirit gel to my nostrils to dull my sense of smell. I saw a television programme that showed some forensic doctors doing just that before examining a corpse, and I decided to follow their example. Even so, the smell never leaves the house, however much bleach or soap I use. It impregnates the walls, furniture, clothes. The smell of an old man's incontinence pads. It impregnates me too. At bedtime, I just give him a quick wash. The shower can wait until morning. A shower wakes him up, and what I'm trying to do is make sure he goes to bed feeling dog-tired. So that he won't have the energy to get out of bed and possibly fall over, as he's done before now; so that he won't suddenly decide to remove his incontinence pad and smear shit all over the room. This has been my daily schedule, my timetable, ever since I had to let you go, Liliana. It always amazed me that performing these tasks didn't seem to faze you at all (it really didn't). He's so kind, your dad. Mine wasn't

200

like that. I don't miss the people I left behind in Colombia, well, perhaps my mum a little, what I miss most is the countryside, which is just unimaginably beautiful. I look at the palm trees here, and they seem like toys compared to our tall, elegant palms, so thin and erect, they look as if they were reaching up to the sky, and you can't help thinking, how can such a slender trunk support that great plume of palm leaves fifty metres above the ground, and the trunk is soft and smooth and almost blue. I don't know why no one has thought to bring some over here, although they're probably very delicate and need a lot of water, as well as the mild climate we have back there, the high pastures for cattle, the hills where they grow the coffee, bananas, sugar cane and mangoes: the higher up you go, the less intense the tropical heat; it's really fertile there, naturally green and lush, and that's at more than two thousand metres up, where the air is soft and pure. I think that if you could grow those palm trees anywhere, no one would ever plant any other sort. There's no comparison, but the problem, as I say, is that they need tropical heat and altitude, they wouldn't grow just anywhere, it's impossible, I mean just look at how big Africa is and yet, from what they say on the TV, there are very few places in Africa to compare with the conditions we have there, because Africa's very flat, at least in those documentaries, you might get one very tall, snow-capped mountain, but the rest is either dead flat or low hills. Which just goes to show what a topsy-turvy place the world is, there's our country, a paradise, and we have to leave it because men have turned it into a little hell. What with all the bare, rocky mountains you have here and the arid plains I saw in Castile when I travelled down on the bus from the airport in Madrid, you Spaniards ought to be the ones emigrating to Colombia, the way you did all those centuries ago, and yet here we are leaving Colombia and coming to this arid place, where the moment you leave the little fringe of greenness along the coast, it's nothing but dry earth and rocks. What are you saying, Liliana, this is the closest thing to paradise on earth; half the retirees in the world want to live here in one of those little look-but-don't-touch houses, with no foundations and plasterboard walls. But be quiet now, Liliana, no, I'm sorry, but your voice troubles me – I need to think about my own affairs, about the way my father dictates the rhythm of my days, as he always has, and even more so now that you're not here, the two of us alone, and me at his beck and call: cooking his lunch, serving it up, washing the dishes, washing him, putting him to bed, loading the washing machine with his clothes (the all-pervading smell that never leaves the house). While in prison, of course, he had to work for his jailers. They treated us like slaves, he said, breaking up rocks, carrying stones, they didn't have whips like the ones you see in films about the Nazis, but when one of them got angry, he would take off his belt and, with his trousers almost hanging off him, he'd beat and kick the hell out of you just for stopping for a moment to wipe the sweat from your brow. Yes, Dad, but you had to put up with forced labour, or disciplinary labour as they called it then, for only a year or a year and a half, whereas mine has lasted more than half a century, you didn't even have to take off your belt and beat me, just a word or a look and I was like a frightened lamb: it's been a very long prison sentence. Before, Liliana would stay with you – Liliana, who, I believed, was going to look after me as well, who was as much mine as I am yours. You'll always have me, Señor Esteban, Liliana, her *sancocho* stew her pipián sauce the palm trees the background murmur of her chatter, she would usually stay with him until supper, the smell of coffee the smell of cocoa beans the smell of leafy trees cool leaves freshly washed by the tropical rain the explosion of colour of a flame tree, haven't you ever seen one? It's one great mass of flowers, a burst of scarlet fire against the green of the forests; and further off, there's the mauve fire of the jacaranda, and she would feed him and bath him, and that was usually the time I chose to go out and have a card game at the bar. When I leave him alone in the house, sunk in his armchair, I'm always afraid that, during the game, someone will ask after him, will say: how's your father doing? Who's he with, the Colombian woman? I hate having to lie and say yes, he's with the Colombian woman, as you know, I can't leave him alone for a moment, because, of course, the person who's just asked me the question might well run into her a minute later in the street, someone might find out that she doesn't come to the house any more and that I leave my father alone at home. Social services might intervene then and accuse me of neglect, ill-treatment and who knows what else, I might even get sent to prison, people are very ready to demand that others act responsibly, very keen to point out other people's obligations and very reluctant to take on their own, and they're certainly not prepared to lend a helping hand. God, that would be a joke, after spending all my life under his thumb to then, at the last moment, be accused of neglecting him. That would be the final irony if I were to end up in jail, in clink. Although I'm pretty sure they won't arrive in time. And so I lie and say, yes, she's there and my father's being well looked after, watched over. The Colombian woman, that's what my partners at the card game call Liliana. Could you help me fold the sheets? Could you help me put the pillowcases on (our hands briefly touch)? Could you advance me a few euros to get me through the next few days? I haven't even got enough money to buy bread, it's been a terrible month, awful, there's the schoolbooks for the children, the older boy needs new clothes, they grow out of their clothes so quickly, or else they tear them playing football in the playground at school, then there's shoes as well, it's so hard to keep up, and Wilson is having a really tough time finding work. Most construction work has stopped, the bars and the grocers aren't doing much business either, they're firing people left, right and centre, there isn't much work at all and what work there is, is really badly paid (in the bar, during the game, Justino, always eagle-eyed, comments: that Colombian woman's got a nice arse on her), to be honest, I can't say I like Spain, or that things have worked out well for me here, not that I'm complaining, but it hasn't been as I imagined it would be when I arrived, (hmmm, a little low-slung perhaps, but nice and firm, especially in those tight jeans she wears, you can see her bum crack, and all the men laugh, yeah, a glimpse of her nice, firm arse, she looks like she's going to burst out of her jeans, I don't know how the bitches squeeze themselves into them, does she give you a bit of a dip when she washes your father? jokes Bernal, does she change your nappies too? does she sponge you down? yeah, does she rub you down or does she just get you wet? I really don't like them talking about Liliana that way), no, really, it hasn't worked out for me at all, I don't mean with you, of course, you've been like a father to me, but ever since I came here I've had this feeling that something was just about to arrive, was just around the corner, and when I serve my father his plate of vegetables, the omelette with a bit of parsley (*fines herbes* they call it in French restaurants, Dad), or a bit of ham and a big glass of milk, she's there at the table with me, as if she had taught me how to position the glass, the plate, the spoon, the knife and fork, yes, Señor Esteban, I thought it was all going to turn out so well, especially at the start, when my husband and my children finally joined me and we got settled in and I got pregnant with my youngest, but the promise of all those good things has never come to anything: I felt that little thrill you get when you know happiness is about to arrive, but I've never felt real happiness here, do you know what I mean: maybe a bit here and there, when we bought the car, when we took out the mortgage on the apartment, when we used to leave the children with our neighbour and go dancing, but since then, it's been largely a matter of keeping our heads above water, waiting for that something good that never arrives, that's how it's been, Señor Esteban, she says, everything's got steadily worse, and now we haven't even got enough money to carry us through to the middle of the month; and I say: Liliana, my dear, that's how it usually is, you feel happy when you think happiness is about to arrive, when you can sense it coming, but then it passes you by, escapes, is gone. Her cinnamon-sweet voice returns to me as I towel my father dry after his shower: my father's cold body like a paradoxical reservoir that has stored away the warmth of her hands, the same hands that, every day, soaped and rinsed this dying flesh, this relief map of stiff tendons and flaccid muscles, these irregular surfaces full of blotches – a multitude of blackish, purplish, yellowish islands, a kind of map of Melanesia or Micronesia – and somehow infected it with her warmth; I want to forget – no, look, you grab the top two corners while I grab the other two, that's it, now give your two corners to me, yes, I want to forget the edge of her hand brushing mine, soft, brown, warm, just as I want to forget the conversations I had with the accountant, with the tax office, with the bank manager who, when we meet in the bar, looks at me as if nothing had ever passed between us; to empty my head of the discussions I'd had with Joaquín, with Álvaro, with Julio, with Jorge, with Ahmed, and, above all, to rid my memory of the final scene I had with each of them, across the desk in the office.

★

205

She never said anything to hurt me, not once in all those years. Never said anything or did anything. Do you think that's usual with couples? I don't know if it was love that she felt for me, although I was crazy about her, I still am, but she must have loved me a little to have treated me with such respect for all that time. The fact that she did the kind of work she did is another matter, irrelevant. She would go out each night about her business and come home afterwards, just as I went about my business and came home afterwards. I know it must seem strange to you, but I never saw it as anything other than a job; and I think she saw it that way too. I suppose you want to know if she ever felt attracted to her clients, if any of the men she had sex with ever gave her pleasure? I never asked. I don't think I was interested, to be honest. It was like the background noise on the radio when they're broadcasting a match. It's not important. I felt attracted by some of the women who came to fill up on petrol, I would watch them bend over to get in their car or to pick up their purse or their handbag from the passenger seat, their tight jeans revealing half their bottom or their miniskirt revealing most of their thighs. No, I don't deny it, I did have the odd fantasy, I would smile and make suggestive remarks. But I never cheated on her. I never said to any of those women, go into the toilet and take your knickers off, go into the back room, and I'll be right with you; or wait at the exit for me to finish my shift, and we'll find a quiet road somewhere and do it in the car, or we could rent a room for a couple of hours in the Hotel Parada, just down the road. I never did that, and I don't think she met up with any of her clients either. I'm quite sure that she never had sex for free with anyone – and that's what matters. Why would she, when she could charge for it? Or, rather, and this is main point, if she wanted that, why stay with me when she could be with other men who were happy to pay her? No, what she did was her job, and I was her home: me and her son (who I treated better than if he'd been my own son), we were her home. The furniture, the sofa, the smell of coffee and toast when she woke up at midday – that was her home. I don't think that's so very difficult to understand. At home, she never misbehaved, she was never moody or angry, she never raised her voice. And, whether she really wanted to or not, I don't know, but she would let me have sex with her, and I would melt into her arms: yes, she'd have a shower, dab on some perfume and lie back on the bed, and I knew then that she wanted me to fuck her that morning, even though she must have been tired – even sick to death – of doing what she'd been doing with other men just a short while before. But like I say, she never got angry with me, she never raised her voice, she never sulked; probably because she was fed up with the loud voices, the noise, the sound of glasses smacking down on the bar or the clinking of glasses, tired of pretending to pout and flirt, of saying the kind of things whores say: buy me a pack of Marlboros, give me a coin for the jukebox, buy me a drink before I show you the colour of my G-string tonight, the kind of things whores say to put you in your place, so that you know it isn't simply a question of turning up and paying, but that you have to earn them and play the part of the man seducing the woman, even if it's all lies; a way of disguising what's really going on and that everyone takes for granted, that going up to a woman's room is nothing to do with liking or disliking, with feeling attracted or repelled, it's purely a matter of money – the only bulge in your trousers she's interested in is the one made by your wallet – but she likes you to pretend to believe that she just happened to be there, in that bar, because she got bored at home, or she didn't want to go to the cinema with her girlfriends, that she's there because she's been waiting for you for months. It's probably because of having to put on a show all the time that she had a loftier idea of family, because she knew what that other life was like, experienced it on a daily basis, was accustomed to living with lies and pretence, and knew what it means to be cut off from family, at the mercy of the first man who comes up to the bar; having no protection, being somehow exposed to the elements. She was already thirty when I met her, no longer a girl, but there's a market for the kind of woman whose looks are just about to fade, men imagine that, because such women are experienced, they'll have stored up inside them everything they've learned from many hours spent with many men, and imagine their cunt to be a kind of *warehouse of unsuspected vices, and they fantasise that, in some way, they're going to benefit from part of that accumulated capital. It's not easy to live under the same roof with anyone, and yet we were together for eight years.*

He draws the back of his hand across his eyes and then leaves it there for a moment, held up, like a visor, hiding his gaze, expressing a sorrow you might describe as pensive, as if a painful thought had suddenly occurred to him, while I glance at my watch and see that it's getting late. Joaquín will have put the little one to bed and may even have gone to bed himself, watching one of those National Geographic programmes he's so keen on. Obviously I miss her terribly, he says with a kind of moan. He isn't crying, but he wants me to feel the emotion in his voice, in his expression. He's saying to me: I could easily burst into tears right now, or I've cried so often just thinking about her, or I just can't cry any more, I'm all cried out, but I'm offering you this pretence of crying, just as actors repeat with complete sincerity words written long ago by someone else, and they do so with real feeling, as if this were the very first time they were acting out to an audience their grief at being abandoned or their anguish at a loved one's death. He's acting out an old grief for me. In the theatre, that capacity for making one's feelings seem real is called getting inside the character. But how can I trust his version of events? I try to imagine what she was like, this woman who for ten or twelve years prostituted herself in roadside brothels: no, she was never a high-class whore, maybe she started too late for that, she always said she didn't like the pretentious clients you get in private clubs. Business executives are just riff-raff, she used to say to me, far worse than the usual poor losers, soldiers, drivers, workmen, who pay to have sex with me. She was a whore in a club heaving with immigrants who go there in order to squander the little they've earned that week, drunken workers or temps, and drunks pure and simple, that's what he's telling me, he's describing the streets, the atmosphere, I don't know Madrid, I've only been there once in my life when Joaquín and I went to see the musical The Beauty and the Beast. *What this* man is telling me can't be true. I try to find out what the woman was like, to get some physical image of her. What was she like? I ask. And he: What do you mean what was she like? Me: Was she tall, short, dark, fair, did she have a long face or a round one? I even wonder if perhaps she resembled me, if she was the same age I am now, and that this is what triggered those memories and his need to confide in someone: although I'm not convinced by the dress he's busily stitching together to clothe the body of that woman whose character I can only deduce from what he's telling me. Such sweetness, such serenity. It just doesn't ring true. The world she inhabited is just the complete and utter pits. Human traffickers, drugs, gonorrhoea, syphilis, Aids. And there he is describing a kind of flower opening in the dawn light. Spending her thirty-first birthday, her thirty-second, her thirty-third, her thirty-eighth at his side. And every night opening her legs in some miserable little room on the outskirts of Madrid. It's just not credible. In places like that you learn to shout and fight, to hurl insults, to attack and to defend yourself. You learn how unstable everything is, how time is eaten up in the few seconds it takes to knock back a drink or stick a needle in your arm. Besides, a woman doesn't just stumble into that world, she must already have fallen into some pretty bad company, have led a certain kind of life. To sink that low. I don't understand it. I don't understand what kind of woman this is he's telling me about, a woman who never once raised her voice in all the time they lived together; and the child, the child who, to hear him speak, seems never to have said a word, a child who ages along with them, seven, eight, eleven, doing his homework at the table in the living room, having a piece of bread and chocolate or a doughnut and a glass of milk when he gets in from school; asleep in his bedroom, hugging his teddy bear or whatever. The cosy family portrait he's painting can't be true. Or perhaps it is, perhaps they were both so weary that they were like a comfortable piece of furniture to each other, the other person's body a sofa on which they could collapse after an exhausting day, a long journey, the welcoming silence of the siesta; or in their case, the whispers of some morning dream, because *their life in common began when she returned home wearily just as the sky was becoming edged with mother-of-pearl, or when she made her way unsteadily home in the broad light of day, the first rays of sun gilding the furniture in the living room, the kitchen and the bedroom with the sweet, honeyed light of early morning. Was he working in a petrol station then too? Did he choose the night shift so as to be able to spend time with her during the day, or did he try to have his time-table coincide with the boy's, so that he could pick him up from school and make him an afternoon snack? The woman returns from work feeling weary, she closes the shutters in the bedroom, she showers, dries off, and he's there waiting for her with two steaming cups of coffee on the table, with some crisp, slightly burned toast made from yesterday's bread, which she nibbles at indifferently; probably the boy had been treated so appallingly before that he thought it best to stay with this man who never raised his voice or, more importantly, his hand to him, not like other men he'd come across before; better the silent man who, when he came home, unwrapped the shiny silver foil from the slices of cold meat, mortadella or turkey or whatever and put it on a plate with some olives and some chopped red pepper; perhaps a bar of chocolate too. No, that can't be how it was, human beings are worse than that. Nothing can be other than it is. All the colours of the spectrum come together to form one murky stain. Why did I stop to talk to him? What am I doing here? I only popped in for some petrol, or so I thought, then straight home to bed: I've just finished the late shift at the ware-house, and I'm in a hurry to get home, I'm too tired to do anything more than grab a bite to eat, have a shower and go to bed; or rather, I was tired, but his words have made my tiredness evaporate. Joaquín will already be asleep or else listening to the radio on his headphones; it's the sports programme now, it's wall-to-wall football at this time of night. I'm utterly exhausted. Why did I begin this absurd conversation with a man I know by sight because he's served me so often, but who I've never really spoken to, just smiled at perhaps when he gave me the card machine so that I could tap in my PIN. He'd hand me the receipt, return my card and I'd say thank you and put the receipt in my purse. On my way to the door, we occasionally exchanged a few words, then I'd say goodnight and he would repeat this back to me as if his deeper voice were an echo of mine. Today, though, he didn't let me serve myself, but rushed to grab the nozzle from me, so I had nothing to do, and while he was filling the tank, he looked up at me a couple of times and smiled, a kind of bored smile, but that was enough, it was as if he had hypnotised me, we went back into the shop so that I could pay, and instead of remaining silent while I put in my PIN number, somehow or other we got talking, and he came out from behind the counter, sat on a stool and asked about my job, because you always come in about this time, he said, he asked about my family, no, no one's waiting up for me, the children and my husband will be asleep, I said, or else he'll be listening to the football on his headphones or watching a nature programme, now that he's unemployed, he spends all night with his headphones on, and I laughed a nervous laugh, no, he's not much older than me, we're more or less the same age, there's just three years' differ-ence, I said, although I've no idea why, and he told me that he lives alone now, but that he had been married to a woman who was older than him, and who had left him, that he'd had a son too, or almost a son, or more than a son, he said, but he hadn't heard a word from them since, then he began telling me this incredible story about his life with the prostitute and her son. Since I always stop by at the same hour of the night, the man probably thinks I'm lying, that I don't work in the fruit warehouse at all, but in some late-night club or other and, in telling me his story, what he's really saying is that he doesn't care what kind of work I do, nor that I'm a bit older than him. I have the feeling he's trying to draw me in with his story, that he wants to do with me what he says he's never done with anyone and which is probably what he tries to do on the night shift whenever he gets the chance, showing me to the small back room he mentioned, alongside the toilets and the storeroom for the cleaning products, giving me the key to the door and telling me: get your knickers off and I'll be right with you, then, once he's back, bolting the door and putting his arms around me, slobbering all over me, shoving me against the wall, hurriedly removing my clothes, grasping my head with his two hands to keep me crouched there until the very last moment, and then quickly zipping himself up again and saying: you can't stay here because the guy who does the cashing up comes on at one o'clock and it's already half past midnight. Yes, that's obviously why he's telling me his story, and yet I feel drawn to his sadness, which could be either real or fake, and although I think his story is a lie, his sadness is real enough, as is the fleshy hand criss-crossed with black lines that he clenches into a fist and raises to his eyes to wipe away a possibly phoney tear, and the air of hopeless resignation he can't hide, and which I feel suddenly tempted to find out more about, to find out if that sad, serene body is the real him or if it conceals a predator calculating his every move as he eyes his prey. I can't bear not having her, not having the boy, he says, but they just left, and now his voice has groan hoarse, and almost cavernous. You don't know what it's like to go home and find no one there, you're lucky, you have your husband, your children. I feel as much attraction as fear, and I get up and place my hand on his shoulder and he sits there, still and contrite, his hand covering his eyes; between us stands a glass of water with ice and lemon in it, the ice slowly melting, while I wonder why I told him about the problems I've been having since Joaquín lost his job, about the distance that has grown up between us now that we spend more time together. Why did I tell him about my home, my private life? I think that, I, too, am a predator, although what I'm mainly thinking is that I'm completely lost. I want to know more about him.*

Losing his job took Álvaro completely by surprise, well, what's happened to me took me by surprise too – or didn't it? He believed the workshop was as inevitable as the skin on your bones, he never took any interest in invoices, account books or bank balances, and would look at me mockingly whenever I complained to him about any problems or difficulties, whenever I found myself getting in a tangle over estimates and having to do all kinds of juggling to make sure credits coincided with debits and didn't leave me in the red. Doing the sums right or wrong, earning money or losing it. I've made far too many mistakes drawing up estimates for customers since my father stopped doing it, and I've lost too much money as well, and that's what really justified all the time I spent going over and over the figures, adding, subtracting and multiplying, the calculations growing ever more complicated; and then there were all those sheets of paper with hand-drawn diagrams, lines in pencil and ballpoint, with numbers scribbled above and below. Customer's name: F. Delmar. Chipboard 6: 0.35 wide x 8.20 long. 2: 0.40 wide x 2.30 high. Work, like family, is a burden you have to put up with, what else can you do, you just take it for granted, it's the biblical curse in which, since there's no way out, you try to find a few advantages: you tell yourself that it's always going to be like this, it's the law of life, this monotonous existence, especially if you've spent thirty or more years in the same job, shut up for eight or ten hours a day in the workshop, five days a week. It's a real treat going out in the van with Joaquín and Ahmed or with Julio, to do a job or make a delivery, something that needs to be assembled on the spot, a piece of furniture, a wardrobe, some shelves. Sometimes, you even find excuses to do just that, I certainly did. It never even occurs to you to think that things aren't eternal, that they could change from one day to the next. It would never occur to you that your particular hell might mean being excluded from Yahweh's curse – in a place outside the pages of that notebook full of orders, far from the invoice book, the machines and the tools, a modern-day reversal of the old biblical curse: In the sweat of thy brow thou shalt *not* eat thy daily bread, an unexpected, diabolical twist. You discover the irritating calm of mornings with no alarm clock going off, the day like a meadow stretching out towards the horizon, limitless time, an unbounded landscape, no flocks graze in that infinite space, not a building to be seen, not even the silhouette of a tree. Just you walking in the void. Hell is a derelict warehouse, a silent hangar filled only with a terrible emptiness. In the end, the divine curse of earning our daily bread by the sweat of our brow seems almost agreeable, the sound of alarm clocks, water gushing out of taps or showers, the bubbling of the coffee pot, the hustle and bustle of morning traffic, the murmur of conversations at the bar in the cafe where you usually have your coffee and croissant, the voices of the other men in the warehouse, the discussions between colleagues, the buzz of machinery, the sandwich and the small glass of beer halfway through the morning. Álvaro: he arrives at the workshop at eight o'clock, has a coffee break at half past nine; a glass of wine or an aperitif at half past one, then home, where, at two o'clock on the dot, his wife will have lunch ready on the table: a plate of rice, another of salad, some pickles, and beside them, a piece of cheese and the basket of fruit; a quick doze in the armchair as the local TV news begins, then a stroll back to the workshop – good for the digestion – followed by the usual afternoon sloth when movements inevitably grow slower, and then, a few glasses of wine at the bar with friends (although Álvaro always drank alone, out of sheer misanthropy according to some, and out of meanness according to others), then supper, sofa, TV and bed. Now what? He just can't get up the energy. No more smile of satisfaction when he sees that an order is going out on time and that the goods have been delivered in an impeccable state. True, there's no reason why a worker should have an overall vision of a business, that's what people call having a business mentality, a perspective or

214

outlook much more likely to belong to those who own the business or who – if we're talking about larger enterprises – work as directors or managers. The obligations of a worker end once the goods are packed up and loaded onto the truck, which is standing there, the front door open, waiting for the driver, and with the back doors closed. A bit boring maybe, but it has the advantage that you're free as soon as the clock strikes home-time. He never showed the slightest sympathy or understanding, which I would have appreciated on occasion, and he even seemed annoyed if I asked for it. If, over coffee in the Cafe Dunasol, I spoke to him about invoices, delivery receipts or monies due, he would just look the other way and change the subject. I can see him now examining the knots in the wood: he follows every vein, detects any weak spots, touching the wood with expert fingers, his tool-like hands detecting whether or not the timber has been well seasoned: his hands are larger than mine, his fingers nimbler, stronger and more gnarled, they have a certain instrumental quality that mine do not, even though I've been in the trade all my life. My hands are softer somehow: although they're full of calluses, my fingers are fleshier, just as my body is, always on the brink of obesity, while his, when he was a young man, was as flexible as a reed (and inside him lurks the same turbid opacity as the lagoon where the reeds grow) and now his body has taken on the hardness and irregularity of certain particularly knotty tree trunks, an old olive tree or a carob tree. He's entirely focused on his work, oblivious to everything happening around him, above or below, indifferent to the vicissitudes of the business. 'Business' is a dirty word these days; a century ago, it signified action and progress, but now it's a synonym of other words heavy with negative energy: exploitation, egotism, wastefulness. He was surprised when, instead of retiring and leaving him in charge of the workshop with an increase in wages, which would have proved most advantageous when it came to his pension, I remained where I was, behind the carved desk in the little glazed room upstairs that we call the office, which oversees the whole workshop – I can follow Álvaro's every move, watch him using the lathe, the saw, the plane. Indeed, going against my father's principle (we don't live by exploiting other people, but from our own work), I took on Jorge, another carpenter, whom Álvaro thought had come to compete for his position, along with three assistants to help us out, especially with driving the truck and delivering the items of furniture that were easiest to assemble on site, mostly those being installed in the apartments in Pedrós' developments, our developments. I want to bump up my pension a bit, and I've got involved in a really major deal, more work for all of us and more pay for you (all right, it wasn't just more pay he was hoping to get as boss of the workshop, but at least I raised his wages, which wasn't to be sniffed at): dealing with the small jobs, the odd jobs, but, above all, working flat out on the doors and other carpentry work for Pedrós' properties, we'll have to work overtime, you'll get well paid (I didn't tell him that I'd gone into partnership with Pedrós on the apartments he was building, the block that was almost ready for the owners to move in, plus the two other developments he had just begun, one of which was still only at the stage of laying the foundations, I had become a guarantor for his loan by using my plot of land up on the mountain as collateral, and a co-borrower on the loan we took out in order to do the work, *and* a partner in fifty per cent of the new buildings, a condition laid down by Pedrós, not to mention remortgaging the house, the workshop and the land, and putting in all the savings the old man had in the bank as well as any savings I had managed to squirrel away without his knowledge). That's a lot of money, he said, and I had only told him about the

216

carpentry work for the apartments that were nearly finished. It wasn't the right moment to tell him about the other two new developments. Nor, of course, did I say anything about the partnership. And certainly nothing about the loans and the mortgages. I told him I was going to take on some new people. I did tell him that. He gave me a look as if to say I was clearly getting greedy in my old age. You've taken on all the carpentry work for Pedrós? he asked, as if he hadn't understood the first time. I heard him ask this and I heard my father's words: we don't live by exploiting other people, but from our own work. That's what he wanted, he wanted those words to ring in my ears. Álvaro the exception, the son of my father's comrade, doubtless my father's favourite son. Another family member, unexploited. For the first time in my life, I was taking decisions, aspiring to something, showing ambition. Instead of the expected, last few languishing years, what lay ahead were a few months of frenetic activity. I don't want to rely on the pathetic state pension for the self-employed I'll receive when I retire and on my own puny private pension. Yes, you're right, we just end up with shitty little pensions, he said, apparently agreeing. That was all. He didn't say: sell the ground floor of the house, sell the workshop, or sell the whole lot and find a small apartment you can pay for with the interest on what you make from the sale – that is, after you've shared out what you have to share out with your brother and sister; or else build the house you've always wanted on that plot of land you own, then move in and enjoy a quiet life. He could have said that, but he didn't: he was thinking about himself, thinking that the workshop must not be touched, because what worried him, what bothered him, was the possibility that he might not be left in charge. And he wanted me to keep paying his wages so that he wouldn't miss the instalments on the motorhome he was going to buy for himself when he retired. His plan was to sell their present apartment and exchange it for a smaller place, just for him and his wife, why do we need such a big place when the children have all left home and married and it's just the two of us, yes, we could buy a smaller apartment and, with our savings and the money from the sale, buy a motorhome so that we can spend the winter further south, near the beach, filling our lungs with the sea breezes, and in summer, we can find a campsite with a backdrop of snow-capped mountains, where even in August the snow is still only just beginning to melt and where foaming, icy torrents plunge down the slopes. He smiled that distinctly un-frank smile of his, which seems to express not happiness, but some unspeci-fied grief. A man who wouldn't say boo to a goose, a serious, silent, honest man, who we imagine must harbour some deep inner sorrow that demands our respect, a man who has a couple of glasses of wine on his way home at lunchtime and orders a couple of tapas, just for him, standing at the bar (other people don't see this sorrow, they say he drinks alone deliberately, so that he won't have to buy anyone else a drink). That's why I'm surprised at the capacity for loathing he displays when I tell him that the Pedrós deal has collapsed, that we're not going to get paid, and since we won't get any cash back for the materials we've already supplied, we'll have to close down for a while until we've found a way round the problem, until I've thought of a solution that will make sure none of you lose out, recoup the money I owe you and get everyone back to work as soon as possible (that's all I say, but he knows perfectly well that, given my age, I'm obviously planning to close the workshop for good). I don't expect him to shed any tears for me or offer to help me out, or say here I am, still by your side after more than forty years, ready to do whatever I can, I certainly don't expect that from a miserable sod like him, who, when he's drinking his wine and eating his tapas, takes such care not to catch anyone's eye just in case he should have to buy them a drink, no, he drinks and eats as solemnly as if he were taking communion (solid and liquid, bread and wine, flesh and blood: always that trace of blood), although I would appreciate a little understanding, a vague show of solidarity, I would even gladly accept a hint of pity, a gesture or a word of consolation. All right, the workshop has been his life, but it's been mine for even longer. And it's been my house too, or, rather, my father's house – it's where I've always lived. I could accept him saying: poor Esteban. In the circumstances, that wouldn't even seem humiliating; a brief embrace, a sympathetic pat on the back, and a murmured 'poor Esteban'. But no, he shifts instantly from his usual attitude – just concentrating on the job in hand, sawing, gluing, polishing, assembling – to an all-embracing hatred, a universal, all-purpose hatred, and now there is nothing in him *but* hate, a bile that overflows onto me and onto everything around us – the machinery, tools and work spaces that have ceased to be instruments he can use to his advantage – the lathe, the saw, the plane, the polisher, the workshop walls and the fluorescent ceiling lights, everything's an object of hatred, he hates the planks, hates the machines and the tools, hates the place itself, none of it's going to help him now to buy his mobile home and allow him to head off to gape in foolish wonder at summer snows and winter beaches, none of those tools or machines or instruments is going to work to realise his egotistical dream of a life spent circling around the warmest of suns, that infantile dream for which he's sacrificed his life; naturally, that bile is aimed at me in particular and manifests itself physically in the sticky, white saliva at the corners of his mouth, saliva coagulated by rage into a substance like carpenter's glue. It isn't just what he says, it's his tone of voice, his gestures – the violence of his response is conveyed by those tool-like hands, transformed into pincers, hammers: his nails dig into his palms leaving faint red lines, channelling all his rage, he squeezes hard – pressure, as if we had been enemies from the moment we first set eyes on each other, and as if he had always known that I would end up cheating on him; then he falls silent, he's never been open and honest, he's slippery, elusive, murky, but there is now a kind of clarity, a solidity, you could stand on him now and you wouldn't have the feeling he was going to give way beneath you: I've never trusted you and with good reason, your father could always see straight through you too, say his eyes, his tight lips, his nails digging into his palms, in this final explosion of the suspicions that have been brewing inside him for more than thirty years. He entered the house when I went off to art school, my father was left alone, when Álvaro was my replacement, half adopted by my father when his own father died, a boy, a beloved son who arrived to make up for the shortcomings of his own unwanted son; and even though I'm troubled, above all, by what his eyes are telling me, I watch his clenched fists, that seem like tools about to unleash all their force on the glass-topped desk, that supposedly elegant desk, with its Renaissance or Isabelline Gothic carving, made by my grandfather, or by my grandfather and my father, and on permanent display in this tiny office, the desk that my father ended up claiming as his masterpiece, possibly a case of misappropriation. My father behaves as if skills were inherited rather than the fruit of a long, hard apprenticeship. He sees himself as carrying on his father's work. The desk is a fake catalogue intended to seduce the customer, along with the four matching chairs, all apparently the same, but all actually quite different when you look at the detail: the incisions in the chair back, the carving on the back legs, because what on one of the chairs is a kind of geometric hemstitch, on another is a garland or a floral hatching, and one assumes that they are all the work of someone with ambitions to be a sculptor, although, as I say, it's never been clear to me who actually did the work, whether he made it with his father's help or whether his father made it with his help: the version changed depending on the customer, for reasons known only to him; he must have done his calculations and his sums, emphasising either the traditional values of the workshop or his own merits – to each creature its own bait, as his brother used to say; over time, he became more and more likely to offer the first version in which he attributed all the work to himself, with his father as mere assistant or onlooker, and my uncle never cleared up the mystery, as if that would have been tantamount to revealing the murderer who committed the original crime on which the business was built, and as if the confusion served to conceal what really mattered. My father behind the desk: the workshop has been in existence for nearly a hundred years, he's saying when I go into the office to pick up an invoice, and he talks that way because he likes to think he's convincing the potential customer that this is the studio of a well-known cabinetmaker accustomed to using only the very finest woods, lime, walnut, mahogany, and not the workshop of some cheap carpenter, who survives by taking on odd jobs and various other run-of-the-mill tasks, someone incapable of carrying out any really delicate work, although he doesn't hesitate to say that he can – yes, of course, no problem, we've often done this kind of work, why, last year we did something very similar, even more complicated actually, and the customer was so pleased that he still congratulates me on it whenever we meet – yes, taking on such commissions was a cinch, although, afterwards, he would keep endlessly postponing the work until the customer got fed up and vanished. I mean, all the customer had to do was glance out over the workshop and see the materials stored there, the chipboard made respectable with a thin wood veneer, the poorly seasoned pinewood planks, the fibreboard, the plywood. All right, give me your card, I need to think about it and then I'll give you a call closer to the time when I need the work done, says the customer – if he's got any sense. But now I'm here with Álvaro, and his face is fixed in a grimace, with his lips pursed and his tongue making a sound as if he were about to shoot a gob of spit at some particularly repugnant person. He is a gloomy walnut-wood carving of some unnamed devil's face, not Baal, not Beelzebub, not Lucifer, no, another anonymous devil, tense, tormented, one not mentioned in the Bible or in any treatises on esoterics and demonology. That crease in his lower lip. I am that repugnant person, a soft, glutinous being like those green monsters made out of snot or plasticine that you get in children's cartoons. He almost yells at me: What am I going to do now? Do you honestly think that, with the way things are, anyone's going to give a job to an old man who's just turned sixty? He snorts. He lingers over the word 'old man' – a very low blow – and I feel something resembling disgust. He is now the soft plasticine doll. The bastard hates me, and yet he's pretending to be helpless, not angry, not scornful, just so that I won't hit back, won't even put myself on my guard, so that I'll feel sorry for him. What does this son of a bitch want? Does he expect me to burst into tears, when I haven't even wept any tears for myself? I don't like people who want you to take pity on them, for example, beggars who, rather than asking for alms in a digni-fied fashion, instead kneel down, arms outstretched at the door of the church, with some religious image hanging around their neck, and mumble Our Fathers and other fervent prayers. It's not their poverty I find repellent, they just seem morally repre-hensible to me. Frauds. I'm sorry, Liliana, but all too often I just don't like myself. Oh, that's normal, Don Esteban, it happens to us all, I often feel the same way. When I look in the bathroom mirror, I feel like crying, I look so ugly and tired, and then I go out onto the terrace and look up at the starless sky and see only the dense yellowish glow from the street lamps, like an awning of luminous air. Here in Olba, I can't see the stars. Apparently, when she stood at the door of her house, out in the countryside in Valle del Cauca or Quindío, she would look up and it was as if a whole array of possible lives lay before her. That's what she tells me. Each star was like a possible life, a different life from the one she was living. But all she sees here is that whitish, yellowish awning, the spider's web of light from the street lamps, from the roads, from the factories, from the housing developers, shutting off her view, closing her horizons. I say to my husband Wilson: I thought we came here to have a better life. But he just laughs at me: life's the same everywhere, or did you really think we would come here and be walking upside down like in the Antipodes? I sometimes think that, when I came here, I'd been hoping for that something none of us can quite put our finger on, but which we all aspire to in secret: instead, what I've discovered is that there is no paradise anywhere. They say the Spanish brought their God to Colombia, but it seems to me that He abandoned Spain altogether and left to go over there, but that, since then, He's abandoned Colombia too, and escaped somewhere else, who knows where: in Spain, heaven is the clothes you buy, the moisturising creams, the fridge and what's in the fridge, the car you drive to work or to take the children out on a Sunday afternoon, to the beach at Misent, so that they can play in the sand and splash around in the waves, although the truth is they don't get to the beach very often because whenever I ask Wilson, he tells me that the weekend is for lying on the sofa and doing nothing, for resting or watching the football, not playing chauffeur and getting stuck in a traffic jam on the way to the beach. He'd be all nerves and tension then, and not rested at all. No way, he says. The only heaven is this business of accumulating things, and that heaven costs money, money is the key to heaven, and that creates a lot of anxiety if you don't have the euros you need to make the payments. It's just soul-destroying having to keep adding up the bills over and over each month only to end up with nothing, with me asking you for help. Back home, the poor people pray to a little figure of the Virgin holding a child and standing on a half-moon, Our Lady of Chiquinquirá she's called, or to a child wearing a red cape and a crown on his head and holding the globe of the world in his hand, or to that other Divine Child, so pretty in his pink tunic and his little green belt, who holds out his arms as if asking his father to pick him up, but in Olba, there's no point, the saints are just dolls no one believes in, and I know perfectly well that the saints can't really help, but at least they keep you company and give you the illusion that something extraordinary or unexpected might happen, a miracle, something that will come along and change this painful life of ours, the huge lack of love filling everything, because it even fills the kids now, they go off to school in the morning and when they come back, they don't want you, they don't want what you've got and can actually give them, they want things you can't afford or only if you make a huge sacrifice, and they keep asking you for them and throw tantrums when you say you can't afford Nike trainers, an Adidas tracksuit, a PlayStation, the little bit of heaven that costs money and that you can't give them, and when you think about it, you realise that they're right, because why should they love you if you're refusing to give them heaven? It's not so straightforward, Liliana: there are other things too. What, for example? I don't know, the things that bind us together, our conversations. Why don't we have a black coffee, a *tintico* – is that the right word? And no saccharin

224

today, I'll have sugar. That way, we'll be drinking exactly the same thing. United in pain and sweetness. Come over here, I want to show you something, look at this little box. It's lovely, isn't it? Touch it, see how soft it is. Smell it. It's made of rosewood. Open it, don't be shy, I want you to see what's inside. What do you think? Do you like it? It's my mother's jewellery, inherited from her mother, who I never knew. I was my mother's favourite, and I loved her too in my fashion, although I hated the way she was always bursting into tears, but then I would cry along with her. I think she's the only woman who's seen me cry, no, that's not true, there was another one, not that I actually cried in her presence, but she did make me cry. But we were talking about my mother. I think she would have liked to have pictures and figures of virgins and saints around the house, because her family was very devout, but my father couldn't stand that side of her, and she took her revenge by sucking our souls out of us, the mother hen covering her brood with her wings, sometimes I felt I was her son alone, not my father's, she would give you everything, and although she always made it seem that she gave it all out of selflessness, really it was pure egotism, a way of stealing from my father the part of us that belonged to him. Do you like the pendant? And the earrings? It's the only jewellery we own, it's more than a hundred years old. My mother's parents were quite well off, you see, and they never forgave her for marrying a loser like my dad. The stones are sapphires, go on, take them, you've more right than anyone. Put them on, let me see how they look. Oh, yes, lovely, the blue of the pendant and the earrings really suit your complexion. Take a peek in the mirror. No, don't take them off. Keep them on. Today is our little party. But why are you crying? Tell your husband they're a gift from an old man who's very grateful for the care and affection with which you treat him and his even more ancient father. Why would your husband be jealous? Oh, kisses and tears together. Wet kisses. In those hundred years, the stones have lost none of their watery blue brilliance, and the white gold has lost none of its glow. The stability of jewels gives us hope, Liliana. Knowing that there are things that stay the same in a world that's constantly changing and constantly growing more corrupt. There was a time when the Virgin of the Rosary of Chiquinquirá lost all her colour, and then suddenly, one day, it all came back, and she looked more beautiful than when she was first painted. What if a miracle like that were to happen to us? What if all the dirt and murk around us were to be filled with colour? Come on, Liliana, make some coffee. Don't tell me you don't want to drink a *tintico* with me. Did I say it right? Doña Liliana, would you care to drink a *tintico* with me? Sipping my coffee while I gaze on you all bedecked with jewels. We old people enjoy looking upon youth. My Uncle Ramón told me that. I was too young to understand at the time. One day, I'll tell you about him.

Álvaro has greyish-brown eyes, Julio's are a kind of greenish-blue, framed by thick lashes that he uses to great effect, lowering them slowly when he wants to ask a favour, blinking quickly when he's trying to intimidate me, silently reminding me that I've been employing him illegally, without a contract. I'm completely bulletproof though. If he reports me, I'll pay up, but he'll have to give back years of unemployment benefits and social security payments. It's your choice, my eyes are telling him, and he again lowers his lashes. Today, he's all meek and submissive. Ahmed's shining, jet-black eyes float against the backdrop of the whites which in his case are yellowish and emphasise his dark pupils rather than diluting or blurring them.

226

He looks at me with pretend fury, and that pretence is telling me: I know you have to put on this act in front of the others, but I'm sure you'll phone me later on and we'll continue to work together and go fishing in the lagoon and have lunch on the grass: that's what he's saying to me. He still thinks this is all just theatre, a set-up to get rid of someone I don't like (Julio perhaps or, more likely, Jorge). We'll see what happens when he realises it's not an act. Well, I won't see that actually, I won't be here, so what do I care? Jorge's brown eyes, small and bright, are almost buried among folds of fat; sometimes they're wounding and sometimes they oil his words and even his silences; the ever-pragmatic Jorge's eyes laugh, mock, threaten: I'm owed two years' unemployment benefits, they say. Give me a decent severance package, and we'll still be friends. Otherwise, you'd better watch your back. He thinks that, as the skilled carpenter he is, he'll always find work. Being unemployed is just a holiday in between jobs. As for Joaquín, I don't know what to make of him. A bewildered child, his eyes always moist, ready to fill with tears because the toy he was given for Christmas has broken. As I walk along, I have before me those five pairs of eyes, each quite distinct, but over the past few days, seeing them staring at me from across the desk, they've begun to blur into a single pair of eyes, a confused combination of them all, a fragmentary, polyhedric eye, a Polyphemic eye into which I would like to plunge a stake to make it stop watching – accusing, mocking, pleading – an eye that is, at once, jet-black, greenish-blue, dark brown, and an infantile greyish-brown floating in its yellow whites, bright eyes half buried in folds of fat: the eye of all eyes. Plunging a stake into it, blinding the monster and escaping. Because that's what I see now, the monster, the primordial predator, the carrion-eater. I discover the dark depths of mankind: the long-buried resentments. They go hunting and their calculations are based on pure efficiency, getting more for less: it's sheer necessity, devoid of any moral value, economics in its purest form; how to stick the knife in the pig's gullet so that it makes as little fuss as possible when it dies, how to pluck the chicken as quickly as possible; like Francisco's hunting father now cleansed of his youthful misdemeanours, I splash around in the puddle of morality, that higher form of good manners. I speak gently, reasonably. I discover the persistence of what, in different times, Francisco and I would have called the class struggle. But how is that possible? The class struggle has faded away, dissolved; democracy has acted as a social solvent: everyone lives, shops at the supermarket, visits the local bar and attends the concerts in the square sponsored by the town hall, and they all talk at the same time, their voices mingling, as they did in the tumultuous meetings at the Tivoli cinema my father used to tell me about, there is no top and bottom of the heap, everything is blurred, confused, and yet a mysterious order does still reign, and that is the nature of democracy. But in the last couple of years, I've begun to sense a more explicit, less insidious order being rebuilt. The new order is perfectly visible, it's as clear as day who's at the top and who's at the bottom: some proudly leave the mall with bulging shopping bags, they greet one another, smiling, and stop to chat with a neighbour, while others are rummaging around in the bins in which the supermarket employees have thrown the discarded shrink-wrapped packages of meat past their sell-by date, the bruised fruit and vegetables, the factory-produced pastries gone stale. They fight among themselves. And I don't know who I am or where I am, I'm not sure whether I should be stopping to greet a neighbour or rummaging about in those bins, because if there's one person who's been exploited in this fucking workshop, it's me, what about *my* fragile state, does anyone care about that? I want to show them that there is no dividing line separating us. But I can't, because there is. The edge of this desk. I'm on one side, talking about what is and isn't owed, about the redundancy money they have a right to, I'm shuffling their future just as I shuffle cards in the bar, I talk about how much and when *I* will be able to pay and when *they* will receive (I'm lying, I'm lying to them, there isn't a single euro in the till; who is going to pay them their three months of unpaid wages?). But why am I thinking about this now, while I'm walking, why am I thinking about the past? The workshop is done for, there is no top and bottom of the heap, not for me at any rate. Pedros' bankruptcy has made us all equal again, brought us all down to the same level, everyone on the floor, as that would-be coup leader Tejero told the parliamentarians, what could have redeemed us is gone and will soon be nothing at all. I'm at the lagoon, searching the marshes for the best setting for our play, the place where my father once wanted to take refuge. This is not the time for trivial matters, what counts now is the transcendant. Although what am I saying? Is the class struggle trivial? Wasn't it the determining factor that impregnated and marked everything? The great engine of world history? Isn't that what my father and his friends believed, what the young Francisco believed, what I neither believed nor disbelieved, but took for granted? The martyrs, the fallen, the fighters, the people tortured by the politico-social brigade, by PIDE, by the CIA, by the Okhrana. They were the battery fuelling my father's aspirations and those of the young Francisco locked in secret combat with his own father (spitting on the photo of the Falangist, then wiping away all trace of saliva). That's why I've despised my father for as long as I can remember. For putting that at the centre of his life. It bored me to hear him moaning on about it and cursing. About those at the top and those at the bottom, them and us. Yours and ours. About how that's the way it's always been. Although, that afternoon in my office, faced by that Polyphemus with five pairs of eyes merged into one, the language that once bored me to distraction came back to me: they are me and we are them. Enough. Let's get on with things. Take the moment seriously. What *is* serious in this life? Is dying serious? Even newborn babies can do it. Even the stupidest animals know how to die. Don't be afraid, Dad, death isn't a serious matter, it's nothing, the lagoon is like the very softest of laps, and the mud is a warm cradle enfolding you as night falls, a mattress of foaming chocolate on which you will rest, on which we will rest. Haven't you ever seen those tombs of medieval lords at whose feet, carved out of the same marble as their masters, a faithful dog lies curled? Well, that's how it will be here, you and your pup.

'Yes, who wants to be remembered for doing something no one else is fool enough to do, namely, throwing away his money?' says Justino Lecter, repeating an argument I seem to recall had already been put forward by someone else and taking a puff on the plastic mouthpiece of the fake mentholated e-cigarette which, since smoking was banned in the bar, has replaced the cigar he used to smoke during our card games. As if he wasn't always boasting to me about how he throws his money away on caviar, champagne, whores, wine-pairing for complimentary flavours in the same tonality or enhanced to get a contrast effect. But he prefers not to say too much about precisely how he earns the money which he now claims never to squander: multi-occupancy apartments, warehouses turned into sweatshops full of Africans in multicoloured robes, ill-shaven or bearded Arabs, and citizens of Eastern Europe, so blonde, so pale, so clean even when they don't wash: each animal in its own cell, its own cubicle, Russians with Russians, Africans with Africans, Maghrebis with Maghrebis, a perfectly ordered zoo, no mixing of sheep and goats or gazelles and tigers, even though there aren't many gazelles in those crowded apartments: plenty of hyenas and wolves, yes, there's certainly no shortage of hyenas, who travel the country from rubbish tip to rubbish tip, collecting carrion and storing it away. The one constant feature that unites this hotchpotch of languages, colours and races, what all the animals in Justino's zoo share in common, is a transit van that has failed its MOT and which, laden with human flesh or stolen fruit or both, is driven at night with its lights off along the intricate paths of orchards, that and wretched jobs, abandoned warehouses turned into squats, furniture picked up on successive raids on rubbish tips, gas cookers connected by defective rubber tubing and at permanent risk of exploding, washbasins full of soapy water, clothes lines hung with damp rags.

Carlos, the manager of the bankrupt bank, arrived a short while ago and, seated behind us, is watching our game. He smiles all the time as if everything we said amused him. If the play we put on each evening was a morality play, he would represent geniality and fairness: the honest bank manager. Tenacity, transparency, public service. The servant of our most neglected citizens. Wasn't that why banks came into being – to meet the needs of what we call ordinary people? He acts as though he doesn't know that every light casts a shadow, that every day has its night, and that the night is a breeding ground in which evil grows fat and in which the needs of the unfortunate pay for the whims of the powerful. As if he didn't know that all the rhetoric about the common good had gone down the pan. No one believes it any more. He himself is a discreet nest of shadows when he signs the documents, mine included, warning of repossession for failure to keep up mortgage repayments. Anyone would think someone else did that for him. Anyway, I'm quite sure that, this evening, the name 'Pedrós' will not be on his lips, a name he knows to be irremediably linked with mine, because he's in charge of all the files and all the mortgage documents, and he was the one who gave his blessing to our bankruptcy; he looks at me out of the corner of one eye, telling me that I'm a witness to the fact that no one will be able to say he spoke ill of Pedrós. Just for the record. Just in case. So that no one will take him to court for breach of confidentiality. While he's talking, I'm thinking that, from the terrace of my house, I can see the cranes standing motionless above the unfinished blocks of apartments, some still with wheelbarrows hanging from them, and those loads are the seal signifying disaster, my disaster, the end of all my plans, the sign that the cranes are no longer being used and that the company is bankrupt. I see the blocks of apartments, some mere skeletons, others with bare, unplastered walls. I notice particularly those that belong – or belonged – to us, to Pedrós and me: the crane silhouetted against the sky and the wheelbarrow dangling there, swaying like a hanged man at the end of his rope. I try to divert the conversation onto more abstract subjects. Like Carlos, I'm particularly keen to stay well away from any mention of Pedrós:

'Attracting attention is really quite difficult nowadays, but the idiotic fools who appear on those trashy TV programmes want exactly that. They're not trying to attract attention because of something they actually do or produce, they're just attracting attention for attention's sake. It's a kind of imbecilic vicious circle, you're there because you're in the news and you're in the news because you're there, but if you're not, and you're not nice-looking – at least according to current criteria – and shameless too, and you want to jump on the merry-go-round, but don't know how to do anything useful, like inventing a new kind of engine or a vaccine against cancer, then you have to do something really big. I can think of a few things: poisoning your children or finding out that they've been raped and chopped up into little pieces; stabbing your wife and jumping off a viaduct. The possibilities are endless: then you'll be guaranteed your three or four minutes on the news. The newsreader puts on a sorrowful face and says: a horrifying case of parricide, another instance of domestic violence, another sex crime, and there's your ID photo all over the news. The civil guard are looking for you, they're searching the nearby fields with tracker dogs, and when the neighbour tells the reporter that he saw you leap in your car and race off into the mountains, they search the rocky slopes and the caves of Montdor; and if, on the following day's news, they say you've been caught hiding, crouched behind an olive tree, or sprawled at the bottom of a ravine, or hanging from a rope in the shade of a leafy carob tree, then there's a good chance they'll show your photo again. If you don't commit suicide, but hand yourself in, the aura grows still larger: you're back on the screen the day you're taken to court, walking unsteadily, as if you were drunk, you're in handcuffs and your head is covered by a blanket, with a policeman's hand pressing firmly down on it, or else it's concealed beneath a balaclava or a crash helmet. The first time I saw defendants with their heads covered when they went into court was twenty or so years ago: the newspaper showed two smartly dressed men in suits and ties, each wearing a bull's head; apparently they were a pair of American drug-runners about to be put on trial. We were watching in the bar and we all just burst out laughing. We couldn't understand what was going on. Now, we've got used to seeing defendants going into court wearing a crash helmet with the visor down, or a Batman mask or a mask bearing Rajoy's or George W.'s face. You also get to be on TV if you've been murdered in a particularly gruesome fashion: if you get chopped up and the pieces sent in the post to your brother-in-law or your cousins, or they find your butchered thighs in the freezer of an apartment in some rough outlying suburb, and catch the murderer sitting at the table eating your testicles fried in breadcrumbs (much tastier than bull's testicles, he told the police who arrested him, according to newspaper reports the next day); if, rather than being the victim, you decide to be the person doing the chopping up, you're guaranteed to see your face in the newspaper (the headline: CANNIBAL ATE VICTIM'S TESTICLES, and the reader gets all excited: how big were they? a meal in themselves? how did the murderer cook them?), but this comes at a very high price. The photo is no compensation, not even if your entire family album is handed over to be used in a TV debate about the decline in law and order and the rise of a new kind of crime, or about serial killers or cannibalism in the modern world. Or a panel of gastronomes and nutritionists discussing the advantages, as regards taste and nutritional value, of human flesh over lamb, mentioning the Mayans, Caribs and certain African or Polynesian tribes, who all had a passion for a delicacy available nowadays only to a privileged few.'

'The only recourse left to the bankrupt is violence, unless he's a decent sort, then he can always sell his own body. In the Third World, people sell a kidney or an eye just to earn enough money to make it through to the end of the month. They sell themselves off piecemeal.'

Carlos:

'Freixenet's New Year ad for their best cava costs more than you will earn in your entire lifetime. Suicide and crime are the revenge of the poor: you're promoting the one business asset I have, this body-cum-tool for whose labour you fuckers pay a mere pittance. I've filled more TV hours today than Coca-Cola. The relatives of the victims meet every year and leave candles and flowers *in memoriam*, and in doing so, they remember me, the murderer. They want my wretched name never to be forgotten. And I'm glad to help, and grateful too, because that sudden multiplication of my market value as a source of labour (we're talking about my death here and the deaths of a few more, so nothing very important) benefits my widow and my children, who, with the help of a good PR man, can turn a nice little profit by taking part in a few reality shows over the coming weeks. PLEA FOR FORGIVENESS FROM FAMILY OF MULTIPLE MURDERER WHO ATE HIS NEIGHBOURS. LIVING WITH A MONSTER: HIS WIDOW SPEAKS. They bring in the right to hire and fire, increase job insecurity, or just sack you, and you respond by multiplying to infinity your market value. EXCLUSIVE: THE GOODBYE NOTE THE MONSTER WROTE TO HIS DAUGHTER.

Justino:

'It's best if they take a while to find you. That prolongs the game a little: MURDEROUS MANIAC ON THE LOOSE. And so on for a couple of weeks. A few minor attacks, a few explosions that put the authorities on their guard, before the major suicide bombing. And afterwards, you're the subject of interviews, they talk about you in debates: the well-known Cordoban psychiatrist Giménez de la Pantera reveals the personality of the nursery-school suicide bomber. Tonight, *exclusively* on Channel 8. Can we have absolute security and still have democracy? Are freedom and security incompatible? An impassioned debate between Judge Camarón de la Ventisca and Professor of Ethics Eloísa de Bracamonte, introduced by Mercedes Corbera.'

Kindly Carlos is concerned about the future of the murderer-victim:

'The trouble is that if they carry you out all blown to pieces and with your guts all over the floor, you provoke more disgust than pity . . .'

Justino:

'Oh, I don't know, people like to see a nice loin of pork in the butcher's window, a sirloin steak. In the supermarket, they gaze in ecstasy at cuts of meat they can no longer afford thanks to the crisis. The newly-bankrupt dream about them just as, during the post-war years, that comic-book character, Carpanta, used to dream of eating roast chicken. Seeing a dismembered corpse on the telly is a bit of freebie nosh. People can afford to consume it and they do; then – and this gives them even greater pleasure – they tell other people about that act of cannibalism: didn't you see that guy on last night's news? God, he was in a terrible state. Like he'd been ground up in a coffee grinder. Honestly, the images they show on the news just when you're sitting down with your family for the evening meal, it's enough to turn your stomach. They should ban them.'

Bernal:

'But if they ban them, you won't see them at all, and that would be a real bummer. You won't get to gobble it all down. You're left with nothing but a miserable chickpea stew. Lenten fare. And who doesn't like a good stew made with bacon, black pudding and marrowbone?'

Francisco:

'It's risky though. Whether you're the victim or the killer, if they dig out some old snapshot of you with your wretched Neolithic peasant parents, or with friends from your youth at a party, complete with paper hat and party horn, you just look like a complete moron. Your fellow wild-eyed, wild-haired, gawping partygoers still stink of cheap wine thirty years on. A terrible image. You sometimes see photos like that in the magazines funded by local councils as a way, they say, of making sure we don't forget what village life used to be like, when what it was, and what it still pretty much continues to be, should – as that nineteenth-century reformer said of El Cid's tomb – be locked up with seven locks and forgotten.'

Bernal:

'Not that the photo on your ID card is a great improvement, that look of terror we all wear whenever we come face-to-face with officialdom (the police no less), the frightened eyes of a bull trying to pass itself off as a tame cow so as not to arouse the suspicions of the always overly punctilious superintendent (I mean, who doesn't have something to hide?); and in the photos taken during your military service, there's the same cheap wine and soda as in those pictures of you and your friends at a party, except that here you're surrounded by strangers who appear to be either mentally or economically retarded, brutes straight out of one of Lombroso's albums of criminal types. Why do all the people one knew during national service look like mental defectives? With images like that, you fall far below your own aspirations, however modest. Best to have no biography at all, or, if you press me, best not to exist.'

Carlos, the bank manager, who was transferred from Alcázar de San Juan:

'Oh, you're right there. You look like such a hick in photos even just a few years after they were taken! The more modern you try to be in the present, the more dated you'll look in the future. You become a symptom. That's what comes of being born in a poor country and in an even poorer village. Your face is like a shop window, displaying all the tons of lentils and chickpeas that made up your ancestors' nourishing diet. Nothing fresh, just tough old vegetables and stiff strips of salted cod.'

Francisco:

'You say that because you're from Castile. Here it's still beans and lentils and the omnipresent rice, but there's plenty of fresh stuff, light soups, vegetables and fish. The diet may be different, but the pain is the same.'

Me:

'It's all a matter of social class. The passage of time suits the rich just fine, transforming them into historical figures. Remember all those British period pieces that get made into films or TV series, *Brideshead Revisited* or *A Room with a View*. The passage of time suits the rich just fine, transforming them neatly into historical figures.'

Francisco:

'No, you're ignoring some crucial differences; yes, as you say, there are rich and poor, those at the top and those at the bottom, the British and the Spanish, north and south, Europe and Africa. Because Spain, my friends, however hard we try to deny it, is still the Africa that begins at the Pyrenees. The last fifteen or twenty years have been a complete illusion. Haven't you noticed that, with the crisis, even the Spanish cars are starting to look more Moroccan than Swedish or German?'

Justino:

'You're all using terminology that went out with the ark. Mentally defective, Neolithic. What are you talking about? English hooligans in action are profoundly European, and when you see them on TV, they bear more and more resemblance to clearly inferior species: pigs, oxen, newly shorn sheep. You guys just don't get it. People today don't care if you feel sorry for them, as long as they get talked about. Mothers who suffocate their children, children who decapitate their parents or their sisters with a machete, and people who demonstrate against them or in favour, using them as an excuse to be able to appear on TV for a few days, complaining about the rise in crime or calling for the death penalty for everyone, including the suspect's mother-in-law and sister-in-law, the suspect usually being an illegal immigrant who just happened to be passing by.'

Francisco:

'Mothers, mothers-in-law, daughters-in-law, sisters-in-law. That's a whole other subject: the continuing importance of the family in Mediterranean countries. As the economic analysts keep saying, it's thanks to the family that we don't notice the five million or so unemployed. Spain is surviving the crisis with the aid of the family, thanks to the solidarity shown by members of the clan, help from parents, grandparents, siblings, cousins, aunts, uncles and in-laws. If it wasn't for the big dish of pasta that Mum puts on the table every day to feed her unemployed son's kids, violence would long since have erupted onto the city streets. The whole country would be in flames, which wouldn't be a bad thing actually. A new beginning. Out of the ashes the light will rise again, the gospels say, or something like that, or was it St Paul? I can't remember now. I haven't read the Bible in ages. A return to the old system of fertilising the earth by burning the stubble.'

Me:

'Just think how hard our mothers had to struggle to disguise a poverty there was no way of disguising, and which everyone knew about anyway.' My words sound almost like an insult. Did Francisco's mother struggle? Did Bernal's? They were definitely caught up in a war, but a different war, or, rather, they were on a different side with different objectives. 'But now it's the opposite. If you're not completely destitute, you're nobody; if you're not the victim of some domestic tragedy: a violent husband, a child with some rare disease, a foreclosure notice' – I try not to look at Carlos – 'you're nobody. It's the only way people can get anyone to notice them. These days, who *wasn't* raped by their father or their grandfather? Even high-class writers talk about it in their books. Yeah, my grandpa used to stick it up me. Well, that never happened before. I don't know anyone of my generation who was screwed by his or her own grandfather. All right, the priests used to touch us up sometimes and fondle the altar boys, especially in boarding schools. You were at boarding school, Francisco, and you've talked about it sometimes, but we took it all as a bit of a joke, not an emotional trauma: you mean, you let Don Domingo handle your willy, you great poofter.'

Justino:

'If poor families remember the past, it's with feelings of profound shame.' He knows what he's talking about, he's from humble beginnings like me. 'A whole catalogue of horrors: eating cats, dogs, rats, potato peelings, rotten melons, maggoty meat. That's what our parents did. Worse than that, they starved. In those museums of memory you find in other countries, they never include a CD with a recording of the rumbling from someone's starving innards or the miaowing of a cat rising up from the depths of a shrunken stomach. Has anyone ever been taught to listen for that music? No, the background music is always Vivaldi, Mozart, Bach, or, at most, some ballad taken out of context or García Lorca's "The Four Muleteers" or the old national anthem. Never any miaowing.'

Carlos:

'Sorry to interrupt, but I just wanted to tell you that Laura,' his wife, that is, 'is pregnant. It's a boy and he's due in April. I'm going to be a father.' Smiles, glasses raised in a toast. 'Esteban, you're the only one who hasn't taken the plunge yet. It's still not too late. Andrés Segovia had a child when he was in his eighties, and I think Julio Iglesias' father kept reproducing until quite late in life.'

'Well, it's good to know that Carlos has finally reached the chapter on sex ed in his Citizenship course and has been doing the exercises,' says Justino mockingly. 'We all learned more or less the same kind of thing, but we did it behind a wall and under our own steam.'

The little monk from the bank, who is leaving half the village homeless because they haven't kept up their mortgage repayments, has just called me a eunuch. I hope he's not going to add that I'm also a bankrupt. Francisco says nothing, indicating by his silence that this conversation is beneath him. I keep talking. Better to talk about sex than about Pedrós' (and my) bankruptcy:

'The very idea of sex education is so weird, as if you could teach sex, as if it could be controlled and wasn't always a restless,

240

untameable thing. I don't know why people describe it as a source of pleaasure. They're lying and they know it. If someone says he wants to screw you or give it to you up the arse, he isn't telling you he wants to give you pleasure. If someone asks you to pick up the soap for them, expect the worst.'

Now and then, when he waxes sentimental, Francisco says that I've been lucky to have spent my life here, in the workshop:

'You've had a quiet life, and I envy you. Twenty or thirty years ago I couldn't understand your decision to stay here, but now I'm convinced that you made the better choice. John Huston used to say something along the lines of blessed are those who have never had more than one town, one god and one house. I've traipsed all over the world and generally taken an interest in what's happening on the planet, but what have I ended up with? Nothing. I'm all alone. The Fates carried off Leonor, and Juanlu' – your son, the wretched child Leonor *did* want to have and that *wasn't* mine – 'has set himself up in some business or other and about which I know nothing, and Luisa, my daughter, spends her time glued to her computer screen, watching the ups and downs of the stock market. My son would complain whenever I took an interest in his affairs: leave me alone, I can't stand you trying to manage my life, when *you've* always done exactly what you wanted. That's my son talking. Anyway, I took him at his word. I don't give a moment's thought to his future now. He hated the fact that his mother wanted to leave him a flourishing restaurant at the top of its game; or, if he'd wanted, he could have carried on the business under my hard-earned name, because, I don't want to boast, but it's a highly respected name in the world of restaurants and the gastronomic press, in the gourmet food and wine trade; he could have had a nice fat bank balance and the chance to borrow whatever he needed to set himself up on his own. But he didn't want that, and now here I am all on my ownsome.'

He complains because he has no one to whom he can bequeath all his hard work, which will die with him. In a hundred years' time, no one will appear on the TV or in the press declaring: I am the fifth generation of the Marsal family, the gastronomic dynasty founded by my great-great-grandfather. The poor thing, alone on his yacht, a Robinson Crusoe adrift on a small island, as small as one of those deceptive clumps of vegetation you find floating in the marsh; alone in his mansion, a monk spending each night in his Trappist cell; a Tuareg nomad riding his BMW through the infinite desert of indifference. Ridiculous. Yes, I actually saw Francisco's eyes welling up with tears – true, he *was* a bit drunk – it was not many months ago, on the terrace of a bar in Marina Esmeralda, where we sat perched on uncomfortable minimalist chairs next to a palm tree on the quayside (the water in that harbour isn't exactly emerald green, by the way; at night, under the spotlights, it's more a dazzling mixture of phosphorescent yellows, poisonous greens and neon blues: the debris from oil, fuel, suntan lotion and detergent: it should really be called the Marina Química or Marina Kuwait); the masts silhouetted against the sky beneath the waxing (or was it waning?) moon, are traditional wooden masts, even though they're harder to maintain; no aluminium, no carbon fibre.

'We must cling to the few principles we have left. Paella rice must have that golden caramelised crust at the bottom we call *socarrat*; foie gras and truffles must come from Périgord; and vinegar from Módena.' He's joking now. 'The new principles, the last thing we have to hold on to, serve to help us choose good wine, wooden masts for our yachts and ammunition for our hunting trips. That's what ethics and aesthetics come down

242

to now, and as we know, they tend to be one and the same. Your ethics are the suit you wear, the shoes you put on, the wine you drink, and whether you choose freshly caught fish or a slice of frozen halibut caught in some godforsaken place surrounded by glaciers. Wood is ethical and aesthetic' – thanks for the compliment, Francisco – 'and glass fibre is unaesthetic and unethical. Times have changed.'

Of course times have changed, Francisco. Life is constantly changing, it *is* change. It has no other purpose but to change and to keep changing, the Greeks knew this and I imagine even their ancestors knew it too, you never bathe twice in the same stream, you don't even bathe the same body, today there's a pimple that didn't exist yesterday, nor did this varicose vein which, for long hours, has been making its way to the surface, or this ulcer in my groin or on the sole of my foot, and which my hyperglycaemia won't allow to heal; they are all lying, those utopians who say that this troubled life of avarice and lust will be succeeded by a peaceful world in which we will all be brothers, and where, as in the Golden Age Don Quijote described, we will, in a spirit of fraternal love, dine on a shared meal of acorns. There is no heavenly peace possible beneath the sheltering sky, only a permanent state of war in which everyone is pitched against everyone and everything against everything. The problem is that with so much change, every-thing somehow ends up pretty much the same. Francisco sobbed – my life, a failure. The things you say when you've had a few too many. But what do you expect your life to be when you're about to turn or have turned seventy? A failure of course. Irremediably so? Yes. Today is worse than yesterday, but better than tomorrow. Such are the diary entries of a seventy-something. Leonor Gelabert triumphed, because the only triumph is to die a timely death, or had you forgotten? Those whom the gods love die young. She got where she was through sheer hard

243

work, she never doubted for a moment that the end justifies the means, a principle attributed to the Jesuits, but which I'm sure the ancestors of the Greeks knew about too, the means, what you have to do, the bitter pills you have to swallow, but also what you have to sacrifice, the things you have to discard, even if that involves giving them a good kick: a carpenter with too good a memory, a small red globular thing that gets flushed down the toilet, are, were, part of her purification process, stages on her ascent of the culinary and social Mount Carmel. If someone were to write a well-documented biography of her, the biographer would speak of sacrifices, of the painful decisions she had to make, her rigorous asceticism when it came to achieving perfection in the kitchen and, thanks to all those sacrifices and renunciations, her moment of plenitude. She was lucky enough to die up there on the heights, not like us egoists and cowards: even though our moment of plenitude is long since past, we stubbornly go on living, it somehow never seems a good moment to disappear, we pretend not to have reached the place where the only way is down, and then we complain about our declining health, our miserable life, our medicalised, chemically assisted survival: pills, serums, drainage tubes, nasal cannula, a catheter up your cock. We snivel on about it. But what did you expect? That your cock would still keep growing at seventy? That you would win a triathlon? Leonor was struck down by lightning on the very summit of the mountain, an enviable scenario, although, since, in life, things rarely go quite according to plan, her final chapter lasted far too long, chemotherapy, repellently high doses of poisons, vomiting fits, you told me all the details, her hair coming out in clumps in her hands, her nails coming away from the skin, her body covered in black marks, her tongue and the roof of her mouth broken out in sores, and she got very little joy out of that irritating rash or boil that was her son. While I'm talking to

244

Francisco, I'm thinking to myself: the chef she had inside her was probably flushed down the loo. Her first child proved useless, or, rather, her second child, manufactured or, rather, uterised by the factory that was, she said, her sole responsibility – I'm not telling you again: this has nothing to do with you, it's *my* problem, so just leave me in peace. You don't have to do anything or accompany me anywhere. Subject closed. But there she was at all the panel discussions about haute cuisine, at gastronomic summit meetings, not just here, but in San Sebastián, Barcelona, Copenhagen and New York. Especially after she was awarded that second Michelin star, our chef's career really took off or, as her husband would say, rocketed. Student chefs, or those simply wanting to improve their technique, would put their names down on a waiting list years in advance just to have the chance of serving an apprenticeship with her; the children of the filthy rich and the children of parents who were in the arts or politics would try to wangle letters of introduction to get their child a job as a mere washer-up at the restaurant, and yet, as it turned out, the Marsal-Gelabert couple's first brat, who had all those things within his grasp from the day he was born, loathed both the profession and the world of restaurants. Millionaires were willing to pay a fortune to get their boy in, and once in, he would keep one eye on the potatoes he peeled, the onions he chopped and the rubbish bin he wheeled back and forth, and the other on Leonor's amazing hands, which knew how to put the finishing touch to a plate, checking the garnish, adding a few thyme leaves, or leaving the dish under the grill just the few seconds longer it takes to achieve the perfect *gratiné* effect, the gastronomic miracle.

'Juanlu could have been anything he wanted, he could have been an Adrià or an Aduriz or like one of our more local chefs, a Dacosta, for example, but they all worked really hard to get where they were, and he didn't want to work or wash dishes or peel potatoes or get blistered hands from the hot oil spitting out of the frying pan. Adrià peeled potatoes while he was doing his military service, in the barracks, not at a cookery school in Lausanne, and the rest, of course, is history. Juanlu could have been a celebrity chef, a writer of articles about wine and cookery, he could have studied at the best school in Lausanne or at the Cordon Bleu in Paris, with all the big shots in France: Besson, Robuchon, Guérard, Senderens, Trama. Leonor knew them all, and I knew them ten years before she did, when I started in the early eighties, when almost no one here had heard of them. Obviously, I wouldn't expect you to know them, but for a gastronome, each of those names is what the Pope is for a Catholic, because gastronomy is polytheistic and doesn't have only one God or only one Pope: cookery is, inevitably, materialistic, secular, a federal republic. They were all gods officiating in their respective temples, and they were all friends of mine and they all adored Leonor. I was offering my son a ready-made life; if he didn't want to stay in Madrid after working in all those kitchens, he could go to Tokyo, Singapore, Hong Kong, Shanghai or Dubai and set up a restaurant in one of those up-and-coming cities if he wasn't comfortable with more traditional locations; others have done so since, and now the dragons of the Orient enjoy the very finest cuisine, the big names are all eager to open a restaurant in one of those almond-eyed cities, because gourmet cooking goes where the money is.'

His cigarette was burning down between his fingers (he had left his cigar half smoked in the ashtray); he was close to tears, not for his son, but for himself, because all his shady dealings would come to a full stop with him, and it's really distressing to have done all those dubious things – well, let's just say: the end justifies the means – in order to do others of which he was very proud, and for all of that to come to nothing, to fall into other people's hands, to be wasted – after Leonor died, the Cristal de Maldón closed: a restaurant *is* its chef – he felt like crying, and I'm not sure what I felt like doing; perhaps telling him about the son who could have been born before Juanlu and who might have turned out to be a hard-working student, a skilled chef, the son who was just a little red ball that got flushed down the toilet when his wife pulled the chain in that apartment in Valencia.

The thing being disposed of was part-payment for her imminent overland trek away from Olba and towards her new life in Madrid: but how could you possibly believe I was going to stay here forever? *Such* a promising future: a shotgun wedding, with all the women speculating: hmmm, she must be knocked up, with the baby born five months later, and then an eternity of nothing stretching out before me for the rest of my life. You're a bit late coming home tonight, love, you've probably been drinking with your pals in the bar and the rice is ruined. Never mind. Do you really see me in that role? You should know me better than that by now. Me, sobbing: But I love you and you said you loved me too. Leonor: People say all kinds of things when they're fucking, but that doesn't count. We've kept each other company in the desert and had a few good times together, that's all. Did I ever promise you anything more than that? I'm leaving, and you should find some way of leaving here too and not waste your life in that shithole of a workshop, with a father who, forty years on, still believes we're in the middle of a war and that the most interesting battle is yet to come.

That wasn't the only time Francisco spoke to me in that complaining tone. This failed Francisco first confided in me a few days after he came back to settle here, having already arranged to buy the Civera house (he didn't mention this to me at the time, not a word), he came to retire here like a humble peasant (our very own Josep Pla), and marked his return to the simple life by acquiring the best house in Olba, owned so long by the former lords of the village, and already had his yacht moored in the Marina Esmeralda a few yards from the terrace cafe where we met on subsequent occasions, and, again, I knew nothing about the existence of that yacht and he never mentioned it, because he used me – isn't that what old friends are for? – as a shoulder to cry on, while, to others, he spoke only of his triumphs. That's friendship for you. With me, he wanted admiration with a pinch of pity. He used to come and see me at the workshop, sit down on the other side of the polisher and speak of the joy of getting back to the simple life, trying to convince me how hard his working life had been: those free flights all over the world, tasting wines from Médoc and Burgundy, from South Africa, Australia and California, snoring the night away in five-star hotels, eating for free in Michelin-starred restaurants, and indulging in the usual energetic, lubricated pastimes that keep human beings entertained on all five continents. He would tell me about his sexual experiences with the natives and then, a couple of minutes later, his eyes would fill with tears and he would say how much he missed his wife, how disappointed he was in his son, how distant he felt from his daughter, and how much, over the years, he had missed us, we imbeciles who had stayed put in this village, scratching our arses, with no Atelier de Joël Robuchon, no Maison Troisgros, drinking wine from the local cooperative (which, a few years ago, bore no resemblance to today's wine, three glasses of the stuff and you'd throw up), eating rice cooked in a thousand and one different ways – in the oven, as a risotto, in a paella, with a fish stock – as we have all our lives (the very recipes he's collecting together for the book he's writing

248

— an encyclopedia of the food and cuisine of the region, over a thousand pages, part literature and part research — recording our customs just as anthropologists record the customs of the mountain peoples of Puerto Rico) and playing cards and dominoes in the evenings with the same bastards who have been screwing us over big time for the last fifty years, because Olba is a small village, which means that, when it comes to the theatre of social life, this is a repertory company, with the same actors appearing in a variety of different plays. Today Othello, tomorrow Lear, the day after that Romeo, and if necessary, you put on a wig and play Lady Macbeth because the leading lady has come down with a sore throat. You see them in a bar and, a while later, in one of the other ten or twelve bars that exist in the village, you pass them in the street, meet them at the funerals of other locals and at bullfights; whether in their work clothes or in their Sunday best, they're always the same people. True, in each place and on each occasion, they're playing a different role. But they're always, always the same people. And he wanted *me* to feel sorry for *him*. He complained that he was lonely, as if I had really struck it lucky living with Tutankhamun's mummy, my father and comrade, who, years later, I would have to feed, dress and wash, the broken digital pet who neither laughs nor cries, and doesn't even say Mama and Papa, as even the cheapest made-in-China doll will do. He wanted me to feel sorry for him, this man who, thirty years ago, used to tell me about that restaurant built on undeclared money given to him by a brother-in-law in some high government position, and would talk me through the script of the get-rich-quick years in which he played an active role, the golden days of Miguel Boyer and Carlos Solchaga, the happy times when — according to the then social democrat minister for the economy — Spain was the country in Europe where you could get rich quickest. I was filled with a mixture of anger, scorn and envy, and yet I would laugh and say: No, Spain is the country in Europe where some people, like you and your friends, can get rich quickest, because the workshop is having a really hard time of it (the late 1980s were disastrous for the region, the World Expo in Seville – Spain's biggest ever urban building project, he would say excitedly – and the Olympics in Barcelona swallowed all the available public and private capital and stole all the tourists: workers here started emigrating again, like in the 1950s, because, in Spain, all the money flowed down those two great drains: Seville, such a wonderful place, and Barcelona, *bona si la bossa sona* – good as long as there's money in the purse). In my house – that's how he referred to the restaurant: my house, it was fashionable to do so at the time, famous chefs did the same in any newspaper interviews they gave: in our house we eat, in our house we only serve – in his house, he had only the best; the vice president had moved into an apartment in the same building as the restaurant and dined there most nights. Anyone who wanted to do any kind of deal by, with or for the government, and always at the government's expense, had to be seen at the Cristal de Maldón, it was a real gold mine, they had it all worked out. And then there was that business created with money from ICEX, the Spanish Institute for Foreign Trade, to promote and export Spanish products throughout the world, a front for getting subsidies that were shared for eight or ten years with a secretary of state who had placed his wife in charge of the institute, and this was quite apart from the wine and hotel scams he was involved in and his position in that powerful publishing group. But here we are in Bar Castañer, talking about this and that, so as to avoid talking about what really matters, and I speak out in defence of Tomás Pedrós, as a form of self-defence and also to see if I can, once and for all, put paid to the subject: 'At least Pedrós has always looked for his real friends among people he liked, people he enjoyed chatting to at the bar, having a few drinks with or going out on the town, never thinking about whether or not they could be useful to him or help him out if he got into difficulties, or, indeed, whether they might even cause him difficulties. As for his other relationships, with politicians, and other such public friendships, it was clear that those were merely business relationships, ways of getting contracts more easily. And today's society can't tolerate such naivety, it's a difficult balance for anyone to maintain, and it's rejected by most people, who regard certain acquaintances as ill-advised or suspicious, simply because they don't belong to the approved circles.' I should bite my tongue, bite it right off, what am I doing defending the bastard who has ruined me, just as a way of saying he was a good guy really, then quickly changing the subject and talking about something else? But that wasn't the only reason. In fact, I fired that shot across their bows to see if it would shut them up, those creeps, those brown-nosers, who always latch on to the most useful person: I know all about Bernal and Justino. And I imagine the little bank manager is no different. And I take it for granted that it's the same with Francisco. He's never told me who he's had to run after or crawl to, there's no need. The relationships he tells me about, those secretaries of state, or the minister who visits the Cristal de Maldón each night and asks for his woodcock *bien faisandée*. After all, I don't know any of those individuals and have never set foot in the world they move in, but I know him.

Justino pours a little pessimism on my words:

'The people most likely to distrust someone like that are the ones he's given his friendship to. They'll think: why does he want me by his side when I have nothing to offer him?'

I don't know whether to take this as a counter-thrust or not.

He bends down to pick something up and, in doing so, his shirt rides up, and in the gap between trousers and shirt, you glimpse part of a kind of split globe, dark as a world without sun, and which grows darker the further south you go, with a thickening jungle of hair: he generously reveals this human landscape to you whenever he bends down on the golf course too: a troubling ravine between two wooded slopes that conceal their mysteries beneath his trousers. This split globe is the accumulation of all the succulent lipids consumed over years of eating expensive food, which is why – whether you want to or not – you assume it must be different from that of the new player who has just joined us at the table to replace Bernal, who has gone outside to speak to someone on his mobile phone: the newly appointed bank manager, a pear-shaped young man, who was sent from La Mancha to this rather unfrequented branch (he says he turned down the Misent branch, yes, I bet), and whose pale flesh – he is as yet unaccustomed to the life of this Mediterranean Florida: toasting oneself in the sun at the beach or on the golf course – is sustained by the adobe of tons of *gachamigas*, dozens of sheep's cheese sandwiches, mountains of vegetables (he said the same himself only a moment ago) and slices of traditionally cured bacon (with only a suggestion of fine ham from acorn-fed Iberian pigs – Cumbres Mayores, Guijuelo or Jabugo: the ham he's received as gifts during the year he's been branch manager). The conversation continues on the theme of how people nowadays set about achieving fame with the least possible effort. And I am the one who continues to mine that seam, which suits me fine. Anything, as long as we steer clear of Pedrós.

'The Islamists have found a really sure-fire way of appearing on TV. Your name isn't mentioned, of course, because you're just an anonymous individual in a collective story, which was also the aim of the people who wrote about the Russian revolution, the ideal of the great utopianists. They'll call you The Suicide Bomber Who Blew Himself Up. But, as a nod

252

to the new narcissism and to technology, a few hours before you blow yourself up, you can post a video on YouTube showing you standing in front of a sheet daubed with a verse from the Koran and holding a Russian- or American- or, indeed, Spanish-made machine gun (they come from all over), so that the followers of the Faithful of the Blood of the Sacrificed Lamb can admire you.'

Francisco says:

'Isn't that business about the lamb part of the Jewish tradition? Or is it Christian? Anyway, it's definitely one of ours. In Misent, they worship the Precious Blood of Christ, it's their biggest festival, and that's what they call it, the Festival of the Precious Blood, and just to confirm the horrible actuality of blood worship among Catholics, I read in the newspaper the other day that before John Paul II died, they extracted a small amount of blood from him and put it in a little bottle, just in case he's made a saint, which he obviously will be. How could he not be made a saint, when he was the victor in that clash of two armies made up of hundreds and millions of soldiers – the Christian armada versus communist atheism? If a victory like that doesn't get you a place in the calendar of saints' days, what will? Pope Leo X persuading Attila the Hun not to invade Italy pales into insignificance in comparison. Removing the gangrene of communism from the face of the earth is easier said than done. I mean, damn it, there was a time when more than half the planet's inhabitants either already were or were about to become communists. We've forgotten that in the 1960s and 70s we still didn't know on which side the coin would fall,' says he, who'd himself watched very carefully indeed to see how it fell. With one foot in the Communist Party and the other in the social democrat camp, he always stayed very firmly on the fence.

Justino nods in agreement.

'Yes, I read that too. The newspapers reported about the few vials of blood taken from the man who fought a battle that took three or four hundred million prisoners: yes, four hundred million wolves transformed into cheap labour. It completely changed the world economy. The crisis we're in now is simply the definitive redeployment of that new legion of man-tools in search of an owner to set them to work.'

'And now the communist wolf has turned vegetarian and eats grass from the hands of the man of peace, Wojtyła, a new St Francis of Assisi.' Carlos says this sarcastically, making it clear that he is speaking ironically, because he himself is determinedly secular. I imagine him fleeing like a fallow deer before the hypothetical advance of the pack of communist hounds he now finds so charming. Given the hundred or so foreclosure notices he has signed, I doubt very much that he would escape with his life. Or would he end up being undersecretary for finance in the new regime? I don't think he has what it takes to be a minister, although with wheedling hypocrites like him, you never can tell.

Me:

'Communists: a labour force crying out to be exploited – and they have been.'

Bernal takes up the earlier theme:

'The idea of going down in history as *The* Suicide Bomber would be quite enticing if you were the only one who'd had the idea, but every day, somewhere in the world, there are dozens of bombers blowing themselves up. Besides, what's the point: once you've blown yourself up, you can't go back home so everyone can congratulate you on being on the television news that evening. If you're going to become a jihadi suicide bomber, you must either be very very bitter or have a deep faith in God.'

'Or both,' says the bank manager.

Justino takes up the argument:

'You'd have to be a pretty nasty piece of work too. The

Madrid bombers have set the bar very high. A bomb that kills half a dozen people is nothing. You have to kill at least fifty before they'll give you a few minutes' coverage on the TV news or put your photo in the newspapers, whether it's at the gates of a barracks in Karachi, an airport in Moscow or a metro train in Madrid; if it was Madrid, you'd definitely make the front pages in Spain. As for Karachi, Lahore or Kabul, the press there is probably so fed up with acts of carnage they don't even bother reporting them. They'd run out of paper if they had to report every massacre. No, you have to kill dozens or even hundreds. Even the drug dealers have been infected with this media frenzy. In Mexico, fifty thousand people have died in the drug wars. They want to be talked about. Individual murders are mainly the reserve of vulgar old domestic violence; but not necessarily, there are men who take their rifle down from the gun rack and clear the house of children, stepchildren, in-laws, the ex-wife's new boyfriend, and even the dog if it gets in the way. Killing is like eating, it's all a matter of beginning. It's hard to swallow the first mouthful, but the rest goes down easily enough.'

The image of the dog lying in a pool of blood makes me shudder (what will become of you and your innocence, Tom?), but I respond sarcastically:

'Don't tell me you have difficulty getting past that first mouthful too. I thought it was just me.'

General laughter.

I go on:

'Yesterday in the paper, there were reports of floods in Pakistan that had left I don't know how many thousands dead; then, in Afghanistan, a bus had plunged down a ravine, another thirty dead; in Iraq, a bomb exploded outside a police station, killing another fifty. And all on the same day. In this avalanche of news, the report from Iraq seemed to me, in a way, both wilful and naive: I thought to myself, why bother with these attacks when Allah kills quite enough people on His own account?'

'Pariahs of the Earth that Fanon, Mao, Lenin, Marx and Che all vainly tried to save (they won't let themselves be saved, they're hopeless cases), and because the heart has reasons that reason cannot know, they continue chanting suras to Yahweh-Allah, the bearded one, and even diligently help Him in His task as the Great Executioner. So why bother trying to figure it out?' says Francisco.

Secular Carlos says:

'Someone once said that the people who believe in God are the ones who have least reason to.'

'Poverty is naturally pessimistic. The poor are always convinced that, however hard a time they're having, something far worse is lurking just around the corner. As a human being you're basically born guilty, and God only confirms that pessimistic view, especially if you happen to be born in a shanty town or in some bad neighbourhood on the outskirts of town, or go hungry from the moment your mother offers you her withered breast to chew on and sends you out to work as soon as you can stand. If you lose an arm, the priest, rabbi or ulama is quick to remind you that you could have lost your head, and if you lose your head, he'll persuade you that it would have been far more serious if whoever it was had chopped you up into little pieces, because then there would be no body and no funeral Mass. Even without a head, your relatives are happy and give thanks to God that they still have at least most of the corpse that they can take to be buried and thus feel superior and sorry for the neighbours who haven't found so much as their loved one's parson's nose. Poor wretches, they think, because they have no one and nothing to which they can dedicate a Mass, not even a consoling bit of spleen or a thigh or a kidney,' I say, pleased with the direction the conversation has now taken.

256

'I think the upper classes are more sceptical as far as the virtues or qualities of a corpse are concerned. It can easily be replaced with cocktails at some deluxe funeral home or, if their grief is more intense, eased by a shopping trip to New York, or, perhaps more fittingly, a melancholy stroll among olive trees, cypresses and ruins on one of the Greek islands,' says Francisco, adding: 'It's touching the way the poor search so desperately for their dead, even though there's nothing left of them. They don't care if they stink, if they're mutilated or rotten; they want to take them with them, to collect the corpses before the municipal cleansing department picks up, or whoever it is who has to deal with any carrion. There's probably some distributive justice going on here: the poorest families from the poorest countries are the richest in corpses. They have no money, no villa in Cap Ferrat, not even a modest pension to look forward to, but they're the owners of a rich variety of macabre biomass: those who have died in accidents at work, of an overdose, of malnutrition, Aids, cirrhosis of the liver, hepatitis C, domestic violence or a mugging; people who have died because, unable to stand it any longer, they've blown their brains out or hanged themselves on an olive tree. They're the owners of a whole varied legacy of corpses, which they defend tooth and nail. Suffer the poor to come unto me, said Jesus.'

'He said suffer the little children to come unto him not the poor.' It's Carlos again, our Secular Pear.

Me:

'Of course, but he was probably referring to the children of the poor, because no rich man would allow his son to approach a stranger. The poor man would, though, because that meeting might be the beginning of some profitable transaction. The poor tend to exist below the threshold invented by the Protestant bourgeoisie and that they call morality.'

★

It's the sour smell that predominates: in summer, it gets mixed up with other stronger, more unpleasant smells, the smell of decomposition, of dead meat, but the most unbearable of all is the smell of rotting fish or seafood. Leave a hake out in the sun for a couple of days, or an octopus or a few mussels, or the remains of the fish you've just eaten, leave them out in the rubbish bin during those suffocatingly hot summer days, and you'll see what becomes of the meal you so enjoyed eating and for which you would pay fifteen or twenty euros in a restaurant or a bar: not that our rubbish collection is exactly perfect, partly because people are totally unscrupulous about what they put in their bins, we've even found dead dogs, the putrefying bodies of cats or rats, when people know they're supposed to put their rubbish in bags, not loose, and certainly nothing dead, especially not in summer, the towns can't cope with all the crap produced by the thousands and thousands of tourists, the bins aren't big enough, they either overflow or sit there surrounded by bags that the dogs or the rats gnaw at, scattering the contents everywhere; the streets in the town centre stink, and so do the residential areas: it's a kind of uniformly funereal smell that mingles with the smells from the flowers and the gardens around the apartments and houses, and with the smell of petrol, and ends up becoming a single smell, the smell of the coast. I was paid to put up with it, and although some of my colleagues used to wear a mask, I never bothered, I've got a fairly robust sense of smell or maybe it's simply that I'm not very sensitive, but I do find it odd that tourists come here and pay good money to spend a month next to those stinking bins. They're probably used to it, because their cities smell the same or even worse, after all, the same things rot everywhere, the same brands from the same chains, bought in the same superstores all decorated in the same style. Not that I care. According to one of my fellow rubbish collectors, Nico, who came as a child from a village up in the mountains, it's the smell of the twenty-first century, neither good nor bad, it's simply what the new age smells like, the twentieth century was one smell and now it's another, he says. Until quite late into the twentieth century, the smell was wet grass and basil, but also the dung from donkeys or cows, and dirty clothes, and unwashed crotches (don't you remember being told how the old ladies in the village really stank, they'd never washed in their life, because washing was for whores, how they stank of pee or decades of concentrated menstrual blood; and how the old men smelled of pee, as well as dried cum); now we've become like animals, and our lairs stink because of all the stuff we keep in the fridge until it absolutely has to be binned; I shouldn't think the caves and huts of primitive men smelled of Chanel No. 5, and can you imagine what the streets of the big cities were like two thousand years ago? And imagine what ancient Rome was like: animal bones and guts rotting in the mud along with vegetables and bits of fish, all thrown out into the street, buckets full of the night's excretions tossed out of the windows with a cry of garde loo, assuming of course that the emptier of the bucket had the courtesy to warn passers-by. Rome's refuse collectors had to pick up dead animals abandoned on the highway and throw them onto the carts, and sweep up real shit, and, from what I've seen in that TV series, Rome, they would probably pick up three or four human corpses every night – another corpse for the cart, I'll take the arms and you take the legs, and one, two, three and UP, God, what a weight – bodies left on street corners, with their guts hanging out, smelling of shit, or already half rotten, the flies green as emeralds forming a buzzing cloud around the corpse; if a rat, which is only about the size of your hand, smells bad when it rots and provokes a swirl of bluebottles and wasps around it, imagine what a rotting body weighing ninety or a hundred kilos must smell like, and imagine the swarm of insects around that. You see dead bodies in films and on the TV news. They don't smell, but those rotting bodies, swollen as wineskins, washed up on the banks of the river that runs through Rome and whose name escapes me, well, imagine the stink of that, and the refuse collectors didn't have gloves or masks then, no hi-vis jackets so that they wouldn't get knocked down in the dark by a runaway horse. I guess they would only collect refuse during the day, because it would be just impossible at night, too dark, don't you think? Mind you, it doesn't exactly smell of roses here in the summer. In winter, it's different: there are fewer people, the bins don't overflow with rubbish, except on the holidays: Christmas and New Year, or days when there's a lot of present-giving, Mother's Day, Father's Day and so on, but not many; apart from days like that, the bins are plenty big enough, and there are some areas it's hardly worth bothering with, areas where there are mainly holiday homes, apartment blocks near the marina or housing developments up in the mountains, where, in the winter months, the bins are empty or pretty much so, and the air you breathe there is very different from the summer air, the cold freezes the smells, makes them less potent, keeps them in their place, stops them spreading; when it's cold, it's the things themselves that smell, each separate thing, not the air; if something smells bad, it's just that one thing that smells, not like in summer, when the smell really spreads, like gauze impregnated with the stench of filth, and that gauze is everywhere, wrapping about everything. On winter days like today, when I used to ride on the running board on the back of the truck, bumping along the streets of those developments built along the coast, or in among the elegant houses up in the hills, there were some nights when I felt as I imagine people who go waterskiing must feel: the slap of cold air in your face, the smell of wet grass, resin, damp earth, the solitude of the night and the darkness (and we're the only people out in those streets edged with walls or railings lush with vegetation), whole districts where there's not a single light in the windows, and in some parts, the council doesn't even bother turning on the street lamps. It's like a ghost town where you feel you're the only man alive, the king of all you survey. These days, now that I've got nothing to do since I got laid off at the workshop, I go there for walks and a cigarette, because it's a way of calming down or escaping, instead of spending the whole day thinking, how the hell are we going to live on my wife's wages and my last few months of unemployment benefit? We should never have bought that new TV, we gave ours to the kids, but now they're always squabbling because they each want to watch a different programme: the cure is worse than the disease, my wife says, and more expensive too, I add, just to wind her up, because it was her idea to buy a new TV; we should never have bought the new Peugeot either, but it seemed necessary at the time, because, of course, while I was working as a refuse collector, our timetables were compatible, with her working during the day and me at night, but after I started at the workshop, it was different, I had to be in Olba at half past seven in the morning, and she had to get to the biscuit factory in Misent by eight, and once we'd got the kids up and dressed and made them breakfast, it was impossible for us to coordinate things, of course I could have made do with my old moped, after all, it never gets that cold here. Or we could have arranged things so that she changed to the evening shift, as she did later on, then I could drive her there in the car after lunch. When they closed the biscuit factory, she managed to get a job at the fruit warehouse, which was lucky, although, depending on the day, she doesn't finish work until midnight and sometimes even later. And now that I'm unemployed, she's the one who needs the car, the one who uses it. It's just as well we didn't move to Olba, which she always preferred to Misent: you'd be nearer your job, she'd said, and it would be better for the kids. It would have been disastrous, because we even looked at a couple of semi-detached properties: they're about half the price of houses in Misent, and they're better built, better finished, and with a little garden too, she said, looking out at the handkerchief-sized patch complete with a tiny palm tree, which the red palm weevil would doubtless kill off in a matter of months. I kept thinking, why is she looking at house prices and comparing them with prices in Misent, when we've never even owned an apartment in Misent and have always rented? I just hope to God we can afford to go on doing that.

I like going out in the rain. I put on my cagoule and walk the deserted streets. On rainy nights, we'd be hanging on to the back of the truck, and my colleague Nico used to say: Right now we're the masters of all this, we can enjoy it more and at a better time of year than those idiots who pay a fortune to come and spend the worst two weeks in August here. I wouldn't come and spend August here if you paid me; I'd go north, somewhere with green fields and a clean river and a tiny village with about twenty or thirty inhabitants and where you can buy good bread and get the local dairyman to provide you with fresh milk, although nowadays you can't get any peace and quiet even in those semi-abandoned villages (in summer, all the emigrants come back from Madrid, Bilbao or Barcelona, talking loudly, getting their wallets out in the bar so that you can see how stuffed they are with euros, and legions of tourists come too, looking, like you, for some peace, but completely ruining it for each other), you can't even buy fresh milk, they won't sell it to you because it's not allowed and farmers risk getting a big fine slapped on them; so there you are, practically standing next to a cow, and you're buying cartons of skimmed milk, enriched with calcium or with added isoflavones or whatever those vitamins are they're always coming up with. You can see the cows grazing in the fields, but you have to buy the same milk you'd buy here. It makes you feel like running up the hill, crouching down under the cow and sucking on its udder. That would be great. I don't know what they would accuse you of if they caught you at it, but I'm sure they'd accuse you of something: animal cruelty, non-consensual sex, molesting a mental defective, who knows. But wouldn't that be great, squeezing and feeling the milk gush straight into your mouth? I used to enjoy drinking my wife's milk. Did you ever try that? It's sweeter than cow's milk. I figure most of us have drunk some of the milk intended for our children. We humans have a tendency to want to eat and drink each other. Haven't you ever seen that picture of Saturn eating his children? Didn't you feel like eating your kids when they were just tender little pink piglets? Don't be so disgusting, I would say. And he'd bellow out: We're the kings of the streets. And I would think: beyond our kingdom, behind the bins and the street lights and the plants climbing up the railings and fences, are monkey-puzzle trees, palm trees, wisteria, hibiscus, swimming pools, covered and uncovered, bubbling jacuzzis, ultra-slim plasma TVs, houses and gardens to which we would never have access, not even to collect the rubbish. And so I would say to him: The only thing we're the kings of is the rubbish, and not even that. We're actually the slaves of the rubbish, the real queen of the rubbish is Esther Koplowitz, who owns the company with all the fat contracts. I wouldn't mind being employed to tidy the gardens of some of those rich wankers, but no, they're too mean, instead, they employ Ukrainians or Romanians and pay them ten or twelve euros a day, but once the Ukrainians and Romanians have pruned their roses and trimmed their palm trees, they get even for being swindled by hitting their employers over the head with an iron rod or a hammer or else knifing them, then stealing all the jewellery from the safe along with the latest household appliances. Confessors and judges call it restitution. The rich pretend to be protecting themselves, but in fact they're drawn to danger, walking on a knife-edge or on the wild side, like in that Lou Reed song Esteban says he's so fond of, Doo do doo do doo do do do do do doo: they invite the thief into their house just to save a few euros; God or nature or whatever must plant in their genes that overwhelming instinct in favour of obligatory redistribution as a counterbalance to their greed. The rich enjoy stealing and get a small thrill when someone steals from them, a feeling of danger that doubtless confirms them in their desire to keep everything under lock and key, makes them value their posses-sions even more, hurriedly replacing any stolen goods and hiding them away still more effectively, and thus continuing to accumulate loot. Nature is very wise.

All that was in my days as a refuse collector, but then the same company made me a road sweeper, a better job, they said, cleaner, more gentlemanly, ballroom dancing with a broom: that's what they tried to fob us off with when it was announced that they'd be moving us to a different section, and from the nocturnal trip on the truck to a diurnal stroll with a broom over our shoulder; it was better, they said, more ecological, using only human fuel, a promotion, really, which was all very well, except – and they didn't tell us this, we only found out later – not only were we paid less per hour, but there was no real overtime, and the truth is that in jobs like ours, overtime is crucial. You can't live on the seven hundred euros they pay you in wages, but, as a rubbish collector, they would often give you thirteen or fourteen hours of over-time a week, and then of course you'd earn quite a lot, especially in summer, what with the tourists, the bars, the food and drinks stalls, or at fiesta time with the stands and the people boozing in the streets, until the new mayor arrived and, according to the company, he was looking for an excuse to give the refuse collection contract to another company owned by a friend, because every mayor is in the pay of someone, and when a new mayor arrives, he naturally wants to get his pals on the gravy train (that's what they were saying, but how likely was it that anyone was going to take the contract away from the Koplowitz family, who have the contract here in Olba, and in Misent, and in the whole region and in half of Spain?), what they also told us (and here we had no alternative but to believe them), was that the new mayor had said it was an absolute scandal that we were routinely being given a few hours' overtime every blessed day of the year, and so they cut our hours, and even got rid of some of us and made others, whether we liked it or not, into road sweepers. Anyway, that's what happened. My wages were cut by nearly half, and I couldn't complain either, I was one of the lucky ones, I mean, at least I still had a job, because they fired more than a third of the rubbish collectors. We intend to respect the rights and the seniority of those who remain, they said, and we will also be taking family circumstances into consideration, and since I have three children, the company did me a favour and let me keep my job, but, of course, by downgrading me from rubbish collector to road sweeper, they took away my overtime: it was a nicer job, less stressful, none of that jumping on and off, loading and unloading I'd had to do before, because I'd be completely knackered after my night's work, although now the foreman was always hurrying us along and, on Friday and Saturday nights, what with young people binge-drinking and everything, the place was like a latrine, a pigsty, you can't imagine the things you'd find in some areas, and these are young people who've finished secondary school, done their baccalaureat, even already going to university, but they're real savages, far worse than any labourer: one night, they pulled up the entire avenue of palm trees that had been neatly planted that very week in readiness for the visit of the Catalan president, who was coming to inaugurate the new garden; another day, they'd uprooted all the rose bushes in the park: and yet another time, removed all the leaves and branches from the little trees in some new square, leaving only the trunks, I saw that for myself: you go there one day and see the garden looking all pristine and lovely, and the next day, the beautiful trees the gardeners had planted a couple of months before are just thirty or forty bare stakes without a leaf or a branch on them, I mean, what possible pleasure can those wankers get from ruining trees, because it must have taken them a long time too, it's sheer malice. And yet that malice seems to get the bastards going, they don't do a stroke of work all day, and so, come nightfall, they're full of energy, because they must have been busy all night with a saw, an axe, a chainsaw or whatever; every weekend it's the same story: filth, vomit, urine, broken glass, even shit: they shit in the doorways or behind the bushes, by the walls or in the sandpit or on the grass, and the next day, children arrive with their mothers and start playing in the sand and go running to their mums with their hands all covered in shit, and then the mothers complain to the town council, saying how filthy everything is, that there's even human excrement in the parks, and we road sweepers get the blame, as if it was our shit. Those infantile sons of bitches will shit anywhere, out of necessity sometimes, because they stuff themselves with all kinds of junk, which upsets their stomach and gives them diarrhoea, but they do it out of spite too, to spoil things for other people, basically, they're just little shits (in every sense); there were times when I thought I'd been better off as a rubbish collector: you had your route, your job, certain bins to empty, and that gave you a routine, a feeling of security, although you did get the occasional surprise, but being a road sweeper, it's one permanent surprise, and on market days or when the town council put on a dance or some special event, bloody hell, then I thought I'd have been a hundred times better off collecting rubbish, although there were also times when I thought the exact opposite: on bright winter or spring mornings, there you were all alone with your broom, as if you owned the whole village, cool mornings, sunny mornings, the streets empty, the people still at home or working, the children at *school, just the occasional old lady out with her shopping trolley, smiling at you and saying good morning, dear, then you hoped you'd live forever and you'd get out your sandwich and your can of beer, sit on a park bench and eat and drink a toast to the winter sun or to the spring shade of some pine tree: it was hard to believe you were being paid for that. On the mornings when it was my turn to clean up outside the school where Iván, my youngest, goes, and it was playtime, at first, I'd feel embarrassed when he'd call to me and run over to the fence to give me a kiss (although I was pleased too, of course), but then it would really make my day when all the kids ran over with Iván to say hello, and skipped around me, shouting and laughing in the natural, joyful way kids do, because, at that age, there's not an ounce of malice in them, and they like costumes and uniforms: they'd see me in my uniform and the little angels would say that when they grew up, they wanted to be street cleaners too and wear a uniform like mine, because, of course, they still weren't old enough to know what that uniform meant, although their mum or dad would explain to them later when they got home, what do you mean, you want to be a street cleaner? That's the lowest of the low, sweetheart, no, you'll be an engineer or an architect or a singer or a footballer like Ronaldo, or a Hollywood actor like Brad Pitt. It'll be the same with Aida, my oldest, or Aitor, who's my middle child. Their fellow students will have been told what a street cleaner does, and that there are uniforms and uniforms; at their age, if they see you in the street in your street cleaner's kit, they'll wish the earth would swallow them up, and try to hide away somewhere although that's not actually true, that's what you'd think, but the truth is very different: whenever Aida has spotted me on the street, she's run over and given me a kiss, although I can't imagine she enjoys her friends — because you know how stupid fourteen-year-old girls are nowadays, all pretending that they're the daughters of lawyers, when really their dad is just a labourer mixing cement (the rich girls and the semi-rich go to private schools) — anyway, she can't have liked her friends knowing that her father's a road sweeper, even though the other girls' fathers are only bricklayers or plumbers who spend all day unblocking pipes; Aida is the more affectionate one: Aitor is colder, more stupid in a way, well, he's a boy, but even he comes over to give me a kiss. He'll leave the gang of nitwits he's sitting with on a bench somewhere, plotting something or other, never anything good, and slouch over, head down, to greet me. And at home, he'd often say: I know who pulled up the palm trees or who burned those three rubbish bins, but I can't tell you; they're real bastards, Dad, they burn the bins, the postboxes, they shit in the street and take a video, crap and all, on their mobile phones, and I wondered sometimes if those bastards weren't his friends, those same creeps sitting on the bench with him, sucking on a joint all day, a faint smile on their lips, looking jeeringly at you and at anyone else who happened to pass. I've never been ashamed of being a road sweeper. It's an important job, what would things be like if we didn't work our socks off, although that's a lie, I've felt ashamed sometimes, when I've seen those supposedly unemployed men taken on by the town council (where they happen to have useful contacts) sloping off and hiding behind a bush in the park or sitting in the bar mid-morning, stuffing their face and drinking, and people saying: only lazy sods become road sweepers, but they don't care, they just laugh, water off a duck's back; and often they themselves will joke with some complete stranger about how little work they do. Then I'd feel ashamed of being a street cleaner, but only then, though that was often enough because those incidents were pretty frequent. It makes me even angrier now; when I see them, my blood boils, here I am unemployed and there they are, the ones with all the right connections, taking it easy and having a laugh at our expense. No, the bad thing about being a street cleaner, the reason I left, wasn't because I was ashamed, but because they stopped paying overtime: if there was a dance or a fiesta put on by the town council, or some binge-drinking party out in the street, you simply had to work faster, and if you couldn't finish on time, that was your problem. You slogged away, then had to put up with people complaining about how dirty the streets were, but that wasn't the worst of it, the worst was ending up with just seven hundred euros a month. But I never felt ashamed, no. My father: I can't believe you really want to be a road sweeper for the rest of your life. It's no job for a man of forty, he used to say. And me: Dad, things have changed. My mother: Leave the boy alone. I got sick to death of seeing him puffed up like a turkey, his drunkard's eyes glinting mockingly, making fun of my job, and one day, I couldn't contain myself any longer. I said: And what have you done with your life? You've been a* collidor, *an orange-picker — you hardly need a university degree to learn how to handle the shears or how to carry the crates around like a mule, worrying about whether it's going to rain, because if it rains, you don't get paid, and you have to put food on the table every day, oh yes, and as if that wasn't a miserable enough life, then you go and get a slipped disc and have to walk around all bent. And what became of your pension, huh? You get the bare minimum. Or even less. Nothing. We go at each other then, me and my dad, as he counters with: Yes, but at least shears are* a man's tool and *you work with other* men *(that was then, I said to myself, now it's all Romanians picking the oranges, more women than men, women pick more quickly and carry more crates, and if you don't watch out, the foreman, who tends to be a forewoman now, will shout at you and tear you off a strip; I've seen it happen), and picking oranges and pruning and burning dead leaves and scrub and carrying crates and putting them on a truck are jobs men have always done, but trailing around with a broom and leaning on street corners, that hardly seems like a job for a man, I mean the only people I've ever seen sweeping the street are old women sweeping the pavement outside their house, but I know you've always preferred that to carrying wooden beams, climbing up scaffolding, hefting bags of cement, or even driving a truck, you soon got tired of all that; your mother and I gave you a good strong body, and you could have earned as much as you liked these past few years, when there was bags of money to be made in the construction business, like you did when you drove the truck, but, no, you never wanted that, you may have a strong body, but you lack oomph. I told him to go to*

268

hell. Are you calling me a fairy? And you, you call yourself a man?
You never even made it to the end of the month on what you earned
and then you'd spend all day whingeing on about how your back ached
from all that bending and lifting and carrying, despite mother's hot
salt baths, and rubbing your back with herbs and oils, calling the doctor
every five minutes because you'd got a sore throat (it's because they're
exposed to the damp air in the orchards all day, it's because there was
such a heavy frost this morning, it's because: yes, every day she had an
'it's because your poor father'), or taking you to the clinic because you'd
pulled a muscle, and you didn't even have the balls to go to the doctor's
on your own, the sight of the hospital corridor and the stretchers was
enough to make you practically shit yourself; if I am a coward, then
I've inherited that cowardice from you. You're not a man. You've been
a slacker all your life, and you've been treated like a slacker and paid
what a slacker should be paid. It's not even really a job, picking oranges,
you've never really been able to say: I have a job. You had a job the
day they took you on and lost it the day they didn't take you on — you're
just a tame dog, trailing after the first person to offer you a few euros,
wagging your tail, and it was pour us another brandy, another glass
of wine, and if no one offered you work, then you'd be in a foul mood,
grumbling on about how you hadn't been picked for any of the teams
because it was raining or because the bastard on duty (they were all
bastards according to you) had chosen someone cheaper and — of course
— nowhere near as good as you, or because there were no more oranges
left to pick, and then you'd take it out on her, raise your voice and
your hand to her, but not to those bastards who had failed to choose
you. You've been jobless all your fucking life, a permanent job-seeker:
every night you'd go to the bar, every day to the main square on the
lookout for work, showing yourself off the way whores do, smiling at
the man doing the choosing, trying to get into conversation, to see if
some jerk would notice you or like you better than someone else and
take you on. Clowning around so that they'd pick you rather than
another man. Desperately telling jokes. Saying you'd buy the guy a drink

or give him a cigarette, when he had enough money to buy a million drinks and a million cigarettes. So they're all men, are they, that bunch of losers you get together with in the bar, all of them with a chip on their shoulder, their pensions too small to get them through to the end of the month, but criticising anyone who attempts to improve his lot? Haggling with the waiter, noticing who pays for a round and who doesn't, and whether they drank a one-euro glass of wine or a brandy that cost one twenty-five. Are they men, those wretches who spend all day watching what others do with their lives, as if, by talking about other people's lives, they could forget what they've done or failed to do with their own? Because you didn't exactly equip me with the right weapons for this war. Not me or my sister. You were far more interested in your game of cards, in having a late breakfast with your friends on Saturday mornings and a brandy every evening after work, than in what I had or hadn't done. So don't you fucking lecture me. I feed my kids and I take them to school and I'll pay for their studies for as long as I can. You had me working as soon as I was old enough, it didn't matter what kind of work. You just wanted the money earned by your fourteen-year-old son. You shameless . . . My mother hurled herself at me, covered my mouth with her hands to stop me talking. I pushed her away: you keep out of it, it's none of your business. She started crying. Her solution to everything. But all I wanted was to be able to earn a little more so that I could live the way I had up until then. And that was when I got lucky and started working at the carpentry workshop. Or, rather, I thought I'd got lucky – that I had, at last, found a nice, quiet, stable job.

When I arrange to meet them in the office, the other four already know what I'm going to say, because Álvaro has told them, even though I asked him not to. I want to be the one to tell them, I said, so that they find out from me, I don't want

270

them to think I'm hiding, afraid to show my face. But all pacts have been broken, nothing binds us together any more. Jorge is very sure of himself and of his skills as a carpenter. Ahmed and Julio, on the other hand, have no very high hopes. They live from hand to mouth. Joaquín just seems bewildered. But Álvaro, sitting opposite me, apparently gazing at me meekly, is merely pretending to be resigned to his fate. Don't expect me to feel sorry for you, his eyes are saying. He's the one who referred to himself as 'old' just to make me feel bad, and yet he's the one refusing to pity me: you surely don't expect me to help you, do you? he said when I asked him to keep the secret to himself for a few days, and he again purses his lips and tut-tuts when we're all gathered in the office. Again, he looks as if he's about to spit. At me. By warning the others about the situation, he was doubtless doing what he logically had to do, being loyal to his colleagues, class solidarity and all that, but I've worked with him for forty years, we've often had lunch down by the lagoon; together – again that endless tape running inside my head – he and I made many a furtive fishing or hunting expedition on a Saturday, although lately I've been going there with Ahmed instead, because Álvaro, as a father and a grandfather, had family commitments, social obligations, or so he said – excuses, lies, his children hardly ever go to see them, his wife once told me bitterly – and suddenly all those days we've spent together don't exist, but the painful memory of them does. He said: you can't do this to me, not when I've only got another four years before I retire. You know what you are, don't you? He seems convinced that I'm deliberately losing everything just to annoy him, that I'm doing this just to him. He'd figured I would retire five years ago, when I was sixty-five, but would keep the workshop open, leaving him in charge, the effective boss, giving orders to an assistant, who would

do the heavier work. I would presumably have hired that
assistant and have kept coming down to the workshop each
day and generally carry on as normal, keeping in touch with
customers, checking the accounts, etc., because if you take
Álvaro away from the cutting-machine, the lathe, the polisher,
the drill or the rasp, if you take him away from the varnish,
he hasn't a clue what to do, he has hands, but no head. He
thought nothing would change, that it would all stay more
or less the same, the only change being me drawing my
pension from the bank on the twenty-fifth of each month and
him getting a large increase in salary because he was taking
on more responsibility. The workshop closing, the dismissals,
the pre-bankruptcy embargo, that was all totally unforeseen,
and he can't forgive me for that – none of them can – as if
I had closed the workshop and fired them all on a mere whim.
They hate me because I've smashed the milk jug they were
carrying on their heads: the jug is in pieces and the milk has
spilled everywhere, filling the cracks in the tiles; but I'm not
to blame for their dreams, I didn't encourage them. As I would
have said in my young days with Francisco: I exchanged money
for labour. We each contributed our labour and fulfilled our
part of the bargain. No dreams were in the contract: they're
the responsibility of the individual; and each and every one
of the disappointments, disruptions or discomforts they'll
suffer as a consequence will hurt me with a pain that goes
far beyond the economic, not that they'll believe that, they
don't understand and there's no reason why they should;
they've been left without work, their calculations have all
proved wrong; I imagine what these were: the payments on
Álvaro's motorhome so that, when the time came, when he
and his wife both retired, he could embark on the happy life
of the wanderer; on that day, the day he received his pension,
then I could close the workshop. It didn't matter about the

others. And what was to be done with the instalments on Joaquín's Peugeot 307 Break, with the communion party for his daughter or his son, I can't quite remember now if it was the boy or the girl who was due for first communion, but he told me months ago that he'd already booked the restaurant for the spring, Las Velas, one of the most popular – and most expensive – places for such occasions; he told me: you have to book a year in advance, because, otherwise, they won't take your reservation. I want to give my son the very best, everything I didn't have as a child; you see, my wife works in the biscuit factory (or the fruit warehouse – I'm not sure now where Joaquín told me she was working) and earns a nice little wage. Not that we're well off, of course, but we can afford it. And what about Ahmed and his plan to bring his widower father over from Morocco, where he lives alone, because his other brothers have emigrated to France and Belgium, and his idea of buying a four-bedroom house, one room for him and his wife, another for the father, and one for each child, because they're a boy and a girl and it's not right for children of different sexes to share a room, however young they are. It's immoral and, in the long run, dangerous, Señor Shteban. A Muslim doesn't want that, he would explain when we went fishing together, doubtless hoping to touch my heart and get me to say: I'm going to give you a loan that you can pay back gradually, when you can – these Arabs think money grows on trees here – or that I would, at least, guarantee a loan as a down payment on one of those apartments he'd seen; or an advance on his wages, he would suggest, as we approached one of those moments of togetherness that happen when you spend the morning in the countryside alone with someone; Julio's Saturday suppers (or Friday suppers in Ahmed's case and at his house) and Jorge's season ticket to watch Valencia play; or the christening party for Álvaro's grandchildren. And Ahmed: Mulud, circumcision, the nightly feasts during Ramadan, spicy harissa perfumed with the coriander he buys in the halal shops – the other day, I noticed they're selling coriander in the local supermarket too, well, money's money, and coriander has an expanding niche in the market, the Latin Americans use it too, as I know from Liliana – dates, almond cakes, the parties he holds when they kill a lamb and roast it in the oven in the courtyard, and to which they invite their Moroccan friends from Misent, parties that he's told me about – he even invited me to one. Roast lamb, salads, honey-glazed fritters, almond cakes, Coca-Cola and all the tea you can drink. Were those invitations intended to pave the way to that advance on his wages? I will leave this world without ever knowing, not that it matters. It's a bit late to find out who genuinely cared about you, and who was motivated entirely by self-interest, who was nice to you purely because he wanted something, like my brother Germán's wife, the hypocrite who fooled us all, even my mother, who was initially jealous because she was taking her eldest son from her, the handsomest one too. Álvaro, Joaquín, Julio, Jorge, Ahmed. Jorge, his pink face, his little eyes sunk in fat: meals with friends, feasts with relatives, birthday celebrations, a season ticket to the football, bus trips to the Mestalla stadium in Valencia with other fans from Misent, wearing the team scarf and singing the team anthem, *amunt, amunt València*, Friday night or Saturday afternoon visits to the La Marina shopping mall. H&M, Zara, Massimo Dutti, Adolfo Domínguez, Movistar and Vodafone, and then a family visit to the pizzeria or the cinema, the latest *Avatar* in 3D or the second season of *Millennium*, you could spend all weekend in the mall, apart from going to the football; and if it isn't pizza, it's hamburgers with the kids in Hollywood at the entrance to the mall, and then there's the medieval bouncy castle, the pretend horses

274

and immodestly rocking plastic bulls, on which the children practise riding for the first time; as well as the swings and inflatable slides. Julio, Jorge and Ahmed are not the same as Álvaro, who has worked with me all my life, or as Joaquín, who I would like to have taken on permanently, had time not been against us. He's a born worker. I know how thrilled he was to exchange sweeping the streets for driving the van and assembling furniture in people's homes along with Ahmed (who is also a good guy). He's the kind who can't wait to show you his driver's licence: I've got the full licence, I can drive any kind of vehicle – he shows you the pink card bearing the relevant symbols, truck, car, motorcycle – and I'm strong enough to carry any load. When he says this, he raises one arm and flexes it, imitating the strong man in the circus. When they finish work, he and Ahmed give each other a high five and then have a beer in the bar. He's no genius, but he's as strong as an ox and very willing. Yes, I would have kept him on. And, at a pinch, Ahmed too. Not the others though (Julio is just a nobody; Jorge is too proud and thinks he knows more than he actually does). Ahmed thought he was my favourite because I took him fishing on Saturdays, let him drive the 4x4 down the narrow paths around the lagoon, spread the tablecloth on the ground by the water, open the cans of tuna and make a salad. We used to barbecue lamb chops over a fire, using olive twigs I kept in the car as skewers. The day before, he'd say: I'll buy the lamb chops, Señor Shteban, because the Moroccan butcher, who's the best local butcher, slaughters the lamb as it should be slaughtered, and then he'd pause, expecting me to hand him a twenty-euro note and say, go on, keep the change; he was apparently just being helpful, but the truth is he hates to eat meat that hasn't been slaughtered in one of their slaughterhouses, I don't know, these Moroccans, after all the hunger and hardship they've endured, now they go all delicate on us: if it isn't halal, I can't eat it. The animals have to be facing Mecca when their throats are slit, then they're bled to death. There's no shilly-shallying, no quick blow to the head for a chicken or a rabbit, or a harder blow if it's a lamb, and, needless to say, no euthanasia in the form of an electric shock, they don't even allow strangling: no, they slit the animal's throat, praying to God as they do so. Islamist terrorists also favour throat-slitting. Machine guns and explosives are mere substitutes, albeit highly effective, but there's nothing like slicing open a throat and having the blood spill onto the ground. It's in the Semitic genes: Yahweh asked Abraham to cut the throat of his son Isaac, then let him swap the boy for a poor lamb who happened to be passing: the important thing is cutting throats and soaking the ground with blood. The crackling flames from the dry branches placed on top of a bed of damp grass, the sizzling fat as the lamb roasts, a lamb that was turned to face Mecca before it had its throat cut and was bled to death by a circumcised butcher. The smell of burning fat and wood mingling with the sickly-sweet air of the marsh. He used to drink with me too (he had nothing against Christian wine and beer, only wrongly butchered meat), and so we'd always put a few cans of beer in the ice chest.

But Álvaro should understand the situation better than any of them: he was as much a part of the business as I was (he who was like a son to my father, the son he inherited from his best friend) or as I once was, he can hardly complain about the death of a limb when the body has died. The firm collapsed on the very same day for him as it did for me, not a day sooner, I waived all privileges. The same day and the same hour for the carpenter's actual son and for the guy who was like a son to the carpenter. I didn't jump overboard and start swimming to see if I could reach the beach a minute before him. I stood on the deck until the very last moment so that we would go down together. If the business goes under, then so do we. I go under and Álvaro goes under. We go under together. That's how it is. The others, the ones I took on more recently – Joaquín, as I say, is the exception, a very strange fish indeed, a complete mystery, who knows what lies behind that eternal smile of his? – the others were merely birds pecking at the elephant's fleas, despite Álvaro's alarm when he saw how skilled Jorge was. The business consisted of my father, Álvaro and me. Isn't that right? We don't exploit anyone, we just do our work, isn't that so, my friend? It doesn't matter that Álvaro has grown-up children and even a few grandchildren and has paid off his mortgage. Losing his dream of a motorhome is not so very grave either. They can use the car they've always used. A seven- or eight-year-old Renault Laguna, which he bought, apparently, because the magazines said it was the safest car on the market, and Álvaro's very keen on safety. It's not bad at all, it's perfectly fine. If he's looked after it – and I know he takes more care of it than he does of his wife, checking it, studying it, cleaning and caressing it – it could last him another ten years. And I think his wife has a car too, because she drives to work. He'll get two years' unemployment benefit too. That's not bad at all. Two years. Many people would happily sign up to a guarantee that they'd have that much time in the world. Besides, his wife has worked for years at Mercadona, which is about the securest job you can get at the moment, and even though she's been off sick lately because of depression – or has been suffering from depression after being diagnosed with heart disease or one of those rare illnesses they diagnose people with nowadays – she'll still get her disability pension. I know it's not the same thing, of course it isn't, but if they've been left jobless, so have I, and it's far worse for me, because the workshop and the machines no longer belong to me, not a single one of the planks in the stores – which have presumably all now been impounded – is mine. Those twats don't yet know that even the bed I sleep in is no longer mine, not even the showerhead I use when I wash my dad. My account books have been impounded. I got so tired of creditors ringing me up, I decided to rip out the landline and throw my mobile in the lagoon – there's no point going through the rigmarole of cancelling my account – and thus I have joined the long list of the lagoon's destroyers and contaminators. Yet another one. Criminals throw incriminating weapons into the marshy pools; recently, acting on a tip-off, the police dragged one of the lagoons and found a veritable arsenal, I read about it in the local newspaper, dozens of guns with their serial numbers erased and the barrels sawn off, thus removing all the bore marks, which doubtless correspond to bullets found in bodies dumped on rubbish tips, on empty building sites, in the boots of cars or abandoned on the pavement or inside a bank after a robbery; police divers even found a car submerged beneath the water, it's really nothing new: years ago, Bernal used to offload asphalt roofing felt into the lagoon. But what was I saying, ah, yes, the telephone has drowned, the workshop is shut, the bank account is frozen, the Toyota will be clamped by the local authorities in a couple of weeks' time, because that's the deadline for me to hand over all the relevant papers to the judge (not that I'll do that, no, I won't be giving the incumbent of Court Number Two in Misent that particular pleasure) and as for the house, there's a foreclosure notice that will come into force in a month: they'll confiscate all the furniture, thus adding to the problems at the court warehouse, which, in this, the age of foreclosures and evictions, is already full to bursting. They've run out of space for all the confiscated electronics, furniture, machines and tools, for the old cars that are no use to anyone, but that have been seized simply to comply with a court order, whose sole aim is to punish the owners for having failed to keep up with their mortgage repayments. There just isn't room for all those cars, and so they stay out in the street, slowly falling to pieces, getting covered in dust and rust, and at the mercy of predatory scrap merchants. What matters is ensuring that the owner is well and truly screwed. Every now and then, auctions are organised to try and get rid of some of that junk, but even auction vultures aren't keen to take on those particular bargains: apartments, mattresses, computers, cars with five or six thousand kilometres on the clock. What had once seemed so necessary is now excess to requirements. Yes, the courts will take everything, imposing a distraint order that my brother and sister will challenge as soon as they find out that my father's ghost continued to sign cheques, guarantees and loans right up until his final moments. Oh to be a fly on the wall when they realise there's nothing left, because, in order to get the necessary loans that would allow me to take on the extra work for Pedrós, I forged my father's signature with, as my accomplice, the bank manager, the one who preceded the Secular Pear, and into whose office I dragged the old man, who was clearly in no fit state to sign anything. It cost me a fat bribe, a fancy dinner and a couple of bottles of French white and Spanish red. We sat in the manager's office with my tamagotchi father, whose signature I forged several times, signatures that appeared on every page of every contract, copies and all, as well as I don't know how many other documents and cheques. I can imagine my sister Carmen's fury when she finds out, although, if she and my brother have any sense and get themselves a good lawyer and an expert to certify that the signatures are forgeries, and, above all, if they don't get flustered or lose their heads, they just might win the case. And then they would be far better off than me, because I am about to abandon them, not in order to swim to shore from the sinking ship, nor even to have the satisfaction of saying 'fuck you'. They are only a small part of the theatrical company

I'm bidding farewell to, because that's what's required by the particular play my father and I are performing. They're welcome to their unemployment benefit or, indeed, their tantrums at the lack of it or, in the case of my brother and sister, their properties, always assuming they can wrench them from the bank's greedy grasp. My future would be a pension, of which I'd only be able to hang on to six or seven hundred euros, because anything above that would have to go to slowly reducing a debt that could never be paid off in a hundred years, and a second count, as the judges say in their summings-up, of forgery, fraud, misappropriation of funds, or whichever term the penal code would use to describe what I've done – I didn't bother to consult it before forging all those signatures – and a subsequent prison sentence. And I really don't see myself doing time in the can at my age: in winter, in Fontcalent prison, you could probably get by, a bit of sun warming the exercise yard and a couple of blankets to keep you snug at night, but in summer, it must be unbearable, a frying pan where you fry in your own fat. Álvaro's fucked, but not because of my finaglings or my failures. He gambled his life away just as I did, no, he's fucked because his sole ambition in life was to stay in a stuck-in-the-mud, dead-end carpentry workshop for more than forty years. Can a lazy bastard also be a hard worker? Álvaro is living proof. Slogging away out of sheer idleness and indifference, because it's easier, because you can't be bothered to walk thirty metres to find yourself another more instructive, more exciting job, with more prospects and possibly better pay. Such workers used to be described as model employees, and they'd be presented with a gold-plated medal on the day they retired: fifty years in the same company and what do you get? A ribbon round your neck and a medal. Fantastic. An idler who has sat in the same chair or stood at the same machine for fifty years. Now it's mobility that gets rewarded. Loyalty is seen as lethargy, a lack of get-up-and-go; you get brownie points for betraying your various bosses, and with each new betrayal comes more money and promotion. Ahmed and Jorge have two quiet years ahead of them in which to rethink their lives, I don't know what Joaquín's situation is, whether he still has some unemployment benefit owing to him from previous jobs, and then there's always child benefit, worth four hundred or so euros for anyone who's been long-term unemployed and so is no longer eligible for unemployment benefit, and then there are the short-term contracts given out by the town council to do cleaning, gardening – which is something he knows about – or bricklaying. Julio won't have that possibility, but that's his fault for choosing to work illegally, because it suited him to receive unemployment benefit and child benefit or help for the long-term unemployed on top of his wages, which meant that he could easily afford his rent or his mortgage or whatever; I don't honestly know what his situation is and, frankly, I don't care. At least he has youth and time on his side. I'd happily swap places with him. No question. His future for mine. It's a deal. I hear them talking about their lives, telling me about their dreams, as if I were a wizard who could grant their every wish, a fairy godmother with a magic wand capable of turning pumpkins into golden carriages. You know, Don Esteban, last Sunday, after my husband hadn't even bothered to come home the previous night, I took my two kids to the park, and there beneath the clear blue sky, I sat listening to the band and watching my kids playing on the swings and the slides and in one of those rope maze things, and I was thinking if only I could have been born in a place where you could just sit and listen to a band on a Sunday morning and watch your children playing, rather than having to up sticks and leave everything behind. I thought, too, that I didn't really need him, Wilson, I mean; God knows where he'd got to, because he was out all Saturday night and didn't come home until Monday. Just me on my own, listening to the music and with my kids there with me. Don't cry, Liliana, because when you cry, I don't know what to do with you, I feel like touching you, caressing you, putting my arms around you as if you were a little girl, come on now, let me dry those tears, I cry too sometimes, but I don't like anyone to see me. Don't cry, my child. What's wrong? Are you worried that he'll have spent all his money during those two nights on the razzle, like he did last month? That's it, isn't it? And you're afraid it'll be the same again, because he got paid on Friday and, so far, hasn't given you a céntimo. Don't worry, we'll find a solution, where there's life there's hope. How much do you need? But, first, dry those tears. No, no need to kiss me (I'm lying, kiss me, kiss me, even if it's only a daughterly peck on the cheek). We should all help each other out when we can. And one of these days, I'd like you to come in wearing the earrings and the necklace I gave you so that I can see how pretty you look, although I know you come here to work and not to party. Liliana in my arms, her lips kissing my cheek, a couple of kisses moist with tears, and the pressure of her body against mine, seeking protection, and while what I feel is infinite tenderness, a kind of corporeal pity kicks in and I begin to notice a discomfiting thickening of the blood, but I don't know how to move away discreetly so that she won't notice that involuntary movement of the flesh, which would sully what really is genuine pity, you're my little girl, Liliana, and I want to protect you, I don't want you to suffer because that makes me suffer too, I say, but body and soul are at odds, or perhaps pity is just an unsavoury form of desire. That embrace, that feeling of plenitude, and now nothing but emptiness, a void, something akin to what a woman must feel after giving birth: completely empty, her body hollow as a bell. Yes, Liliana, a feeling of emptiness: the workshop gone, you gone, and this silence, but a feeling of repose too, of being at peace. My head is no longer filled with invoices, deadlines, loans, designs, numbers, nothing, I'm no longer in pain, I can't even feel the emotion that used to fill me whenever I saw her eyes well up, when I held her close, nor the descent into the lower depths when I watched her say goodbye, not even bothering to close the door behind her, no, now I don't even have you, Liliana. The other day, I turned and escaped down the nearest side street when I saw her in Olba, walking along with that ball of over-cooked fat, her husband, who had one great paw resting on her shoulder, when I saw their apparent affection for each other – because they were walking along together laughing and kissing, and she returned his kisses – an affection financed by me. None of that need bother me any more, I feel only rest and certainty. The calm that rushes in on a pervert the day after he's been castrated, but describing it in those terms has other murky implications, when in this case there is – and was – only a paternal feeling. Having a business fail must be the male equivalent of having an abortion. You see, Leonor, how we are bound together by similar experiences? You and I united by a rushing stream of water carrying away part of our inner self. After all, shit is also part of our inner self. Sometimes we give things an importance that only exists inside our head. How much do you need, Liliana, would five hundred euros be enough? Here, make that seven hundred, that way you won't have to worry. No, really, you can pay me back when you can. The workshop lived inside me. I didn't mean to stay, Leonor, you knew that. I wanted to leave as well, but when I came back, I realised that I just didn't have the strength to leave this house that has always been my home, even though it's never really been mine, it's my parents' house that I used as collateral – along with the orchard and the land in Montdor – for part of the loan I applied for, supplemented by the money I withdrew from the bank in order to become an equal partner in Pedrós' latest building venture. I, who had never owned my own house, was suddenly part-owner of several dozen houses. I've never been allowed to buy furniture and arrange it in the rooms as I wished, I've never been able to bring a friend home, I could never have brought *you* home with me, Leonor, and shut myself up with you in my room, our room, we could never have come out of the bathroom and walked down the corridor naked or sunbathed on the roof terrace or made love without worrying that someone in the next room might hear us sigh or moan, or hear the mattress creaking, never, I could never even masturbate in peace, my mother was always watching and listening: I don't like you locking yourself in your room, Esteban, I'm always afraid something might be wrong. My father's harsh voice: we're not thieves in this house, you know, there's no need to shut your door. But it wasn't just because the carpentry workshop was part of the house I've always lived in, it's more because I've carried the cross of this business for more than forty years now, I mean, what else have I done with my life? Fishing, hunting, a few games of cards in the evening, going out drinking on Friday and Saturday nights – as I did for a few years – preceded only, during the time when I managed to be defined by neither house nor workshop, by a short walk on what I thought was the wild side (the Rolling Stones, Lou Reed, David Bowie, Crosby, Stills, Nash & Young, Creedence Clearwater Revival, Jimi Hendrix); and yet what should have been part of the sentimental education of a hero of our times – as it was for Francisco – turned out, in my case, to be of no importance whatsoever: Can't you hear the music, Leonor? It's playing now, you must be able to hear it, all those groups playing at the same time and driving me mad. I could multiply that list by ten, doubtless because I lack judgement or still have no confident, mature sense of what I like, because I'm incapable of saying, as Leonor did, this is brilliant and this is rubbish, then heading straight for the thing I've chosen without caring what or who I trample on the way. I sampled this and that, and it all seemed good, nourishing stuff to me, but I probably lacked focus, character, get-up-and-go, or whatever. That break during the mid-sixties did get me out of here, but I didn't have the courage or the intelligence to convert that experience into the embryo of another way of life; like Álvaro, I gave in and chose the easy chair: at first, I called that easy chair Leonor – fool that I was, because she was restlessness personified, constantly choosing between this and that – but Leonor made her choice and left, while I stayed behind and made the workshop in Olba my solitude. I didn't even go to the bar (a recurrence of the symptoms of the infection inherited from my father), I saw no one, spent whole weeks without leaving the house; yes, I was a true heir to my father, he returning from his war and me from mine; he from icy Teruel and me from the cold, rainy boulevards and orange lights of Paris. Two defeated men. As he locked the workshop door from inside, I would go upstairs to my room, where I found myself in a kind of nowhere-land; initially, I felt claustrophobic shut up in there, listening over and over to the fifty or so LPs I'd brought with me, plus those that Francisco brought me on his visits later on. It wasn't enough to open the windows in order to drive out anxiety, because there was a wall surrounding Olba, I could almost see it in the distance, to the south, the boundary line: the houses in Misent, the cliffs blurred by mist, the little shapes of the fishing boats coming back as evening fell, followed by a flock of seagulls; and on the other side, the stony slopes of Montdor. From the roof terrace, I could see those boundaries stretching to the north as well, the great void of the lagoon, the endless reed beds; the curve of the beaches that, over time, have disappeared behind the many blocks of apartments and houses; I gradually got used to it: a couple of times a month I'd get spruced up and take the workshop van: Are you off out again? Can't you just stay quietly at home or go for a walk in the hills? Walking's good for the health: my father. Sometimes, I would put my wellington boots and the rifle in the van too so that he'd think I was going hunting, and then I'd turn up at the club in the early evening, when you're unlikely to meet anyone you know, and if you do, it's because they don't want to meet anyone they know either, a time when the girls are just starting to take up their positions at the bar. Even now, that's the time I usually choose to go there, when they're chatting to each other, sharing the music they've recorded on their mobiles, exchanging songs and ringtones, and I quickly select one of them (aren't you at least going to buy me a drink? what's the big hurry?), diversions that have never touched the very kernel of my rat-like existence, clinging desperately to a passing piece of wreckage and jockeying for space with my fellow rats, competing for salvation. The gloomy workshop, whose destruction I should see as a slave's freedom papers, but which feels instead like a painful mutilation. The way a woman must feel when her child is torn from her: that was my first thought. A child given to me in adoption has been torn from me. Does that sound familiar, Leonor? We have each, in our own way, suffered a loss; I know, I know, your loss was an exercise in emptying yourself out, whereas I have merely removed an excrescence, no, you're right, it isn't the same: your loss was insignificant or, rather, liberating, while all I'm losing is an innocuous, transmissible bit of property inherited from my father, and which he inherited from his father, an undernourished, ill-fed piece of property; the workshop closed its doors during the years he spent in prison, and only the odd jobs my uncle did kept things going until my father, on his release, rather reluctantly took up the reins again. I wouldn't have had anyone to leave the business to anyway. If Álvaro were to keep it going for a few years longer, it would still be a business run by two old men. Or 'two poor old men', as he would say, growing wrinkled and decrepit and already beginning to rot. While my father was away, my uncle, an adolescent at the time, did odd jobs in people's houses: mending doors, building tool sheds, making chicken runs or rabbit hutches on modest roof terraces (the post-war years brought farming into the villages, just so that people had something to eat); my father started the business up again in the face of great difficulties – so he did still have some ambition when he left prison, his apathy was a bit of a pose really, even if, as an artist turned labourer, it meant that he was unable to fulfil his possible aspirations – but that was also when the business first fell prey to the disease that brought it to its later state of decay, symptomatic of the times. And left in my hands, it has died without issue. Yes, Leonor, the tale of a barren creature. Liliana: you don't understand because you don't have any children of your own. Very true, I know nothing of such things.

Neither the pain of loss – knowing that I will never really have anything of my own – nor the peace that seems to fill me bear any resemblance to the sense of repose felt by a mother when she finally gives birth, when something that was part of her, that lived and breathed thanks to her, suddenly begins to breathe on its own, to move independently, to live its own life. The empty space inside her is the beginning of something, a willing surrender, whereas what I'm experiencing is an ending: the piles of wood, the motionless machines, the silent workshop, they're still there, not that I'm allowed in, because they've sealed the doors to stop me taking anything away, as if a load of planks would be of any use to me where I'm going. Not that it matters. I can close my eyes and see it all, not just the machines, the equipment, the small glazed office and the steps up to it, the filing cabinets and the desk carved by my cabinetmaker grandfather or by my carpenter father with ambitions to be a sculptor (I've never really known who made that desk, it was, for some reason, kept a deep dark secret). No, I could see every bit of wood in the stores as well, every plank: I have a horribly photographic memory, which was a real boon over the years when it came to finding what I needed in that shambolic workshop, and which is now – all too vividly – helping me to feel what an unfortunate wretch I am; because when I look at all those things, I don't see something I myself created in order to give back to life, I see only what I've buried. Once they've been used, the roadside whores are thrown back in the gutter. When a driver abandons them, they become available again to give pleasure to others, to provide some sexual release for the drivers who park their cars or vans next to the reed beds, half hidden away, their licence plates covered by vegetation so that no one will recognise them. Being spotted haggling with a whore at the roadside means being accepted as a companion in the last circle of hell, a being unable to control his lust – or, far worse, a wretch unable to control his money, who can afford nothing better – and thus condemned to catch one of the many infectious diseases transmitted by those women. And what else is a bankrupt business but a transmissible disease that has never given pleasure to anyone? Clients and providers pretend never to have had anything to do with it, they conceal all previous connections, because even the mere suspicion of contact contaminates: having sent invoices or delivery notes or IOUs bearing that name, having exchanged letters of credit, having supplied materials, all those things make you a suspect being. I'm talking about the business, but I could just as easily be talking about myself. How many years have I spent in this godforsaken place? I remove the judicial seals and – what the fuck – tear off the orange tape criss-crossing the door connecting the workshop and the house, then once again contemplate the workshop, the machines, the stacks of wood. I sit down at the desk in the office or on one of the stools in the storeroom, surrounded by all those materials, which are even more like corpses than me, useless and abandoned and just about to begin the process of putrefaction. It will all be put up for sale at risible prices at the next auction, and probably won't even find a buyer. The instability of things, the emptiness of words. Yes, my eldest son will only eat hamburgers and he'd eat them all the time if he could, he's always on at me to buy them. I refuse, of course, but I know he buys them anyway with the pocket money I give him, even though I give him a hard time, because he's really fat, I mean, he's only twelve and he weighs almost as much as that great fool of a father of his, he's actually obese, and that's a reason nowadays for them to take your child away from you if a teacher reports you; children want nothing but pizzas and pasta. And do you know why children like pasta so much? No, how could you if you don't have children of your own? She says: you don't have children of your own, as if I were some very meek domestic animal, as incapable of causing harm as of giving pleasure; and her words fill me with a sense of worthlessness that restores to Leonor the guilt from which death should have freed her. A carpenter is expected to be a peaceable fellow, a cuckolded St Joseph, 'they', the others, have to manage businesses, cope with stress, do dirty jobs in a factory, dangerous jobs on a building site, exciting work at a lawyer's desk, and they think of carpentry as a harmless profession, with the golden filter of the sun gilding the sawdust floating in the air, like the splinters of gold from a goldsmith's chisel, the pleasant, soothing smell of wood, pinewood, cedarwood, resin, even the smell of glue is pleasing to the nose: all lies and clichés of course. Even the most serious accidents seem relatively minor in a carpenter's workshop, not like truck drivers who might get burned to a crisp inside their cab; or bricklayers who fall from scaffolding twenty metres up and land on the pavement, their head split open like a melon; or metalworkers who, tragically, trip and fall into a blast furnace: here, at most, you might inadvertently saw off your fingertip or bring the hammer down on your thumbnail, minor wounds received during a domestic war and that further consolidate your image as a peaceable man who has honed his skills in honest toil, as if the commandment 'Thou shalt not kill' didn't apply to you, simply because you're incapable of killing anyone.

I put down an ace of spades and reach out to pick up the cards scattered on the small green baize mat in the middle of the table, and, as I do so, I brush Francisco's hand. That almost imperceptible contact evokes an image. In the dark of the cinema, Leonor nibbles my ear, licks it, pokes her warm, firm tongue inside, where it echoes, half crackle, half murmur. That damp, moving warmth tickles the cartilage, and that warm, vibrant, sticky feeling spreads like a shudder through the rest of my body and makes me catch my breath, or to be more precise, gives me a hard-on, it's true, and I am panting like a steam engine. Francisco laughs at something he has just said, and which I didn't even hear, as he throws down his two remaining cards, admitting defeat. This evening he has spoken with unusual frankness. Normally, if he criticises someone, he avoids naming names. He says 'him' or 'that guy'. He leaves an apparent freedom of interpretation to his listener who he has just injected with a dose of poison. He places the burden of guilt on him: it's up to the listener to put a name or a face to 'that guy', and thus become the thinker of evil thoughts, the betrayer. He merely provides the clues, much as one buckles on one's seat belt in the car – just in case. Or as if he were speaking with the knowledge that someone has turned on a tape recorder or placed a microphone in a hole in the plaster ceiling or underneath the table. He must have learned these linguistic precautions at the courses he attended when he was a member of the JOC or the JEC.

Justino stubbornly returns to the leitmotif I'm trying hard to avoid:

'Tomás' problem has always been his wife, but then that goes for all of us.'

And looking thoughtful, like someone who has just made a discovery and is pondering what exactly it might mean, he goes on:

'The clifftop house with the infinity swimming pool must have cost him a fortune, and then there's the designer furniture, and the Gucci and the Prada. I'm not just saying this, I'm not inventing it. She herself tells you when you meet her.'

'She tells *you*? Amparo tells you that she's wearing clothes from Prada? Are you buying them for her?' asks Bernal.

More laughter.

'No, of course she doesn't tell *me*, because I don't talk about clothes with her (I'd like to, but she won't), but she tells my wife. She does it very casually, while she's talking about something else, dropping a name here and there, and if you were to ask my wife what all those bits and pieces were worth on *The Price is Right*, she'd win hands down. You know what women are like. They see a woman wearing a nice blouse and it's, Minuccia, silk, three hundred and twenty euros, from Vanités, Avenida Orts in Misent; or Marqués de Dos Aguas in Valencia; or Madison Avenue in New York. Ah, but those shoes are fake Blahnik, only a hundred and fifty euros. Identical to the real thing and, if you press me, I'd say they were better finished too, but they're as false as Judas.'

Bernal:

'He's nuts about her and has simply let her spend, spend, spend.'

Justino:

'She must be forty-five if she's a day, and when she wears one of those blouses showing off her nice, firm, perky tits, you just know they must be silicone, because they could be the breasts of a twenty-year-old; but when she wears those skin-tight jeans, her arse still looks like an apple you'd like to bite into.'

'If you had enough teeth left.'

'Oh, I've none of my own, but my implants have given me back my adolescence. I do have to be careful, though, because when I bite, I can't always tell how hard I'm biting.'

'But what exactly are you biting and whose whatever-it-is are you biting into?'

More laughter.

Time to hear another fragment from Francisco's hidden – and falsified – autobiography:

'Women are always man's main obstacle.' I'm sure this isn't what he thinks of Leonor, who was hardly an obstacle in his life. I don't think he'd ever have got to the second rung on the ladder without her. 'They're the main brake on our actions. Fall hopelessly in love, and you're lost.'

Who could he have fallen so hopelessly in love with? While Leonor was still alive? After she died? I don't mean did he fall in love with her corpse, like an Edgar Allen Poe protagonist, but did he fall in love with someone else when Leonor was already dead or while she was still alive, or has he perhaps fallen in love more recently? When he shuts himself up in his house for the night, does he receive calls from that woman, do they talk dirty on the phone, does he invite her out on his yacht on those days when he disappears from Olba and all the shutters on his house are closed? Or do they lock themselves up in the house for weeks on end? I don't know that he was ever in love with Leonor, the marriage suited him – it suited them both – he used her – they used each other – economically, socially, eugenically. All right, their son didn't quite turn out the way they wanted, but they certainly can't complain about their daughter, an economics whizz. He says he finds her coolness towards him wounding, but I figure she's intelligent enough to know that if she does talk to him, he'll only start nagging her. He and Leonor were business partners, like Tomás and Amparo, but Tomás is mad about Amparo: theirs is clearly a sexual relationship (I know this, you can tell), they share a taste for sex, vice, luxury and doubtless even drugs. Pedrós is always touching his nose when he talks, and I imagine she's the same, the kind who lets someone else put the powder on the mirror, then, apparently reluctantly, sniffs it up, just to be polite of course, but if no cocaine is on offer, she'll be sure to mention it, in case someone else is willing to share theirs. And they've accumulated money together, which is how they've managed to live the way they do; I can't imagine Francisco and Leonor sharing any vices; I've always had the impression that his vices occupied a separate, clandestine world, although who knows? And what about her?

Bernal has now stopped playing with his mobile, having missed the last part of the conversation. He says:

'It's hard to be really in love with a woman *and* do anything useful in life. Anxiety eats away at you. There's no point getting hooked up with a woman who's hard to get, that's tantamount to spending the rest of your life climbing Everest. You should marry a woman you can keep without too much effort. You can always pay for the company of a real beauty if you want to. For a few euros you can have an eighteen-year-old Russian girl who's better-looking than any film star. You fuck, you pay and you go back home to have supper with your family, with your wife, who's a good cook, but lousy in bed, and who would never dream of leaving you, because, quite apart from anything else, no one is interested. She goes to parents' evenings at school, is a leading light of the PTA or whatever they're called – you know, all that social democratic rubbish that the Partido Popular gleefully copies because it fits their modern-responsible-happy-family image with just a touch of Opus Dei – plus she keeps the children in line and knows which is the best detergent to buy and the best cheese and the best local foie gras. She irons your shirts and sews on your buttons, or can tell the maid how to do it, having first put her through more trials than an Olympic athlete. That's what a man needs, because it takes a lot of courage to live with a woman who's your equal and makes you cook the vegetables and hang out the clothes, as well as being insatiable in the sack and screwing you dry. Hard work. No man could stand that.'

'Amparo is too much of a woman for Tomás or for anyone. It's not just that she's drop-dead gorgeous, but if she's arranged to meet someone at seven o'clock, then, rather than arrive even a minute late, she'll leave whoever she happens to be with in mid-fuck. She has character, style, independence. As well as nice tits and a nice arse. It's really hard to cope with that at home on a daily basis, having to fight off marauders – because that's what it's like these days,' says Justino, who is known to be something of a marauder himself and, doubtless, one of those men Amparo has, on some occasion, left high and dry in mid-fuck.

Bernal again:

'She's certainly an important factor, but less so than you seem to think. He knows how to have fun too, how to live it up. Amparo played only a small role in the collapse of Tomás' businesses, all right, there were the facial peels, the nails, the spa treatments, Revlon, Dior, Loewe, Miuccia Prada, and all the rest, but that's normal for any bourgeois bit of pussy. The wife of any small-time property developer, car dealer or owner of a chain of petrol stations or an apartment block will be sure to have acquired that designer stuff over the last few years. Or are there wives who don't go to those shops, wear those clothes or indulge in aromatherapy massages and hydromassage baths? *He* was the real problem, what with his extravagant tastes, his desire to impress, the money he lavished on social or should that be municipal events (not forgetting the usual backhander paid to the local councillor); and then there were the wines from Burgundy, the seafood, the champagne, and so on, not to mention the Russian girls, and the cocaine,' – ah, so the secret's out, I always suspected that he took cocaine from the way he kept rubbing his nose, I shoot a quick glance at Francisco, who remains impassive – 'because the bastard certainly hasn't stinted himself.'

Justino:

'He's screwed the best prostitutes in the region. Not the ones in the clubs, who charge fifty or a hundred or two hundred euros. No. He only used to go there on work outings with his employees or to impress small-time suppliers. He's always gone for the kind of woman who appears to be working for herself, but is, in fact, just one tentacle of a mafia octopus, the kind of woman you find at the Marina Esmeralda lying on the deck of some yacht, which might belong to a friend, male or female, who has lent it to her, crew included, to enjoy a few days of rest. Rest from what, though? From business deals, catwalks, boutiques, photo sessions or some other sort of session. At least that's what she'll tell you when she gets you in her sights. The kind who always has bottles of Moët chilling in the fridge, a forty-inch flat-screen TV and a jacuzzi in a 200-square-metre apartment with a sea view or a clifftop villa in Xábia or Moraira, owned by mafia from Eastern Europe or possibly Western Europe (you'd have to check whose name is on the deeds, and even then you'd never know for sure who's hiding behind the ostensible owners). Pedrós has often bought himself a few weeks in one of those villas, telling Amparo and us that he's away travelling, phoning home on his mobile to complain about the rain in Vigo (it hasn't stopped all week) or how cold it is in Pamplona (enough to freeze your balls off), and that he's staying another few days so as to sort out the distributor's accounts (they're a complete mess, I'll tell you about it later), when, in fact, he was opening and closing a pair of silky legs. He's taken those women out to supper at Quique Dacosta's, at the Hotel Ferrero, at the Girasol when they had that Swiss or German chef working there, or to spend the night in the Westin Hotel. He's been seen in those places on more than one occasion and word has spread, after all, it's a very small world here, and everyone knows everyone else. And he's learned a lot from you, Francisco, I think. By now, he probably knows more about wine than you do.'

Francisco leaps on this statement like a Bengal tiger:

'Don't I know it. He loves showing off to me: Olivier Leflaive's Corton-Charlemagne with the *amuse-gueules*; a Chateau Cos d'Estournel with the *plat de résistance*; and a Coutet Sauternes with the dessert or the foie gras: mere nouveau-riche posturing.'

Justino interrupts:

'Don't forget the cognacs: Martell, Delamain, Camus, because his other vice – apart from prostitutes – is cigars and cognac, even more so than wines. He loves sitting around after a meal, one hand on his belly, his legs stretched out under the table and his lips pursed, blowing out a great cloud of cigar smoke. He uses wine to give him a veneer of class, but cognacs are his true love. I would say that he's spoiled Amparo rotten because it suited him to. Husbands who cheat always take great care to make sure their wife lacks for nothing. If you do get caught out at some point, you can always save yourself by saying: but I'm crazy about you, don't be silly. Don't I bow to your every whim and treat you like a queen? Besides, anyone can make a mistake.'

Francisco can resist no longer. Falling into the trap of

discussing what wines and cognacs Pedrós drinks has hit him where it hurts – in his wine expert's liver. He can detect direct competition; all that talk about Corton-Charlemagne and Delamain; and hearing someone say that Pedrós knows more about wine than he does is tantamount to challenging the emperor for his crown. And so he adds:

'It's one thing to say Amparo is still gorgeous, even at her age, and that she's intelligent and has good taste, but basically he, well, he's just a fucking plumber. He may have fitted the bathrooms of his Russian clients with gold taps, but he's still a plumber. That's how he started out. He knows nothing about cognac or wine. He knows names and labels, but that's a very different matter. He's quick on the uptake and notices what the genuinely rich people he mixes with are drinking. He's the sort who keeps a little notebook and goes into the restaurant toilet to note down the labels of the wines being served with the meal, or which were the most expensive ones on the menu, along with the brand names of the clothes and shoes his fellow diners are wearing, he even notes down words he doesn't know, but which he notices are considered to be chic. He was on at me for months to teach him about *denominaciones*, wine merchants, good years and bad years. He bled me dry, like a vampire. Not that I'm criticising him, mind. At least he did his homework. He's a conscientious fellow. Hard study can turn even an ignoramus into a sage,' Francisco declares, closing his speech with an unexpected defence of the plumber Pedrós. Like Christ with Lazarus. The Lord taketh away and the Lord giveth back. The Lord is God-like in his generosity.

Justino yawns and stretches voluptuously, undulating his body like an odalisque in a harem, then he scratches his crotch and sighs:

'It's such a good feeling when you do rein yourself in and stay faithful to your wife. I'm faithful most of the time, and only occasionally do I allow myself to succumb to temptation, but how delicious those occasions are, no?'

Bernal continues:

'They're each as bad as the other, it's been pretty much tit for tat between Tomás and Amparo. She's done her fair share of over-spending too and hasn't gone without certain other things either: trips abroad, shopping sprees, days spent who knows where (best not ask); solo visits to Paris, exhibitions, although, having said that, their marriage does seem pretty indestructible. Or it has been as long as the money kept flowing in. We'll see what happens now. But I think that, at least for the moment, their bond will remain strong as long as they still share financial responsibility. What really binds a couple together are the business deals they have in common or the loans taken out in joint names and that have to be repaid. If you sign up for a twenty-year mortgage, you're pretty much guaranteeing your marriage for the same period of time. That's true love. Not mere words that the wind can carry away. The banks don't keep words in their safes; you can't buy anything with words or use them as a guarantee.'

Justino:

'When things go wrong, that's that. Like they say, when poverty comes in at the door, love flies out the window. Unpaid bills put paid to love. The water of debt short-circuits the electrics of passion. Wow, that sounds like something straight out of an old-fashioned novel or some high-falutin' essay! You're the writer, Francisco, take note. Who knows what goes on between husband and wife, it's forbidden territory, not even a lover has access to the secrets of the marital bedroom, the bedside table with the family photos, the alarm clock, the little boxes with ear plugs in them, tampons, KY jelly, it's years of accumulated habits and obsessions, you get their different versions of events, but you don't know what really matters, what they owe each other, what money they have, where they keep the safe and who has the keys; that's what you can't know, what's in her name or her father's name or the name of some spinster aunt above suspicion, they won't tell you that even if they fight like cat and dog, I know, or I think I know, that they've agreed on separation of property. And this bankruptcy could well just be a cover.' He speaks as what some people say he is, one of Amparo's spurned lovers.

Francisco:

'It's obvious that the only happy marriages are marriages of convenience, which work like well-oiled machines, with no friction, each partner aware that their aspirations are progressing well thanks entirely to that alliance. It's really good to see such couples working as a team, having grasped the idea that matrimony is tantamount to being a publicly traded company. They do well in the world, providing each other with total support, each one specialising in a different activity so as to get maximum return on their investment, because they know that whatever one of them gains will benefit them both. Public arguments, disagreements, announcements of a separation make the price of shares on the social stock exchange plummet, damaging the domestic economy, so forget all the rubbish that young people and other imbeciles proclaim to the winds, not realising that they're devaluing what they have. They believe in being in love and falling out of love, in betrayal and jealousy, unaware that, as soon as what novels and romantic magazines insist on calling "love" gets in the way, you're buggered. Screwed. An end to all peace of mind. When someone says "I'll love you for ever", the affair has already begun to take in water. A mountaineer can't stay on the peak he's just conquered, because he's already reached the highest point. What next? You know that now you have to climb down again and find another K 8000 mountain to climb. Your newly married neighbour, the office colleague you'd never even noticed before, become new targets. It's the same with everything. The flames melt it. It's what happened to the Twin Towers. They melted. At boiling point, the stock in the pan soon evaporates and the stew you were so lovingly preparing burns dry. Ardour only serves to scorch things. The lovers themselves, if they're truly in love, are in a hurry to end that torment and do all they can to free themselves from it. They force matters. If a marriage is to last, you must never swear eternal love. Rather than a rolling amorous boil, you need a steady selfish simmer on a medium flame.'

Francisco – quite unintentionally – is telling me about his marriage to Leonor, but Justino, despite his radical distrust of all things human and, indeed, of the whole of divine creation – he's the sort who hears a goldfinch singing at the window and rushes to close it because he thinks it's the screech of a rat on heat – gathers his strength, sensing that now is the moment to begin to make light of the charges against the accused: you never know who you might be talking to; he's probably noticed that I've only opened my mouth to defend Pedrós and this makes him uneasy. He must know that I'm a partner in Pedrós' business. And naturally he knows about all the work I've done on his properties. As for my bankruptcy, he must be more than aware of that, how could he not know what everyone else knows? Besides, he has direct access to the intimate details of the Pedrós household, not through Tomás, but through her, through Amparo, who he criticises – his usual strategy – simply in order to conceal their likely relationship; and, quite probably, because he's a tad jealous, given that Amparo has vanished along with her husband and hasn't stayed behind, waiting for him, despite the rumoured separation of property. People have always said that there is or was something between them, and that some of her disappearances coincided with his business trips. At this point, the conversation – doubtless purely as a precaution – changes in tone. Justino says:

'I know Tomás well. He's spent money because he had the money to spend, but above all because it suited him to do so. For every euro he's squandered, he's earned a hundred. He's used it, let's say, for PR purposes; that's how he's always earned his money, by sticking his nose into other people's businesses and involving millionaires in his various projects. Why else would he invite a whole legion of old crocks onto his yacht? To get money out of them. Retirees who have chosen to end their days by the sea – Germans, French (the English out here don't have yachts, they're too low-class), and who everyone else ignores. They're bored rigid here and feel sad because, in old age, they have finally come to the realisation that money doesn't bring happiness (as if old age were not a stupid addendum to life proper). He takes them out for a sail, provides them with a hammock on deck, serves them a plate of salted tuna when they're on the high seas, a few toasted almonds for their very white false teeth to bite into, a little glass of wine (well, a little glass of wine never hurt anyone, it's recommended by cardiologists, rheumatologists and endocrinologists), tries to make them feel comfortable, cared for, listens with interest to the problems they have with their children, grandchildren and daughters-in-law, and simply by listening he becomes the ideal son, grandson and son-in-law, they adopt him as the son they would like to have had (what son would ever treat them so well?), they spoil him as they wish their grandson would allow them to spoil him, they love him just as they would love a daughter-in-law if she was all she should be, the kind to prompt a few erotic dreams. He offers them the understanding and complicity they wish they received from their wives. The trouble is that now with the crisis, Pedrós' yacht barely leaves its moorings because fuel is so expensive. The banks aren't giving out any more loans (now, they're in the business of getting loans from the government) and going for a weekend sail beneath the blue Mediterranean sky costs a fortune what with the soaring price of fuel, and so, he wasn't even able to try to save himself by casting his net in the fishing ground of the elderly, though they wouldn't have rescued him anyway, because it's one thing to wheedle the occasional tip out of them or to ask for a helping hand when necessary, but quite another to stand before one of them and say, point-blank: Herr Müller, I need eight hundred and fifty thousand euros. What's giving a bit of small change to their boy entertainer (a letter of reference for some new project, a 'loan' of eight or ten thousand euros, a box of Moselle wine, even a Patek Philippe watch as a birthday gift)? That's quite different from actually getting out your wallet and handing over a large wad of money. That's a serious matter – requiring careful consideration, evaluation and expert advice. They may be capricious and old, but they're not stupid – they'll pay for a toy, but at a toy price. They'd been prepared to keep shelling out just enough to make sure the fun would continue, but not a euro more; they've made their investment (as people usually do), thinking of the profit they might make (opening doors locally). We've known for centuries that there is no such thing as a generous rich man, generous people tend to run aground in the stages preceding wealth, when, for a while, they point wildly back at the coast, but then they drown. Their corpses disappear forever, buried in the sea of the economy or the sea of life, which comes to the same thing. They die in poverty.'

Francisco:

'A few days before he disappeared, Pedrós came to see me in tears. It's not the overspending, he said, as I know people are saying, but the lack of income that's done for me. I swear to you on my daughter's life, and she's the person I love most in the world. I haven't gone out on the town or been to a brothel or with anyone else in months. I swear. I spent money while I had it, when I could afford to spend. But now it's all gone.

Paying for materials, paying wages, paying for publicity, of course, but with no money coming in. You pay, but no one pays you, that's the problem. Anyone who tells you otherwise is a liar. I'm not the only one who's been caught. Do you know how many local businesses have disappeared? Not closed, but simply vanished, gone: you go to the office to get your money, and the office isn't there, I don't just mean that the doors are closed, but you look through the window into an empty room, with papers and boxes strewn all over the floor, and when you try to find out who is (or was) the owner, no one knows. And the guy you dealt with, the one who signed the receipt, had no right to sign it, he wasn't even an employee. That's the worst thing. It's as if you've been working with ghosts, phantoms from the other side. I'm not the only one bankrupt either, Tomás told me in tears. Fajardo's, the building suppliers in Misent, has closed, and Magraner's has fired half its staff and is about to close. I know this for a fact. And Sanchis, the furniture supplier and Vidal who used to sell blinds. And Ribes. And Pastor now does his own bricklaying when anyone asks, because he's laid off all his men, more than fifty of them. And Fajardo's has auctioned off all their material, for which they got a pittance (I mean, who's going to want to buy building materials, machinery, a backhoe or a crane nowadays?), and they've paid what creditors they could and shut down. And Rodenas has gone back to Jaén or Ciudad Real to pick olives alongside Moroccans and Romanians and Poles, can you imagine, a developer working with immigrants, with scum, his poor chilblained fingers frozen on those icy Andalusian mornings.'

While Francisco is talking, all the while carefully avoiding my eyes – which means that, during that conversation, Pedrós must have mentioned me among the victims of this chain of disasters – I can't help thinking that, if this were the jungle, we would be watching the lianas beginning to twine their way around the window frames of the closed shops, to climb the walls of abandoned apartment blocks, smothering the empty penthouse suites with their foliage and thick woody stems. A lost city, like in the adventure films we enjoyed when we were kids. For days and days you hack your way through the jungle, then, suddenly, you stumble upon a vast city, all overgrown with leaves and scrub and full of temples, statues, buried treasure. The fantasies of Jules Verne and Salgari.

My friend concludes his speech:

'I don't know how this is all going to end, Pedrós said, whether the country will emerge from the crisis or not, but what does it matter to you and me, Francisco? There's no way out of our crisis, we know that. It's like Carlos Gardel says in the song: Downhill all the way. He was feeling terribly low. I felt really sorry for him.'

Bernal:

'What did he mean "*our* crisis"? Is that what he said? Is he seventy years old, like you? He's only about forty-four or forty-five. God, he's a sly one. He really has a way with people, trying to draw them in. You and him, two retirees contemplating their final days together. As if he wasn't already plotting some new deal. I bet he is. This bankruptcy business is probably just some new strategy or other and it'll turn out that all they've impounded is pennies, because anything valuable is in Amparo's name.'

Yep, everyone here is still talking about Pedrós, even though, as far as I know, they're not among his creditors – although I'm not sure where he stands with Justino – and the suppliers he hasn't paid will be talking about him for months, and so will the people who hated him and are pleased to see him go under, and the employees he sacked and their poor families; and by the ones who'd have given anything to be invited to go for a sail on his yacht. That's his lasting bit of fame. Better than nothing, I suppose. I may be doing my best not to mention him, but I think about him all the time. I may not be making any contribution to his long-term fame, but I do keep his memory alive. The people who talk are the ones who would've gladly paid a fortune to watch him go under, as well as those of us who did pay a fortune for him to watch us go under with him. I take my last sip of beer, listening to them discuss Tomás' fall from grace, and think that I should be able to get at least a couple of hours' sleep tonight. The alcohol's doing me good. I glance at my watch, and Justino notices. He says: It's after eight o'clock, Esteban, time for your Colombian girl's shift to end. During the game, I drank a black coffee with a dash of brandy and two glasses of punch. Then, when we left the card table, and continued chatting at the bar, I'd had three glasses of beer, or was it four? More or less what I usually drink in the evening. I don't know if that comfortable feeling that wraps itself around you when you leave the bar is thanks to the card games or the alcohol, but you leave the bar as if borne along, floating on a cotton-wool cloud. I consider suggesting to Francisco that we have a gin and tonic together, from one of those bottles of Bombay Sapphire or Citadelle that the barman keeps especially for him.

Early the next morning, before going out, I took the goldfinch up to the roof terrace and opened the cage door. The bird hesitated for a few moments: initially, just sticking its head out, fluffing its wings as if preparing to take flight, then turning round and going back into the cage to peck at the seeds in the feeder; after a while, it again hopped over to the open door and, this time, it barely paused before fluttering over to the rail, where it remained perched and hesitant for a few more seconds. It turned its head nervously this way and that, repeatedly glancing across at the cage door, moving its head as if an elastic spring had gone wrong. And then, it flew off, slipping away into the faint morning mist softened with dawn light, growing smaller and smaller until it merged with the blue of the sky. My eyes filled with tears as I watched it vanish, and I felt a strange mixture of feelings: while it was beautiful to see the bird flying free, I felt very sad to lose it. And a knot formed in my throat to think that the goldfinch would not escape disaster either. Unaccustomed to finding its own food, to defending itself against any tiny enemies it might meet, it would have great difficulty surviving. And yet it was beautiful to watch it plunging into that diaphanous winter sky: the slight morning haze, the bird's precise flight, the fragile light of the rising sun misting the blue with gold. The whole episode provided an illusion of freedom, of untarnished joy. We human beings also go out into the world with certain handicaps.

Again my eyes fill with tears – I feel like crying. I bring my fist down hard on the steering wheel (watch out for the airbag, a blow like that might trigger it), before opening the door of the Toyota to make enough room for putting on the wellingtons I left on the floor in front of the passenger seat. While I'm putting them on, I again imagine the bird growing smaller and smaller until it's lost from view. Liliana's face: you know, I had that warm feeling you get when happiness is about to arrive, as if something's about to happen, a kind of inner hustle and bustle, like someone tidying the house for some important visitor – putting things in their proper places, dusting the furniture and cleaning the windows, while, from the kitchen, comes the smell of a special meal being prepared. Now it's Álvaro on the other side of the desk in the office: You might have warned me. Do you really think I knew this was how things would end? The conflicting feelings are evident in his moist eyes. I taught Álvaro to hunt and fish at the lagoon – about forty years ago – just as my uncle had taught me. Yes: in the mid-seventies – Álvaro is a keen worker, who does all the jobs at the workshop to perfection. Despite the paternal ghost hovering over us, we establish a kind of friendship. I'm just back from my most recent escapade, and he's the same as when I left – my father's loyal son. Sometimes he comes with me on a Saturday morning, we have lunch together and I teach him how to handle the rifle and he's surprised at all the things I know about the lagoon: as you see, time debases everything, erases it, what can I say? Álvaro and me like two brothers, if only we had been, I wish things had turned out differently between us, of course I do, and for you too, although you can't really complain, you've had a steady job without too much responsibility, a house, a family. What I regret most of all is that things didn't turn out differently for me – if only, rather than spending decades feeling that everything was just temporary, and then realising too late that life is nearly over and things have never gone as we expected, and that they're beyond our control, yes, if only, if only . . . It's his eyes, the glint in his eyes that I see in the glow of the sunrise. The bird growing smaller and smaller, becoming one with that same glow. Álvaro's eyes. The glint in his eyes, the tiny spark that lights up the pupil, surrounded now by a wash of blood. The pupil floats in that reddish liquid, just as the sun did a few moments ago, as it emerged from the sea: a red ring floating above a pool of blood. Why am I surprised to find that Álvaro hates or despises me? I don't like my own father, and yet I've spent my whole life with him. Álvaro came with me on dozens of days like today, when you can breathe in the clean winter air. The two of us alone under the clear sky, walking through this luminous space, the light outlining every object, emphasising every shape, making each one stand out against the landscape like a paper cut-out: after the first autumn rains, the heavy air of the lagoon grows thinner, and the putrefying smell of the stagnant water is replaced by another more vegetable odour, the odour of fresh, newborn vegetables. That's what I can smell now, like a stimulant, a tonic that helps me walk more energetically, swing my arms higher, more vigorously, take longer, faster strides, step more firmly; for a moment, I look like a man determinedly going in search of what he wants. I advance along the path: the only sound is the whispering of the reeds as I part them, the soft murmur as they swish against my shoulders or brush against my rucksack as they fall back, the monotonous sucking noise of each boot lifting up from the squelching mud. The cawing of a crow, the fluttering of the coots: they jump out almost between my feet, I frighten them and they startle me too when I hear the beating of their wings, the whirr of the air. The dog races, mesmerised, after those fluttering wings, then stops at the edge of the water and turns to watch two ducks taking off. He barks. These noises shatter the glassy air; the splashing of some creature launching into the water: a frog, a toad, a rat; the barking of the dog amplified by the glass dome of the sky. I walk and feel as if I were immersing myself in a world apart, inhabited by other beings and ruled by other laws. Like my father, I feel a sudden desire to stay here forever. Like him, I am a divided being when I leave this labyrinth for the outside world. The dog runs excitedly up to me, overtakes me, then comes trotting back, wagging his tail; he stops, jumps up and puts his front paws on my belly. Filled with emotion, I stroke him, rubbing his head and back. Our guilt is going to take away your innocence, little dog. The wind has dropped, and the silence is almost painful, a warning of the great silence to come, the silence that will fill everything. On some winter days, the north winds bring with them the hum of traffic from the nearby main road or – more loudly from the motorway – cars and trucks passing incessantly, a sound amplified beneath the wintry dome of the sky – noises which, on the other hand, the summer mists seem

308

to swallow up the way blotting paper or a sponge absorbs liquids. Not today, there's no wind today, no noise, not a breath. The welcome knife of the cold wind stopped. I move with a sense that I'm walking along its motionless blade. I've parked the 4x4 further up, because I want to enjoy the walk, but my contemplation of the landscape, my thoughts, are not a distraction from my goal, I know now how far I'll be able to drive with the Toyota, I've calculated the width of the half-overgrown path, the state of the surface, I've checked that I'll be able to drive the car up to the point where the water blocks the path, the bend in the lake, the kidney-shaped pool that, in the summer months, is cut off from the rest of the marsh: for years, my uncle and I used it as a pantry, a natural fish farm, which, tomorrow, will find its nutrients further enriched with meat to nourish its watery inhabitants, at the same time contaminating or poisoning the little spring my uncle showed me I could drink from; once again, good and evil all mixed up together. This was where I baited my first hook, cast my line and caught a couple of tiny fish (I can't remember what they were, mullet or tench, I imagine) that my grandmother cooked for supper that evening. A stew of potatoes, garlic, sweet peppers and a bay leaf. The fish are for the boy, because he caught them. On the way home, it began to rain and we had to take shelter in the ruined building where we had left the bike. When we saw that the rain showed no signs of stopping and the sky was growing ever darker, my uncle decided to get on the bike, with me sitting on the crossbar with his waterproof cape covering me, head and all, and the rain drumming on the fabric and me inside as if in a glasshouse; I can still feel the warmth of my uncle's body and the plip-plop of the ever larger raindrops on the cape. In these days of heavy autumn rain, or during winter, you can hear the roar of the waves even in the marshes, because the waters of the sea swell the lagoon, reaching up into the mouths of the river and the drainage canals, and then the mirror of the lake shatters into a thousand pieces, which, like droplets of molten metal, shift and jostle nervously, constantly changing shape and position. The lagoon comes alive, everything moves: the water, the reeds, the shrubs, everything. I've seen it dozens of times, but my memories focus on that one afternoon when the sky suddenly grew dark, and the day turned into a strange night bathed in a pale light that seemed to spring from the surface of the water. Light emanated from the leaves, the reeds, from the vegetation on the banks, an inverted light cast upward into the great, black clouds, like a photographic negative. My uncle holds my hand as we walk through that nightmare landscape as far as the ruined warehouse where he left his bike. I hear the rain hammering down on the roof tiles and see the ghostly light, like an optical illusion, on the brick wall nearest the entrance, which suddenly glows intensely red, highlighting the rough surface.

This morning, however, the calm is absolute, no engines, no voices trouble the air, and the still water reflects the blue of the sky, the passing clouds and the vegetation on the shoreline, duplicating the changing landscape. While I walk, it occurs to me that my uncle taught me pretty much everything. Handling a rifle, choosing the right bait for the right fish, laying traps baited with rotten giblets that quickly fill up with crabs, setting the nets to catch eels, even what carpentry I know I learned from him. Yes, he taught me almost everything, except my despairing view of the world, the certainty that every human being is guilty as charged. That's in the blood, my father's blood, which I inherited along with his harsh voice and gaze. As Leonor would say: he's a man who still believes we're in the middle of a war and that the most interesting battle is yet to come. That's what my father taught me, and he wouldn't allow me even that one ounce of innocence you need if you are to aspire to anything. I was neither a sculptor nor a cabinetmaker, which the dictionary defines as a skilled joiner who works with high-quality wood, a maker of fine furniture, Renaissance writing desks like the one created by my grandfather and my father, cupboards with mouldings in the form of acanthus leaves or the petals of a flower, bedheads carved with the shapes of poppies, marquetry work, rosewood bedside tables adorned with lilies or geometric art deco designs in noble oak or ebony, none of which anyone has ever asked me to make, and none of which I would have known how to make or even wanted to. So I haven't even really been a carpenter. Ever since I abandoned art school (after all the sacrifices I've made, he said: I've given you the chance Germán never had, the chance to do what I never managed to do, later, I discovered this wasn't strictly true – I was a substitute for Germán, and we both failed him, more fuel for his bonfire of resentments), my father never suggested we create something together, never taught me how to be my own man and become the kind of cabinetmaker who leaves behind him a few pieces of furniture that others can admire and enjoy. When I rejected his plan, he gave up on me altogether. And I gave up on myself. In his youth, my father did have aspirations, ambitions: he wanted to get a few rungs further up the ladder than his father, who had been a good cabinetmaker but, because he'd lived here and not in a big city, had lacked the opportunities to develop his skills. He had, nevertheless, left a few good pieces, some of them still in this house that has never been mine and in which, until recently, I lived like a resident in one of those old boarding houses, who gets told off if he uses too much water when he showers, if he turns on the heater or reads until late into the night with the bedside lamp on.

My uncle's justification would be:

'I was just a boy, more willing than able, and I would knock a few things up for local people who still remembered the workshop run by your grandfather and your father and where

311

I'd already begun to work as his assistant. During that difficult period when I was left alone, without my father, without my older brother, the people who gave me work didn't expect much from me, they ordered things more out of solidarity with my family, or pity perhaps, than because they thought much of my abilities. They would ask me to make a shed to store their bits and pieces, or a rabbit hutch, or a pigeon roost for the roof terrace. I never made anything for inside their houses, because even in the poorest houses, those places are still considered noble somehow, and furniture represents some kind of dignity or decency. My mother and your mother both got work scrubbing floors and washing clothes, and in the fruit-picking season, they worked as packers. When your father came back, there was almost nothing left in the workshop, most of the machines and the materials had been stolen and any furniture destroyed. The walnut chair and table that your grandfather made, and the desk of course, only survived because we hid them under hay in the shed. The other bits of furniture, a wardrobe and a dresser, were also stolen and doubtless still adorn some house in Olba.'

'But didn't my father make that furniture?'

'Your grandfather started making them, and your father did the carvings.'

'And didn't he do anything after that?'

'As I say, we saved that furniture at the very last moment, he'd just come back from the front and was so weak he could barely stand, but between him, your grandmother and me, we managed to get it all out into the yard –'

'And what about my mother? Wasn't she there too? Didn't she help?'

'– and we buried it in the hay, there was piles of the stuff, right up to the roof, and then we used tools and boxes and old planks to disguise it. They came to plunder the house, although it seems ridiculous to apply a word like "plunder" to a house in which there was barely enough to eat, but there were those machines and tools and, above all (some neighbour must have informed on us) the furniture carved by my grandfather – his pride and joy, his life's work that he never finished, the treasure of a poor, wretched household, quite out of keeping with the rest of the furniture, but his plan, over time, had been to furnish the whole house, making the dining table, the beds and bedside tables, the wardrobes, he had it all there in his notebooks, he used to show me the drawings. The men who came were so drunk they spent their time chasing the chickens and hauling the rabbits out of their hutches – they didn't even bother with the shed, with that load of old hay, assuming it wouldn't contain anything of value.'

I looked into my uncle's eyes and seemed to see in them what he as a child had seen.

'But what did they do?' I asked, 'What had those eyes seen, Mum?'

'Nothing, just those drunks plundering the house and then walking drunkenly past the window a few times.'

'And they didn't come back?'

'They came back to search for weapons, but, of course, there weren't any, because we'd buried your grandfather's hunting rifle, the one your uncle used to use, the one he gave to you, we buried it in the olive grove on the outskirts of the village. They came looking for papers and books too, but we'd burned or buried those a few days before.'

'But did they come back after that?'

'No, they never came back,' she replied sharply.

Funny, isn't it? 'Never' usually seems such a terrible word, but in those circumstances it brought hope: they would never come back. You will never come back either, Liliana, never, and I'm not sure if, in this instance, the word is terrible or hopeful, just as I don't know if I will ever stop hearing your voice. I imagine I will: after all, in the end, everything fades, although it will take some time; as you know, bitterness lasts rather longer than love, your voice. No, today I'm not going to say anything because I don't want to worry you, I told you I was crying over some problem I've got, but don't ask what it is, like I said, I'm not going to tell you, and that's that. But you've already told me, your eyes are telling me, look at me, that's right, lift your chin and look me in the eye, you're crying again, how can I not worry when I see you crying like that, in fact, if you don't tell me, I'll be even more worried, let me guess, you don't have to say anything, just nod if I'm right. Wilson's spent all the money again, is that it? You didn't nod. Is it something worse? Did he hit you, you certainly shouldn't let him get away with that, and if you report him, the state will protect you and automatically grant you Spanish citizenship. He didn't hit you, did he? Or has he just left? Forgive me for saying so, but if he has left or if he did hit you, and even though you'll be sad at first because he is your husband, the father of your children, and you still love him or did love him, he will have done you a big favour, because that man is more of a hindrance than a help. That's not my view, it's what you've told me yourself. You're shaking your head. So he hasn't left you and he hasn't hit you. Well, whatever it is that's happened can be sorted out, then. As I always say, neither good luck nor bad luck ever comes to stay, they stop with us for a while and then leave, head off somewhere else, have other people to deal with, other households. Luck is very fickle. Come here, no, don't look away, let me stroke your hair, my poor child, my poor Liliana. What's wrong? You're still shaking your head. I don't want to tell you the same thing all over again, I feel ashamed. But what's there to be ashamed of, what shame can there be between father and daughter, come here, let me put my arms around you, that's it, rest your head on my chest, you have such soft hair, thick and soft. You're like your hair, strong and soft at the same time, because you know what suffering is, life has toughened you up. Don't be frightened, child. That's it, have a good cry, cry out all the sadness. Crying relieves and relaxes. Let me get my handkerchief out of my pocket and dry those tears, that's better. It's just that I feel so ashamed to come to you again and again with the same story, month after month, I mean, you're under no obligation to help me, and I'd completely understand if you get fed up and tell me to go elsewhere, that it's my problem, always the same old story: the fridge is empty, I've got nothing to give the kids to eat, no money to pay the rent. It gets boring, and I understand that. I'm so afraid you'll get tired of me one day. But how can you say that, how could I ever get tired of you, you don't get tired of a daughter, it's not the kind of love you can pick up or put down as you wish, you carry it around with you, that's right, have a good cry, rest your head on my chest. How much do you need this time?

What am I doing out of bed? What am I doing wandering about the house that is only dimly lit by the moon when I walk past the windows in the dining room and pitch-black when I go down the corridor and past the door to my brothers' bedrooms? Perhaps I woke up and, seeing my uncle's bed empty, set off to find him. I'm five years old. To the right of the corridor are the stairs that lead down to the workshop. To reach the door handle, I have to stand on tiptoe. I manage to open the door. I don't know what I think I'm going to find. At the bottom of the stairs, there's a line of light beneath the door into the workshop, and I advance slowly towards it, afraid I might fall, feeling my way along the wall, feeling carefully for every step, and when I do finally open the door, there is my uncle, sitting, head bowed, eyes fixed on something I cannot see, but which, as I approach, I discover to be a little wooden cart, which he's holding in his hands. Filled with excitement, I race over to him and he looks up, surprised. I grab the cart and try to wrench it from his grasp, but he holds on tight and looks at me, amused, making the wheels of the cart spin with one fingertip, and I release my grip and discover, lying on the bench to his right, a very thin piece of wood which is, in fact, the silhouette of a horse. The first thing my uncle does when he sees me is to hide the horse beneath a cloth next to him, but when he realises that I've already seen it, he smiles resignedly, sets the wheels spinning again, gently pushes away my hands and returns to the task he was immersed in when I entered. He's making the horse a pair of reins, threading a slender piece of leather through the tiny hole next to the horse's mouth. I was expecting you. Father Christmas's little helper woke you up. Father Christmas says you can see the cart and touch it for a moment, but that you must then go back to sleep so that he can leave it at the end of your bed the day after tomorrow, which is the day when children get their presents. Now I'm the one making the wheels spin with one finger, looking at my first real toy, it's the first time Father Christmas has ever visited the house. I celebrate the fact that on this night I've left my room, walked down the dark corridor, feeling my way along the wall, before being drawn to the line of light under the workshop door. He takes me back to my room, turning on the lights as we go. How did you manage to come down the stairs in the dark? You could have fallen and cut your head. Now let's both go back to bed and go to sleep, you and me, he says as he draws back the bedclothes so that I can get in, then pulls them up to my chin. Imagine walking about barefoot on such a cold

316

night, he says. Then he sits down on his bed and starts taking off his shoes. Why did my father, who either did or didn't carve the elaborate desk, never once make me a toy, a cart, a Pinocchio with a long nose, a wheel? I don't remember him making any of us a toy, not even Carmen. I'm thinking this as I once again see my uncle's hand as he accompanies me to the fair and wins a prize at a shooting gallery, a small tin truck hanging on a wide strip of paper that he took just two shots to perforate and tear. The man running the booth congratulates him on his marksmanship and asks: Are you a hunter? And my uncle turns to me: You've enough to set up your own transport business now and earn your living, he says, laughing, you've got a cart, a horse and a truck, all you need is some petrol. Then he places one hand on my shoulder and guides me towards the dodgems, where we both climb aboard. The metallic sound of the music blaring out from the loudspeakers, the lights, the coloured Chinese lanterns, the grown-ups dancing, the music, I can see it all now and hear the music, the couples dancing beneath the lights and the little Chinese lanterns, the songs of Antonio Machín and Bonet de San Pedro, the songs my mother sings as she does the ironing, and now I can hear my uncle's voice, twenty years later: always remember, great oaks from little acorns grow. I've finished my military service, I've abandoned art school, and I've told him that I want to stay and work as a carpenter in the workshop, and he says: small things are the embryo of larger things, just as every fully grown man starts out as a foetus. And on this sunny morning, I think he was right, happiness can be summed up in that skinny wooden horse and its cart, the tin truck, the lights of the fair and the metallic clang of the dodgems and the sparks crackling from the web of wires criss-crossing overhead. And the smells of the fair: candyfloss, toffee apples, the burnt oil from the stall selling fritters.

He says:

'Esteban, we cannot make large things without first making small ones, for example, the maquette that a carpenter makes contains the whole building the architect then goes on to construct, there are no big professions and small professions. I'm glad you've decided to stay here with us in the workshop, but you must remember that. Don't forget: God sits on a chair, eats at a table and sleeps in a bed, just like anyone else. He can make do without the altarpieces and statues and books dedicated to Him – including the Bible – but He can't manage without His chair, table and bed.' My uncle was trying hard. He wanted me to feel at ease with my profession, to begin to love it. He thought I felt like a failure for dropping out of art school. He probably sensed that I needed to love myself a little. But to me, it sounded like empty rhetoric – which it was – because I had just started going out with Leonor and she was what I loved and, through her, I was learning to love myself. I was learning about my body with each part of her body, and my own body was gaining in value because it was part of hers, her complement, I thought we shared two bodies that could never be parted, could never live without one another. We saw each other whenever we had a free moment. When I finished work I would race off to find her. My father: And where are you off to in such a hurry? We would take refuge in the back row of the cinema in Misent (we would go in when the film had already started and the lights were down, so that no one would recognise us), we would make love in the sand dunes, we would rent rooms in boarding houses where sailors went with whores. I brought her to the marsh, and her body was the only one that never made me feel I was soiling the place. Her mud-smeared body was beautiful, even when it smelled of the putrefaction in which we'd been lying. We would wash at the spring, where the water was cleanest, the excitement of treading on that soil slippery as snake skin, the caressing touch of the plants floating in the water, the green filaments clinging to her white flesh and making her body look as if it were wounded and begging for a little tenderness, the faint smell of slime and putrefaction. My uncle's rather laboured hymns to the lathe and the saw seemed to me as futile as my father's gloomy complaints. Ah, the cool water of the untruth, so easy to drink. But truth was that flesh I could touch, her saliva, her teeth biting into my neck as she moaned with pleasure, the moist, sticky body I embraced in the mud. I didn't want to stay in the workshop, but then I had no idea what it was that I did want.

The back of the calendar for 1960 kept hidden away by Esteban's father in one of the many invoice files piled up in the cupboard in that glazed room known as the office and which was reached by a set of steps. Only the first page of the calendar, the cover, is missing, but one can safely assume that it does date from 1960 because – even though the year doesn't appear on each month's page – on the very bottom of the last page, December, in tiny print, is the name and address of the printer and, underneath, the date when the calendar was presumably printed. September 1959. Since his father wrote these notes, no one has had access to them, not even Esteban, who hasn't bothered to look through the mountain of old papers that fills nearly the whole cupboard, which has eight shelves and is about five and a half metres wide by three metres high. The twelve leaves of the calendar are illustrated with images of women in regional dress posing before familiar landscapes or well-known attractions or sights from the area they represent. The explanatory note for the January image says: Castilian woman standing outside the city walls of Ávila; February: A Navarrese woman from the Valle de Ansó. March: A Catalan pubilla *outside her farm; April: A young woman from Seville standing next to the Torre del Oro. May: A Valencian woman in traditional dress. June: Fisherwomen from La Coruña. July: Woman from Coria (Cáceres). August: 'Dulcinea' standing near the windmills of Campo de Criptana. September: Basque housewife. October: An Aragonese woman dressed to dance the* jota *at the Fiesta del Pilar in Zaragoza. November: Woman from the Canary Isles next to the thousand-year-old dragon tree. December: Woman from the Balearic Islands. The handwritten notes are on the back of the pages from June to October (inclusive). The pencilled notes are in tiny writing and some parts have faded so completely as to be illegible. That is why they are not included here.*

I'm fifteen years old and I'm listening to my father. He's home on leave from the front for the first time, I touch his soldier's uniform admiringly, not noticing that it's made from bad-quality cloth and looks as if it were meant for someone ten centimetres shorter than him and weighing twenty kilos more. I do not yet know that, very shortly, I will be wearing the same one. The war has just begun. He's in a hurry to tell me what he knows. He takes it upon himself to educate me, about what it is that surrounds every life and gives it meaning, what frees you from notions of destiny or so-called Divine Will and makes you into a man capable of making his own decisions: you're the only one who can make the best of what nature has given you, you're not obliged to do more than that — but you must do nothing less either; that's what he tells me over and over. Knowing that he'll soon have to return to the front, he thinks he may only have a brief time in which to teach me what he knows. Everything seems to happen very quickly during the war and no one makes any long-term plans.

*But if I think of him even ten years before that, I see the same peda-
gogical impulse: I go back to when I was eight. He's holding my hand
and telling me about the origins of the wood piled up in the port of
Valencia: the forests of the Congo, the Amazonian jungle, Scandinavia,
Canada or the United States, places I saw later on in films and on
the newsreels. I think he's making it up. I don't know if the timber
arriving in Valencia at the time did actually come from so many
different places. Or perhaps I'm the one distorting my memories and
putting in his mouth words he never said, but I don't think so. I can
relive that afternoon in the port of Valencia as if it were yesterday,
but quite why exactly we'd gone there, I'm not sure. It was the first
time I'd ever seen a big city. Later, during the war, I was in Madrid
and Zaragoza, and a few years before the war, I had been on an art
school trip to Salamanca. But that was all — then it was prison and
after that and ever since, Olba. I think we went to Valencia to visit
one of my grandmother's sisters, because she was ill, and my grandmother said she wanted to see her one last time: a family trip. We
had lunch in a little apartment that smelled of medicines, of alcohol
and iodine and cat pee, of pills and potions kept in chestnut-wood
drawers. An old person's apartment. In the afternoon, the tram travels
down the long avenue leading to the port, and from there, we go to
the pier where you catch the boat that takes you past the docks and
as far as the estuary. During the whole trip, I feel my father's hand
resting on my head, gently guiding me, pointing out the cranes with
their dangling loads of wood and the piles of timber on the wharfs
that we can see from the boat. The trunks look enormous. When we
leave the boat, the others stay on the beach: my grandmother and her
sister, my mother, the wife of one of my father's cousins, who used to
live in Valencia and who was also there that afternoon with her two
children, two boys I don't recall ever meeting again, and three other
men, I'm not sure who they were, but probably more of my father's
cousins. We were on Las Arenas beach, near the hotel and the beach
huts for rich people. The memory of my father on that happy day,*

the day when he gave me the gift of a train journey, of a visit to a big city with its lively streets, elegant women and cars; I get on a tram and a boat and he's there with me, holding my hand or guiding me, the palm of his hand resting on my head, and his presence in the memory is part of that gift. The two old ladies, who can't crouch down, sit on the hired beach chairs. The others lie or sit on the sand, my mother on a towel so as not to stain her skirt, which she tucks up between her knees against the wind, Ramón (who would be, what, two or three years old?) is playing with the sand, running barefoot through the fringe of foam left by the waves as they slowly retreat. They're drinking – beer and anise for the men, horchata for the women and children – and he separates me out from the group, not even taking my cousins with us – we have some business to attend to, he says by way of an excuse – and he takes me for a walk along the wharfs: from the cranes hang huge tree trunks, white, golden, reddish, dark brown. There's a book in the office that describes all the woods piled up on the wharf and that my father is now telling me about as we walk past train carriages, vans, carts pulled by great Percheron horses, the drivers idly smoking as they lean against the back of their carts or sit in the driver's seat, and stevedores bustling back and forth like busy ants. I compare those trunks with the images in the book: there, on the wharf, I see them for the first time life-size and in full colour, dark or pale, brown or honey-hued, not in black and white as they appear in my father's book. Back home, sitting beside him in the workshop, I read, guided by his finger that pauses beneath each word as I pronounce it: the maple tree originates – Dad, what does 'originate' mean? – in the Rocky Mountains and Canada, it is a mellow brown, excellent for hard floors, roller-skating rinks or dance floors; rosewood comes from Brazil and is much used in the making of luxury furniture. The Paraná pine or araucaria also comes from Brazil and is highly prized for its unusual honey-coloured wood and because it lacks growth rings; the pino amarillo or yellow pine also comes from the Americas and, because it is so strong, has been widely *used to provide rafters for the houses in our region. His finger resting on the illustrations shows me the wood that I can now see lying on the concrete and other kinds of timber that, forty years on, I have still never seen. While I'm reading, I keep asking him the meaning of the words I'm saying out loud. Many I don't understand: originates, excellent, mellow, rafters. But the mystery contained in that unknown vocabulary only increases my curiosity. I will spend weeks trying to introduce those words into my conversation and so I say things like: milk originates in a cow or this bread is excellent — that makes me feel like a grown man who knows certain secrets.*

During his leave, my father tells me that in order to love a job, you must have a thorough knowledge of it, understand its purpose, know everything about the materials you work with and respect them — their qualities and defects — as well as the hard work that went into growing and harvesting them: we're not artists, we're artisans, although, when all this is over, you'll be able to go back to the School of Arts and Crafts and become an artist, if that's what you really want. Always remember, though, that a good carpenter isn't someone who performs miracles with wood, but someone who makes a living from it; survive first, philosophise later, or make art, but whatever you decide to do, make sure you can earn enough to live on; you also need to know the precise use of each tool: look, touch this chair — he rests his hand on the back — it's born of the combined labours of nature and man, it was made by people who speak and think, it took a lot of work. The furniture you make supports the bottom or elbows or hands as well as the papers and tablecloths and plates and glasses of someone, intelligent or stupid, rich or poor, but someone, who, thanks to your work, allows himself the little bit of comfort that offers him relief from the hustle and bustle and weariness of each day, just as the headboard on a bed protects sleeping bodies — whether beautiful or misshapen it doesn't matter — during thousands of nights, it keeps you company while you sleep or if you're ill, and it's there, supporting the pillow on which you lay your head the day you die, so you see how important that headboard is. With a bed or a bedside table, your customer has given you access to a world no one else is privy to; more than that, you work with wood from trees that have grown on other continents and were felled by men using specific tools, the trunks of those trees have travelled thousands of kilometres to get here, they required the work of lumberjacks, dockers, drivers, warehouse workers, sailors, they've been hauled along by carts drawn by oxen or by mules, in trucks driven by drivers, in wagons pulled along by a steam engine whose boiler was stoked by a stoker, like the stokers on board the ship that crossed the ocean. When you think like that, then you begin to understand the importance of your work, not because you're a genius, but quite the opposite, because you're just one link in the chain, but if that link fails, it will ruin the work of all the others. Man is only his own consciousness, he makes himself. If you don't know what you're made of or what the material you use or transform with your work is made of, then you're nothing. A mere beast of burden. Knowledge gives meaning to your work, makes you a thinking man, because man is what he thinks. For millions of people, work is the only activity that teaches and civilises them. For others, it's a form of self-brutalisation in exchange for food or money. Yes, people are beginning to live a little bit better now — although this war is sure to bring back poverty — and even we enjoy a few more comforts, but we're also less as people, the rebel generals doubtless have furniture made of rosewood and walnut wood in their houses, but they're just mules, they don't understand the value of work, they think a worker is a mere tool to serve them, unable to think for himself and with no freedom to decide his future, they don't know the value of what they use, only what it costs, how much money they paid for it. Do you understand what I mean?

I nod.

★

The war ruined everything. I had to tell my son Germán before he went off to do his military service – doubtless to show him that I myself had fought in a great battle, but also because he would have a war of his own to fight – it will be no easy thing to keep your dignity among the fascist pigs you'll meet in the barracks, especially when they find out who your father is. Expect the worst, I told him. When I was about ten years old, my father taught me how to carve wood, he kept me by his side while he was making some of the furniture for the house. Then he wanted me to go to school to learn more. He had chosen me. He said to Ramón: once your brother has learned, it will be your turn. I was the oldest, just as you're the oldest now. There was an order to be followed. There wasn't enough for all of us. At least one would be saved, and that one would have to help the others along. Once one of us is out of the water, he can throw the others the rope that will save us all. That was the agreement. I learned a few things in the months I spent at the School of Arts and Crafts, how to use a gouge for example. I don't know whether I would have been any good, but I would like to have been a sculptor. Then the war came. The light went out. I had to abandon everything. For me, it was too late. At first, when I was in the trenches, I held fast to my ambition. I carved a few figures that I sent to my wife via a neighbour – I made my father a really beautiful key ring, a five-pointed star with a hammer and sickle on it – they all got thrown away or buried or burned before the Nationalists arrived in Olba, because they were politically charged images – the head of a militiaman, a fist, two crossed rifles, secular imagery, substitutes for the medallions of saints and virgins that people wore around their neck or hung on the walls before the Republic arrived. As well as medallions, I made small plates, key rings with patriotic, revolutionary motifs. All that's left are those little wooden figures on the sideboard, not much bigger than chessmen (a woman in profile, with her hair caught back, a medallion showing a horse, another on which I had carved a vase of flowers). I continued making them in prison, where I would work with any piece of wood

I came across; I made a chess set that kept us entertained for hours and, of course, I made spoons and forks with bits of boxwood I managed to smuggle into the cell or the block, because, at first, we weren't even held in cells: we were all crammed into a kind of warehouse where we had to sleep taking turns because there wasn't enough space for us all to lie down. I made key rings and those small secular medallions that prisoners hung round their neck on a bit of string or a shoelace: a name, an initial, a flower, a leaf from a plane tree. The political symbols had all vanished; we didn't even think to use the symbols that had accompanied us over the last few years. It was usually the guards who gave me the wood so that I could carve something for them. When I came out of prison, though, I stopped carving altogether – I did try occasionally, I'd pick up a piece of wood, make all my preparations, but then I'd just sit staring at it like an idiot, I think it was because everything I'd lost would suddenly rise up before me. It was like reliving the whole experience. I said to Germán: Look, I may have failed, but you could be a great cabinetmaker, I can't afford to send you to art school, as I would have liked, but I'll show you everything I know, all the rudiments, and the rest you'll pick up as you go along, you'll see. Who knows, maybe one day, we'll be able to afford to pay for some courses or you could go and become an apprentice to some master cabinetmaker. Perhaps when you come back from military service, and with your brother helping me in the workshop, we'll be able to afford to send you to art school.

That was the first time I'd spoken plainly to one of my children about what had happened to me during the war. He gave me a hard look and said:

'But I don't want to be a cabinetmaker, and when I've finished my military service, I have no intention of working here or studying. Besides, my military service isn't going to involve going into battle, this is peacetime, they won't be sending me off to war, but to a barracks, and I see that more as an opportunity than a punishment, it's a way of leaving home, escaping from Olba, meeting people, getting some *training, because I'm going to get my driver's licence there, an all-purpose one for buses, trucks, everything, and then I'm going to ask if they can put me in the repair shop, so that when I get out, I can set up my own garage and become a mechanic. Military service will be like school for me. I've got it all planned. I can learn everything I need to know there.'*

My eyes clouded over. It was all I could do not to slap him. I was torn between giving him a good beating and bursting into tears.

'Well, it's up to you,' I said.

This son of mine has inherited his mother's lack of guts, although I don't think it's really a matter of genetics, but more the times we live in. And the others? At least Esteban should turn out like me, even though physically we're so very different. He's more heavily built, a different physique altogether – he's stronger and more imposing than Germán. I don't know how bright he is, but he certainly has the physique of a man who can contain his will and his anger. But it irritates me to see him hanging around with that Marsal boy, I don't trust that family an inch, I don't even dare to tell him about what went on in the war, just in case he mentions it to his friend. He says they go to the Marsal house and listen to music. I told him I don't want him to go there again, but he probably won't pay any attention. I'll have to talk to him one day and tell him how things were. And just who his friend's father really is – so polite, so proper, butter wouldn't melt in his mouth. And this business with Germán doesn't help. As for Juan, I don't know what to think, he's too much of a child, and not just because he's the youngest. But, as I say, what do body types or genes matter? All the children have lost the heads they were born with and been fitted with new ones, tailor-made – yes, it's still going on. I live in my house with my wife and my children, and I feel like a stranger. It makes me ashamed to write this, but it's as if I were surrounded by enemies in my own house. I so miss the conversations I used to have with my father, and with my friend Álvaro, but they're both gone. Álvaro was a broken man when he came out of prison, I had a hard time too, but, perhaps I was luckier or just stronger, because when he got out, he was so embittered and so ill that he didn't last long. I've learned to live with the bitterness and somehow stop it ruining my health. Anyway, I'm from another planet. That's my choice, though, or the only choice available to me.

Stone carving seemed somehow a superior art, it frightened me, made me take a step back. Stone, I felt, was for truly great artists, and I really didn't feel I qualified. Wood was different, I'd lived with wood my whole life, but stone was something else entirely. I told the teacher that I didn't want to learn what he was asking me to learn. I felt I didn't have the skills. I just couldn't do it. The teacher tried to talk me round, saying that appearances can be deceptive: you're the one in charge of the stone, you pick up the mallet and the chisel and you patiently measure and shape and work, file and rasp and polish: the stone is a compact mass that you can split or pierce using your own strength and with the help of the right tools. Sculptors can make anything out of stone, even the finest filigree. In Bernini's statues of women, the stone becomes soft flesh into which a man can plunge his strong fingers. As with wood, the main thing with stone is to get to know it, know how to choose it, to know its density, its qualities, how it will behave, although that's something we can never entirely predict. My teacher was right. The important thing with wood is to know how to season it, how to work it when it's just dry enough, how to follow the grain, although nowadays I don't know if even sculptors bear those things in mind, and, of course, we carpenters now work with wood we know nothing about, where it came from or how it was treated. Some stone is so very hard and so very difficult to work with — my teacher told me — that you'd think any statues made from it would be condemned to eternal life, but in no time at all they get worn away by water or changes in temperature or bacteria or fungus. Other types

328

of stone, like the sort we saw in Salamanca, actually get harder when exposed to the elements. Salamanca was the one class trip we made during the Republic, thanks to a grant given by a Swedish or Dutch foundation, I can't remember which now. But I've never forgotten that city, it was like a magnificent open-air sculpture museum made of a stone that can withstand the elements: San Esteban, the cathedral, the university facade, the Patio de las Dueñas. The extraordinary sculpted figures covering entire facades, the beautiful colour of the stone that changes with the light, pale in the morning and an intense coppery gold in the evening. Almost five hundred years after they were first carved, they're still intact thanks to the quality of the stone, called Villamayor after the village where the quarry is located and from which they extract a stone that's easy to carve when it's just been cut, but which, with exposure to the weather and the passing of time, forms a kind of patina which, instead of attacking or dissolving the stone, as happens with other kinds of sandstone, preserves and even hardens it. It's nearly thirty years since I saw Salamanca and yet, if I close my eyes, I think I can still see it.

'And then there are those impressive sculptures cast in bronze or iron, which we find so amazing,' the teacher went on.

At the school, they showed us the works of Mariano Benlliure, and I almost died of envy, he was still a fashionable sculptor then, despite his statues of the king. What I had done up until then was little more than what shepherds all over the world do, whittling the handles of walking sticks, I had worked with my father in the workshop, and he'd taught me various techniques, but what we were looking at now was art, although my biggest surprise came when we visited an altarpiece by Damià Forment in the School of Fine Arts; that was when I realised my teacher was right, wood really could compete with the grandeur and perfection of stone and metal. My teacher told me: you've already worked with wood, so you've done the hard part, or do you imagine that Forment didn't have enormous difficulties to overcome? As I said before, you have to understand wood, even more than you do stone, *you have to find out what it can offer, its qualities, what it wants of you, where it's leading you, the grain, the differences in density that alter millimetre by millimetre; it's a warmer material than stone, there's more of a flow of energy between your hand and what you're sculpting, which is precisely why it often makes more demands on you, it won't be deceived, it asks you to understand it, to care for it, it asks you what a friend asks at the beginning of a friendship; although I should say that, for me, the most beautiful material – my teacher was getting carried away now – because it's the one closest to man, is even humbler than wood. I mean clay, which adapts itself to your hand, is easily marked, clay is a prolongation of yourself, after all, you yourself are clay and will be clay again one day. When you work with clay, you understand that. You realise that you are dust and will return to dust. A fragile creature working with a fragile material. And yet, in books, we see those terracotta figures from Crete or made by the Etruscans – still beautiful after thousands of years – and which, by their mere existence, show that, with intelligence and hard work, the fragility of man and clay becomes strength. Stone and metal won't necessarily last longer than clay. When you finish making a clay object, you have the feeling that you're letting go of a part of yourself. Rodin modelled his sculptures in clay, that was Rodin, then he cast them in bronze and it became industrialised.*

At the art school, we used to go to class equipped with a sketch pad, an inkwell, a pen, a pair of compasses and a set square. We learned by drawing the capitals and bases of Greek and Roman columns (Doric, Ionic, Corinthian and Tuscan), we copied engravings from Vignola's treatise on architecture, we copied the Piazza Sant'Ignazio in Rome, the Pantheon dome, the Parthenon frieze, the elevation of the temples of Paestum, the relief work on the Ara Pacis Augustae. I drew all those things and yet I've never seen any of them, I've never been to

Rome or to southern or northern Italy, I've never really left Olba, and both the desire to see those places and the possibility were buried the day they put me on a truck and sent me to the Teruel front at the age of seventeen, part of the so-called nappy brigade. When I came home on my first leave, I tore up all those drawings – my fingers gnarled from the cold and full of cuts and callouses from digging trenches with pickaxe and spade, and my ears still ringing with the noise of the bombs and shells that had fallen around me, and I was pursued by images of the frozen corpses you stumbled over at every step and the screams of the wounded, operated on in the field hospitals without any anaesthetic, and the moans of the dying being carried along on stretchers, I felt like crying or screaming too, even though I wasn't wounded and no one was sawing my leg off; more than anything, I felt like running away. I did weep as the truck took us back to the front that first time, leaving the fields of Olba behind. My uniform fitted me better than it had my father, but I didn't see him that time, my leave didn't coincide with his, in fact, I never saw him again. But I didn't know that then. On some nights, lying on my camp bed, I felt as if my head would explode and I trembled more with fear than cold, and had to repeat the word 'deserter' to myself over and over in order to stop myself from getting up and running away. Fear of the bombs and the bayonets. More horrible even than being blown up by a bomb was finding yourself face-to-face with an enemy, the bomb requires nothing of you, there's nothing you can do, your fate is sealed, but in hand-to-hand combat you are the one who has to act – and my greatest fear was that I might discover I belonged to the secret army of cowards. It troubled me to think I might be a potential coward, although, with time, I realised that any man who finds himself dragged into a war, any man, that is, with a glimmer of intelligence or an ounce of sense, is a potential coward. It's only human to want to desert and utterly absurd to decide to stay there waiting to get drenched in blood, yours or someone else's. Not even ideas can drive that thought out of your head. Some will say that you're fighting hard because you know you're fighting for a good cause, but that's not true. Only someone who has been there can speak about these things, only someone who has had that experience can know what I'm talking about – and I'm making no distinction between the people on either side – just whoever was actually there, dragging the weight of his body over those hard, icy rocks – those harsh landscapes of apparently fragile glass: having lived through all that creates a mysterious bond with the enemy, with the man who was and has continued to be your enemy, it transforms him into an accomplice, a comrade, and being transformed into your enemy's comrade makes everything seem even more unsavoury, culpable, absurd, cruel and senseless, but that's in hindsight, when you – on both sides – know what you're talking about and despise the ignorance of those who weren't there and cannot know and yet who speak about war and, like parrots, repeat words like heroism, moral courage, self-sacrifice. Your enemies also know this, although they have won and have continued their cruel behaviour because victory is a potent drug that makes you forget everything, creates new feelings, while mutilating and anaesthetising others, and unleashing pride and greed; as the victor, you want peace to repay you in spades for all that you put into the war, you feel that peace is your personal property. They certainly felt and behaved like proprietors, and yet they know more than all of the people on your own side who stayed here, they understand you better than your family, than your fellow travellers who were lucky enough – or clever enough – to be posted to the rearguard, to barracks, hospitals, offices, arsenals, places where they weren't obliged to fire a single shot in the three years that the war lasted. I missed the first two years, but had to endure the last. I looked at my hands and thought about those two tools, simultaneously hard and flexible, capable of working, sculpting, caressing, but also of punching, smashing, killing. I know that, nowadays, hands are worth less and less, many things are done by turning a knob, moving a lever back and forth, hitting a key, pressing a button, but, at the time, hands were still man's greatest gift, binding him to the creator god, part of the skills given to man by the great sculptor of the universe, whom we know does not exist (although my father used to say: never forget your head – your hand is a like a pair of pliers, just a tool – but the head is the man, the seat of man's mechanism, of understanding, desire, willpower, the ability to withstand the very worst).

END OF THE NOTES WRITTEN BY ESTEBAN'S FATHER ON THE BACK OF THE CALENDAR.

PS When, in a few days' time, they come to clear the house and take the furniture to the municipal warehouse or to some other place designed to keep all the repossessed goods of the last two years, no one, needless to say, will notice this 1960 calendar lost among the piles of papers, invoices, delivery notes, catalogues, newspapers and magazines. Before the furniture is auctioned, which will happen some months later, the men will empty desk drawers and cupboards of any useless objects and throw papers and items of clothing into the rubbish dump, where they will be burned along with other detritus. But that won't be for a few months.

It was impossible to patrol that labyrinth of water, mud and reeds. The pursuers set fire to the vegetation, intending to smoke out the fugitives, to flush them from their burrows as if they were animals (which they were), dogs were sent in along with the patrols that squelched through the mud, but it proved too costly to track the fugitives down, among the pools, bogs and tiny islands that turned out to be nothing but clumps of plants set adrift or vegetation rooted to the lagoon bottom, and, after all, the eight or ten desperados who had taken refuge there presented no real threat, they were not – as they were elsewhere – guerrilla fighters, but, rather, a handful of cornered, desperate

333

castaways, more dead to the world and more forgotten than those who really had died many years before and whose photographs and names their descendants could see on their headstones in the cemetery, although a few women did continue to make secret visits to the marsh to see their husbands or boyfriends. Locals would see them disappear off into the reeds and return, at nightfall, a couple of days later. As children we heard others mention these men under their breath, when they had probably all long since died, and we imagined them then to be amphibious beings with membranes between their fingers, a kind of web-footed creature covered in scales like the sad aquatic beast from a film I saw a few years later, *Creature from the Black Lagoon*, beings condemned to endure a bestial life. Some chose suicide. A revolver pressed to the temple. Or perhaps the muzzle of a rifle placed in the mouth: they would take off one alpargata (although, by then, they were probably barefoot, their alpargatas having long since been eaten away by the damp) and use their big toe to squeeze the trigger. Their comrades would bury them somewhere, or their corpses would be left exposed to the elements, their flesh devoured by animals, and time would eventually cover their bones in mud and scrub. But that wasn't the story my father kept in his head; for him, the life of the marsh fugitives had a nobler aura. I caught a certain note of satisfaction in his words when he spoke to me of those who had shot themselves: they were not poor beasts worn down by despair, but the only locals who still had the right to call themselves men. Caked in mud, bearded, half naked, wearing only rags or a loincloth made from the remnants of old clothes or woven together from leaves. He himself had not had access – or else had relinquished the chance to have such access – to that moment when you are absolute master of your own destiny – that moment when you grip the barrel of a rifle with your teeth, when your lips kiss metal. That, for my father, was the moment when a man was almost a god – the only real contact with freedom that life afforded. And his family, we'd been the ones who had forced him to linger on as a lesser being. Well, today, Dad, I agree with you: you'll never be the master of your own fate, you'll never be closer to being entirely your own man, the dictator of your own agenda. You have accepted that you'll never succeed in opening the eyes of a dead child, not even a god can do that, but you can snatch back from death its arbitrary power, by imposing an order, a time and a date: I may have no control over my life, but I do have control over how long my life will last, I own that decisive moment. No greater power has been given to us – we are able to close forever eyes that would other-wise remain open. Whatever priests, politicians and philosophers may say, man is not a bearer of light, he is a sinister breeder of shadows. Incapable of giving life (how can I say this, when I myself came so close to creating life and when humanity continues ceaselessly to reproduce, but I know what I'm saying), he can kill at will. The greatest power a man can wield is that of taking away life. Squeezing the trigger and seeing the bird that had been flying swiftly across the sky suddenly drop like a stone to shatter the mirror of the water. I close my eyes and listen to my father, the noise of his false teeth crunching their way through a lettuce leaf, grinding away at a biscuit. That noise gets right inside me. It's like the sound you hear when you step on a cockroach. Those grinding teeth, the smell when I remove his incontinence pads, his eyes fixed on mine, although I have no idea what lies behind them. The old may have poorer memories than the young, but they are also the ones who forget least. The soft mud, the smell of putrefaction. Into my head come memories that belong to me because I myself amassed those memories, along with others I inherited, but which are no less vivid for that, part of the vortex of a life: they whirl past on a carousel, protagonists and bit-part players, and not only them, because, this touring theatre company of mine takes with it the trunks containing the costumes and the crates containing the scenery for all the plays that are to be put on, and yes, the props as well: there are the faces, the gestures, the voices (yes, I can hear all those people talking, there's no point covering my ears), but there are also the clothes they wear or wore; the rooms in which they lived, the furniture. My nightmare includes both the facades of the houses and the interiors with their own particular smell, because every room has its own smell; the landscapes, the sounds, the light that changes depending on the time of day or night, the temperature – hot or cold, the dense air, the cloying humidity of evening – the languor that fills you as you watch the rain snaking down the windowpane, my mother holding the iron close to her face to see if it's hot enough, or sprinkling the clothes with a few drops of water that sizzle into nothing as the iron touches them; Uncle Ramón's red eyes as he comes down the brothel stairs, feeling his way along the wall, and when he fastens his seat belt on the passenger side and watches through the window the soulless warehouses, the places where neon signs flash on and off day and night, the shadows of the orange trees, the emerald-green rice fields, their glow prolonged by the last rays of sun as if the greenness itself were giving off light rather than receiving it, the reeds and the bulrushes.

It isn't true what they tell you, that you come from nothing and will leave with nothing. You had something when you arrived, Francisco: a fine cradle, linen nappies, a warm bottle, possibly a wet nurse, and certainly, shortly afterwards, a nanny or a governess. After school, I would often see you and your brothers picnicking in the park beneath the watchful eye of that woman wearing a white apron. Not that this explains very much. What matters isn't how you come into the world or how you leave it, but what you are like now: if you have to worry about essentials or if they just come to you naturally, if things fall into your hands or slip through your fingers – or, worse still, if you never get them at all, if your whole life is a struggle to obtain what you know you can't have. That is the poison. You're pursued by what you can't have. What matters isn't the beginning and the end of the play, curtain-up-curtain-down, but the play itself, how it evolves – life; demagogues like my father tell you that what matters is the beginning – the social class you come from: that's what revolutionaries tell you – or the ending – the four last things – death, judgement, heaven and hell: that's what priests tell you, as people like Francisco do in a way. In both cases, the end – which, for Francisco, was, initially, revolution, and latterly, the creation of a modern, cosmopolitan society – justifies the means, like some modern form of casuistry. Ideologues tell you that it's a matter of beginnings and endings, which are, in any case, inextricably linked, because for the less favoured classes, the suffering of every day also finds its justification in the ending, and both sides devalue the one thing that is of any real value, namely, life itself, the moment: that's what my Uncle Ramón used to say after he was widowed: he made no distinction between revolutionaries and priests, he had lost the ability to choose, to evaluate, the whole world was part of a thick, malignant drool; that's what he thought, but it didn't sour his nature as it did my father's. His despair was strictly for internal use only. Saying that at the end of the road we're all going to die alone and, as Machado said, with very little baggage, is rather like the fable of the fox and the grapes. It's accepting that you won't pick the grapes because you can't reach them. You tell yourself: why pick something that's too green to eat today and that, in a few days' time, will be rotten: you deny yourself the pleasure of possession, of savouring the moment, why have anything if death will take it all away? But what about the icy milkshakes you take out of the fridge on boiling hot August afternoons, the tender steak you slap on the grill when you have friends over in the winter, or the air conditioning that cools you while I'm frantically working away in the unbreathable atmosphere of the workshop? Don't tell me that those things, however transient, are of no importance, I mean they may only last about as long as a cool drink stays cool in summer, but are you really saying those things don't matter? Of course they do, imagine the construction worker on a roof in the August sun, the man cement-spraying the walls of a swimming pool in forty degrees of heat, or me sweating over a saw because the workshop budget would never stretch to having air conditioning installed, and you, Francisco, sitting under an air conditioner or on a recliner on the deck of your yacht, enjoying the sea breeze and sipping a single-malt whisky: you're not going to tell me there's no difference, vanity of vanities, all is vanity, that's what you used to say when you were a Christian and an excitable worker-priest in the making. It's a lie, as you now know and, as you also know, not even the priests believe it, although, for some, faith does manage to override common sense. Faith didn't remove your ability to take action. You fled from the seminary, you ran at a gallop. You saw the essential contradiction in Catholicism: if you're convinced that everything will return to dust, why build those huge churches, marble upon marble upon marble? Marble floors, marble columns, marble facades. The mosaics and coffered ceilings and frescos and gold leaf; the gold and marble altars: Travertine, Carrara, Paros; onyx and marble, red and pink and serpentine and green; lapis lazuli and white ivory, and more gold and cedarwood and mahogany, and yet you're telling me that everything turns to dust once you've slammed down the double six on the marble tabletop at the end of a game of dominoes, when we're left alone at the bar and you tell me – the friend whose shoulder you can cry on – how disappointed you are, how unhappy. Obviously we are dust and to dust will return, but all in good time – we *will* return to dust, but you, Francisco, are afraid that death will take away your material pleasures, that the Grim Reaper will prevent you from going back to your yacht on another luminous day like today, when the sea is utterly calm and blue as blue; in the air, only the crystalline breath of the mistral; or that death might not allow you to eat one last partridge in brine garnished with caramelised shallots, garlic, black pepper and a bay leaf, while, for me, in this workshop, which is blazing hot in summer and damp in winter, the wait for death seems very long and I call on death to see if I can finally get some rest. That's how you need to think, Francisco, if you want us to be real friends, as we once were, you need to start thinking frankly and not hypocritically: watch me eat the grapes, little fox. Yes, me, I'm eating them: see how the pips crack between my teeth, how the sweet juice trickles from the corners of my mouth, how I chew and suck and enjoy. They're muscat grapes. The pleasure of desire and the pleasure of the act. If you're starving, you can't even allow yourself to feel desire, you cut desire off at the root because it's such a painful reminder of everything you lack, while for me – rolling in money as I am – it's the door through which I pass into real life: that's why I cultivate my desire, feed it, postpone the moment of fulfilment, it is the ample vestibule that precedes pure pleasure, a warehouse set apart from the one in which dire need is stored. I prolong desire, just as, when I'm having sex, I prolong the moment before I come, because I prepare meticulously for that small explosion, I make the foreplay last as long as possible so that my orgasm is all the more intense. I enjoy the thirst for possession, and I enjoy, above all, the moment when I quench that thirst, when desire explodes, when that little spring bursts forth, God, it's good that little death, *la petite mort*, that holds you captive for a moment, then returns you back to earth: I think that's what the French call it, *la petite mort*, at least I seem to recall reading or hearing that somewhere. When the journey is over, yes, we will both die, each on our appointed day and at our appointed hour, but you will leave without having lived, while I will have lived my life to the full: that's the difference between us; I will be dust, but, as Quevedo says, I will be dust in love: dust that has eaten, drunk and fucked royally, a dust rich in nutrients, an opulent concentration of the very best that human beings have produced; and maybe, who knows, dust has a memory, a memory that floats obstinately, eternally, above time, and consoles us with the thought that at least we drained life to the very last drop, it's either that or we're desperately unfortunate and we will be plagued for all eternity by the knowledge that life passed us by without our having had the chance to enjoy it. That's how you should talk to me, Francisco – show me that what I have is just so much rubbish and that the sooner the wind rises and carries it all away, the better for everyone, and here I am, saying this to you today as I stand on the shore of the lagoon and gaze out over the water made still more beautiful by the blue sky, as if nature wanted to seduce me into playing with her for a little longer; and yet, I can assure you that, even while gazing on all this beauty, I feel eager to know what it will be like to cross the threshold and step into the kingdom of shadows, yes, to cross that threshold for good.

From the top of the dunes, I can see fragments of beach between the distant buildings. Since the crisis began, the frenzy of cranes, cement mixers and derricks has stopped, and the landscape swept clear. There are half-finished buildings, where work has been abandoned, and none are still under construction. None. In winter, you can walk quietly beside the sea, feeling your feet sink into the sand, almost alone, except that the solitude of the beach is an inhabited solitude: there are fishermen, as well as English and German retirees either jogging or striding along the shoreline moving their arms energetically in what they imagine to be martial fashion, but they succeed only in looking deeply weird: rapid steps, elbows close to the body and forearms stiff, or else swinging their arms vigorously back and forth; as I say, they just look rather pathetic: old people moving clumsily, mechanically, like automatons, or like lunatics throwing a completely pointless tantrum in the face of death. I find it faintly repellent, this determination among the elderly to keep fit by running from one place to another or cycling along the concrete path that skirts the beach and which is supposed to be the esplanade (that's what local councillors call it when they're interviewed on the radio). Most of these winter athletes are vigorous old people who, one can't help thinking, would be better off sitting in front of the TV in an armchair and taking stock of their past life, preparing for the big encounter, before the lights finally go out, but who decide instead to risk their lives – which are, after all, already lost and, for the most part, wasted – as well as those of others, many of which might still have some value. They pedal along these narrow paths, full of bends and hills that test their spent hearts, some cycle along the twisting local roads in groups that even spill over onto the opposite lane. Others cycle alone. It really makes me cringe to see one of those solitary, ancient cyclists huffing and puffing up a hill. The terrain is very rugged here. The mountains dominate the horizon beyond the plain and come right down to the sea to form steep cliffs. The plain only widens out towards the north, where the orchards meet the marsh and the beach. It's an unpleasant sight, those old men hunched over the handlebars, sweating and panting; scrawny, bird-like thighs encased in tight, garish Lycra, flabby bottoms drooping over the saddle or skinny ones pointing skywards like bony, avian prows. I no longer enjoy strolling by the sea, not with all the tourists, restaurants, open-air cafes, snack bars built along the seafront, where, in winter, the waves beat against the walls of the many apartment blocks, and where, each spring, trucks bring in tons of fresh sand to replenish the beach: the sea here is a dirty, violated place, where mere passing tourists, people who come from who knows where, pee, defecate or ejaculate, and into the sea are emptied the bilges and toilets of the oil tankers that dot the horizon on their way to the port of Valencia, along with the Mediterranean cruise ships laden with retirees enjoying a falsely luxurious lifestyle or, rather, an illusion of luxury – the ports of call are announced in the newspapers: Tunis, Athens, Malta, Istanbul, the Amalfi Coast, Rome-Civitavecchia, Barcelona – leaving whole tankfuls of filth in their wake. The sea is like a great lung of salty water constantly being oxygenated, and the briny wind expelled by that respiratory organ simultaneously purifies us and cleanses itself, that, at least, is how we think of the sea, a body that is always pure because it's washed clean by every storm, but my sense now is that it's impregnated by the kind of sticky muck that remains in a body after it's been violated, the cement from the buildings next to the beach, the rubbish that accumulates against the breakwaters built to keep the storms from carrying off the sand; to me the whole coast looks worryingly like the aftermath of a banquet; besides, you're never free from prying eyes; as I say, I do still walk alone along the sand, but there's no real solitude. The flatness of the beach leaves you exposed to view; you can make out the movements of other tiny human figures from a long way off, their comings and goings; you yourself provide a permanent visual display for other walkers or for those peering out of the windows of the hundreds of apartment blocks. One day, a layer of ash will fall on all of this, covering it up, an ash whose qualities we cannot as yet decipher. In its neglected state, the marsh restores some sense of privacy to me, makes me think of the 'houses' we used to build as children to shield us from the eyes of our elders, places safe from prying adult eyes, where we could set up our own system of laws, play more or less forbidden games under the tablecloth, under the bed, or inside a large wardrobe. In the marsh, you can create your own world outside the real one. No one jogs, still less cycles along the muddy, potholed paths, which smell of stagnant water, rotting vegetation and the cadavers of dead animals: a snake, a bird, a rat, a dog, a boar; the locals no longer deposit the corpses of their pets here; they used to, not so long ago, but those country houses that haven't collapsed have been refurbished and are used only as weekend retreats, and so very few animals are kept there. Customs have changed, and a different sensibility is abroad, there's more vigilance, more neighbourhood watch, the modern name for tale-telling, which has become ever more wide-spread. People are keen to denounce anyone committing some offence, however minor: no one would dare to ask a neighbour to lend him his van to transport the body of a dead horse or a dog. This is now considered socially reprehensible.

I've parked the 4x4 next to the water, climbed up the slight incline to the right that conceals the vehicle from view and, from there, I've been contemplating a landscape partially concealed by mist and by the smoke from the bonfires in the orchards, where they've been pruning the orange trees. The smoke lends a watercolour quality to the sunny winter morning: the greens of the past months have been replaced

343

by yellows and coppery browns, the light has a quality that is, at once, delicate and sharp; it emphasises the shapes of the distant buildings, making them seem nearer, just a stone's throw away; it carves a chiselled line around the whitewashed walls of the huts – some of which still have brick chimneys – where the rice-growers on the edge of the lagoon store their agricultural equipment, including their irrigators. In summer and at certain times of day, the water takes on the earthy colour of tea, but on this sunny winter morning, it's an intense blue, in marked contrast with the dun-brown of the dry scrub and the reed beds: the lagoon seems to have gone back to being a bay open to the sea, a status it lost centuries ago. Where it touches the water, the sand of the dunes glitters, becoming a multitude of shining particles, like gold, mica, silver. I'm aware of the subtle, stimulating vitality of the morning, a morning that gives one a sense that everything that is about to disappear is being made anew. Even I seem to have been infected by a youthful air that makes the whole situation utterly absurd. What am I up to? What am I about to do? The beauty of the place lends an unexpected slant to the whole situation, a sort of false euphoria that overlays the gloom into which I am about to plunge and that has been waiting in the wings. I walk along with a spring in my step, pushing aside the reeds that brush my face. The shifting wind – a cold, almost imperceptible mistral that seems to cut through the air like a cheese wire – mitigates the marshy smells, mingling or alternating the sickly aromas from the stagnant water with the salty pangs carried on the breeze from the nearby sea, and with the hushed breathing of the grass, a damp emanation from the night dew that is fast evaporating beneath the warm breath of the sun. Flocks of sparrows cross the sky in formations that look as if they had been drawn by a geometrician. A distant rifle shot rings out. Someone is

344

shooting ducks or the wild boar that come down from the mountain to drink or to hide their litter among the reeds, although they usually only arrive as dusk is coming on. I've watched them at sunset with my Uncle Ramón. Next to the road, at the top of the dune that runs alongside it to the left, is a well. How often have I lifted the wooden lid as I'm doing now? As soon as I do, a moist exhalation rises up from within, I can see the wall thick with maidenhair ferns, I take the bucket down from its metal hook, throw it into the well and hear a watery splash as the bucket hits bottom. As I struggle with the rope, the pulley above my head creaks and, from down below comes the echoing slosh of water as it overflows the bucket each time I give a tug on the rope. The metal bucket emerges misted with the cold water, which I drink, scooping it out with my hands, which, in turn, grow numb and intensely red. I splash my face, feeling the shock of sharp crystals on my skin. This clear, cold water bears no resemblance to the slimy stuff you get in the lagoon. When we used to drink it or pour it over our heads on hot summer days, I was always astonished at how cool the well water was and it still surprises me that, despite the depth of the well, it's completely untouched by the salt sea nearby. What limestone corridors does it follow? How did my uncle know that down there, beneath the marshy mud, was a layer of rock and, beneath that, flowing water: the knowledge of old country folk, of water diviners who have passed on their experience, but who also have a nervous system able or trained to pick up energies and vibrations that we never notice. The well connects with some of those underground rivers born out of the rain that seeps through the calcareous rock of the nearby mountains and that then follow their subterranean course for dozens of kilometres beneath the sea. There are places where a fisherman can throw a bucket into the sea and find fresh water to drink.

Yet, all around me lies dark, boggy earth composed of thousands of years of rotten vegetation.

While your voice, Liliana, is drowned out by the contemporary racket – the future that is fast approaching and no longer includes me – they come back to me and occupy the space you have vacated: they return to perform their dance, Ginger and Fred. I see them dancing, hand in hand, leaping, turning. He's wearing a top hat and, holding her hand above her head, he whirls her around like a spinning top, her skirt swirling about her thighs. They are, of course, taking an active role in the big closing number, just before the curtain falls to rapturous applause. They walk with the others to the front of the stage, and the whole cast bows to the audience. They've clearly rehearsed this beforehand, and the applause continues as the curtain rises two or three times more, before falling for the last time: she is like a piece of pale gauze, she looks as if you could easily pass straight through her, as the strange light from the spotlights does, impregnating whatever it is she's made of, if, that is, the bluish fingers that take his hand, not mine, really are made of matter. They always appear to me together, as if they were just one person, they remind me of the Siamese twins joined by their beards who appeared in a fantasy film I saw as a boy, *The Five Thousand Fingers of Dr T.*, or the two inseparable detectives in the adventures of Tintin. But it isn't true, they're not joined together, and this fact could and does console me. The performance continues for Francisco as it does for me, a torrent of memories bursting through the floodgate, Leonor has escaped downstream, free, belonging to no one, and this grants her a redeeming weightlessness. As the nightmare ends, the scissors have snipped the

346

couple in two, and Ginger has left Fred all alone, setting him unexpectedly adrift. She leaves without so much as a wave of the hand, without saying goodbye. Leonor, too, left without saying goodbye, without a word of warning as to what she was about to do (you should leave as well, she said, and I thought she was talking about the future, about her and about me too); after the operation, she vanished from Misent and, shortly afterwards, I learned that she'd gone to live with Francisco in Madrid. I just couldn't understand it. I didn't know then that women have a sixth sense telling them where best to invest in what one might call the human futures market. They see in a man the germ of what he will become, a bit like the barely perceptible red speck in the yolk of an egg indicating that it's been fertilised. Some people believe the maternal instinct activates that impulse in women, that eugenics search. Who knows? They came back for a few days and were seen together everywhere: the bars in Olba, the restaurants, cafes, the beach at Misent, various bank branches. Francisco was shown off like a trophy. She – the daughter of a fisherman – stayed at the Marsal house. She did not, as Francisco believed, leave Misent with a hook through her lower lip, but had gladly taken the bait that best suited her. You've caught me, but just wait and see how hard a catch I prove to be, how much I wriggle before you put me in that basket. The instantly acquired air of superiority (she proffered her cheek for me to kiss, *mwa mwa*, as if we were passing acquaintances who hadn't seen each other for a while, while a beaming Francisco looked on), as if that marriage had been just one of the possible options open to her, when, in reality, what future awaited her in Misent? Becoming a dressmaker? Going to the warehouse with the other women to sort, wash, wax and wrap oranges? Packing persimmons? Joining the other employees for their coffee break in the bar opposite the biscuit factory? Running to get to the shop before it closed and buying a couple of chicken thighs and wings after work? Racing home to warm up the food prepared the previous night, before the kids get home from school? At the very most, becoming a schoolteacher, which was, you said, your true vocation. Day after day, writing the word 'Dictation' in careful script on the blackboard, trying to explain that most inexplicable of things, according to which the letter pi equals 3.14159; that *baca* is written with a *b* when you mean the rack you put on the roof of the car and with a *v* when you mean an animal whose meat and milk is used to feed human beings (that's what teachers used to teach then, although, shortly afterwards, things changed, and I've no idea what they teach now). Or making the most of her elementary knowledge of arithmetic to keep the accounts in my father's – and her father-in-law's – poky carpentry workshop. Another option – almost the same, but considerably worse – would have been to marry one of the local fishermen, a fisherman like her father, like her eldest brother, for whom the wife waits with the supper ready so that he can eat as soon as he gets home, having first drunk a few rounds of beers and anises in the local bar. A lovingly prepared supper left for hours with a plate covering it to keep off the flies. She could sense who would provide her with a safe nest, who would promise security for any children that might come along. Placing any chicks who were born – and who would, this time, be loved and wanted – on a high enough branch to keep them safe from the inevitable predators prowling below, that's the law of the jungle. Placing herself on that same high branch, her wings spread to cover her chicks: you see, I'm not like you, she seemed to be saying when she came back. And I was just one of many. I remember her getting out of the car, wearing a silk scarf tied under her chin, revealing a couple of strands of blonde or dark hair, she went light or dark depending on her mood. She showed her white teeth in a smile that appeared to be directed at the universe, while he removed the suitcases from his Volvo and placed them on the pavement outside the front door, designer luggage, a leather weekend bag, another small suitcase; she was wearing a full print skirt or perhaps, more daringly, a pair of tailored trousers (in Olba at the time, it still took a certain degree of courage for a married woman to wear trousers), her chest moulded by a tight-fitting Breton sweater, blue stripes on a white background. The perfume that lingers in the street for a few long minutes. The smell of burnt petrol from the engine of a car far beyond the reach of most of us in Olba, and the smell of perfume that pursued me for weeks like a thorn in a finger that has become infected. Her and Francisco. A brief hello, her proffered cheek, my brief kiss. As if nothing had happened between us. He smiles. My subordinate position. Forty years later, when he returns to Misent, Francisco still carries the guilt I placed on him, I can't help it, whereas Leonor has received the forgiveness bestowed by irreparable loss. Her lightness – she is only a shadow now – exempts her from guilt, death has snatched her away. Death, the supreme dealer out of justice. After that, there is no guilt, no sin. She has passed through all the stages required by purifying asceticism: suffering and illness, the anointing with holy oils (or, in place of the oils, endless manipulations by doctors and nurses), music by Bach and the cortège with the long hearse climbing the hill up to the cemetery and parking a few metres from the place where my grandfather's body was found. *Requiescat in pace.* The sordid nature of the disease – her hair coming out in clumps in her hands, sores in her mouth, her nails coming away from the skin – has cleansed her of life's miseries, has tamed the flesh, transformed desire and anger into pity. Something similar is happening to the marsh;

349

its fetid, unhealthy state helps it to remain intact, preserves or redeems its innocence, and constitutes its own peculiar form of purity, a variant on the lightness that comes from its unwillingness to fit into a world different from itself (and yet, it isn't exactly pity I feel for her, no, though I do feel infinite pity, but as if covered by a *gratin* of resentment, what did you do to me, what have you done to me?). Francisco began to visit Olba more often after Leonor died. After the packed funeral, attended by journalists, Michelin-star chefs and the odd politician, and where the locals gazed in amazement at the abundance of wreaths heaped inside the hearse and the car escorting it, he had a pink marble headstone erected, a rather vulgar declaration of his supposed love for her – he wept inconsolably as the coffin was lowered into the grave – one of the few elaborate graves in Olba cemetery, which is otherwise a modest place: simple graves and niches, a couple of dozen cypress trees and three or four old family vaults (new arrivals like the Marsals and the Bernals haven't dared to compete with them) as befits the egalitarianism of the region, where, as used to be said a few years ago, no one has too much, but everyone has something (the last ten years have put paid to that social equilibrium). He screwed up his face and his nose twitched nervously just as it did when he was sniffing a glass of wine, uhhmmm, uhhmm, making unpleasant sucking noises with his mouth, swilling the wine noisily around inside: oh, hm, gorgeous, just a faint touch of violets, ah, yes, and a hint of aquatic flowers beginning to fade, can't you taste it? Water lilies, irises (but Francisco, my friend, don't aquatic flowers smell a bit like rotten fish? – you've been to the marsh with me and know perfectly well that water lilies give off a disgusting scent, yes, the same *ninfées* that Monet painted so obsessively and deliciously, because they do make a wonderful subject for painters. I'm going to make you smell one so that you remember the vile stink from our childhood). Floral, silky, full, fruity, intense. That wasn't so very long ago. What? Six or seven years? When you tightrope-walk along the fragile thread of the seventies, you realise that ten years is nothing, and that even twenty years is no big deal. Nor are the seventy years you've been alive. Life is gone in a breath. I think Leonor died in 2003. Perhaps shortly before. Francisco had stopped visiting Olba after his parents died and his siblings moved to other towns and sold the family house to make way for an apartment block. But she, it seems, said – and even wrote in her will – that she wanted to be buried in Olba. I don't know why, because she had no family here. Her brothers, with whom, as far as I know, she had lost all contact, live in Misent as her whole family always has; the fisherman brother came to the funeral with his wife and children, looking serious and solemn, but he didn't shed a single tear; the other brother didn't even bother to come. Olba is Francisco's territory, although for a few hours it did occur to me to wonder if perhaps my presence here could have had something to do with her last wish. That she had felt a sudden pang of nostalgia for her first love. Why not? As we get older, we have a longing to put things right, to correct the mistakes of our childhood or adolescence, as if such a thing were possible. We often wonder what's become of that girl we once knew. This doubt-less happens because we are aware of our own inability to correct anything in the present. You don't want to accept that the girl you once knew will now be an old lady with dental implants or dentures like yours. At night, you're besieged by memories of people who are no longer here, by stories you can share with nobody, because the ones who lived through them with you are gone. Yes, I did foolishly think that perhaps she'd chosen to come back to Olba out of melancholy, as a homage to her own youth, to the rooms in cheap hotels, our mingled saliva, the darkness in the dunes, the moonlight on the water and the water on her skin: a longing for the happiness of those years of which I was, I presume, a part. I even thought that I would, at last, have her near – as if a dead person can be near or far – and I imagined myself walking up to the cemetery each afternoon to talk to her, as some widowers do, yes, making a daily visit to his wife's grave, kneeling down next to it, keeping it clean, polishing the glass protecting the wife's photo, and placing a little bunch of flowers on the headstone. Not everything had been lost – there were still the ashes from the bonfire. Life was trying to correct a few mistakes. She had come back. All too often, it's the dead who impose meaning on the living. The grave of the beloved, who, after her sojourn in the world, decided to return to rot in the place where she had experienced her first love, her first exciting discovery of the flesh.

A few days ago, when I drove past the cemetery, I noticed an enormous rat creep out of the shrubbery and crawl over the wall, doubtless attracted by the stink of the most recent burials. With the crisis, people are now getting buried in really cheap coffins that don't always retain the rotting bodies. When I saw the rat, I swear I jumped, jolted by a tremor of fear for you, afraid the rat might harm you in some way, although I doubt there's much left to gnaw on beneath the stone bearing your name and your photo, but who knows, rats will give anything a try: the wooden planks of the coffin – even top-quality ones like yours – or bones or any remnants of cloth that have survived the pervading damp. Because here it's damp in summer too, even on really hot summer nights, when the temperature is more tropical than Mediterranean, sultry nights when you toss and turn, unable to sleep, nights that seem interminable even though they're the shortest of the year, when, as I lie in my bed, I can hear the night dew dripping from the roof onto the pavement.

You flail about between the damp, burning sheets, stewing in the heat, your face glued to the pillow with sweat, as sticky as the still air around you. And as you drift in and out of sleep, the blinding light of the sun suddenly appears, unannounced, and the crushing heat of day falls on the scorched grass and the whirring cicadas. No, Leonor, this isn't Sweden or Germany or gentle Brittany, those shady, Gothic, nocturnal places, where sex seems to take on a metaphysical density. There's no room here for the tale of a lover returning to her first love. For a while we used to have sex together, then you chose someone else to keep you company in bed, and that was that, there's nothing melancholy about it, nothing that needs to be put right, nothing to feel nostalgic about, such rhetoric is quite simply unthinkable: this is the Mediterranean, where all mysteries shrivel up and die in the excess of light. No romantic metaphysics can survive under such a sky. Not for us the vast, shady forests, splendid deciduous trees, or sad, solitary, wandering souls, no poetic penumbras. Our trees are more gnarled than leafy, have more wood than leaves, are more grey than green. You have to keep your feelings to yourself, because they fade fast beneath this impertinent light. But surely everyone knows that. And so the only person to visit and leave flowers on her grave every month or so was her husband. As is only right and proper.

I often see him pass the workshop on his way to the cemetery, and I think that the flowers he's carrying are partly mine, not because of the love I may have felt for Leonor, nor because of any part of myself that may have remained inside her (for we leave part of ourselves, our saliva, our fluids, our bacteria and viruses inside the person we love, we leave certain gestures, certain vices: therefore, I must have been present during whatever may have gone on between them, certain words, a certain deft way of touching, of setting off certain springs in the body, all of which we learned together), but

353

those flowers contain the empty space she left behind, because I am what I lack, what is missing, what I am not. I can hear Leonor saying: this is mine, it's inside me. I'm the only one who can give you permission to poke your nose into my business, and, as you see, I'm not going to. She even refused to allow me to make a contribution towards the cost of that intimate piece of butchery. I think of the bloodstained doll floating briefly in the toilet bowl, but the truth is, I didn't see it, I don't know what it actually looked like, I'm talking about how these things happen in films and documentaries and magazines, but I had nothing to do with it. I don't know where she went to get it done or who did it, who paid or how much. I prefer to think she went alone, that, at the time, she was still alone. I don't even know if she returned to Misent afterwards or if she got on the train and went straight to Madrid; if she had prepared her escape beforehand as previously agreed with him, or if she sought him out once she was there. I can picture an apartment in Valencia, on one of the many housing developments, and I can even see the room, with all its windows closed, but I've never known for sure. Like my father with his war stories, she decided it was none of my business. What *was* my business? Francisco used to come back from Madrid, eat in some of the bars in Olba and visit the cemetery, until he decided to return for good, and, in the process of restoring the house and moving in, he gradually forgot about the grave which had, it seems, been more of an excuse for him to come back: to smell the orange blossom in the spring, to stick his spoon into a paella, to go sailing on his yacht on calm days: my children have their own lives to lead, but here, I at least have her, the only thing I truly do have; besides, Olba's a nice, quiet place, and if you want a bit of excitement, you've got Misent about ten kilometres away, Benidorm fifty kilometres away and Valencia a mere hundred kilometres. You can even get on a boat in Misent and in a couple of hours, you're in Ibiza, although you'd need to be forty-five or fifty years younger to cope with the club scene there. While he was giving me this spiel justifying his return, he would laugh, taking sips from his glass or swirling the wine around and claiming to be able to detect the smell of broom and scrubland and sun-scorched rock roses, of animal pelts (all the animals we know locally have been to school, we used to say when he wasn't there, and we'd laugh and imitate his mannerisms, raising our glasses, studying the contents and swirling them around), of tanned hides and tanneries. I remember him at the Saturday-morning brunches we organised; that was when I still used to occasionally go out on the weekends: these partridges would go really well with a Marqués de Riscal 86 or a Tondonia 88, since I don't think we're going to be able to stretch to an Único de Vega Sicilia (and I won't even mention a Latour, that would be going a bit far). And still talking, he would head off to what he rather pretentiously called the cellar, the garage-cum-dining room he had installed in the free-standing annexe where he kept his wine along with any tools or equipment: we never went upstairs, or only once and one at a time, his Olba friends were not allowed, it was reserved for a different kind of guest, although each of us believed that we were the only ones to have been given the privilege of visiting the finer parts of the Civera house, until we discovered that he had, in fact, shown them to us all, but always swearing us to secrecy. Vanity has always been his weak point. Anyway, he would stroll off to the cellar and, *voilà*, as if by magic, would emerge bearing two bottles of Vega Sicilia and show us the faded, yellowing labels on which one could still read the year: he would point at the date several times, assuring us that it had been a very special year and that, in a recent auction, someone had paid

20,000 *duros* for a bottle like the one we would be drinking in forty-five minutes or so (for the wine to be perfect, we need to let it breathe, and, meanwhile, we can set the table, prepare the salads, drink an aperitif and grill the meat). Some of the wilier guests would make a mental note of the date and the way the wine was described, so that they could repeat it later on like a parrot when they were at a meeting with suppliers or clients, or use the information in situations where such knowledge would gain the most brownie points, for example, in the office of the bank manager from whom they're hoping to get a loan so risky that not even the boss of Banco Santander would sign off on it: perhaps he can be seduced by all that talk of coffee, cedars of Lebanon, water lilies, autumn leaves and fruits of the forest, and with the remark: I was with Marsal the other day, you know, Don Gregorio's son, the one who used to edit that foodie magazine, what a guy, eh, he's travelled all over and you'd be amazed what he can taste in a wine, he showed me a box full of little bottles containing maybe eighty or ninety different smells, or was it only sixty, but still, sixty different aromas that you can find in a glass of wine, my friend's wife – God rest her – (and thus they add Francisco's esteemed friendship to their CV) used to run a two-Michelin-star restaurant in Madrid, the Cristal de Maldón, you must have heard of it, it was in all the magazines and on the TV, anyway, as I was saying, the other day, we were having brunch with some other friends, and he brought out two bottles of Único de Vega Sicilia, I can't remember the year now, and they're convinced that by telling this to the bank manager – who, before he came to Olba, had probably never drunk anything more expensive than a twelve-euro bottle of Jumilla – he will be persuaded that the person asking for the loan is not some poor wretch in need of a few euros, but a man of the world who got out of bed this morning hoping to do business with another man of the world, a fellow entrepreneur, the loan really being more of an excuse to sit on the office sofa and smoke an expensive cigar with him in private and drink a glass of this Martell brandy I've brought for you, no, wait, wait, it's here in my briefcase, no, let me serve you, and you keep the bottle, I'll be offended if you don't. You know how snake-like bank managers and agents are: when confronted by someone who can persuade them that he's actually rolling in money and is only asking for credit on a whim, simply to have the pleasure of talking to him for a while, they crawl and fawn and remove all obstacles and don't even ask for guarantees; if you can make them feel small enough, you've got that impossible loan in your pocket, guaranteed by a guy without so much as an ID card to his name. However, if you go there explaining that you need a loan so that you can carry on working, so that you won't have your car repossessed or be evicted from your house, they'll just snort scornfully and show you the door. I was never that impressed by Francisco's little act. Sniffing out the next opportunity with that sensitive hare's nose and that reptilian brain of his, not soul, because he doesn't have a soul; neither do I, we share that idea in common, we cannot have what does not exist, there is what there is and it lasts as long as it lasts. Then, it's over. So what's the point of putting flowers on her grave and standing there grim-faced, your eyes full of tears? What are you doing standing there in front of something that is nothing and expects nothing? Or are you just crying for yourself, you jerk?

My boots sink into the mud, which has a kind of rubbery consistency, the path is almost impassable, I can barely go any further, I don't know how I'll manage to get my father this far, even though it's only a matter of a few metres, there's no way I could get a wheelchair along here. In this glutinous clay, the wheels would be more of a hindrance than a help; for cyclists, the marsh is a real trap, some paths remain deep in mud all year round, and it's a particularly sticky mud, the enemy of rubber tyres that get stuck fast as if in a sculptor's plaster mould; other paths – most of them – turn to mud as soon as a little rain falls, and some stretches are so overgrown by vegetation that only walkers can fight their way through. I could pick him up or let him walk very slowly to the shoreline. It would only be about ten metres. This is the unspoken pact I have made with him, to return him to the place that we forced him to leave. No one comes to this deserted area of reed beds, in which, if you're not careful, you find yourself stepping into a patch of treacherous quicksand, into which you sink a little deeper with each step you take. It's not a very attractive place to go for a walk, unless you know it really well and are drawn to it precisely because of its difficulties, plunging down dubious paths flanked and overshadowed by reeds. The bustle of life is only a step away, but still safely outside. This is a very discreet, secretive corner of the world, where we will be together. The dog stops and turns his head, looking at me with his honey-coloured eyes; he trots back towards me, brushing against my leg. He's panting and keeps looking up at me. I pat his back, crouch down and press him to me, I feel very emotional again, on the point of crying. I'll drive the car up to this point and, before I conclude my task, I'll move it back a few metres, onto the side of the dunes, so that the fire won't spread to the reeds. I pat the car too. And the dog? I look away, I can't bear to see him, but the dog is part of the family. I couldn't possibly leave him alone. I would say that even cars are part of the family too, and it would be cruel to abandon them. They can't be separated from the people who drive them, they contain our memories, our DNA, which is at the disposal of any policemen who might want to find us. It would be immoral to leave the car in the grubby hands of some auctioneer.

The past transformed into an alien that keeps swelling in size, an agglomeration of faces and voices that create an unbearable pressure inside me. I'm going to explode under my own weight, and meanwhile, everything is becoming noiseless, fading, growing thinner, fainter, about to vanish, disappear: the faces looking at me and the voices speaking to me are upbraiding me for my fifty years of solitude here, when I tear off the tape on the workshop put there by the local officials and go downstairs (after all, what more can the judge do to me now?), when I sit down in front of the TV or wash my father. The solitude of the night in my bedroom: best not think about the night. The night becomes theirs, it's their time, they are in charge. They occupy the whole room, I can feel them cleaving the air, and I have to turn on the light and sit up so as not to suffocate, and so that they return to the walls from which they have escaped. I sit up, gasping for breath. In the darkness, I hear them moving about, they brush my skin with their tattered clothes, their fingers. I feel the air they dislodge touch my cheeks, and when they have, at last, gone, they leave behind a cold blade of air, as if someone had left the door of a deep freeze open. The light switch. The brightness of the light bulb drives away those bodies I touched, returns them to their airy state, shuts them up in the walls they have escaped from, dissolves them into the nothing they should never have left. I get up, take a sip of milk from the carton in the fridge, make myself a cold drink, turn on the TV in the living room, smoke a cigarette, inhaling deeply, and then, I return to my own room and get back into bed, but spend the rest of the night with the light on so that they don't return. Apnea, I think the doctors call that sudden pause in breathing while you sleep, a kind of mini-death that makes you wake suddenly, gasping for air like a fish out of water. An obscene smell hangs in the room. I manage to get to sleep, and now I'm walking along passageways that tunnel into the earth in all directions, that meet and mesh, forming a labyrinth of suffocating burrows, an outbreath of damp earth that mingles with the vapour given off by weary flesh. In the nightmare, my footsteps ring hollow. Each step draws from the earth a dull thud. Empty steps, sounding ever further from my feet, pale reflections of themselves. And again that smell of dampness, of mustiness, of decomposing vegetation. It's the smell of the marsh on a hot day; and yet, even though I'm sweating, the room feels cold and damp. I walk aimlessly on, trapped in the network of passageways, which feel as if they were inside something indecipherable, like the convoluted guts of some enormous animal. But inside what? Inside where I am? The viscous crust of the earth – or whatever it is I'm walking on – contains a kind of vapour that is slowly dissolving until vapour and earth become one slimy substance. I walk on that vapour and my feet sink further in with each step. When the nightmare ends and I wake up, I realise that the outside world offers me no relief, that what stretches endlessly out beyond the shutters and windows that I fling open in the early hours, in the hope of breathing in some clean night air, makes no difference, I can't reach what lies on the other side. Outside, I am not myself. It's an alien place, the stage on which other people act out their lives, people who have arrived after me, too late to take part in the play of which I am the protagonist or, rather, in which I have been only an extra. The writer hasn't even given me any words to say. A character who enters and leaves and, when he appears, leaves a tray on the table, empties the ashtray, places a vase on a sideboard, or hangs some item of clothing in the wardrobe. Those who arrive now cannot know – they're not authorised either – anything more than the ending, which isn't going to interest them one bit. But what are they hoping to see, if this is no longer the play, but what happens afterwards, the removing of the costumes and putting them back in the trunk, picking up brushes and make-up sticks, helping to dismantle the scenery, fold up the curtains, tasks which, although hard work, mean very little, it's just part of the process: closing the workshop, closing it on the customers whose work has been left unfinished, employees and suppliers who have not been paid, the accountant to whom the bank returned the last three cheques, the bank employees who want to get everything sorted out as soon as possible. Above them all, like in the religious services that used to be held in the theatre at school, there appears the eye of God inside a triangle, the fateful eye that sees everything, and from which there is no point hiding anywhere in the city or even the countryside. Cain, where is Abel, am I my brother's keeper? And Pedrós is the eye, a kind of contemporary God, the eye inscribed above the stage on which grownups are putting on a play, my familiar god, my domestic god, my household god, the one who has changed the ending and become the owner of the diary, ahead even of my father: whether you like it or not, my father's diary has the innocuous nature of the private, while Pedrós' diary has all the seriousness of the public: topographers, valuers, notaries, lawyers, judges, bailiffs, prison officers. Pedrós elbows aside the old boss, changes the script, alters the dialogues in the final scene and, above all – and this is what matters now – he determines and manipulates the ending. Curtain. The whole company is on stage now. The main characters rub shoulders with those who appeared in only a couple of scenes and then exited, those who are no longer alive and those who survived, those I still see – or did until a few weeks ago – and those I met fifty years ago on the journeys that constituted my brief summer of love, and who could be anywhere. Those wearing tracksuits, skirts, shoulder bags, bomber jackets, fashionable trainers, either with genuine designer labels or bought in street markets, made here or imported from France, Italy, America, China or India, coexist with those wearing only dark rags clinging to their scrawny flesh and bones. What were once white shirts with collars, cuffs and starched fronts, are now, as you see, mere threads attached to withered skin or worn bones. There are so many other characters. They pass quickly, a motley, pressing crowd. I'd like to put names to them, but there's no time, so quickly do they pass, and so fragile is their presence, I can't even remember their names; and not being able to name them, not finding their names in my memory however hard I try, fills me with anxiety. Fruitlessly I rummage around in what should be a warehouse, but which has become a rubbish dump: a missing or squandered heritage. Life as waste, isn't that one of your central ideas, Dad? On sleepless nights, they have probably vainly racked their brains for my name too, tried to relive scenes in which I played a part. But the floodgates have opened. We are emptying ourselves out. I notice that I have included Liliana in the cast, when actually she's part of the disappointing present, part of contemporary theatre, a character – like Pedrós – playing an undesirably prominent role in my dénouement, the protagonist of her own play, which will, foreseeably, take a few years to reach its climax, a climax I won't be around to see. I won't see what she's like at fifty: her body will change, her voice will lose its silken touch or the silk will wear thin – you gave me a preview of that particular transformation, Liliana – her smile will fade – it already has

– her tears will dry. I won't see you, and seeing or not seeing you won't be the result of any decision or whim of mine. The other day, in order to avoid you, I turned and walked in the opposite direction when I realised that, otherwise, we would bump into each other near the main square. (Olba is so small, such encounters are almost inevitable.) You were alone. Not arm in arm with your husband. And so that's what I did, I turned down a side street, I just couldn't bear to see you; I didn't even know what I would do if we did meet, whether I would speak to you or look away. By then, though, when the time I've been talking about arrives, I won't be able to see you, even if I want to; or, rather, I won't even be able to want to see you; I won't hear your voice, I won't inhabit any memories: I collect my little girl from the nursery and then pick up my youngest boy from school, because I can't be sure he'll make it home on his own, there have been so many awful cases involving children lately, I go to the supermarket to do my shopping, drop in at the Colombian shop where I buy stuff that may or may not come from Colombia, but which is the same as what we get at home, wild bananas, guayaba, yucca, sweet granadilla, sweet potato and so on. By the time my husband gets home, me and the children have already had supper and they're either doing their homework or have gone to bed, and I've sat down to watch TV; sometimes I wait to have supper with him and, at others, I keep his supper warm for him, one plate on top of the other, and you have no idea how sad they make me feel, those two plates on the kitchen table, when I look at them as I turn out the light, when I've been waiting up for him, because, since he's been unemployed, he arrives home later not earlier, and he's nearly always drunk too (where else do you think I'm going to meet people and find out where the jobs are, he grumbles – while I'm folding up the clothes I've just ironed – here on the sofa? Do you

363

really think someone's going to drop by and offer me a job just like that?) That's what you tell me, Liliana, and hearing your words is like watching a recent performance, one that may be depressing for you, but which opens up complicated emotional spaces in me, rooms I thought had long ago been sealed up. Your sadness feeds my hopes: my arms offer you a refuge from your disappointments, which I caress and make mine, making the warmth of your sadness mine too, and that excites me, and I don't know if that excitement is clean or dirty, you're my daughter, and yet I'm filled with desire, a desire to have your small body in my arms, a desire to look at it, as my Uncle Ramón used to do when he went to visit whores, he would look at them as if they were daughters or mothers, and like him, I myself never appear on stage naked, it must be a family thing or, more likely, my age: I press your warm, supple body to my chest – now that is dirty; you are living out your own play, a play written solely for you, and my play is from another age entirely, the timescales don't coincide, it's what the French call *décalage*, my play has gone cold, a bad scriptwriter has made the plot too long, the audience is getting bored, and yet I have to go on until the end now, we have to perform the final act.

"Sweetie," he says, or "sweetheart," and he plants slobbery, wet kisses on my neck. Stop it, you're tickling, I say, but actually I find his breath disgusting, it stinks of cigarettes and booze; I've felt even more disgusted recently, ever since I've smelt different perfumes on him, different from the ones I use. He seems so laid-back, but he's always got an eye on the main chance. He pretends not to care, but as soon as there's something he wants, there's no stopping him. He can be sitting quietly watching television and, suddenly, he'll glance over at the clock,

leap up, get dressed in no time and off he'll go, having spent the entire evening lolling on the sofa as if he had nothing better to do. Where are you going? Out. And I'm sure he's got a date. He's arranged to meet someone and doesn't want to tell me who. I look at my watch, ten past eight. And I know he must have arranged to meet someone somewhere at half past. He appeared to be bored, but actually he was waiting, he's been waiting all day for that date at half past eight, but who with? There's no point asking him, he wouldn't even bother to invent a lie. Out. I'm going out. And if I insist, I know he'll look me up and down, as if I disgusted him, the way a caged tiger looks at the keeper who has him imprisoned and yet is so far beneath him, and he'll either say nothing or start shouting at me: What do you expect? Do you want me to stay home all the time? I just can't win — I'm wrong if I go out and I'm wrong if I stay in. If I go out, I'm up to no good and a drunkard, if I stay in, I'm a lazy useless son of a bitch. There's no pleasing you. I'm minding my own business, all right, looking for work so that I can feed you and your children. And I stay home with the kids, seething with rage, knowing that he's off somewhere having a good time, drinking, or worse, screwing around. It's just awful knowing someone so well and being torn apart by jealousy: you know exactly what he'll be saying to that woman he's screwing, the gestures he'll make, the words he'll say, the same words he used to say to you, you see his body, every inch of it, see how he gets out his cock and even how the other woman takes hold of it, and the little movement he makes with his hips in order to enter her, his mouth half open, his tongue between his teeth, it's awful, jealousy is sheer torture, and it's not even as if that bitch was taking something you want, because you hate that body — you wish you could be rid of him once and for all, but you always feel it's not quite the right time, it never seems to be quite the right moment. The other night, we went out dancing. So there I was, having just sat down at a table, a drink in my hand, and up he comes and says: Come on, we're leaving. I said: But we came here to dance, didn't we? We haven't had a single dance — you drank too much this afternoon and now you're feeling sleepy. He replied: Look, I said we're leaving, and he grabbed my elbow, his fingers digging into me. But why? It's still early, things are only just beginning. Let's dance – just one song. No way – I'm leaving and you're coming with me, he said. Later, he told me that he'd seen me sitting at the table surrounded by plastic cups with the dregs of drinks – Coca-Cola and gin and tonic and whisky – left behind by the previous occupants, and he felt I looked too exposed, available for anyone to look at, surrounded by someone else's rubbish, the cups all sticky with someone else's saliva, and that he was the only one who had the right to look at me the way it seemed to him the other tipsy or drunk or coked-up men were looking at me, randy as rabbits. He said they walked past me, looking at me as if they wanted to do what only he can do with me.'

'I know, Liliana, but he was probably thinking about all the men who had looked at you during the months he was still in Colombia, and about the other hands that had touched you, about what they'd done to you.'

'I always made them use a condom. Besides, I was defending the family. I was paying the price of having them here with me, don't forget, the price of their airfares, I was buying what they would need so that I could have them with me again, don't you see, Susana?'

'Well, men say those things when it suits them, they pretend they don't know, but they're simply storing it all away, piling up all that information like wood to burn you with later on.'

'He grabbed my elbow and dragged me to my feet. The chair fell over, but being only plastic, it didn't make much noise, and anyway the music was blasting out at full volume and everyone was talking at the tops of their voices. What's wrong? I said. When he pulled me to my feet like that, he didn't just knock over the chair, but some of the plastic cups too, and the contents spilled onto the table and dripped onto the floor (Coca-Cola, soft drinks, orangeade, pineapple juice, lemonade), and one of my shoes got stained and they were new shoes, and I felt like crying, and he was staring at me in this really horrible way. When we got out on the street, he kissed me, but it wasn't how

366

a husband kisses his wife, it was a drunk's kiss, the kind of kiss those men in the club were wanting to give me. Without even thinking, I wiped my mouth with the back of my hand, wiping away his saliva, and he saw me do that and, although he didn't say anything then, he gave me a really frightening look. When we'd walked a little way down the street, he said: What's up? Do you only like that old man's kisses now? That's what he said, and I felt like slapping him, but I knew that, if I did, he'd beat me to a pulp right there and then. He's a really nasty piece of work, at least when he's behaving badly, although lately, even though he's been trying to behave a bit better, it just makes matters worse somehow; but the truth is he probably doesn't give a shit about other people's feelings and does exactly as he pleases, whatever suits him best, and as the mood takes him. I remember the look of pleasure on his face when he turned up with a puppy for the little one, how he opened the door, carrying the dog in one hand and kissing and petting it, and with a broad grin on that great round face of his. The boy started screaming with excitement and jumping up and down, let me have him, let me have him, and my face just dropped, how can we possibly keep a dog here, I said, there's barely enough room for us in here, what on earth were you thinking of? I said. Turn round right this minute before the boy gets too attached to the dog, and take it back where you found it. Give it back to whoever gave it to you. Of course, the boy started crying, he's mine, he's mine, Papa, and the smile on Wilson's face became more like a tiger's grin, his lips curled back, baring his teeth, and the language, the swearing, fucking hell, fuck the lot of you, screw you, I can never do anything right in this fucking household. Happiness isn't allowed here. And it's your fault, you're the one who turns everything sour, you're the witch, the bitch, who spoils our lives, who pisses us all off. And I said: Well, if I'm the witch-bitch, you're the bloody ogre, me and the kids never know what mood you're going to be in next, it's like I'm slaving away, doing the cooking and the washing for an ogre who'll just end up eating us all. And I added: Plus you're a really stupid ogre. And telling him he's *stupid is the worst thing you can possibly say, the thing guaranteed to offend him most. Well, you should have married an engineer, then, if you're so smart, he said, elbowing the little one in the mouth as he stood on tiptoe to stroke the puppy, and the boy hit his head on the table and started screaming and stamping. You could have fractured the child's skull, I shouted, and you wonder why I call you an animal. Now he was the one manhandling the dog, and the dog didn't even bark, its eyes wide with terror, realising suddenly what kind of new home this was turning out to be, and how this man, who had started out so affectionate, stroking and kissing him, how he was treating him now. It was the same with me, little dog, I thought, first, he was all sweetness and light, and then . . . Then Wilson said: Oh, go screw yourselves – the dog, the kids and you – and he suddenly squeezed the dog's neck, I heard a click, and the dog lay there in his hands, his legs all limp. He'd strangled it; because I think he knew it was already dead when he hurled it against the wall, as hard as he could. The little creature ended up lying in the middle of the living room, along with various ornaments from the sideboard: it lay there, bleeding from every orifice and surrounded by broken glass. I snatched up my little boy, who was about to rush over to the dog and cut himself on the broken glass, and Wilson left, slamming the front door. The worst part, I thought, will be when he comes back, boozed-up and furious, after going over and over all the shit in his head, I even considered putting the security chain on, but that would only have made things worse, because then he would just kick down the door, with the chain on or off, and would even tear out the door frame, because he's very strong, but there was a time when the same strength that frightens me now gave me a sense of security. It drives me to despair seeing that body of his, so full of energy demanding to be used up, lying on the sofa or slumped in the armchair and dragging that great body from there to bed. He's not the big lad I used to really fancy when he led me onto the dance floor, the one who made me feel safe in his arms, like a bird in its nest. Now I'm afraid of his hands and his arms and,*

*do you know what he reminds me of when he gets angry – he reminds
me of a fat, furious old lady. I told him so one day: you're like a big,
fat woman, I said, because his hair and even the hair on his legs looked
to me like a woman's hair. He hit the roof. Don't you dare make fun
of me, not unless you want to feel the back of my hand. I've got enough
problems being unemployed without you coming and winding me up.
I said: Out of a job, you say? Well, there are more than enough jobs
for you here, doing the cooking and the washing, hanging out the
clothes, but no, you do fuck all. All you ever do is lie on the sofa and
drink beer. He reached out one arm and punched me softly in the
buttock. It was almost a caress, but I said: if you ever hit me again,
I'll report you to the police and you'll never see hide nor hair of me
again. My voice sounded shrill and strange. Prevention is better than
cure, I thought. If that punch to the bum is a warning, then I'm going
to issue my own warning. You wouldn't be missed, he said. No, you
probably wouldn't miss* me, *but you'd miss the steaming plate of pig's
trotters and greens at lunchtime, and the cold beer and the clean shirts,
you'd miss that, and all the time I'm saying this, I'm washing the dishes,
making a real clatter with the water and the glasses and the plates as
I put them in the draining rack, just to remind him that there is
someone in the family who works and goes back and forth, carrying
shopping bags, picking up the little one from school, cleaning this
apartment and other people's, putting on rubber gloves and sticking
my hand down other people's toilets to scrub away the accumulated
dirt, smelling old people's shit and feeling it all squishy on my gloves.
I sometimes think he's such an evil bastard that the devil will have a
hard time finding volunteers to burn him in hell. Nobody could stand
being with him twenty-fours hours a day, besides, I heard recently that
the Pope had said there is no devil, but if there's no devil, then there's
no God. Given the state of the world, this doesn't surprise me. I'll
have to ask my late aunt next time I talk to her.'*

*'You're not still going to see that clairvoyant, are you? You're crazy.
How can you believe anything that old witch tells you?'*

'I miss all the people I left behind in Colombia and the ones who've passed away since, and the ones who died before I came here. I feel so alone here and frightened about what Wilson might do to us one day.'

'Look, love, say what you like, but I can't see what pleasure there can be in contacting the dead, I don't understand why you spend a fortune on paying that woman, why not spend it on jewellery instead, or, if you like, get yourself one of those Cuban boys you see on the TV. Talking to the dead is a complete waste of time and money. The ones who speak to you, assuming they do, are the poorest of the poor, they have absolutely nothing, they can't give you a loan, you can't even use them as guarantors, they're useless. I can't see why you bother. All that nonsense about how she's seen your Aunt Manola or your cousin Purificación and even spoken to her, or your aunt from Barranquilla who drank too much brandy and died from bleeding of the oesophagus, or chatted with Grandma Constanza, who often thinks so fondly of you and your brothers and is as happy as a lark up there in heaven; or worse, that she's really fed up because some devil has taken a dislike to her and won't leave her in peace and keeps prodding her with his trident day and night. What's so interesting about all those disgusting things, those incurable diseases, those grudges that still rankle, people you used to avoid like the plague when they were alive? And you pay good money to be told all that rubbish or other equally horrible things? Because the most those dead people can tell you is that they're fine, thank you, and send their best wishes, and then what are you going to say? Hi, Aunt Corina, I'm glad to hear you're well and that you're praying for me, because we really need your prayers now that Wilson got fired and we're about to be evicted. You pay money to say that crap? You'd be better off saving up for an emergency, because Wilson's unemployment benefit will be coming to an end soon, and then what are you going to do, with him making a dent in the sofa 24/7, except, of course, when he's in the bar, and with you scrubbing stairs with a three-month-old foetus in your belly, a present from his brother, who, very conveniently, has gone missing, having fled back to Colombia where he's doubtless busy getting some

370

other stupid woman knocked up, and is probably already planning to sell the baby to someone, because that's what he's like, always assuming he hasn't ended up in prison or been shot and is lying bleeding in a gutter somewhere, because, from what you told me, he squandered half the money you sent him on getting drunk and on shirts and shoes. Liliana, you'd better just pray that Wilson doesn't start putting two and two together and begin to suspect that the bump in your belly isn't his. Luckily, he's so vain that it wouldn't occur to him to think that, having experienced the joy of sex with him, you would ever try your luck with someone else, so you're fortunate in a way, or rather, unfortunate, because there's no way you're going to get rid of him; with those size forty-sixes of his on the sofa — I mean, you need a sofa with feet that size — what with the cans of beer, the day's football match, your apartment is turning into a real hell, phone the Pope up and tell him, tell him you've found the hell he lost, and about the devil pursuing you with his trident, tell the Pope you have the devil's address, because Wilson really is a devil and he's got it in for you, and there you are, frittering away your money on talking to the dead. You must admit it's not exactly logical, talking to your grandma and your dad and your aunties who died and are now in the next world, as if you hadn't had quite enough of them when they were still in this world. Leave the dead in peace, and let's just assume they're all right because they haven't shown any signs of life and haven't come begging either. I don't know why we poor people are so obsessed with the dead, the rich buy apartments, yachts, jewellery, stocks — they have no interest in talking to the dead, they want to live among the living. They're just not interested, they haven't got the time. And you haven't even reported your husband for harassment and cruelty, and it's high time you did. Did you know that if you make a complaint about physical abuse, they can't deport you even if you're here illegally? The state will then look after you, find you a safe apartment to live in, give you food and pay you a wage.'

'Yes, the old man told me that if you make a complaint, they'll give you Spanish citizenship.'

'Liliana, you had the chance to leave him and the kids in Colombia and make a new life for yourself here; you could have started over. Your parents would have looked after the kids, because he *certainly wouldn't have, after all, your mum was still alive then, and he'd soon have lost interest in you when you stopped sending him any money, you could have vanished and started all over. You'd been through the worst and could have started to enjoy life, but no, you paid for their airfare with the sweat of your you-know-what: you paid for your own misery, you little fool. Your husband didn't want to know how you earned your money and so he pretended he didn't know and never even asked. He pretended not to know because it suited him that way, but he must have known, just as he knew that his brother used you as a drug mule when you first came to Spain, how much did you bring in, by the way? And Wilson said nothing, because you were still sending him money, no, he said nothing and didn't even tell you that, when he came to Spain, he had a few grams of drugs up his arse too, he kept you completely in the dark about that, and I bet he never said anything to you about how much he got for those drugs either. He kept any money to himself, for his nights out, for those Friday nights when no one knows where he's been, but which he returns from smelling of sour sweat and other women's perfume. And now he has you scrubbing stairs and wiping old men's bottoms. You poor little girl. Come here and let me comb your lovely hair, let me touch it, it's so soft, what a shame you've given it to a brute who doesn't even appreciate it, let me unpin it, that's it, let it cascade down, the way those femmes fatales do in soap operas, let me just fluff it out a bit so that it falls on your shoulders like shiny, curly, black water, and it smells so good too, hmmm, let me bury my face in your hair, let me kiss your soft neck, what do you mean, it tickles? Doesn't he ever kiss you there? The old man must have kissed you while you were working for him, I mean, he gave you those earrings and that lovely necklace, which you told me your husband got rid of in a matter of days, and how the old man kept saying he wanted to see you wearing them and you had to keep*

making excuses because you didn't have them any more. Even the old man dumped you in the end, he obviously wanted to have sex with you too, but then he just got rid of you.'

'I can come and see you whenever you like now, because there's no work any more and every bit of money helps, that's what I told him on that last day, when the old man told me he couldn't keep me on. I can't pay you a wage, he said, and, please, call me Esteban. You don't work here any more, so now we can be friends. I said: in Colombia we tend to address older people as Don or Doña. And he: I mean we can still see each other, just drop round whenever you want, so that we can see you, so that we can see each other, I wouldn't expect you to do any work, I can't afford to pay for that now and I don't know if I'll ever be able to again, but that's all I want, Liliana, just for you to pop in now and then for a chat and a coffee, a tintico, *that's all: it's my turn to cry today and your turn to console me. You see, I'm bankrupt, I don't even have enough money to pay my mortgage, well, that isn't exactly how it is, it's a long story; but I'd be so grateful if you could come and keep me and my father company sometimes, now that we're going to be so alone. Of course, Don Esteban, of course, I understand, but you know how busy I am and that I barely have time for me or my husband and my children, so it's quite hard to find time for anyone else. I have to earn a living. I can't come here if you don't pay me. That's what I said, and he opened his eyes very wide as if he was going to have an attack or something. The look on his face really frightened me. I thought he was either going to hit me or be ill, and then, suddenly, out of nowhere, came this hard, gruff voice: Well, you'd better be off then. You don't want to waste your time with me. Go somewhere where they'll pay you. It really shook me. Did the soft old thing really think I'd go on wiping his father's bum and chatting to him for no money? That's what he expected, but I summoned up the courage to say: You just be thankful I never told my husband about you touching and kissing me, you know: give me a hug, give me a little kiss, go on. That's between you and me. I left then, and he slammed the door behind me so loudly, I bet the whole street must have heard. The old fool started weeping when I*

said that. He probably just wanted me to feel sorry for him and make sure
I didn't say anything to Wilson, although I do understand how lonely
those two old men are, but tough. I'd already pocketed the money he gave
me as a kind of bonus for firing me, because he really wasn't a bad old
guy, and as for the money he lent me before, well, he's in for a long
wait before he gets that back.'

'You mean he lent you money? A lot? You must have done something
in return. If you had told Wilson about the kisses and the money, he'd
have killed him, but then he would have killed you too.'

'Oh, I doubt it. When I brought home the earrings and the necklace,
he just grunted: Why did he give you those, then? If that old bastard
comes on to you, I'll kill him. But a week later, the earrings and the
necklace were gone, and I still don't know whether he sold them or
gave them away. Kill me? After what I've had to put up with. He's
pissed as a newt most nights. When he does come home on a Saturday,
because often he doesn't get back until Monday, I have to take off
those great clodhoppers of his and lift his legs onto the bed, where he
lies snoring for hours, like a very noisy corpse, no, it's certainly not
the pale pink and green tulle they wrap you in on your wedding day,
damn right it isn't, and then there's that sweetish, sourish smell that
kind of creeps under your skin if he happens to come home feeling
randy and wants to kiss you, the God-awful stink of sour saliva, tobacco
and alcohol, and him filling your mouth with his hot, disgusting saliva
and that sour waft of indigestion. Sometimes he gets up in the early
hours and drags himself off to throw up in the toilet and when he
comes back to bed, he licks your face, thrusts his tongue in your mouth,
as hard as a muscle, and then his saliva tastes of vomit too, because
he hasn't even had the courtesy to wash his mouth out, and this happens
night after night. When I first met him, he smelled of shaving lotion,
eau de cologne, and his mouth smelled of toothpaste and his saliva
and his breath of fresh mint. Of course, at the time, you see him as a
suitor, as a fiancé, who bathes and shaves and perfumes himself before
coming to see you, and you see this radiant man and you're fool enough

to think things are bound to get better, that he'll mature and soften and won't fly into a howling rage as he sometimes does, you think: he's still young, but when he sees his first child or, rather, when he holds his son in his arms, when he holds in the palm of his great big hands that little scrap of warm flesh moving and laughing and crying, he'll mellow, he won't have those worrying tantrums, he'll be the handsome, perfumed, affectionate man who touches you gently as you dance. But no, the child who he finds captivating at first, who makes him laugh, the child he plays with, later on, just seems to annoy him. He says brusquely: Can't you shut that brat up or change his frigging nappies, because he stinks, I've never known a child whose shit stank like that, it's like an old man's shit — as if he himself wasn't related to the producer of that shit. And you answer back and say: How would you know what an old man's shit smells like? I do, because of the shit I have to clean up every day so that you can go out drinking, all you care about are those good-for-nothing friends of yours at the bar, that's the only smell that doesn't seem to bother you, because you even find it disgusting when it's my time of the month, you get angry if you touch me and find your fingers all sticky, but that's how it is with women, and if you don't like it, go and find yourself a man, who doesn't have a period, and give it to him up the arse and then see how your cock smells when you take it out, you bastard, well, that's what I wanted to say to him, but I didn't dare, because I knew he'd smack me in the face.'

'Pink tulle, the loving bridegroom, that's straight out of those rubbishy daytime soaps you have time to watch now that you don't go and look after the two old men at the workshop, and that's what's feeding your fantasies. You're going mad.'

'It's true, Susana, when I've got a free afternoon, now that I don't go and see the old men, I listen to the radio and watch TV, and that's how I know more about what's going on. I think I heard that stuff about God on the radio and heard it again in the fishmonger's or the shop where I buy limes and chillis for the ceviche, yes, while I was waiting in the

queue, I heard a woman say it, and, according to her, even the Pope agreed. She'd read it in some newspaper, she said, and the Pope had stated that there was no hell, and if there's no hell, then there's no heaven either and no God, and that's why all these bad things are happening.'

'What a thing to say! I mean, in that case what are you doing talking to the dead? Where do you think they are? If the Pope agrees that God is dead, then he should give Him a decent burial and join the queue at the benefits office. After all, isn't he God's representative on Earth? Anyway, as you well know, gods don't die, they're immortal. Our gods back home and the ones the blacks brought with them on the boats from Africa are all immortal, yes even we are: we die for a while, as if we were having a long sleep, but in time, we wake up. We will wake up.'

'But how? Where will we wake up? Will we wake up here, surrounded by all these damn Spaniards, or will we wake up in Quindío or in Caldas or in Risaralda, on the banks of the River Cauca, or in Magdalena? We'll probably wake up downstream, in Cartagena de Indias, in one of those discotheques full of rather pathetic, lukewarm Spaniards looking for a bit of Caribbean fire, or else in the middle of the ocean. Will we wake up one warm spring afternoon, lying in the shade of a big mango tree or among the flowering coffee trees or the guamo trees, and will we wake up to be confronted by the faces of those same bastards who drove us out?'

'How should I know? But we will wake up. I know we will, because the gospels say so. It's a matter of faith. If it's not true and there's nothing after death, then what's left for us? After all our suffering . . .'

'But who's going to wake up those half-eaten bodies, the ones the vultures tore the guts out of probably a hundred years before? No one comes back from the dead, no one ever will.'

'I feel sorry for you, you know. You may have your head stuffed full of TV soaps, but you've no imagination, that's why you can't believe in God, only in your ugly old dead people, you can't believe that this life will change one day, that life can be different. I believe that one day I'll get lucky and win the lottery, and I pray for that to happen and praying comforts me. I would pray even if there wasn't a God. Just in case.'

'No, you just don't want to admit that what's happening to us here in Spain is even worse than that. We don't even wonder any more if miracles are possible or not, whereas we used to in Colombia, or if we'll ever see justice or understand the truth or if you can achieve happiness simply by doing your duty; we don't even ask ourselves now what the meaning of life is, only if any of this makes any sense at all. There's no time, we can't be bothered, we just can't do it. Those questions have grown too big for us.'

'But, in that case, you can't even have the consolation of a good cry. People cry over something they've lost or something they want. Neither of these applies to you. Do you see what I mean? So why are you crying? You've suffered a lot, I don't deny it, and that's what's troubling you: all that past suffering. But so what if you had to work the streets in order to bring over your husband and son? There's no shame in that.'

'Don't be cruel, don't remind me of those things. It's water under the bridge. It happened. Necessity made it happen, but it's over. It no longer exists. OK, a new life will come along, but we also have an old life that's been and gone. All right, I agree, I too believe that we'll wake up after we're dead. It's a matter of faith. A better life. Otherwise, what else have we got? We'll all have suffered for nothing . . .'

'I know, Liliana. For the moment, on this damp, misty afternoon, when the cold really seeps into your bones, God is a good, hot, aromatic cup of coffee, made with freshly ground and roasted beans; in summer look for God in an ice-cream cone – one of those turrón- or chocolate-flavoured ones; or else papaya or mango, because the Spanish do make papaya and mango and guayaba ice cream now, and one day they'll have durian-flavoured ice cream too, although I think they find the strong smell a bit disgusting. Not that I like the smell much either, but the fruit itself is delicious. Just think of the ice-cream shop on the square as a little piece of the heaven we dream of or a heaven that is at least within our grasp and hasn't yet been taken away from us. Sit

377

down with your kids on the chairs outside as the sun is going down on an August evening, and order a lovely creamy mango ice cream and you'll find the God of summer right there, just as, in winter, he's there in a hot cup of coffee. When the Spaniards came to occupy our country, we knew there wasn't only one god, because there are lots of them, one for every thing, for every day, and we tried to teach them that, but no, they were so pigheaded they had to frighten the other gods off so that theirs was the only one left, and what did we gain from that?'

'And yet why do we ask ourselves when will we meet again and where and how? Do we want to suffer and suffer and go on suffering even once all the suffering is over? I mean why go to Mass? Death brings rest, it frightens us because it's the unknown, because we can't imagine what it means not to be, but you just have to think of it as a chance finally to rest, and that's that. I don't want to find myself back inside this same body in a million years' time, Susana, a body that makes so many demands and that allowed itself to be deceived by the useless twat who has ruined my life. All this stuff about heaven is so relative: spending all eternity with God; think of the number of people up there, and you don't get to choose your neighbours either, you know, they could be anyone, it must be even more of a jumble there than it is down here, everyone with their own language and food and peculiarities, and every day for all eternity, they'll all be jostling for a chance to see God.'

'What a great idea! Yes, you'd have to wait your turn, like you do in the supermarket, with those numbered papers that they give out at the fishmonger's to make sure no one jumps the queue, so you'd know when it was your turn to spend a little time with the Lord, but to do what? Imagine all those people waiting like vultures to be alone with God because they've seen Him in paintings and pictures looking so handsome, with that long, fair hair of His; and what if, instead, you were with God all the time, just you and Him, alone, because there was enough God for everyone, which is what they say about the host, and He was everywhere all the time and with everyone, every single individual, then what would you do alone together, go back to your old ways? Another

husband, but with the major disadvantage that He would never die. I mean, after your experience with Wilson, would you ever marry again? The prospect of widowhood has been woman's one great consolation. Did you know that for every widower, there are ten widows?'

'It's a bit less than that now, what with cancer and accidents, because women smoke more, work outside the home and travel alone and sometimes crash the car on their way back from the supermarket or from work. But, yes, ten times more widows than widowers.'

'It must be even more that way in Colombia, do a quick headcount and think how few men are left, you know they can't resist a shoot-out there – as people say: what's a party without a death or two? No, to be honest, I don't find the Christian heaven very convincing. Apparently, Arab men get seventy houris each when they die, and that would be exhausting for any man, not even drug dealers want that, because they're not really into sex, they're too coked up, they tend to toy with girls, they beat them and torture them, because they like to see them suffer, to see the look of fear on their faces, they even film them on their mobile phone or camera, yes, coke makes men randy, but then they can't get it up, and the poor girls pay the price, I mean, have you seen what they do to girls in Mexico? They kill them and make videos of the poor things dying. We women aren't easy to put up with or to please, I mean, if you really like a man, you never tire of fucking, you'd like to have him inside you all the time, but there, in that Arab paradise, I think the same thing would happen as what goes down on those drug dealers' ranches, it would be a paradise for the kind of man who enjoys seeing women suffer and where it's always the man who gives the orders. The priests say that, in heaven, there's no unemployment and no poverty. Well, I think you should name as your household god your other brother-in-law, the one who sorted out your paperwork and has come back now with dollars in his pocket, and who, I hear, is doing very nicely, thank you, although it's probably best not to ask how. Hang on to him, pray to him. Ask him to divide himself up like the God of the sacred hosts, a little bit of his body *for each of us, and meanwhile, grab your own little piece, don't let him escape.'*

'I don't believe in God for myself, but I want to believe in God for my children's sake, they're so small and helpless. I want to be sure God won't abandon them, just as I don't want their teachers to leave the school. I know them, I talk to them, I know they're good people and care about the kids. Yes, God is a service I can't do without. If you can't entrust your children to God, who can you entrust them to? Who else is going to love them in this God-awful place? It doesn't bear thinking about. Some pervert probably. Poor little things. I have to make sure they're in good hands.'

He gets his servants to do the shopping, even if all he needs is some bread or a newspaper, he sends the maid or the gardener who looks after the courtyard, the kind of big courtyard you only find in the old houses built here originally for the wealthy bourgeoisie; it's got a palm tree, a jacaranda, orange trees, an araucaria; and there's a pergola overgrown with a thick thatch of bougainvillea and jasmine that provides protection from the sun's rays for two wicker chairs, upholstered with cool cotton cushions and cream-coloured antimacassars embroidered with flowers; it's one of the few courtyard gardens left in Olba. He's had it restored so that it's just as it was when the Civera family lived here, in the fine tradition of all bourgeois families. Yes, he sends the servants, even though the bakery and the news-stand are only a couple of hundred metres from his house. He gives – or wants to give – the impression that he hasn't left much behind him despite all the years he spent in Madrid, and all the travelling he's done. He doesn't seem to have many visitors, although he may be in touch with people by phone. He doesn't bring his mobile to the bar with him, which, for a modern-day man, indicates little or no work activity and a complete absence of any social life. There are, of course, those escapes from Olba, about which he says nothing, but which leave the blinds of his house closed for weeks at a time. In our conversations, he occasionally mentions the person who was his wife – she wanted, she did, she decided, she would have liked, she couldn't bring herself to – and I find it odd that I feel nothing, no vibration, no inner stirrings, no tremor. I slam down the double six on the marble tabletop or strike the table with the back of my hand when I throw down a card with the angry gesture all players affect. It's a way of saying 'I'm a man', a faint memory of when these games were played by armed men. Francisco mutilates her lovely name, Leonor, abbreviating it to Leo, and, in doing so, he makes it ordinary. It seems incredible to me that a writer should show such a lack of sensitivity. After all, he calls himself a writer, so you'd think he'd be aware of the importance of words and their music. Or is that mutilated name part of a demolition strategy that continues beyond death? Making it clear that, without him, she is not a complete woman, not the woman who got out of the car, keeping her knees together and showing off her elegant high heels, her beautifully cut skirt, and, a moment later – when she got to her feet after that initial gyratory manoeuvre that allowed her legs to appear first – her patterned silk blouse or a tailored jacket in a soft pastel shade. Not a trace of the original stuff she was made of. She was another woman, an outsider with no history. What was their relationship like during all those years when I hardly had any news of them? Did they continue to lie together, to interpenetrate, to form that shameless eight-limbed creature I cannot bear to imagine? A deformed beast, a monstrous graft, because while she continued to be Leonor, I was no longer me. So many years have passed, and I still reject the image of those two well-lubricated, tongue-and-groove pieces pistoning away, an action

I knew so well, and yet in which one of the parts has been replaced by another, just like when you take your car into the garage to be repaired. Were they in love? Did they feel affection, friendship, camaraderie for each other? Or desire? Or is that just another way of saying the same thing? The question that wounds me most is: did they desire each other right until the very end, with her ill and him penetrating her, rising and falling above her until she could no longer move (I read in a newspaper that, in Egypt, they want to make it legal for a husband to have sex with his wife's corpse, a kind of macabre farewell), or did they focus, above all, on maintaining shared strategies, business deals and bank accounts? No one will ever know. It's part of what I don't know and will never know, like the names I've lost along the way and whose forgetting provokes such foolish anxiety in me when I wake in the early hours, along with the anxiety of knowing that, however much I might want to, I will never see Liliana when she's fifty or hear her fifty-year-old voice. My nocturnal apnea. The return to wakefulness, that hand held out in extremis to pluck you from the grave into which you were falling. My sudden awakening. In the middle of the night, the image comes back to me of the two of them locked together, a single body, and then I feel as if I'm suffocating. One more night. I sit up in bed and fumble for the light switch. I'm drowning in all the stuff leaking out from that crack in the floodgate of my memory, the tank containing everything that was and that is now draining away. It seems that only the most painful things are destined to remain. I read somewhere that the cross was originally a representation of the sexual act: the horizontal, the woman's body; the vertical, the man who has her nailed down. The cross that, for a time, was composed of the two of us, Leonor and me. The cross that kept me nailed to Olba, or that I've come to think of as the excuse that kept me nailed to Olba. Did they live permanently nailed to that cross as we did during those months of our youth? If that worked for them, then everything else must have worked too, the overwhelming power of sex, although now that I think about it, that's not true, it certainly wasn't in our case. She always aspired to something more. I couldn't understand it at the time. When Francisco talks to me about her, it's the plenitude of the cross he's trying to express, that he wants me to believe, but, at this stage, nothing he can tell me is of any help. The mark of her teeth on my neck, her tongue drilling into my ear, her nails digging into my back, the drumming of her heels on my buttocks, the hoarse, rattling moan. That is my story, reserved for my own exclusive use. That's how it was and how it ceased to be. Anything that Francisco can tell me now is an entirely biased, mutilated version. I would need to know the part he doesn't mention, what he didn't see, doesn't want to see or couldn't. Just as I couldn't see what it was that suddenly drove us apart. To see through the eyes that gazed at him – the same eyes I used to gaze into as I thrust deep inside her, eyes that once gazed back at me – secretly hoping to confirm that what I see is the memory of a relationship that wasn't even unhappy (because that would at least grant it a certain nobility), but simply banal. That consoles me. But those eyes are no longer here, they're nothing but darkness. I can't retrieve what they saw of me. But you said you loved me, Leonor. She laughed: People say all kinds of things when they're fucking. It's all part of the game, just as we play tute, brisca and dominoes. And when Francisco, for whatever reason, mentions her name, I feel not a tremor, not a flicker of emotion, I remain as cold as a slab of fish or as a scaly reptile, but I see her just as I can see her now as I walk over the soft, damp, tender grass, so well watered by the autumn rains (it rained torrentially a couple of weeks ago, the last of the season's storms), a face, a body that moves and breathes behind glass: her hair floats around her head, weightless, unreal. Her skin has a greenish, bluish quality. Fish in an aquarium look like that, surrounded by that special, underwater light, a milky, fluorescent mist. Yes, her hair moves with the weightlessness of the inhabitants of an aquarium. Although now, this vision of Leonor is more like a melancholy echo of the voice hammering away inside my head, the voice of Liliana, who is still dense, fleshly matter: *¿le provoca un tintico*, Señor Esteban? Ah, you laugh now, but the first time I said it, you protested, because you thought I was offering you *un tinto*, a glass of red wine in the middle of the morning, when what I was offering you is what we Colombians call a *tinto*, a cup of coffee. A coffee made from beans grown in the shade of the guamo trees. Do you know what a guamo tree is? Of course you do, I've told you before. The guamo trees are the ones that shade the coffee plantation. They protect the plants from being scorched by the sun, just so that you can drink this *tintico* I'm making for you now. We speak the same language, but we speak differently, people say it's all Spanish, but we call our mosquitoes *zancudos* and we call you Spaniards *godos*, but that's not a nice word. It's a bit like here when you call us *conguitos* or darkies. The guamo trees protect the plants from the harsh sun. They shelter the coffee plantations, just as you have so often sheltered me. The shade protects us. And that voice, your voice, is leaving me alone and helpless. Fuck you, Liliana: fuck you and your guamo trees.

How old am I? Four or perhaps five? I'm sitting on my uncle's knee, watching as he folds the sheet of paper and hands to me, like a lavish gift, the possibility of being the one to put it in the envelope, then stick on the stamp that will allow this newly written business letter to reach its destination: I can feel again the tremor of excitement as I run my tongue over the sickly, gluey surface and give the stamp a good thump with my fist so that it's firmly stuck down; once that's done, I gaze, entranced, at the coloured design. I wish I could keep it for my collection, but these stamps are all destined to leave, to disappear into the mouth of the box in which I myself post the letters. Whenever he sends a letter, he always lets me lick the stamp with its sickly taste of glue, and then thump it down firmly with my fist. I don't like dull stamps bearing the face of some old man – now I know they were politicians, writers, painters, musicians or scientists – but sometimes they're brightly coloured and represent flowers, birds or flags. At night, I can feel Leonor nibbling my ear in the darkness of the cinema, the damp, moving warmth of her tongue tickles the cartilage, and that warm, vibrant, viscous feeling spreads like a shudder through the rest of my body and makes me catch my breath. Adrift in the night are old photos, me and my classmates standing outside the school, or me sitting alone at my desk with a pen in one hand and the map of Spain on the wall behind me. Photos of her, of Leonor: in one she has long, shoulder-length hair. As the poet says: We sing what we have lost. She's wearing a very short skirt, in a pale fabric, and a floral print blouse; the top two buttons are undone to reveal a hint of cleavage. In another, she's with her father – she gave me that photo because I told her it was the one in which she looked the prettiest; her father: dark shirt, large hands as hard and stiff as if covered by a carapace, a man of the sea. I burned those photos. They're only there in my head now, where they will remain for just a few hours more. In my memory, Leonor's brothers are also hard, sinewy youths, I still see the older one occasionally, he's a fisherman in Misent, like his father; I remember the other two wearing overalls: they would leave the garage with them on, I remember them walking home or standing chatting in the local bar. Of the two, one died young, and the other opened his own business in Misent – apparently, later on, he bought my brother's garage from my sister-in-law Laura after my brother died – and now he owns a car dealership, I remember them then as serious and compact, pure sinew: they hadn't yet acquired their father's opaque air, his breadth or weight. He reminded me of the French actor, Jean Gabin; the older brother, Jesús, the fisherman, has filled out since, grown heavier; the second brother, José, never reached the solidity to which he was predestined by his genes, because destiny cut short the evolutionary process – he died test-driving a car on the sharp bends of the road to Xabia; that was over thirty years ago now, his slender, muscular body lying, headless, next to the car, I didn't see him dead, but others have talked about it hundreds of times in the bar, describing his death in detail; so many people claimed to have seen it that I ended up seeing it too, and can see it now: his decapitated body and the overturned car, its wheels still spinning. So much time has passed since then, and here I am, seeing these images in the dark, seeing Leonor, who always looked like a modern young woman, as if she belonged to a different family, she had a more urban beauty, as if, right from the start, she was destined to escape from here; she had, above all, a slightly affected vivacity: in another of those now non-existent photos, you can see it in her face, in the way the neck of her striped polo shirt – she looks like a petite urban matelot – reveals the soft skin at the base of her throat, her short hair, she's a little matelot straight out of a sewing magazine or a musical, and not the daughter of a fisherman, which is what she was; not the daughter of a boat-owner, but the daughter of a fisherman whose wages depended on how much fish he caught each day, the kind of people who formed a small, marginal population within Misent, or, rather, in one corner of Misent, because they lived right on the seafront, in small, crammed-together houses protected from storms by low dykes built parallel to the facades so as to shield the steps that led up to the front door on the upper floor, where they lived and had their furniture and any objects of value, because every year, come the autumn storms, the ground floor was flooded. I can see faces and bodies, as well as the old houses that were demolished years ago now, I can also see the sea, which I don't think resembles today's sea, something has changed, perhaps the colour, no, that's not possible, how could the colour of the sea change? That's absurd, but the sea does seem different. Alien. Faded. Perhaps my capacity to distinguish colours has changed. The marsh remains the same in its degradation, when I look at it now it seems identical to how I remember it; it smells the same. In my nightmare, it's gradually taking on the form of a huge, dark hand that I can see from the air, as if I were riding on the back of one of those migrating ducks. The duck flutters its wings and shakes its back, as if trying to dislodge me and hurl me into that dark watery hand – that's another night when I wake up, anxiously reaching for the light switch. It takes me a few attempts to find it. I grope around. I'm submerged in the dark water of the lagoon, the giant hand is squeezing me, until, at last, I find the switch. Only then do I relax, make myself breathe regularly and try to empty my mind, but I can't. A while ago, I was the little boy dozing peacefully, lulled by the dull regular thud of the iron on the blanket covering the ironing board: the child closes his eyes and has a sense that this is true happiness, the warm, damp, soapy smell filling the room in which he lies drowsing while his mother does the ironing, the moment when his mother holds the iron close to her cheek to see whether the iron is hot enough, and soothed now by the light of the bedside lamp, I am the old man who closes his eyes and begins to breathe more easily because the

387

woman is ironing by his side and singing to herself, *ay mi Rocío, manojito de claveles*, she has a very clear, almost childish voice, *capullito florecido*, and beneath the blanket, all is safe and certain, warm as a nest, I can close my eyes now, because the woman with the child's voice is protecting me, and a limitless future opens out before me. I can be whatever I want to be and achieve whatever I want to achieve. The old man splashing along the marsh paths feels a pressure in his chest that grows and thickens like the kefir the Turks use to ferment milk. I reject the old man's anxiety. I want to be in those memories, to enjoy them before they vanish: my mother crossing my scarf over my chest before I set off for school. I can see the diaphanous light, the thin, fragile, winter light, like today; I can feel the cold air on the parts of my face not covered by my cap and earflaps and scarf; suddenly, it's my father who's at my side, watching how I hold the plane; he takes my hand so that I'm holding it properly, not like that, like this, he says, and his hand, that hand-cum-tool, grips mine like iron pincers, and his sour voice drills into my ear, but from behind comes my uncle's voice, leave him to me, I'll show him how to do it, and I immediately feel his large, warm hands, like a rough bird's nest, enclosing mine. Simultaneously hard and soft. He never shouted at me, and I could count on the fingers of one hand the times he raised his voice above his usual grave, calm tone, my father never shouted at me either, or hit me, it was just that harsh voice, which seemed to emerge straight from the ill-shaven cheek that sometimes brushed roughly against mine. My father. Tomorrow, I'll make him sit on the toilet until he has a proper bowel movement, and then I'll give him a thorough wash. We must be clean, Dad. I wouldn't want our trip to be sullied by such sordid details, by excrement and foul odours. We'll go to the place where my uncle taught me to fish and to drink the clear water from the spring, the place where I caught just a glimpse of the thing we seem to have spent our lives looking for. It's a shame, though, to poison the waters. Tomorrow: I'll put on my latex gloves to remove his incontinence pad before turning on the shower, then take off his pyjama jacket. I can't help feeling a certain distaste when I press my bare chest to his. I sit him down on the stool, struggle to remove his pyjama trousers, help him up, then remove the incontinence pad. The stench fills the bathroom. I put the pad in a plastic bag and tie it up before throwing it in the waste bin next to the sink. I hold his hands to help him walk. He's in front of me now, I can see his back, I watch him stumble unsteadily forward and warily place his feet in the shower basin, excrement sliding down his thighs, I press lightly on his shoulders to make him turn to face me, all the time talking to him. He stares at me blankly, as if he didn't understand what I was saying. He groans and moans and waves his hands about, rubbing his eyes with his fists: his shrunken chest, hard as a board, the wrinkled, bluish nipples of an exhausted mammal, his chest a cracked board that still has a troublingly youthful pallor. I have him in my grasp, I grab his shoulder, support him with one hand so that he won't fall and, with the other, run the sponge over his face, I lift his chin, see his eyes sunk among the wrinkles and, in among the wrinkles, the whiteheads, like fossilised nodules of fat; I rub his chest, and I do so with unnecessary vigour, a vigour into which I channel all my anger and weariness at having to do this every single morning; I see the fuzz of hair barely visible beneath his navel, but which grows thicker around the pubis, grey hairs that immediately merge with the soap bubbles left by the sponge. I wash around his balls, and with the tips of two fingers, push back the foreskin of his penis and rub the place that rubbed against and entered my mother's body, the topographical origin of me, the genesis of the lines on my face – partially disguised by fat – and the geography of age spots, more and more like his, on the backs of my hands. My father stares down at my gloved hand, with a look of astonishment that masks some unknowable emotion; I have the impression that the number of skin tags on his back and on his reddened buttocks – as wrinkled as those of a newborn baby – are increasing on a daily basis – and yet on his thighs and on the areas that are usually clothed and have never been exposed to the sun, the skin is surprisingly delicate, like marble, not newly carved Paros or Macael marble, but marble that has been exposed to the elements for centuries, exposed to the wind and the rain, which have worn it away and created a slightly porous texture, with a patina of curdled milk. I rub the rough sponge over his penis, a sponge that doesn't so much rub as scrub. I begin gently, barely brushing the crinkled skin around his balls, but then rub harder, almost fiercely and his skin becomes covered in blotches, not red or pink, but a bluish or even intense iodine yellow, the colour of stagnant or slow-flowing liquids, pent-up human fuel. The skin tags on my father's body make me think of the ones that, for some time now, I've noticed appearing on the base of my neck, in my armpits and the inside of my thighs. If, when I take a shower, I look in the full-length mirror in the bathroom, I see reflected in the mirror over the wash-hand basin a mottled, milky-white back. My skin has the same deathly pallor as his. My brown hand stands out starkly against the white skin of this man rhythmically repeating the same feeble groans of complaint. I know it hurts, but I have to give you a thorough wash, I tell him as I continue scrubbing away at the areas that were covered by the incontinence pad. We have to wash away all the muck that gets lodged in the pores, so that you'll be as clean as a newborn baby. If it was up to him, he would never bathe. Ever since he first began to lose his reason, even before he had the operation on his trachea, he's developed a hatred of water; the struggle begins as soon as I start propelling him down the corridor to the bathroom. It's sheer torture trying to undress him, he puts up a fierce resistance, folding his arms so that I can't take off his pyjama jacket and kicking his legs when I try to remove his trousers. He falls into a sulk each morning when I tell him it's time for his shower. It seems that the slightest contact or pressure hurts him, and he complains when I grab his elbow and make him raise his arms so that I can wash his armpits. It hurts him to stretch up; his muscles – his dwindling muscles – are painful, like his joints. And yet, for his comfort, I always try to dress him in a bath-robe and in pyjama trousers with a drawstring waist that are easy to get off; in summer, he wears just a light robe that reveals his blotchy legs. I look at his wrinkled hands, his gnarled, calloused fingers, with their irregular, deformed tips, the hands-cum-tools that have so often, pincer-like, gripped mine: the tip of his left thumb is missing, as is the tip of his right index and middle finger. The tip of my right thumb is missing too, I've also lost part of my left index finger, and my right index finger is somewhat squashed. Do you know any carpenter who hasn't suffered these minor mutilations? The benign wounds of kindly St Joseph's peaceable profession. I look at those hands that were once strong and skilful, and stroke them chastely, as if I were simply washing them, but which I am, in fact, caressing. I suppress the urge to kiss them. Hands are no longer important, the concept of being good with your hands, once so respected, has vanished, things now are made by machines or made somehow or other by anyone – some better than others – you just have to see how clumsily the bar staff serves coffee or beer, sticking their thumbs in the empty glasses or the full plates. Waiters are incapable of carrying a tray properly. Hands no longer have the sacred importance they once had: they were necessary for work, but they also blessed and consecrated, hands were laid on the sick to heal them. When an artist, a writer, painter, sculptor or musician, was on his deathbed, a mould often used to be made of his hands. Used to be. Was. Were. Had. Everything is in the past tense. My mother is ironing, my uncle is making me a cart pulled by a little wooden horse, he lets me stick on the stamps and takes me to the fair. I see him at the shooting gallery, the butt of the rifle hiding part of his face. He's aiming at a strip of paper on which is pinned a small tin truck. The festivals where coloured Chinese lanterns were hung from the cables that hung above the dancers' heads, the sort of lantern you could open out like an accordion and close again using the wooden sticks at either end, like flowers, and we children thought they were really beautiful. Bonet de San Pedro, Machín, Concha Piquer. the metallic clang of the dodgems and the sparks crackling from the web of wires criss-crossing the ceiling. My mother is singing. *Capullito florecido.* The smell of burnt oil from the stalls selling fritters, the smell of toffee apples and candyfloss. The blaring music. The noise of the pellet guns used to knock over the ducks that circle endlessly round and round at the back of the stand, or to sever the strips of paper on which were pinned a packet of cigarettes, a bag of sweets, a tin car. The music that booms out metallic-ally from the dodgems, the equally metallic voice of the man announcing the tombola prizes. I don't know if these things still exist, they probably do, and are more or less the same, although it's been years since there was a fair in Olba. My hand holding my uncle's hand as we did the rounds of all the stands. Can happiness be located so very far away? So far away in time, I mean; in terms of perspective, it's neither near nor far, happiness is something one waits for, looks for, and just when you begin to tire of waiting for your rendezvous with happiness, it turns out that the owner of the place where you've been waiting is in a hurry to close (hey, don't push, please, no pushing, let me at least finish my drink). The door he's pushing you towards is right there, and outside is the night you must face alone, the darkness the child is afraid of, and you really don't want to go out into that blackness.

Dunes at the mouth of the estuary, which is really more like a drainage canal and, in rough weather, overflow from the battering waves. When the wind from the Gulf of Lion is blowing hard and the waves get really big, the sea tries to recover what has been stolen from it by nature's own sedimentary contributions and by human silt. The whole marsh was once a vast bay: the sea penetrated inland to form an arc that mirrored the one formed by the mountains, and the waves licked the foot of the mountainous amphitheatre whose peaks I can see now above the reeds and beyond the cultivated areas that extend beyond the oxide-rich wetland. In winter, the boundaries are clearer, unobscured by the greens of spring and summer: first, the ochres of the overwintering reeds, then the dark green of the orange trees and, on the slopes, the very slightly lighter green of the pine trees; and above them, the bluish tones of the limestone. The bay has gradually been closing in on itself as the belt of dunes has grown higher and more extensive. The feeling one gets from this confused landscape – in which water alternates with mud that is sometimes more like shifting sand, and with terra that is only more or less firma – is that of an unfinished world (and it is: nature is slowly continuing the silting process, the mud remains part of the lagoon even as it's swallowing it up; it is, simultaneously, birth and death), an unreliable still photo of the moment when God began to separate the waters from the earth, a shifting geography still in the process of being made, halted on the morning of the third day of creation, assuming that being made is different from being destroyed, for the same process that brought the marsh into existence is contributing to its disappearance. What engenders the marsh is also condemning it to extinction. It is, in any case, an undefined space, a half-made world, progressively becoming blocked by the heaps of sand deposited by the waves and by the mud brought down by the streams swollen with the autumn rains, with the sediment of corpses of millions of plants and animals, in short, putrefaction, what is now known as active biomass, to which we humans add our own residues; the remnants of our various projects linger like scars: canal-digging schemes that were failed attempts to drain the whole marsh and convert it into cultivable land, walls that were supposed to act as defences and that are now mere ruins, rusty piping abandoned among the scrub, the remains of irrigation pools that lie unused or were never used, rubbish dumps, tips, dunes worn down by bulldozers or by machines that blithely carried away tons of sand for construction work; but also fresh dunes on which grow endemic species of plant that resemble cat's claws and some of which are, I believe, called just that. The bulky torsos of the mountains – whose feet, centuries ago, were licked by the sea – seem like bits of distant, abandoned scenery, the ruins of some ancient edifice. Before me, in the foreground, lie drifting spots of colour, botanical detritus floating on the greenish mirror of the water, pushed gently along by the sharp knife of the mistral; at certain points, the peaks on the horizon seem to emerge out of nothing: beyond are the reed beds, which stand plumed in white like feather dusters, they float on the flat surface of the water that the mud and the water lilies either disguise or adorn.

The passing clouds reflected on the surface create an illusion of a world in constant evolution, but which is, in fact, motionless, fixed as if in an old photograph, whose sepia tones precisely match the rusty colours of the winter reeds, faded yellows and ochres and a brown so dark it's almost black, and which forms sooty clumps, the melancholy tombs of giants.

3

EXODUS

'Will we one day find ourselves nostalgically recollecting the good old days?'

The ten o'clock brunch, with salad, pickles, salt fish drizzled with olive oil (dried octopus, mackerel, fine slivers of salted tuna and tuna roe), a few lamb chops, cold meats, wine and beer, finished off with whisky or coffee or, in my case, a good cognac (no, I won't have whisky like the others, give me a Martell out of that bottle you keep just for me); this is followed by a post-prandial conversation at the same table, which lasts until the pre-lunch aperitif (shall we get up and stretch our legs, I'm stiff as a board) and then the paella (God, that brunch went on a long time, we might as well have lunch here too, no?), some succulent risotto or else a dish of fideuà, which arrives when the clock has just struck three. Around the table, builders turned developers and other owners of prosperous businesses — glassworks, plumbing, carpentry, furniture shops, building materials, paint warehouses, haulage firms, men with independent incomes from various sources — meet together in peaceful coexistence, good people who receive — like the golden rain from a slot machine — the surplus value that, with every hour that passes, falls upon them from every shop assistant, every secretary tapping away in front of a screen, every labourer — Spanish, Peruvian, Colombian, Moroccan, Bulgarian or Romanian — working hard laying bricks or perched, like birds, on scaffolding. Some of those birds, as well as producing money, *sing songs learned back in their own country or heard in the car – on the way to work or going home – on the radio or on one of those channels for migrant workers that have started broadcasting locally and that play vallenatos, salsas and merengues, often preceded by dedications to our Colombian friends, our dear fellow Ecuadorians, all the Peruvians in Misent, Olba and the neighbouring towns, to a Guatemalan, you know who you are and you know who I am too, the person who's dedicating this song to you, just so you know I'm thinking of you. You can hear their unappealing warblings above the hammering of the carpenters or the metallic clank of the men nailing up the steel reinforcement mesh.*

The waiters have not yet finished clearing away the plates piled high now with the discarded shells from the seafood, but they have already placed on the table the steaming coffee cups and the glasses of cognac, whisky or sloe gin. The colleague seated on my right, a developer-cum-builder, tells me that every time he hears the clock chime on the wall opposite, he imagines he can hear the chink of money pouring into his pockets. I can actually hear it, he says, and it's pure joy, sheer paradise. Of course, I say, no harps, no angels, no ghosts or spirits or theological disquisitions, no, yours isn't a Catholic paradise, it's more of a Muslim one: all tasty titbits, tempting human flesh and alcohol. According to this very talkative developer, he spends the day buzzing about here and there, doing nothing very much, and, at the end, he does his sums: if twenty or so Moroccans or Romanians or Africans, or a group of other men of different nationalities, each work eight hours a day, that's 160 hours. I charge the client – averaging out the cost of a skilled worker and a labourer – about fifteen euros an hour per man: that comes to 2,400 euros, and I pay the labourers six, seven or eight euros an hour (depending on whether the guy's a friend, how long he's been working for me, whether I like him or not, because now that I work for myself and not with that bastard Bertomeu, I can do what I like, I'm my own boss) and I pay the skilled workers twelve euros an hour (take it or leave it), so, as I said, that averages out at eight euros per man, which comes to 1,280 euros, and once you subtract that from the 2,400 I charge the client, that leaves me with 1,120 euros: which means that, on this very pleasant afternoon, something over eleven hundred euros have clinked their way into my pocket, not bad, eh – especially when you bear in mind that more than half the workers aren't registered for social security, and with those who are, I've arranged that they pay me the equivalent of the contribution out of the money they earn. That's as far as I go, because arithmetic isn't really my strong point. The calculator does the work for me. He rambles boastfully on: What I'm saying is, that, sitting here in this restaurant beneath the air conditioner, before these empty plates being taken away by the waiter (careful now, don't drop the lobster claws), as I'm watching those hands removing plates heaped with the debris of prawns, fish bones and skin, bits of rice and breadcrumbs and aioli sauce, I can still hear the clink of that money, which is why I'm ordering another whisky – to toast my amazing good luck – and proposing to my dining companions: Let's all go off to the Lovely Ladies Club. It won't be open yet, says one man, best have a game of tute first, or poker, oh, and by the way, there's another line of coke for you in the toilet, you'd better hurry, though, before that dickhead behind the bar spots it, the bastard's always on the lookout for trouble, snooping around, seeing what he can find out. That's the trouble with living in a village like Olba. There's no privacy. The clock chimes again: clink, clink, clink, the endless tinkle of coins falling into my pocket, the way they fall into the little tray on slot machines, when a row of cherries or bananas or oranges lines up; I can almost hear them, can feel them against my thigh, the sixty or seventy euros every hour, clink, clink, clink, clinkclinkclinkclink, the three oranges, plus I charge twenty euros for every hour I spend in here, because, in theory, I'm conducting business, buying materials, drawing up plans, dealing with work-related matters, a meeting with suppliers, for example. I go out into the street for a moment while my whisky's being poured over ice, shouting into my mobile phone, giving orders. I tell someone off, then get him to put me on to someone else and tell him off too. I pretend to be angry – honestly, where would you deadbeats be without me chivvying you along? – to be anxious about the sheer number of problems I'm left to deal with because of their incompetence. So that the workers can see I'm on top of them, watching their every move, breathing down their necks, making sure they're not slacking off: come on, lads, get stuck in, and in a couple of weeks, we'll finish that house in Benalda, have a fancy meal to celebrate and then on to the next thing. The bungalows in Serrata, where work should have started a month ago, are still bogged down, I keep a labourer on site, looking busy, so that the owner knows I haven't forgotten him, that I'm thinking about him, but he'll have to wait anyway. When I meet the owner, a bulldog-faced German, I swear to him that I'm so worried on his behalf that I'm not sleeping or eating, ha ha. Well, for someone who doesn't eat, your belly's getting bigger by the day, you bastard, he says, and I laugh again, but the trouble is, you see, I've got too much work. Anyway, since there's no way he's going to find another builder, who cares? We're going great guns, we are, up to our ears in work. My father could never have foreseen such a brilliant future for his son, I mean, when I first started working for him as a labourer at four-teen, he was always telling me what a useless wanker I was. You can't even carry a bottle of milk without dropping it, God knows what we're going to do with you. Well, surprise, surprise, Dad, you didn't need to do anything, I've done it all on my own, all by myself; alas, I can't do anything for you, Dad, because where you've gone, you've got no needs, no anxieties, no problems. Yes, I did it all myself, the family idiot learned damn fast. I've got twenty blacks slaving away, perched on some scaf-folding, I drive a 4x4, and I'm lying on pink silk sheets, my private parts newly washed by this lovely Ukrainian girl, who is now moving her hand up and down my cock and drumming on it with her fingers, working away, trying to get some response, but what with the drink and the coke, I just can't get it up, and yet I'm happy (oh yes, look how easily it slips in, oh yes, do it again, look how hard it is now), I like to watch my cock sliding in and out of that sweet mouth, with not a thought for my wife or the kids, who'll be off doing what they do best, namely, spending money: they've got used to having all the good things in life, the tennis club, the rides around the bay in a catamaran belonging to friends, regular facials and manicures, Saturday-night suppers with a bottle of *Moët & Chandon* for starters, followed by a bottle of *Ribera del Duero*; Sunday brunch at the Marriott; what is brunch? says the radio ad, trying to civilise us: very simple, it's half breakfast, half lunch, you see, neither fish nor fowl, we had brunch last Sunday and we'll go again this Sunday – the Ukrainian or Lithuanian girl is still at it, come on, keep going, but not so rough, you stupid bitch, keep working, that's what I'm paying you for – followed, of course, by a round of golf – fucking hell, woman, slow down, careful you don't bite, there's no rush, no hurry, all in good time.

I interrupt him: please, my friend, spare me the details, you're almost splashing me. Time to stop the tape. Your life isn't so very different from mine, although sometimes I have to put on an act, move in rather higher circles, but in the autumn, I go to the Marriott on Sunday mornings too, haven't you seen me there? I've certainly seen you. A clear blue sky, straight out of a tourist brochure, the miraculous Mediterranean light when the mist has gone and everything stands out so clearly, silhouetted by the sun's rays, me with my baseball cap on back to front, American-style, me and the kids wearing Nike and Adidas (I don't like Lacoste, that's more your spoiled rich kids' style, better suited to a banker or an office clerk or an architect, but not an independent entrepreneur like me, I favour the sporty, informal look), and Amparo in her Italian straw hat (well, the straw comes from the next village actually, where they make a lot of stuff out of wicker, straw and rattan, or did, because now everything's imported from China, but she tells her friends she bought it in Florence), her sunglasses covering half her face: my lady wife looks like a model from a TV show, slightly faded perhaps, but a model nonetheless, the problem is that she wants to look like one of those gaunt-faced TV glamour girls, whereas she's got a naturally round face, and she's getting really scrawny too, what with dieting and Pilates, she's still got nice tits, though, and those plump red lips of hers, which she applies to the straw in her Campari as eagerly as that whore sucking your prick; on the seat beside her, a Louis Vuitton bag; and then, of course, there are the Dior shoes, the dress *by Versace or Carolina Herrera. With men it's watches that matter. From my sunlounger, I can see how the men keep stretching out one arm so that the others can see their watches, I mean, how naff is that, the wristband tight on their sunburnt wrists, because most of them are just upstarts, builders like you, my friend. You can tell how a man votes from his watch: a big fat Rolex with all kinds of chronometers and barometers on it indicates a PP voter, a right-winger; while a stylish Patek Philippe, which is what Felipe González wears, indicates someone more drawn to the socialists. Patek Philippe, a good cigar, a neat, toned bum, and a gin and tonic served with a stuffed olive – heaven. And perfectly consistent with socialism too, which, after all, represents wealth, well-being and money for everyone.*

I can hear the developer's murmuring prattle and my own, and I can even see the scene, the day we met in the restaurant, I can't remember the man's name, but I look back sadly now on those innocent times. I wonder what's become of him and his warbling workers. The golden age was just around the corner, we could almost touch it with our fingertips, it was so very close, but it never came, and when we jumped up to grab it, we fell flat on our arses: it's all gone, the money that fell from the skies (for my friend the developer, it fell from the scaffolding, whereas I had various springs from which it bubbled up), the multitudinous suppers, the cocaine, and the whore who would come blow your horn; and the paddle tennis and the squash and the Pilates and the brunch. It lasted as long as it lasted, and we really can't complain, the thousands of generations who came before us never enjoyed a single day like that, and now we're left with the hangover, that nail drilling into your head (an occupational hazard, no pleasure without risk and no such thing as eternal happiness), and all because the grasshoppers failed to store away any food for the bad times and, at the moment, it isn't just that we can't afford a whisky or a cognac, we can't even afford a jar of instant coffee or some frozen lamb chops, let alone a piece of line-caught hake or grouper, in your dreams, it's a time of wailing and gnashing of teeth, a time of repentance: where are the euros of yesteryear? What became of those lovely purple notes? They fell as fast as dead leaves on a windy autumn day and rotted in the mud: they fell on the casino tables, onto the claws of the lobsters and crabs we used to crack open with a nutcracker (yes, I did the same, I was one of the first, several rungs higher, but it was basically the same: don't make the rice with fish stock today, and it's better to use lobster rather than crayfish, that's even drier than the chicken breasts my wife grills so as to keep to her diet), they fell on the rickety beds in brothels; on the lines of white powder left on toilet cisterns (I always went for really expensive beds, for mirrors and little spoons and tubes made from silver or from 500-euro notes, but it wouldn't be the same for everyone, and it wasn't): those lovely purple 500-euro notes, ubi sunt? *Where are they? Everyone's looking for them and no one can find them, those of us who are entrepreneurs are looking for them and so are the taxmen, but they're nowhere to be found. They search lawyers' offices, private homes, false bottoms in car boots, in the hulls of yachts, but the notes aren't there, they were flushed down the bidets where those women washed away the remnants of the human effluent they had so expensively coaxed out; down the plugholes of sinks where you washed that incriminating nose of yours, which has begun to bleed again; down restaurant urinals, restaurants in which tons of rare veal steaks from Ávila, Galicia, Cantabria or the Basque Country were eaten, along with whole crates of line-caught hake, suckling pig from Segovia and lamb from Valladolid, fish or prawn risotto, and paella made with lobster; along with wine from Ribera del Duero and whisky from a Scottish distillery in some wild glen somewhere (there again I differ from most people in that I prefer French wine and cognac). It all went down the drain, down the toilet, into the holes of cunts just coming into bloom and already grown calloused from all that friction. Do you really think it's any different with life itself, our life? The whole world is being washed down the drain, but how we miss all those things that will never come back. The snows of yesteryear, the rose that opened this morning and will have faded by evening, and whose petals will fall when the sun shines on it tomorrow, leaving only an ugly dry ball, a miniature skeleton that crunches between your fingers when you squeeze, the princes of Olba, the ladies of Ukraine. Where did they go, all those people who passed so swiftly before our eyes, where were they going, where did they end up? Water swallowed by the drain, by the labyrinth of pipes, sewers, filters and water-treatment plants, pipes that flow out into the sea.*

That is how the time granted to you on this earth was spent, my friend. The same goes for me. Now we have to live life's afterlife.

These new times are less frantic, people no longer drive back and forth in powerful cars, in trucks laden with merchandise, in vans rushing to make an urgent delivery, it's quieter, more restful, less physical (there's less carnal traffic, the rooms at the Lovely Ladies Club stand empty, no one lies down on those pink sheets, no one is queuing up in the offices of notaries to sign property deeds: it's the butterfly effect) and, of course, these are also far less chemical times, there's not much cocaine around and what's available is very bad quality and hardly anyone buys it. Well, we're hardly in a position to waste our money on coke! Obviously, we live less whoring, less rascally lives, have fewer hangovers after nights on the town. One can sense new values in the air, Franciscan virtues: a taste for life in the slow lane, a quiet evening stroll, so good for the heart, we even view poverty differently: I'd go so far as to say that it's fashionable to be poor and to have your house and car repossessed (but what can I tell you that you don't already know, my friend. I imagine you're in more or less the same situation). If you appear on TV because you've been evicted or fired, you become a hero; and it's no longer cool to rev your engine as you pass some cafe on the Avenida Orts in Misent, so that everyone turns to see you at the wheel of your Ferrari Testarosa, it's considered bad taste to be caught by a local TV crew in a five-star resort, playing golf or having brunch, that mixture of breakfast and lunch (the news spreads like wildfire: the bastard says he doesn't have enough money to pay back his loans or his creditors or the men he's left unemployed, but he can apparently still afford his golf club membership), and if you have a business meeting with someone, it's best to leave your Mercedes 600 in the garage and take the Volvo instead: it's important to appear unostentatiously substantial, the worker-owner rather than the speculator; oh, yes, these are definitely duller, drabber times. But what do you expect? I break off my thoughts because Amparo's tapping me on the shoulder:

'Wake up, Tomás Pedrós, you're falling asleep and snoring and dribbling too.'

I open my eyes and find her wiping the corners of my mouth and my chin with a Kleenex, I'm touched at such evidence of love in these difficult times. In these new conditions, we have learned to appreciate small kindnesses. On the other side of the window, I see one of those enormous long-distance planes taking off. Another one emblazoned with the profile of the mythical Garuda bird is taxiing up to the passenger walkway. Amparo, my beloved Amparo, throws the tissue in the bin beside her and asks: What currency do they use there? What a wonderful woman, always with her eye on what counts. The real? The sol? The bolívar? The quetzal? The rupee? I smile at her as one might smile at an angel: it doesn't matter, my love: money has no homeland, just make sure you've got plenty of convertible euros or convertible dollars (is that what they call them?) in your handbag, and try, above all, to store away those gold ingots, because they've been around for centuries now, for millennia, along with jewels, gems, rubies and sapphires – they retain the value they had on the eighth day of creation, when Eve saw a serpent and picked it up, thinking it was an emerald necklace.

Beniarbeg, July 2012

TRANSLATOR'S
ACKNOWLEDGEMENTS

I would like to thank the author for his immense patience with my queries, as well as my usual helpers, Annella McDermott and Ben Sherriff, for whose advice and support I am forever grateful.

AFTERWORD

As a young boy, Rafael Chirbes was sent to an orphanage for the children of railway workers after his father died, because his mother couldn't afford to keep him. He was born in 1949 in a small town on the shore of the Mediterranean, Tavernes de Valldigna, Valencia, to a Republican family – his grandfather was a basket-maker – on the losing side of the Spanish Civil War. Beleaguered, considered traitors and 'Reds,' his father committed suicide when Rafael was four and his mother, who worked as a pointsman, was eventually detained. Yet before he died, Rafael's father taught his unusually bright son how to read, and at eight the boy was sent away from the sparkling blue seaside, muscatel vineyards and liberal-minded rural town, where they showed films without censoring them for the children and celebrated bawdy, pagan-infused spectacles during which vedettes' breasts would fall from their blouses as they danced in defiance of the suffocating national Catholic dogma imposed by Franco. At least that's how Rafael Chirbes remembered the warmth and earthiness of the Mediterranean world from which he'd been uprooted to find his way alone in the severe, snowy, landlocked plains of Castile during some of the darkest, most miserable years of the dictatorship.

His peripatetic life began in towns like Ávila, Salamanca and Leon – the dour lands of Santa Teresa, where her pruny reliquary finger presided 'like a fruit peel' over life and 'celebrations' transmogrified into ominous religious processions with waxy virgins and proselytes dressed in habits, cinctures, olive uniforms, widow's black or penitent purple. This contrast between the coast versus the famous rainy (often in fact quite dry) plains of Spain (which Chirbes – who went on to become a gourmand with friends like the writer Manuel Vásquez Montalbán, founding the magazine of literature and gastronomy *Sobremesa* – described as 'fresh vegetables versus dried legumes and salt cod') is a recurring motif in some of his early novels.

Just to be on the safe side, his grandmother had warned him when he was taken away that dare he return in priest's garb, she would strangle him. What he came back dressed in thirty years later, though, was the Spanish language as well as a uniquely obsidian sentimental education that would chisel one of the most renegade and uncomfortable literary testaments of Spain – for both the establishment and anti-establishment alike. 'Who do I write against?' Chirbes once asked rhetorically: 'I write against myself. If you stand yourself up against the character you most despise, you'll find your own contradictions staring straight back at you'. His novels sprout from a deep human disquiet and this inexorable process of self-examination – novels as private passions that take a public form. Writing as a means for making sense of things that seem incongruous, as a way of broaching that nagging question that won't go away. First comes fixing the perspective, the way of looking, the point of view from which the story is to unfold, and once he catches sight of the figure trapped in the marble, Chirbes takes no prisoners in the carving, the shaving, the filing, the telling. Not even himself.

It's not hard to imagine how these years went into crafting

a certain narrative distance in his writing, which is an essential feature; the objectivity and detached scrutiny of a solitary, acutely observant child stunned by the weirdness of a strange new environment, the alienation of a new language with its new possibilities. Not merely the desire but also the ambition to make sense of it by naming and appropriating and organising the derangement of a peculiar alternative domain. Though stripped of his native Valencian, he gained the high artifice and syntactical precision of Castilian, a language he fell in love with and a literary tradition he absorbed copiously – along with the French – and with which he was in constant, intense conversation throughout his life; from his revered seventeenth-century Baltazar Gracián – whose philosophy of scepticism influenced Schopenhauer and Nietzsche – to a forty-year love affair with the writing of Benito Pérez Galdós and of his beloved Mexican-exiled French-German-Jewish-Spanish experimentalist Max Aub. *No hay mal que por bien no venga* (all clouds have a silver lining) Chirbes said of being sent away as a boy; it caused him to relinquish any identification with a single place on earth. He became a stateless writer 'freed of any romantic baggage' that would wax syrupy on the orange-blossom breeze of Mediterranean writing and disregard the ripe stench of its marshlands. *On the Edge* is set in Valencia, yet its intentions are closer to how Gracián 'works everyday language in a way that deviates from it enough that it neither falls into caricature nor mere reproduction'. He also pointed to Jonathan Swift's 'A Tale of a Tub' for the indulgence of its digressions, and closely identified with the intentions of John Dos Passos. *On the Edge* is a poetic spasm, an epic of the rubbish dump written by a witness who breaks the underclass's legacy of silence during a crisis that is not merely economic, but social and acutely moral. The song of the property siren from its debris-ridden cesspool, the swan-song of the hope that was deposited in a generation, his generation, who held the country's future in their once-militant hands and yet quickly betrayed those who, with a modicum of dignity, had struggled before them during the years of the regime. There's no dignity in the struggle against greed in a world where values have shifted away from the human. You're just poor. But Chirbes would quote Hermann Broch: 'Was there ever a time when values were not in crisis?' He believed that the novel as a form is inescapably a creature of its time and that any writer who considers it to have some supreme value-in-itself as a piece of artifice reduces the form to something banal, a paltry toy. Even in language's search for what's on the inside, there is a relationship, a tie, to what's on the outside. Writers who don't understand this connection, Chirbes felt, yet claim to inhabit literature as if a sacred temple, are really living in a doll's house. And like selfish children they are negating the novel's public concern, cancelling its role in civil accountability.

At a precocious sixteen, and despite the stacked odds, Chirbes moved to Madrid where he studied Modern and Contemporary History at Universidad Complutense. There he joined an underground student group and became involved in clandestine, anti-Franco activities that landed him in Carabanchel prison. He also worked in several bookshops, notably Tarantula in the early seventies, which fed his voracious reading habits and exposed him to many of the books prohibited by the regime that were kept hidden away in a special room, like a speakeasy its bottles of whisky: Sade, Miller, Marx, Lawrence, Aub and Juan Marsé, among many other delicacies. History, politics, social movements and literature converged in these years, and crystallised his perspective as an eyewitness. He spent the rest of his life narrating – in a great, twirling kaleidoscope of voices – the annals of this generation of young rebels who grew into tentative democrats: how many of them fell into the habits of their predecessors, how daily life is much harder to bear than putting up a good fight, how hard it is not to betray the ideals they had fought for as students when it came their time to make life choices. As the French writer Jean Genet quipped when asked what he would like from the world, 'I would like for the world not to change so that I can be against the world'. For many, fighting against Franco had been much easier than forging a democracy, which obliges thinking of the greater good.

Chirbes went to Paris for a year and became a consummate Francophile, devouring all of Proust and declaring himself a 'Proustian Leninist'. He read the *maudits*, Zola, saw the films of Renoir, Ophüls, Godard, listened to Debussy, Satie. 'Balzac, Flaubert, Stendhal, Maupassant are in me, they are in my novels, they are me. I admire Sartre and Camus in some books, but others are boring. I admit that Braudel is magisterial. I like Carrère's *Limonov* and *The Wound* by Laurent Mauvignier'. From Paris he headed for the Morocco of Paul Bowles, Jean Genet and Mohamed Choukri to teach the history of Muslim Spain in a school in Fez without knowing 'a potato' of Arabic. Chirbes was searching elsewhere for paradise; Franco had died and the free-for-all atmosphere disturbed him. He quickly discovered Morocco was no nirvana either, but the experience spurred the writing of his first published novel, the alcohol-infused *Mimoun*. The novel oozes sexual tension and debauchery and an idea that 'life is dirty, pleasure and pain sweat, excrete, smell. No human is anything more than a badly stitched sack of muck'. His lifelong fascination with the work of painters like Francis Bacon and Lucian Freud should come as no surprise. His writing eventually worked into a style that broke with any conventional idea of realism; his sharp-edged hyperrealism moves into the poetic, the revealing detail so excruciatingly exact, existentially emblematic, that it becomes unbearable, searing. In his later novels, the ageing human body serves as a symbol of the decadence and decay of the political and social body, too. It was the novelist Carmen Martín Gaite who first discovered his work. She sent the manuscript of *Mimoun* to Jorge Herralde at Anagrama, who called immediately and encouraged Chirbes to present the novel for the Herralde Prize. His debut was voted the runner-up. Herralde continued reassuring Chirbes at a crucial moment in his creative life, and Chirbes never forgot it. The relationship between writer and editor would last his lifetime and produce several novels and essay collections.

History for Rafael Chirbes was the key that opened his creative spigot, the present was the crystallisation of the past and a writer was an antenna able to capture what Chateaubriand called an epoch's *esprit principe*. He embraced Walter Benjamin's concept of the moment of danger, 'for every image of the past that is not recognised by the present as one of its own concerns threatens to disappear irretrievably ... In every era the attempt must be made anew to wrest tradition away from a conformism that is about to overpower it ... Only that historian will have the gift of fanning the spark of hope in the past who is firmly convinced that *even the dead* will not be safe from the enemy if he wins. And this enemy has not ceased to be victorious'. Benjamin is one of the ghosts, the deceased writers that Chribes talked to, listened to: Cervantes, Tolstoy, Montaigne, Yourcenar, Lucretius, Virgil, Döblin, Faulkner, Eça de Quierós.

Chirbes had always been attracted to literature and cinema, but found the vastness of formal abstraction terrifying. History was a system, it tied things down and grounded them, brought things from the fanciful into an initial structure that allowed him to pose questions through literature and use the form of the novel to seek knowledge, to place an object in the light, to apprehend it long enough to distinguish its mechanics and intricacies. History was a boomerang – the past through the light of the present and its projection into the future. 'You can't see anything without history because if you don't comprehend the evolution of things, you'll never understand anything. Either you bear witness to your time, or you become a symptom of it'.

After returning to Spain, Chirbes settled into a tiny 400-soul town in Badajoz, Extremadura. He wrote travel and culinary pieces to get by, but plunged into eleven years of fervent reading, rereading and writing. By night, he would frequent the town's profusion of bars and argue with the local socialists about how the cause had been sold for a few measly government contracts. He produced a fine second novel, *En la lucha final*, and a third, *La buena letra*, written in the feminine voice against the 'new pragmatism' which he said could be summed up perfectly in a phrase by Deng Xiaoping: 'Black cat, white cat, what does it matter, as long as it hunts rats'. He wanted his storytelling to pierce the marrow of the transition, hit that quivering moment when the scales balance and the novel finds its vantage point, its aura, firing an infinitude of meanings. 'Beautiful penmanship is a costume for lies,' his protagonist laments. Chirbes believed that literature is like a lover, either you go all the way or you'll be left alone.

When his fifth novel, *La larga Marcha*, came out in 1996 it became a *casus belli* among certain sectors of the critical apparatus in Spain. It was translated into German, and the critic Reich-Ranicki melted into a paroxysm of accolades, establishing Chirbes as the 'model to follow' for the great German novel that was coming. It was 'the book that Europe needed'. Chirbes became an instant bestseller there, winning prizes and a veritable phenomenon. For many years his most ardent readership was German while in Spain he was still a 'cult' writer. 'I'm not a priest or a politician, I'm not writing to console readers, but to awaken contradictions and disquiet'. This is part and parcel of what made Rafael Chirbes the consummate outsider in Spanish letters, the prickly, unrelenting social conscience of his generation: his was an intimate knowledge of the age-old underbelly of the human condition, he knew that victims become executioners and 'no human being can be considered free of guilt'. In this he echoed Camus's famous dictum: 'In such a world of conflict, a world of victims and executioners, it is the job of thinking people not to be on the side of the executioners'. It's what suffuses his work with its potent edge, its sense of urgency and grit. For years he was described as a 'secret' writer, which in Spain is often a euphemism to describe someone emerging from the underclasses, but as he well knew, eventually the readers are the ones to decide who is a great author, not the establishment. Chirbes the reader's writer, Chirbes the witness of his time, Chirbes the historian: he always understood the artistic act as an ethical one, and the novel as a potent artefact for describing a particular time and place on earth, as a microcosmic representation, as a fractal, of the universal.

Novel after novel, Chirbes continued pushing form, experimenting, and became one of the greatest prose stylists of the language, forging new and original forms to renovate the boundless European tradition of social realism, adding modern, original twists to the sweeping fresco style of writers like Galdós, Balzac or Musil. Early in the new century, Rafael Chirbes returned to the Levante of his childhood, and found a solitary home in the small town of Beniarbeig, Alicante, living as a near recluse with his two dogs and two cats (he had been afraid of dogs earlier in life, and one can follow their presence throughout his novels). His tipping point came in 2007 with *Crematorio*, his eighth novel and a force to be reckoned with, like it or not. By now it was too dangerous for the establishment to flaunt ignorance of a writer of such a categorical stature. However uncomfortably, even the audacious few establishmentarians who still believe that history can keep a secret, yes, even they were forced to pay attention – the man isn't going away and he writes like the devil. And Chirbes's work proves that history cannot keep a secret. A tepidly conceded finalist for the City of Barcelona Prize that year, *Crematorio* landed the wildly applauded National Critics' Award. It was about time. The novel was then adapted for television, becoming one of Spain's most successful series ever.

In an essay (Chirbes has four books of essays) focusing on the work of one of his totem authors and a fellow member of the underclass, Juan Marsé, Chirbes writes: 'He devoured his predecessors, ground them up into little pieces and built a new height over their remains from which to observe'. This is what Chirbes did in his last two books that are linked like bubbly (*cava*) and a hangover; *Crematorio* describes the Spanish soul at the beginning of the twenty-first century, particularly on the Mediterranean coast during the heyday of the property bubble. But if *Crematorio* was about bling and bigger-than-thou yachts and beachfront properties, *On the Edge* takes a swan dive into the putrid bog left behind when the bubble burst. The main character is the marsh, the poisoned quagmire where the mafias dump their hot guns and cars, where toilet bowls float with construction site debris, where corpses were hacked and disposed of. It chronicles in human terms the consequences when the tower of cards came tumbling down and asks very difficult questions: Are the underclasses any better off now, than they were under Franco? Do we remember how much they struggled? 'I dream about the dead people I knew when they were alive,' Chirbes said to me in Xalapa, México: 'I've touched them, even, and now they're nowhere, and knowing that they're not here and that I can't talk to them or hear their voices distresses me when I go to bed. Some nights they take control of the room: their absence leaves me breathless and I have to turn on the light so I don't suffocate'. What has his generation done with the new democracy they were given? The word 'carrion' appears in the last sentence of *Crematorio* and in the first one of *On the Edge*. 'The wind has dropped again, and in the ensuing calm, from the place where the dog is scratching, a sickly smell of old carrion rises up, impregnating the air'. 'The first one to spot the carrion is Ahmed Ouallahi'. The young Moroccan sees a dog chewing on something. Other dogs try to take it away. He draws closer, apprehensively. It's a human hand.

On the Edge is a masterful example of writing at the top of its form, a centrifugal novel with sentences like sticky tentacles that clutch onto readers and suck them into a swirling, tempestuous, pulsating centre. The tension comes from the language itself, from the myriad stories of his characters all told in his characteristic torrential, terse, powerful prose, whose cadences echo his beloved American writers, Faulkner, Mailer and Dos Passos. Language that is as theological as it is diabolical, that keeps a surreptitious network, or builds a web, like a dictatorship. *On the Edge* garnered a second National Critics' Award and, finally, the National Prize for Literature.

Rafael Chirbes, who died in August 2015 after being diagnosed with incurable lung cancer, accepted his role as the defiant, intrepid author who bears witness, who acts as counterbalance to the forces of power, of corruption and of greed and misery, yet writes lucidly, and even at times tenderly. 'Literature obliges a radical practice, it demands a form of aloneness that yes, at times can be almost unbearable: but it's a matter of old virtues and harsh discipline'. Writing was his form of observing and expiating his own inconsistencies and primal urges – sex, power, money – in their modern iterations – property speculation, prostitution and human trafficking, political debauchery – and challenging readers to look into his pages as into a dark mirror, to see the ghostly reflection of their own faces looking back. What redeems these scathing truths – for a writer with this experience and depth of insight – is art.

Valerie Miles